OKANAGAN UNIV/COLLEGE LIBRARY

03273141

PS 1294 .C63 A6 1999
Chopin, Kate,
Bayou folk ; and, A night in
Acadie /

N ACADIE

uary 8, 1850, in St.
from the St. Louis
later she married
w Orleans. They
r they moved to
s Parish, in north-
ghter was born in
their plantations
bor, but abruptly
ars she had begun
he published two
)9)—and nearly a
reviews. Her two
River country of
e (1897), were ac-
, the story of a
was widely con-
short story col-
d on August 22,
in 1991 by Pen-
ing and Selected

pin for twenty-
University, au-
, and editor of
e has also been a

BRODART

Cat. No. 23-221

BAYOU FOLK

AND

A NIGHT IN ACADIE

KATE CHOPIN

EDITED WITH AN
INTRODUCTION AND NOTES BY
BERNARD KOLOSKI

PENGUIN BOOKS

PENGUIN BOOKS
Published by the Penguin Group
Penguin Group (USA) Inc., 375 Hudson Street, New York, New York 10014, U.S.A.
Penguin Books Ltd, 80 Strand, London WC2R 0RL, England
Penguin Books Australia Ltd, 250 Camberwell Road, Camberwell, Victoria 3124, Australia
Penguin Books Canada Ltd, 10 Alcorn Avenue, Toronto, Ontario, Canada M4V 3B2
Penguin Books India (P) Ltd, 11 Community Centre, Panchsheel Park, New Delhi – 110 017, India
Penguin Books (N.Z.) Ltd, Cnr Rosedale and Airborne Roads, Albany, Auckland, New Zealand
Penguin Books (South Africa) (Pty) Ltd, 24 Sturdee Avenue,
Rosebank, Johannesburg 2196, South Africa

Penguin Books Ltd, Registered Offices: 80 Strand, London WC2R 0RL, England

Bayou Folk first published in the United States of America by
Houghton Mifflin Company 1894
A Night in Acadie first published in the United States of America by
Way & Williams 1897
This volume with an introduction and notes by Bernard Koloski published
in Penguin Books 1999

5 7 9 10 8 6

Introduction and notes copyright © Bernard Koloski, 1999
All rights reserved

LIBRARY OF CONGRESS CATALOGING IN PUBLICATION DATA
Chopin, Kate, 1851–1904.
[Bayou folk]
Bayou folk ; and, A night in Acadie / Kate Chopin ; edited with an introduction
and notes by Bernard Koloski.
p. cm. — (Penguin classics)
Includes bibliographical references (p.   ).
ISBN 0 14 04.3681 2
1. Louisiana—Social life and customs—Fiction. I. Koloski, Bernard, 1937–   .
II. Chopin, Kate, 1851–1904. Night in Acadie. III. Title. IV. Title:
Night in Acadie. V. Series.
PS1294.C63A6   1999
813´.4—dc21   98-36398

Printed in the United States of America
Set in Stempel Garamond

Except in the United States of America, this book is sold subject to the condition
that it shall not, by way of trade or otherwise, be lent, re-sold, hired out, or
otherwise circulated without the publisher's prior consent in any form
of binding or cover other than that in which it is published
and without a similar condition including this condition
being imposed on the subsequent purchaser.

OKANAGAN UNIVERSITY COLLEGE
LIBRARY
BRITISH COLUMBIA

CONTENTS

INTRODUCTION

Kate Chopin spent the decade before she published *The Awakening* writing some ninety short stories, many of which she published in national and regional magazines. In 1894 she gathered together twenty-three of those stories in a collection she called *Bayou Folk,* and in 1897 she chose twenty-one others for a collection titled *A Night in Acadie.* The books were well received by reviewers, who lauded them as charming, delicate portraits of Creole and Acadian life, and often compared them to works of the French realist Guy de Maupassant.

Chopin's *Bayou Folk* publisher had encouraged her to write a novel, arguing it might be more popular than another collection of stories. Yet when *The Awakening* appeared in 1899, most reviewers found it disturbing and flawed—disagreeable, unhealthy, vulgar, morbid. Although they praised the artistry of the novel, they condemned the choice of subject matter, especially Edna Pontellier's adultery and suicide. Chopin's reputation was tarnished. Her third collection of stories, to be called *A Vocation and a Voice,* was not published in her lifetime.

Chopin wrote a few more short stories before she died in 1904, but people became excited about her work again only in the 1970s when they rediscovered *The Awakening* and made it among the most often read and best loved of classic American books. Today there is renewed interest in the stories Chopin wrote before her great novel. *Bayou Folk* and *A Night in Acadie* are the two books Kate Chopin's contemporaries most likely knew her by.

The books are celebrations of people in their communities, whether they are inhabitants of New Orleans or of the rural areas of Louisiana, mostly in the 1870s and 1880s. Chopin's characters are

Creoles, Acadians, and "Americans," people of color and of mixed blood, Native Americans and immigrants, adults and children, the educated and the illiterate, the rich and the poor. The stories are strikingly varied from one another and from Chopin's famous novel. Some (like "Madame Célestin's Divorce" or "A Respectable Woman") focus on women's issues—on the restrictions women face in seeking self-fulfillment—but many do not. Some (like "Athénaïse" or "Regret") deal with an awakening by someone—often a woman—to something, but many do not. Chopin centers stories on men ("Mamouche," "Ozème's Holiday") and children ("A Turkey Hunt," "Boulôt and Boulotte") as well as on women. She writes about ethnic distinctions, class, race, money, divorce, religion, sex, and, more than anything else, social possibilities.

Most of the strongest stories depict people striving to establish better lives in their communities at a time of traumatic social change. The Civil War is over but its devastation is evident everywhere. Poverty is the norm, illiteracy is common, and the potential for violence is often palpable. Slavery has been abolished but most African Americans struggle to survive. The once-dominant Creoles have lost their economic—if not their social—power and sometimes work the fields alongside lower-class Acadians and blacks. Many young people are dissatisfied, attracted to newly arrived outsiders who by their very presence suggest fresh options. The ruined economy and social order are embodied in decaying plantation mansions with crumbling porticos.

Yet the stories are mostly bright, animated, full of hope because Chopin's energetic, resilient characters sense possibility in the midst of hardship. They manage to cope, using whatever strategies or tactics they have available. Many of them function as both insiders and outsiders in their communities, intuitively grasping (though rarely intellectually comprehending) the changes going on around them. They recognize opportunities and reach for them. They pass quietly back and forth across the social boundaries that define appropriate behavior by race, class, gender, or generation. It is not coincidental that the child in "Mamouche" tears down fences, that La Folle in "Beyond the Bayou" crosses a terrifying border to save the life of a child, or that the woman in "Madame Célestin's Divorce" hides behind her picket fence while negotiating with a man of a higher social class. It is not surprising that so many children in the stories have learned from adults to be resourceful, to fend for themselves. Characters in the stories appropriate values from others, gaining for themselves and their families experience that helps them build more fulfilling lives.

Chopin brings to the stories a complex perspective that reflects her background. She grew up bilingual and bicultural in St. Louis. Her mother had come from French stock, and French was spoken in her extended family in the 1850s, though her father was Irish (her maiden name was O'Flaherty). As she visited friends and relatives, she learned that there were deep differences between the two communities in folkways and values. Her ability to function in both groups served her well when she married Oscar Chopin in 1870 and lived with him in French- and English-speaking communities in New Orleans and Natchitoches Parish in northwestern Louisiana. After Oscar's death, she moved with her children back to St. Louis, where she wrote all her fiction and where she died at the age of fifty-four. In both St. Louis and Louisiana, she lived among comparatively prosperous, sophisticated, and well-read people.

Chopin composed the stories in *Bayou Folk* and *A Night in Acadie* between 1891 and 1896. It was an ideal time to write short stories. By that time three thousand or four thousand magazines and Sunday newspaper supplements were being published in the United States, and many of them included fiction. Earlier in the century, all magazines and newspapers had been regional, but by 1890 some were national, and at least twenty had circulations of more than a hundred thousand copies. Technological changes in printing and photoengraving had lowered the cost of publication for both popular and high-quality magazines, and an international copyright agreement in 1891 forced magazines to seek American writers because they could no longer so easily pirate British ones. Competition among magazines was fierce. Kate Chopin never earned her keep through her writing—she lived primarily from her real estate holdings—but she was a successful professional writer who made money with her work.

Writing short stories in the 1890s brought prestige as well as money. The short story genre had been established in the United States by Edgar Allan Poe and others earlier in the nineteenth cen-

tury, and in the 1880s literary critic Brander Matthews had per-
suaded influential readers that the genre deserved the same respect
and attention accorded to the novel. The short story became immensely popular. Readers especially liked realistic fiction and local
color fiction. Kate Chopin had firsthand knowledge of a group of
people in Louisiana whom American readers found interesting to
read about, so her stories were well received.

Realists and local color writers pictured ordinary people living
ordinary lives. The larger-than-life characters of earlier romantic
writers, the Natty Bumppos and Captain Ahabs and Hester
Prynnes, had demanded novels, often long novels, to hold them,
but by the 1890s such characters were less in vogue, despite an occasional Isabel Archer. Realistic writers here and abroad were influenced by the work of Sigmund Freud, Charles Darwin, and Karl
Marx. They understood people as molded by psychological, biological, economic, and other forces, as striving in the unremarkable
events of their everyday lives to fashion decent possibilities for
themselves. Short stories, Chopin learned, were perfect for captur-
ing moments in the lives of such people, people like those her readers would meet if they went to Louisiana.

The *Bayou Folk* and *A Night in Acadie* stories show the influence of the realists—and of other writers. Kate Chopin had read
widely, from Aeschylus and Shakespeare to Ralph Waldo Emerson,
Henrik Ibsen, Algernon Swinburne, and Walt Whitman. She knew
the sentimental fiction that prospered in America throughout the
nineteenth century. She studied the work of American realistic writers Sarah Orne Jewett, Mary Wilkins Freeman, Ruth McEnery Stuart, Hamlin Garland, and others. But she was most deeply affected
by French realists—especially Guy de Maupassant and Émile Zola.

Chopin read Maupassant in his original French and loved his un-
adorned phrasing, his frugal use of detail, his irony, and his determination to tell the truth as he saw it. "Here was a man," she writes,
"who had escaped from tradition and authority, who had entered
into himself and looked out upon life through his own being and
with his own eyes; and who, in a direct and simple way, told us
what he saw. When a man does this, he gives us the best that he
can." She adds, "I read his stories and marvelled at them. Here was
life, not fiction."

Zola too she read in French. Although a review she wrote in 1894 is critical of one of his novels, she speaks well of his work in general and admires what he had accomplished throughout his career.

> I once heard a devotee of impressionism admit, in looking at a picture by Monet, that, while he himself had never seen in nature the peculiar yellows and reds therein depicted, he was convinced that Monet had painted them because he saw them and because they were true. With something of a kindred faith in the sincerity of Mons. Zola's work, I am yet not at all times ready to admit its truth, which is only equivalent to saying that our points of view differ, that truth rests upon a shifting basis and is apt to be kaleidoscopic.

Chopin stressed the importance of a writer reaching for the truth. She sought in her stories to depict the "shifting basis" of the truth of life in Louisiana as she knew it during the fourteen years she lived there. And when she assembled her stories into collections she worked to capture in each book the feel of a kaleidoscope, the sense that each story was distinct in itself but composed of the same little pieces of life that made up all the other stories.

As they are arranged in the two books, the stories in *Bayou Folk* or *A Night in Acadie* almost seem to comprise a novel. They share a geographic space, with most set in New Orleans or in Natchitoches Parish, although characters have ties to many parishes (counties, as they would be called in other states): Caddo, Sabine, Avoyelles, Assumption, Lafourche, and others. Moreover, the characters who live in this imaginative world know one another, marry one another, are related to one another, or work together. The Duplan family, mentioned in the first story in *Bayou Folk*, reappears in a later story and then again in *A Night in Acadie*. Members of the Santien family—Placide, Hector, and Grégoire—and the Laballière family—Alphonse, Alcée, Didier, and their mother—figure in several *Bayou Folk* stories. A journalist named Gouvernail plays a major part in two *Night in Acadie* stories (and later appears in *The Awakening*). Many other characters are common to both books.

Motifs and images also recur: houses and outsiders and boundaries are present in both collections, as are poverty, violence, race,
and sex. A 'Cadian ball is a field for choosing marriage partners in
both books. The cross-referencing, the links in content and form,
unify the stories in *Bayou Folk* and the ones in *A Night in Acadie,*
and they unify the two books as well. The stories that open each
collection are especially integrated, full of interconnections—with
other stories in the same book and stories in the other book.

Chopin's planned third book of stories, *A Vocation and a Voice,*
was not published until 1991. With only two or three stories set in
Louisiana, it is not a continuation of the earlier collections. Those
Bayou Folk and *A Night in Acadie* themes and motifs that appear
are distorted and darker, and the sense of balance found in *A Night
in Acadie* is missing. *A Vocation and a Voice* is a fascinating book,
but the stories Chopin planned for it are of a different order from
those of her earlier two collections.

Many of the best stories in *Bayou Folk* are about young people
seeking good marriage partners and better lives for themselves. The
opening story stresses a young couple's determination to balance a
culturally rich life with a personally rewarding one. The woman,
eighteen-year-old Euphrasie Manton, cannot tell what, exactly, it is
she yearns for, any more than *The Awakening*'s Edna Pontellier
can—most of Chopin's characters act more from their instincts,
their cultural dispositions, than from conscious thought—but Wallace Offdean, the businessman Euphrasie will marry, certainly can:
"What he wanted . . . was to get his feet well planted on solid
ground, and to keep his head cool and clear. . . . Above all, he would
keep clear of the maelstroms of sordid work and senseless pleasure
in which the average American business man may be said alternately to exist, and which reduce him, naturally, to a rather ragged
condition of soul."

Offdean wants balance—between work and pleasure, the intellectual and the physical, the body and the spirit. He wants "a life
that, imposing bodily activity, admits the intellectual repose in
which thought unfolds." Chopin writes of such a yearning for balance again and again in *Bayou Folk* and *A Night in Acadie.*

The first three stories in *Bayou Folk* explore marriage possibilities, and all revolve around the Santien brothers—Placide Santien, Euphrasie's rejected fiancé in the first story; Hector Santien, a New Orleans gambler, in the second; and Grégoire Santien, also rejected by a woman, in the third. Each of the Santiens is involved with a woman seeking a better life for herself, and the women are all successful. Euphrasie of "A No-Account Creole" will marry her New Orleans businessman, purchase the old Santien plantation, and reach for the quality of life she knew as she grew up with the wealthy Duplans. Suzanne St. Denys Godolph of "In and Out of Old Natchitoches" will agree to be courted by the planter Alphonse Laballière. And 'Tite Reine, the once imperious "little queen" of "In Sabine," will escape from her drunken, abusive husband to seek the comfort of her family, if nothing else.

But marriage in *Bayou Folk* may lead to a loss of balance and a diminished social life. The Acadian Doudouce in "A Visit to Avoyelles," like Grégoire Santien, encounters a woman whose difficult life affects him deeply. Doudouce's journey to another parish— Chopin is fond of the journey motif—has brought him to a woman who has married an attractive outsider and is now living in poverty. But Mentine has no interest in being rescued. She adores her husband, poor as her life is, and Doudouce, who loved her before she left her community, loves her still.

Among the strongest stories in the collection is "At the 'Cadian Ball," for which Chopin would write a magnificent sequel called "The Storm," not published in her lifetime. The *Bayou Folk* story does not match the sweeping power, the intensity of focus, or the stunning language of "The Storm," one of America's great short stories, but it succeeds as a penetrating look at how two marriages came into being. Marriage is a social as well as an individual matter in the story. The 'Cadians hold all-night balls so young people can test possible marriage alliances. Old people attend the balls, as do married couples and children, but the evening belongs to the young 'Cadian women and the 'Cadian—and sometimes Creole—men who drift out onto the galleries between dances and whisper in the shadows.

The two couples in the story come from different social groups. Alcée Laballière (brother of Alphonse Laballière of "In and Out of Old Natchitoches") and his beautiful but cool kinswoman Clarisse are Creoles—the elite of the region, comparatively wealthy, sophis-

ticated descendants of settlers from France or Spain. Bobinôt and
the seductive Calixta, with her Cuban blood, are part of the Acadian community—poorer, less well-educated descendants of the
two thousand or three thousand Catholics who found their way to
the bayous of Louisiana after the British drove them out of Acadia,
Nova Scotia, in 1755. The possibility that Alcée might persuade
Calixta to agree to a rendezvous in another parish is a dangerous
threat to both couples—and the stability of both social groups. The
intervention by Clarisse restores equilibrium. Balance once again
prevails.

The charming, witty "Madame Célestin's Divorce," focused on a
marriage's end, might seem the antithesis of "At the 'Cadian Ball,"
but Chopin builds the story around a picket fence, suggesting a
boundary that separates the hopeful lawyer from Madame Célestin
and keeps the woman inside her marriage and her community. The
story, like the interaction between the lawyer and the woman he
would like to make his own, is flirtatious, and Chopin masterfully
uses a broom to suggest the power of sex in preserving this marriage.

Yet marriage is not the only subject emphasized in *Bayou Folk,*
and at times balance—with the chance for stability and fulfillment
that it brings—cannot be grasped by the characters in the collection.
In "Ma'ame Pélagie" an obsession with the past interferes. In this
story near the end of the book, Chopin develops the house-
reconstruction motif she uses in the first story, and brings in an outsider as she does there and in other works.

The outsider Wallace Offdean in "A No-Account Creole" will
help Euphrasie restore the old Santien house. But the new person in
"Ma'ame Pélagie"—La Petite, a niece of Pélagie—blocks a restora-
tion effort. Like Offdean, La Petite articulates what she wants, and
her sense of rich social possibilities resembles his: "I must live another life," she says, "the life I lived before. I want to know things
that are happening from day to day over the world, and hear them
talked about. I want my music, my books, my companions." But La
Petite's needs and Pélagie's vision for the restored house are incom-
patible. The young girl will have what she wants, as will Pélagie's
sister. But Ma'ame Pélagie herself has lost her dream, her fantasy,
and lost something tangible as well—her chance to regain for her-

self and her sister the prewar social position upon which her sense of fulfillment depends.

The darkest moments in *Bayou Folk* are in "Désirée's Baby," Chopin's most popular story throughout most of the twentieth century—and one of her few stories set before or during the Civil War. Again a fantasy, one of racial superiority, drives the narrative. But it leads not—as in "Ma'ame Pélagie"—to one person's acceptance of a diminished social position in return for the happiness and fulfillment of a beloved sister, but to a woman's shame, humiliation, and, presumably, death. Nowhere in Chopin's fiction does an inability to balance social and individual fulfillment result in more disastrous consequences.

The story's famous ironic ending hinges on differences between cultures. Armand Aubigny's white father and black mother apparently lived together happily in Paris, so Armand's rejection of his wife and child because the child carries black blood—part, if not all, his own—is a rejection of his parents as well, and perhaps even of himself. It is not clear if Armand knows that he is of mixed race or if he has had a child with La Blanche, his slave, nor is it clear just what Désirée understands about her husband. The story leaves much unexplained, but its stinging condemnation of racism has burned itself into the memory of readers for generations.

The depressing tone of "Désirée's Baby" is echoed at the end of *Bayou Folk*. The youthful optimism of the early stories is gone. "La Belle Zoraïde" and "A Lady of Bayou St. John" are linked stories centered on whites' attitudes toward race and on people's obsessions with fantasies. Both stories—separated by the lighter "A Gentleman of Bayou Têche"—close the collection with a focus not on the possibilities of the future but on the destructive pull of the past.

The principal theme in *A Night in Acadie*, as in *Bayou Folk*, is a search for personal fulfillment and cultural richness. But *A Night in Acadie* is a better balanced book, and its stories are stronger. Kate Chopin wrote other fine stories in the mid-1890s before she started on *The Awakening*, ones she did not include in this second collection—"The Story of an Hour," "Lilacs," "A Vocation and a Voice," "The Falling in Love of Fedora," "A Pair of Silk Stockings," and one or two others—and she wrote some powerful short fiction later in her career, notably "The Storm" and "Charlie." But she would produce little to surpass the works she published in *A Night in Acadie*—"Athénaïse," "A Matter of Prejudice," "Nég Créol," "Tante Cat'rinette," "A Respectable Woman," "Ripe Figs," and a few more. The *Night in Acadie* stories show us a world where life remains as difficult as it was in *Bayou Folk* yet is bursting with possibilities. *A Night in Acadie* is one of America's best nineteenth-century collections of short stories—and one of the most compassionate views of life in American realistic fiction.

The stories in the collection are framed by beginning and ending narratives about a man setting out on a short trip that leads to unexpected results—a probable marriage in the first, an act of kindness in the last. Within that frame is another, comprising two of Chopin's strongest stories—the lovely, haunting "Athénaïse," placed second in the collection, and "A Respectable Woman," positioned just before the little sketch "Ripe Figs" near the end.

The opening title story is a bridge from *Bayou Folk*. The setting is a 'Cadian ball held in a disintegrating plantation mansion, a perfect place for a narrative about young people—their options hemmed in by an oppressive poverty—seeking marriage partners and better lives. Zaïda Trodon, to be rescued by Telèsphore Baquette, himself escaping, at least for the day, from what he sees as the limited possibilities of his own region, is a cousin of the emaciated Mentine Trodon, whom Doudouce loves so desperately in the *Bayou Folk* story "A Visit to Avoyelles." Chopin describes Zaïda arriving at the ball all in white (the young woman plans to elope later in the evening) and, in a skillful touch, notes that even her slippers are white, though "no one would have believed let alone suspected that they were a pair of old black ones which she had covered with pieces of her first communion sash."

Like 'Tite Reine of "In Sabine," Zaïda is spared life with an arrogant man who drinks too much. She has the possibility now for a better match with the prudent, methodical Telèsphore, who adores her. But Zaïda is saved by chance. Without the fortunate appearance of an outsider, she might be in a difficult position the night of the 'Cadian ball, forced into a marriage she realizes would be a mistake.

The story Kate Chopin tells in "Athénaïse"—the longest, and, perhaps, the best story in the two collections—at first resembles

Edna Pontellier's story in *The Awakening*. The title character is a young woman recognizing a new life within her. Athénaïse Miché is miserable in her marriage, despite comfortable surroundings, and unsure about what she wants in place of it. Her Creole husband is polite and attentive enough about some things but insistent and arrogant about others. She herself is moody, impulsive, and headstrong—determined to do things her own way no matter what the cost. She leaves her husband's house, meets an attractive man, and finds her body and spirit suddenly alive, vibrant—full of new possibilities.

"Athénaïse," however, develops in a way that could hardly be more different from *The Awakening*. The man Athénaïse meets on leaving her husband, a journalist named Gouvernail, is drawn to her and would not hesitate to take her as his lover—but he understands better than Athénaïse herself does that what she needs at the moment is a confidant, a brother, so he holds her gently in his arms and tries to be that for her. Her husband, Cazeau, brought her home once before, after she left him, but he is so horrified by the thought of treating his wife as his father treated a runaway slave that he cannot seek her out again. He writes to her saying he will always love her but will no longer force himself on her. Although he believes that he has lost his last chance for happiness, that Athénaïse will never care for him, he writes that he will wait for her to return. The story ends not in separation and suicide, but in pregnancy, reconciliation, and hope.

There is no winner or loser in the narrative. Athénaïse changes, but so does her husband. To be sure, her brother is disappointed that she is behaving in such an "ordinary," "commonplace" fashion by returning to her husband when she learns she is pregnant, and certainly Athénaïse is transformed by the discovery that she is carrying a child. But she comes back to Cazeau not because she is trapped but because she is happy, because she is "steeped in a wave of ecstasy," because the "first purely sensuous tremor of her life" is washing over her as she speaks her husband's name, because she now understands herself as a partner of Cazeau, a coproprietor of their estate, because she has chosen the best opportunity open to her, because she has reached for the best possible life.

Other characters in *A Night in Acadie* are also changed by a child or children. "Polydore," "Regret," and "A Matter of Prejudice" are touching little narratives about the effect of a child on an older woman (and in "Mamouche," later in the collection, the older person is a man). In "Polydore," Mamzelle Adélaïde discovers a "bond of love" connecting her with a motherless boy she has raised as her own. In "Regret," Mamzelle Aurélie learns she has blundered in refusing marriage and the possibility of children. And in "A Matter of Prejudice," old Madame Carambeau—one of Chopin's more memorable characters—forgives her son for marrying an American woman and reaches out to her daughter-in-law and her grandchild.

Old Madame Carambeau's prejudices are part of a motif running through many Chopin stories—the way Creole culture influences people's sense of what is natural. Madame Carambeau "was a woman of many prejudices—so many, in fact, that it would be difficult to name them all. She detested dogs, cats, organ-grinders, white servants and children's noises. She despised Americans, Germans and all people of a different faith from her own. Anything not French had, in her opinion, little right to existence." Yet almost everyone around her yields to her dispositions. When she decides after ten years to reconcile with her son, she insists that Providence had arranged the details and "no one contradicted her." Like Maman Nainaine in the delicate sketch "Ripe Figs," near the end of *A Night in Acadie*, Madame Carambeau speaks with such authority that others accept her view as natural. Creoles—Madame Carambeau, Maman Nainaine, and others—maintain their dominant position in Chopin's Louisiana by virtue of their cultural, if not their economic, power and influence.

Yet Chopin makes clear here and throughout her fiction that such dominance is waning, that among young people French, like other languages immigrants have brought to America, is being displaced by English, and that most mainstream American values will eventually prevail. Madame Carambeau in "A Matter of Prejudice" will teach her granddaughter French, but the little girl will teach her English, and the old woman—having never before ventured into the American quarter of New Orleans—has now passed across the boundary separating it from the French quarter and will surely make the trip again.

Some *Night in Acadie* stories, like some in *Bayou Folk*, focus on people of color. "Nég Créol" and "Tante Cat'rinette" depict the loyalty of former slaves to the families that once owned them. The stories are among Chopin's strongest works in part because of the sensitive, loving portraits of two African Americans of great courage and dignity. Loyalty is a highly prized value in Chopin's stories. In "Ozème's Holiday," the closing work in *A Night in Acadie*, a 'Cadian man gives up his annual week's vacation to help a former slave pick her cotton and nurse her son back to health, and in "Odalie Misses Mass" a young girl stays with an old black woman left alone on a feast day. But in "Nég Créol" and "Tante Cat'rinette" a loyal commitment to others is measured not in hours or weeks, but in years, a lifetime.

Old Chicot, the nég créol, earns his keep in the teeming multi-cultural French Market of New Orleans among Sicilians and Gascon butchers, among Irish, Jews, Choctaws, mulattoes, blacks, and others. Because he is "so black, lean, lame, and shriveled," the merchants call him "Chicot" (stump), "Maringouin" (insect, mosquito), or simply "Nég." Powerless and dominated, he nevertheless builds an identity for himself by proclaiming his association with what he insists is an elite white family and by secretly caring for the diseased, poverty-stricken, seventy-five-year-old daughter of that family.

Tante Cat'rinette's devotion to her former owners is the same. Because she had saved the life of his daughter before the Civil War, a rich planter whom she calls Vieumaite (old master) had given Tante Cat'rinette her freedom and a house in Natchitoches. But a generation later, hard times and sickness have fallen upon Vieumaite's child, so Tante Cat'rinette once again saves her—with her nursing and with a loan of a thousand dollars she earns by selling her house. But the former slave rescues herself as well by avoiding the humiliating loss of her house (it is in poor repair and has become a danger to the community) and by integrating herself again into the lives of people whom she loves and who love her.

Chopin's attitude toward race in these works is complex. Her characters' language reflects the speech of the people in the regions she describes: "Negro," usually offensive to our ears, appears frequently in the stories and "darkey" comes up a few times, as does the hateful "nigger" or "nigga." Her characters' assumptions about the social position of African Americans also mirror those of their communities. Almost everyone in "In and Out of Old Natchitoches," the second story in *Bayou Folk*, accepts the social boundaries that separate whites from mulattoes, and African Americans throughout the stories insist on "maintaining the color line." Marriages between whites and blacks are impossible, as are relationships built on social equality.

Yet Chopin is not blind to racial injustice, any more than she is blind to patriarchal oppression or self-serving assumptions about gender, class, or ethnicity. She describes the racial situation as she has found it. In many stories friendship and trust are common among people of different races, and affection flows back and forth between blacks and whites, especially between black women and white children. "La Belle Zoraïde," "Nég Créol," "Tante Cat'rinette," "In Sabine," and other stories depict individual people of color as loving, sensitive, and strong. The stories capture both the suffering and the triumphs of these black people's lives. Chopin does not apologize for the racial situation in late-nineteenth-century Louisiana, nor does she idealize it. Her family had owned slaves when she was a child in St. Louis. During the Civil War, her half-brother fought on the side of the Confederacy and died of typhoid fever. Her husband joined the notorious White League in New Orleans. The culture of the Louisiana she knew inherited some ugly racial attitudes.

But Kate Chopin functioned in more than one culture and more than one language—and attitudes toward race were not the same from one group to another, so she always sees more than her characters see. She is not a revolutionary; she does not seek to overthrow the social order. She lived her entire life among people suffering the consequences of a violent destruction of their social and economic system. She values her communities, such as they are, because she values the individuals in them. She draws her characters—white people, black people, Native Americans, and people of mixed blood—with respect and dignity. She seeks the truth about the life she portrays. Within such a context—within an imaginative world where compassion and acceptance can be taken on trust, where the goal is to capture what is (though not always what ought to be) the truth—Chopin's limitations of vision as a white, middle-class, nineteenth-century Southern American woman loom not so large.

The depressing nature of race relations does not dominate the ending of *A Night in Acadie* as it does some late stories in *Bayou Folk.* "A Respectable Woman" occupies roughly the same position near the close of *A Night in Acadie* that "Athénaïse" has near the start. Sophisticated as well as respectable, Mrs. Baroda becomes fully aware of how powerful an influence her husband's friend—the journalist Gouvernail, who took such good care of Athénaïse Miché—is having upon her. Sitting alone with him one night, she is deeply disturbed: "She wanted to reach out her hand in the darkness and touch him with the sensitive tips of her fingers upon the face or the lips. She wanted to draw close to him and whisper against his cheek—she did not care what—as she might have done if she had not been a respectable woman."

Gouvernail murmurs, "half to himself," lines from Walt Whitman's "Song of Myself": "Night of south winds—night of the large few stars!/ Still nodding night—." Only after Mrs. Baroda returns to the house does he complete Whitman's "apostrophe to the night." Chopin does not quote the remainder, but readers may be familiar with it: "Press close bare-bosomed night—press close magnetic nourishing night!/ Night of south winds—night of the large few stars!/ Still nodding night—mad naked summer night."

In "A Respectable Woman" Gouvernail approaches the intimate circle of a married woman, as he had done in "Athénaïse," and again understands the woman in some ways better than she does herself. Kate Chopin does not often assign such understanding to a man. In her stories women are generally not only more attractive, graceful, and energetic than the men around them, but more insightful as well. Chopin likes Gouvernail, however, and gives him a small role in her novel *The Awakening.* He attends the party Edna Pontellier throws to celebrate her independence, and he observes carefully the events of the evening. Again he quotes a fragment of poetry—this time a sonnet by Algernon Swinburne—and again Chopin withholds the rest of the passage. But readers who recognize the Swinburne sonnet will see what the sensitive Gouvernail sees: that watching over the wild scene near the close of Edna's party is the brooding figure of death.

Near the close of *A Night in Acadie,* Gouvernail perceives the longing of his friend's wife as they sit together in the darkness. Chopin's wonderful last sentences of "A Respectable Woman" do not specify just what Mrs. Baroda has in mind to do now, but Gouvernail has opened for her possibilities she had not been aware of before.

Chopin is always aware of the importance of children in her communities. About half the stories in *Bayou Folk* were first published in or submitted to children's magazines or have subject matter and themes similar to those that were. "A Very Fine Fiddle" is a children's story, as are "Beyond the Bayou," "Old Aunt Peggy," "A Rude Awakening," "The Bênitous' Slave," "A Turkey Hunt," "Love on the Bon-Dieu," "Loka," "Boulôt and Boulotte," "For Marse Chouchoute," and "A Wizard from Gettysburg." Almost a third of the stories in *A Night in Acadie* are children's stories: "After the Winter," "Polydore," "A Matter of Prejudice," "The Lilies," "Mamouche," and "Ripe Figs." Other stories in the collections might be suitable for young readers. And some of those first published in children's magazines—"Beyond the Bayou," "A Matter of Prejudice," or "Ripe Figs," for example—might be thought of as stories for adults.

It was common in the nineteenth century for authors to write for both children and adults. Mark Twain did, as did Louisa May Alcott, Nathaniel Hawthorne, and Sarah Orne Jewett. And it was common for magazines like *Youth's Companion* or *Harper's Young People*—both of which published Chopin's work—to attract high-quality fiction and for editors of adult magazines to monitor the children's magazines for talent. Some beginning authors wrote children's stories to polish their craft and to impress such editors, then turned away from the genre when they had established themselves. But Kate Chopin continued to write for children throughout her career.

Mindful of her readership, she thought carefully about what to include in her works. "The question of how much or how little knowledge of life should be withheld from the youthful mind," she writes,

> is a subject about which there exists a diversity of opinion with the conservative element no doubt, greatly in preponderance. As a rule the youthful, untrained nature is left to gather

wisdom as it comes along in a thousand-and-one ways and in whatever form it may present itself to the intelligent, the susceptible, the observant. In this respect experience is perhaps an abler instructor than direct enlightenment from man or woman; for it works by suggestion. There are many phases and features of life which cannot, or rather should not be expounded, demonstrated, presented to the youthful imagination as cold facts, for it is safe to assert they are not going to be accepted as such. It is moreover robbing youth of its privilege to gather wisdom as the bee gathers honey.

Chopin writes to inform, to entertain her children's audience, not to offer moral guidance, but, like others writing for children at the time, she chooses her subjects with care. She likes stories about girls becoming adults ("Loka," "A Rude Awakening") and about adults seeking companionship ("After the Winter," "Polydore," "A Matter of Prejudice," "The Lilies," "Mamouche"), and she often dwells on the way children cope with the harsh economic conditions so common in her world ("For Marse Chouchoute," "A Very Fine Fiddle," "Boulôt and Boulotte," "A Wizard from Gettysburg").

Her concern over balance in her adult stories spills naturally into her works for children. A search for balance has been a fundamental element in many classic British and American children's stories—balance between what children are free to do and what they are not, what they wish for and what they can have, their wanting to be home and wanting to run away, their feeling alienated or feeling wanted. All those motifs are present in Chopin's children's stories.

From the time of her childhood in St. Louis, Kate Chopin had the ability to see beyond what those in her immediate community were seeing, to see with detachment and irony, with an understanding that truth looks different from within different cultures, that it shapes and reshapes itself and is not subject to easy generalization. In Bayou Folk and A Night in Acadie she writes both as a member of the communities she depicts and as an observer. Although she generally accepts the values of her communities, she positions herself so that she can comment on those values. She is anything but dogmatic. She seeks to show "true life and true art," as she calls it, "human existence in its subtle, complex, true meaning, stripped of the veil with which ethical and conventional standards have draped it." She has a gentle, knowing gaze—insightful, compassionate, and accepting.

Many stories in *Bayou Folk* and *A Night in Acadie* place people of one culture alongside those of another (*The Awakening* too has an intercultural emphasis; Edna Pontellier is a Kentucky Presbyterian married to a New Orleans Creole). They illuminate the cultural contexts of human yearnings. They explore how people are shaped by life in a heterogeneous, complex, often unjust society.

Chopin understands, as her contemporary Henry James understands, that a person lives in a community, but the community also lives in the person. Like James and other realists, she is aware of the giant biological, psychological, and economic forces shaping people's lives, but her characters are usually free to seek the better existence they yearn for, although what they want is deeply influenced by those with whom they live. Her communities have troubling problems, but individuals—women, men, and children, white people and people of color—cross social boundaries, appropriate others' values, reach with intelligence and confidence for richer, more fulfilling, better balanced lives.

Kate Chopin integrates culture, regional character, race, the power of sex, and the concerns of women into her collections of stories, sensing what Walt Whitman had felt forty years earlier— that cultural differences and racial differences nourish a community, that women as well as men nourish it, that sex nourishes it. She weaves together sex, race, culture, and gender in her stories, celebrating them all, making *Bayou Folk* and *A Night in Acadie* feel at times exotic, like Louisiana plantations and 'Cadian balls, and at times familiar, like the multiethnic, multiracial, multilingual, gender-sensitive, and sexually charged America we know today.

BERNARD KOLOSKI
Mansfield, Pennsylvania
May 1998

SUGGESTIONS FOR FURTHER READING

THE WORKS OF KATE CHOPIN

Seyersted, Per, ed. *The Complete Works of Kate Chopin.* 2 vols. Baton Rouge: Louisiana State University Press, 1969.

Seyersted, Per, and Emily Toth, eds. *A Kate Chopin Miscellany.* Natchitoches, LA: Northwestern State University Press, 1979.

Toth, Emily, Per Seyersted, and Marilyn Bonnell, eds. *Kate Chopin's Private Papers.* Bloomington: Indiana University Press, 1998.

BIOGRAPHIES

Rankin, Daniel. *Kate Chopin and Her Creole Stories.* Philadelphia: University of Pennsylvania Press, 1932.

Seyersted, Per. *Kate Chopin: A Critical Biography.* Baton Rouge: Louisiana State University Press, 1969.

Toth, Emily. *Kate Chopin.* New York: William Morrow, 1990.

CRITICISM

Arms, George. "Kate Chopin's *The Awakening* in the Perspective of her Literary Career." In *Essays on American Literature in Honor of Jay B. Hubbell,* Clarence Gohdes, ed. Durham, NC: Duke University Press, 1967. 215–28.

Arner, Robert D. "Kate Chopin." Special issue of *Louisiana Studies* 14(1975): 11–139.

Bardot, Jean. "French Creole Portraits: The Chopin Family from Natchitoches Parish." In *Perspectives on Kate Chopin: Proceedings from the Kate Chopin International Conference. April 6, 7, 8, 1989.* Natchitoches, LA: Northwestern State University Press, 1992. 25–36.

Birnbaum, Michele A. " 'Alien Hands': Kate Chopin and the Colonization of Race." *American Literature* 66 (1994): 301–23.

Bloom, Harold, ed. *Kate Chopin.* New York: Chelsea, 1987.

Bonner, Thomas, Jr. "Christianity and Catholicism in the Fiction of Kate Chopin." *The Southern Quarterly: A Journal of the Arts in the South* 20 (1982): 118–25.

———. *The Kate Chopin Companion.* New York: Greenwood, 1988.

———. "Kate Chopin: Tradition and the Moment." In *Southern Literature in Transition: Heritage and Promise,* Philip and William Osborne Castille, eds. Memphis: Memphis State University Press, 1983. 141–49.

Boren, Lynda S., and Sara deSaussure Davis, eds. *Kate Chopin Reconsidered: Beyond the Bayou.* Baton Rouge: Louisiana State University Press, 1992.

Dyer, Joyce. "Gouvernail, Kate Chopin's Sensitive Bachelor." *Southern Literary Journal* 14 (1981): 46–55.

———. "Kate Chopin's Sleeping Bruties." *Markham Review* 10 (1980): 10–15.

———, and Robert Emmett Monroe. "Texas and Texans in the Fiction of Kate Chopin." *Western American Literature* 20 (1985): 3–15.

Elfenbein, Anna Shannon. *Women on the Color Line: Evolving Stereotypes and the Writings of George Washington Cable, Grace King, and Kate Chopin.* Charlottesville: University Press of Virginia, 1989.

Ellis, Nancy S. "Insistent Refrains and Self-Discovery: Accompanied Awakenings in Three Stories by Kate Chopin." In *Kate Chopin Reconsidered: Beyond the Bayou.* Lynda S. Boren and Sara deSaussure Davis, eds. Baton Rouge: Louisiana State University Press, 1992. 216–29.

Ewell, Barbara C. *Kate Chopin.* New York: Ungar, 1986.

Fluck, Winfried. "Tentative Transgressions: Kate Chopin's Fiction as a Mode of Symbolic Action." *Studies in American Fiction* 10 (1982): 151–71.

Fusco, Richard. *Maupassant and the American Short Story: The Influence of Form at the Turn of the Century.* University Park: Pennsylvania State University Press, 1994.

Gardiner, Elaine. " 'Ripe Figs': Kate Chopin in Miniature." *Modern Fiction Studies* 28 (1982): 379–82.

Gaudet, Marcia. "Kate Chopin and the Lore of Cane River's Creoles of Color." *Xavier Review* 6 (1986): 45–52.

Goodwyn, Janet. " 'Dah you is, settin' down, lookin' jis' like w'ite folks!': Ethnicity Enacted in Kate Chopin's Short Fiction." *The Yearbook of English Studies* 24 (1994): 1–11.

Gunning, Sandra. "Kate Chopin's Local Color Fiction and the Politics of White Supremacy." *Arizona Quarterly* 51 (1995): 61–86.

Howell, Elmo. "Kate Chopin and the Creole Country." *Louisiana History.* 20 (1979): 209–19.

Jones, Anne Goodwyn. *Tomorrow Is Another Day: The Woman Writer in the South, 1859–1936.* Baton Rouge: Louisiana State University Press, 1981.

Koloski, Bernard. "The Anthologized Chopin: Kate Chopin's Stories in Yesterday's and Today's Anthologies." *Louisiana Literature* 11 (1994): 18–30.

———. *Kate Chopin: A Study of the Short Fiction.* New York: Twayne, 1996.

———. "The Swinburne Lines in *The Awakening.*" *American Literature* 45 (1974): 608–10.

Lattin, Patricia Hopkins. "Childbirth and Motherhood in *The Awakening* and in 'Athénaïse.' " In *Approaches to Teaching Chopin's The Awakening,* Bernard Koloski, ed. New York: Modern Language Association of America, 1988. 40–46.

———. "Kate Chopin's Repeating Characters." *Mississippi Quarterly* 33 (1980): 19–37.

———. "The Search for Self in Kate Chopin's Fiction: Simple Versus Complex Vision." *Southern Studies* 21 (1982): 222–35.

Leary, Lewis. "Kate Chopin, Liberationist?" *Southern Literary Journal* 3 (1970): 138–44.

Lohafer, Susan. *Coming to Terms with the Short Story.* Baton Rouge: Louisiana State University Press, 1983.

McMahan, Elizabeth. " 'Nature's Decoy': Kate Chopin's Presentation of Women and Marriage in Her Short Fiction." *Turn-of-the-Century Women* 2 (1985): 32–35.

Newman, Judie. "Kate Chopin: Short Fiction and the Art of Subversion." In *The Nineteenth-Century American Short Story,* A. Robert Lee, ed. New York: Vision, 1985. 150–63.

Papke, Mary E. "Chopin's Stories of Awakening." In *Approaches to Teaching Chopin's The Awakening,* Bernard Koloski, ed. New York: Modern Language Association of America, 1988. 73–79.

———. *Verging on the Abyss: The Social Fiction of Kate Chopin and Edith Wharton.* Westport, CT: Greenwood, 1990.

Peel, Ellen. "Semiotic Subversion in 'Désirée's Baby.' " *American Literature* 62 (1990): 223–37.

Petry, Alice Hall. *Critical Essays on Kate Chopin.* New York: G. K. Hall, 1996.

Potter, Richard H. "Negroes in the Fiction of Kate Chopin." *Louisiana History* 12 (1971): 41–58.

Ringe, Donald A. "Cane River World: Kate Chopin's *At Fault* and Related Stories." *Studies in American Fiction* 3 (1975): 157–66.

Rogers, Nancy E. "Echoes of George Sand in Kate Chopin." *Revue de Littérature Comparée* 1 (1983): 25–42.

Shurbutt, Sylvia Bailey. "The Cane River Characters and Revisionist Mythmaking in the Work of Kate Chopin." *The Southern Literary Journal* 25 (1993): 14–23.

Skaggs, Peggy. *Kate Chopin*. Boston: Twayne, 1985.

———. " 'The Man-Instinct of Possession': A Persistent Theme in Kate Chopin's Stories." *Louisiana Studies* 14 (1975): 177–85.

Steiling, David. "Multi-cultural Aesthetic in Kate Chopin's 'A Gentleman of Bayou Teche.' " *The Mississippi Quarterly* 47 (1994): 197–200.

Stein, Allen F. *After the Vows Were Spoken: Marriage in American Literary Realism*. Columbus: Ohio State University Press, 1984.

Taylor, Helen. *Gender, Race, and Region in the Writings of Grace King, Ruth McEnery Stuart, and Kate Chopin*. Baton Rouge: Louisiana State University Press, 1989.

Toth, Emily. "Kate Chopin and Literary Convention: 'Désirée's Baby.' " *Southern Studies: An Interdisciplinary Journal of the South* 20 (1981): 201–08.

Wood, Ann Douglas. "The Literature of Improverishment: The Woman Local Colorists in America 1865–1914." *Women's Studies* 1 (1972): 3–45.

Wymard, Eleanor B. "Kate Chopin: Her Existential Imagination." *Southern Studies: An Interdisciplinary Journal of the South* 19 (1980): 373–84.

A NOTE ON THE TEXT

The stories reprinted here are arranged in the order they appear in *Bayou Folk*, published in 1894 by Houghton Mifflin Company of Boston, and *A Night in Acadie*, published in 1897 by Way and Williams of Chicago. The texts of the stories are taken from Per Seyersted's definitive *The Complete Works of Kate Chopin*, published in two volumes by Louisiana State University Press in 1969. Information about editions of *Bayou Folk* and *A Night in Acadie* and about the stories—composition dates, magazine publication dates, earlier titles, differences in wording between manuscript, periodical, and book versions—can be found at the end of the second volume of *The Complete Works*.

BAYOU FOLK

BAYOU FOLK

BY

KATE CHOPIN

BOSTON AND NEW YORK
HOUGHTON MIFFLIN COMPANY
The Riverside Press Cambridge

A No-Account Creole

I

ONE agreeable afternoon in late autumn two young men stood together on Canal Street, closing a conversation that had evidently begun within the club-house which they had just quitted.

"There's big money in it, Offdean," said the elder of the two. "I would n't have you touch it if there was n't. Why, they tell me Patchly's pulled a hundred thousand out of the concern a'ready."

"That may be," replied Offdean, who had been politely attentive to the words addressed to him, but whose face bore a look indicating that he was closed to conviction. He leaned back upon the clumsy stick which he carried, and continued: "It's all true, I dare say, Fitch; but a decision of that sort would mean more to me than you'd believe if I were to tell you. The beggarly twenty-five thousand's all I have, and I want to sleep with it under my pillow a couple of months at least before I drop it into a slot."

"You'll drop it into Harding & Offdean's mill to grind out the pitiful two and a half per cent commission racket; that's what you 'll do in the end, old fellow—see if you don't."

"Perhaps I shall; but it's more than likely I shan't. We'll talk about it when I get back. You know I'm off to north Louisiana in the morning"—

"No! What the deuce"—

"Oh, business of the firm."

"Write me from Shreveport, then; or wherever it is."

"Not so far as that. But don't expect to hear from me till you see me. I can't say when that will be."

Then they shook hands and parted. The rather portly Fitch

5

boarded a Prytania Street car, and Mr. Wallace Offdean hurried to the bank in order to replenish his portemonnaie, which had been materially lightened at the club through the medium of unpropitious jack-pots and bobtail flushes.

He was a sure-footed fellow, this young Offdean, despite an occasional fall in slippery places. What he wanted, now that he had reached his twenty-sixth year and his inheritance, was to get his feet well planted on solid ground, and to keep his head cool and clear.

With his early youth he had had certain shadowy intentions of shaping his life on intellectual lines. That is, he wanted to; and he meant to use his faculties intelligently, which means more than is at once apparent. Above all, he would keep clear of the maelstroms of sordid work and senseless pleasure in which the average American business man may be said alternately to exist, and which reduce him, naturally, to a rather ragged condition of soul.

Offdean had done, in a temperate way, the usual things which young men do who happen to belong to good society, and are possessed of moderate means and healthy instincts. He had gone to college, had traveled a little at home and abroad, had frequented society and the clubs, and had worked in his uncle's commission-house; in all of which employments he had expended much time and a modicum of energy.

But he felt all through that he was simply in a preliminary stage of being, one that would develop later into something tangible and intelligent, as he liked to tell himself. With his patrimony of twenty-five thousand dollars came what he felt to be the turning-point in his life,—the time when it behooved him to choose a course, and to get himself into proper trim to follow it manfully and consistently.

When Messrs. Harding & Offdean determined to have some one look after what they called "a troublesome piece of land on Red River," Wallace Offdean requested to be intrusted with that special commission of land-inspector.

A shadowy, ill-defined piece of land in an unfamiliar part of his native State, might, he hoped, prove a sort of closet into which he could retire and take counsel with his inner and better self.

II

What Harding & Offdean had called a piece of land on Red River was better known to the people of Natchitoches[1] parish as "the old Santien place."

In the days of Lucien Santien and his hundred slaves, it had been very splendid in the wealth of its thousand acres. But the war did its work, of course. Then Jules Santien was not the man to mend such damage as the war had left. His three sons were even less able than he had been to bear the weighty inheritance of debt that came to them with the dismantled plantation; so it was a deliverance to all when Harding & Offdean, the New Orleans creditors, relieved them of the place with the responsibility and indebtedness which its ownership had entailed.

Hector, the eldest, and Grégoire, the youngest of these Santien boys, had gone each his way. Placide alone tried to keep a desultory foothold upon the land which had been his and his forefathers'. But he too was given to wandering—within a radius, however, which rarely took him so far that he could not reach the old place in an afternoon of travel, when he felt so inclined.

There were acres of open land cultivated in a slovenly fashion, but so rich that cotton and corn and weed and "cocoa-grass" grew rampant if they had only the semblance of a chance. The negro quarters were at the far end of this open stretch, and consisted of a long row of old and very crippled cabins. Directly back of these a dense wood grew, and held much mystery, and witchery of sound and shadow, and strange lights when the sun shone. Of a gin-house there was left scarcely a trace; only so much as could serve as inadequate shelter to the miserable dozen cattle that huddled within it in winter-time.

A dozen rods or more from the Red River bank stood the dwelling-house, and nowhere upon the plantation had time touched so sadly as here. The steep, black, moss-covered roof sat like an extinguisher[2] above the eight large rooms that it covered, and had come to do its office so poorly that not more than half of these were habitable when the rain fell. Perhaps the live-oaks made too thick and close a shelter about it. The verandas were long and broad and inviting; but it was well to know that the brick pillar was crumbling away under one corner, that the railing was insecure at another, and that still another had long ago been condemned as unsafe. But that, of course, was not the corner in which Wallace Offdean sat the day following his arrival at the Santien place. This one was comparatively secure. A gloire-de-Dijon, thick-leaved and charged with huge creamy blossoms, grew and spread here like a hardy vine upon the wires that stretched from post to post. The scent of the blossoms was delicious; and the stillness that surrounded Offdean agreeably fitted his humor that asked for rest. His old host, Pierre Manton, the manager of the place, sat talking to him in a soft, rhythmic monotone; but his speech was hardly more of an interruption than the hum of the bees among the roses. He was saying:—

"If it would been me myse'f, I would nevair grumb'. W'en a chimbly breck, I take one, two de boys; we patch 'im up bes' we know how. We keep on men' de fence', firs' one place, anudder; an' if it would n' be fer dem mule' of Lacroix—*tonnerre!*[3] I don' wan' to talk 'bout dem mule'. But me, I would n' grumb'. It 's Euphrasie, hair. She say dat's all fool nonsense fer rich man lack Hardin'-Offde'n to let a piece o' lan' goin' lack dat."

"Euphrasie?" questioned Offdean, in some surpise; for he had not yet heard of any such person.

"Euphrasie, my li'le chile. Escuse me one minute," Pierre added, remembering that he was in his shirt-sleeves, and rising to reach for his coat, which hung upon a peg near by. He was a small, square man, with mild, kindly face, brown and roughened from healthy exposure. His hair hung gray and long beneath the soft felt hat that he wore. When he had seated himself, Offdean asked:—

"Where is your little child? I have n't seen her," inwardly marveling that a little child should have uttered such words of wisdom as those recorded of her.

"She yonder to Mme. Duplan on Cane River. I been kine espectin' hair since yistiday—hair an' Placide," casting an unconscious glance down the long plantation road. "But Mme. Duplan she nevair want to let Euphrasie go. You know it's hair raise' Euphraise since hair po' ma die', Mr. Offde'n. She teck dat li'le chile, an' raise it, sem lack she raisin' Ninette. But it's mo' 'an a year now Euphrasie say dat 's all fool nonsense to leave me livin' 'lone lack dat, wid nuttin' 'cep' dem nigger'—an' Placide once a w'ile. An' she came yair bossin'! My goodness!" The old man chuckled, "Dat 's hair been writin' all dem letter' to Hardin'-Offde'n. If it would been me myse'f"—

III

Placide seemed to have had a foreboding of ill from the start when he found that Euphrasie began to interest herself in the condition of the plantation. This ill feeling voiced itself partly when he told her it was none of her lookout if the place went to the dogs. "It 's good enough for Joe Duplan to run things *en grand seigneur*,[4] Euphraise; that 's w'at 's spoiled you."

Placide might have done much single-handed to keep the old place in better trim, if he had wished. For there was no one more clever than he to do a hand's turn at any and every thing. He could mend a saddle or bridle while he stood whistling a tune. If a wagon required a brace or a bolt, it was nothing for him to step into a shop and turn out one as deftly as the most skilled blacksmith. Any one seeing him at work with plane and rule and chisel would have declared him a born carpenter. And as for mixing paints, and giving a fine and lasting coat to the side of a house or barn, he had not his equal in the country.

This last talent he exercised little in his native parish. It was in a neighboring one, where he spent the greater part of his time, that his fame as a painter was established. There, in the village of Orville, he owned a little shell of a house, and during odd times it was Placide's great delight to tinker at this small home, inventing daily new beauties and conveniences to add to it. Lately it had become a precious possession to him, for in the spring he was to bring Euphrasie there as his wife.

Maybe it was because of his talent, and his indifference in turning it to good, that he was often called "a no-account creole" by thriftier souls than himself. But no-account creole or not, painter, carpenter, blacksmith, and whatever else he might be at times, he was a Santien always, with the best blood in the country running in his veins. And many thought his choice had fallen in very low places when he engaged himself to marry little Euphrasie, the daughter of old Pierre Manton and a problematic mother a good deal less than nobody.

Placide might have married almost any one, too; for it was the easiest thing in the world for a girl to fall in love with him,— sometimes the hardest thing in the world not to, he was such a splendid fellow, such a careless, happy, handsome fellow. And he did not seem to mind in the least that young men who had grown up with him were lawyers now, and planters, and members of Shakespeare clubs in town. No one ever expected anything quite so humdrum as that of the Santien boys. As youngsters, all three had been the despair of the country schoolmaster; then of the private tutor who had come to shackle them, and had failed in his design. And the state of mutiny and revolt that they had brought about at the college of Grand Coteau when their father, in a moment of weak concession to prejudice, had sent them there, is a thing yet remembered in Natchitoches.

And now Placide was going to marry Euphrasie. He could not recall the time when he had not loved her. Somehow he felt that it began the day when he was six years old, and Pierre, his father's overseer, had called him from play to come and make her acquaintance. He was permitted to hold her in his arms a moment, and it was with silent awe that he did so. She was the first whitefaced baby he remembered having seen, and he straightway believed she had been sent to him as a birthday gift to be his little playmate and friend. If he loved her, there was no great wonder; every one did, from the time she took her first dainty step, which was a brave one, too.

She was the gentlest little lady ever born in old Natchitoches parish, and the happiest and merriest. She never cried or whimpered for a hurt. Placide never did, why should she? When she wept, it was when she did what was wrong, or when he did; for that was to be a coward, she felt. When she was ten, and her mother was dead, Mme. Duplan, the Lady Bountiful of the parish, had driven across from her plantation, Les Chêniers,[5] to old Pierre's very door, and there had gathered up this precious little maid, and carried her away, to do with as she would.

And she did with the child much as she herself had been done by. Euphrasie went to the convent soon, and was taught all gentle things, the pretty arts of manner and speech that the ladies of the "Sacred Heart" can teach so well. When she quitted them, she left a trail of love behind her; she always did.

Placide continued to see her at intervals, and to love her always. One day he told her so; he could not help it. She stood under one of the big oaks at Les Chêniers. It was midsummer time, and the tangled sunbeams had enmeshed her in a golden fretwork. When he saw her standing there in the sun's glamour, which was like a glory upon her, he trembled. He seemed to see her for the first time. He could only look at her, and wonder why her hair gleamed so, as it fell in those thick chestnut waves about her ears and neck. He had looked a thousand times into her eyes before; was it only to-day they held that sleepy, wistful light in them that invites love? How had he not seen it before? Why had he not known before that her lips were red, and cut in fine, strong curves? that her flesh was like cream? How had he not seen that she was beautiful? "Euphrasie," he said, taking her hands,—"Euphrasie, I love you!"

She looked at him with a little astonishment. "Yes; I know, Placide." She spoke with the soft intonation of the creole.

"No, you don't, Euphrasie. I did n' know myse'f how much tell jus' now."

Perhaps he did only what was natural when he asked her next if she loved him. He still held her hands. She looked thoughtfully away, unready to answer.

"Do you love anybody better?" he asked jealously. "Any one jus' as well as me?"

"You know I love papa better, Placide, an' Maman Duplan jus' as well."

Yet she saw no reason why she should not be his wife when he asked her to.

Only a few months before this, Euphrasie had returned to live with her father. The step had cut her off from everything that girls of eighteen call pleasure. If it cost her one regret, no one could have guessed it. She went often to visit the Duplans, however; and Placide had gone to bring her home from Les Chêniers the very day of Offdean's arrival at the plantation.

They had traveled by rail to Natchitoches, where they found Pierre's no-top buggy awaiting them, for there was a drive of five miles to be made through the pine woods before the plantation was reached. When they were at their journey's end, and had driven some distance up the long plantation road that led to the house in the rear, Euphrasie exclaimed:—

"W'y, there's some one on the gall'ry with papa, Placide!"

"Yes; I see."

"It looks like some one f'om town. It mus' be Mr. Gus Adams; but I don' see his horse."

"'T ain't no one f'om town that I know. It 's boun' to be some one f'om the city."

"Oh, Placide, I should n' wonder if Harding & Offdean have sent some one to look after the place at las'," she exclaimed a little excitedly.

They were near enough to see that the stranger was a young man of very pleasing appearance. Without apparent reason, a chilly depression took hold of Placide.

"I tole you it was n' yo' lookout f'om the firs', Euphrasie," he said to her.

                              IV

Wallace Offdean remembered Euphrasie at once as a young person whom he had assisted to a very high perch on his clubhouse balcony the previous Mardi Gras night. He had thought her pretty and attractive then, and for the space of a day or two wondered who she might be. But he had not made even so fleeting an impression upon her; seeing which, he did not refer to any former meeting when Pierre introduced them.

She took the chair which he offered her, and asked him very simply when he had come, if his journey had been pleasant, and if he had not found the road from Natchitoches in very good condition.

"Mr. Offde'n only come sence yistiday, Euphrasie," interposed Pierre. "We been talk' plenty 'bout de place, him an' me. I been tole 'im all 'bout it—va! An' if Mr. Offde'n want to escuse me now, I b'lieve I go he'p Placide wid dat hoss an' buggy;" and he descended the steps slowly, and walked lazily with his bent figure in the direction of the shed beneath which Placide had driven, after depositing Euphrasie at the door.

"I dare say you find it strange," began Offdean, "that the owners of this place have neglected it so long and shamefully. But you see," he added, smiling, "the management of a plantation does n't enter into the routine of a commission merchant's business. The place has already cost them more than they hope to get from it, and naturally they have n't the wish to sink further money in it." He did not know why he was saying these things to a mere girl, but he went on: "I'm authorized to sell the plantation if I can get anything like a reasonable price for it." Euphrasie laughed in a way that made him uncomfortable, and he thought he would say no more at present,— not till he knew her better, anyhow.

"Well," she said in a very decided fashion, "I know you' ll fin' one or two persons in town who 'll begin by running down the lan' till you would n' want it as a gif', Mr. Offdean; and who will en' by offering to take it off yo' han's for the promise of a song, with the lan' as security again."

They both laughed, and Placide, who was approaching, scowled. But before he reached the steps his instinctive sense of the courtesy due to a stranger had banished the look of ill humor. His bearing was so frank and graceful, and his face such a marvel of beauty, with its dark, rich coloring and soft lines, that the well-clipped and groomed Offdean felt his astonishment to be more than half admiration when they shook hands. He knew that the Santiens had been the former owners of this plantation which he had come to look after, and naturally he expected some sort of cooperation or direct assistance from Placide in his efforts at reconstruction. But Placide proved non-committal, and exhibited an indifference and ignorance concerning the condition of affairs that savored surprisingly of affectation.

He had positively nothing to say so long as the talk touched upon matters concerning Offdean's business there. He was only a little less taciturn when more general topics were approached, and directly after supper he saddled his horse and went away. He would not wait until morning, for the moon would be rising about midnight, and he knew the road as well by night as by day. He knew just where the best fords were across the bayous, and the safest paths across the hills. He knew for a certainty whose plantations he might traverse, and whose fences he might derail. But, for that matter, he would derail what he liked, and cross where he pleased.

Euphrasie walked with him to the shed when he went for his

horse. She was bewildered at his sudden determination, and wanted
it explained.

"I don' like that man," he admitted frankly; "I can't stan' him.
Sen' me word w'en he 's gone, Euphrasie."

She was patting and rubbing the pony, which knew her well.
Only their dim outlines were discernible in the thick darkness.

"You are foolish, Placide," she replied in French. "You would do
better to stay and help him. No one knows the place so well
as you"—

"The place is n't mine, and it 's nothing to me," he answered bitterly. He took her hands and kissed them passionately, but stooping, she pressed her lips upon his forehead.

"Oh!" he exclaimed rapturously, "you do love me, Euphrasie?"
His arms were holding her, and his lips brushing her hair and
cheeks as they eagerly but ineffectually sought hers.

"Of co'se I love you, Placide. Ain't I going to marry you nex'
spring? You foolish boy!" she replied, disengaging herself from his
clasp.

When he was mounted, he stooped to say, "See yere, Euphrasie,
don't have too much to do with that d———Yankee."

"But, Placide, he is n't a—a—'d———Yankee;' he 's a South-
erner, like you,—a New Orleans man."

"Oh, well, he looks like a Yankee." But Placide laughed, for he
was happy since Euphrasie had kissed him, and he whistled softly
as he urged his horse to a canter and disappeared in the darkness.

The girl stood awhile with clasped hands, trying to understand a
little sigh that rose in her throat, and that was not one of regret.
When she regained the house, she went directly to her room, and
left her father talking to Offdean in the quiet and perfumed night.

V

When two weeks had passed, Offdean felt very much at home with
old Pierre and his daughter, and found the business that had called
him to the country so engrossing that he had given no thought to
those personal questions he had hoped to solve in going there.

The old man had driven him around in the no-top buggy to
show him how dismantled the fences and barns were. He could see

for himself that the house was a constant menace to human life. In the evenings the three would sit out on the gallery and talk of the land and its strong points and its weak ones, till he came to know it as if it had been his own.

Of the rickety condition of the cabins he got a fair notion, for he and Euphrasie passed them almost daily on horseback, on their way to the woods. It was seldom that their appearance together did not rouse comment among the darkies who happened to be loitering about.

La Chatte,[6] a broad black woman with ends of white wool sticking out from under her *tignon*,[7] stood with arms akimbo watching them as they disappeared one day. Then she turned and said to a young woman who sat in the cabin door:—

"Dat young man, ef he want to listen to me, he gwine quit dat ar caperin' roun' Miss 'Phrasie."

The young woman in the doorway laughed, and showed her white teeth, and tossed her head, and fingered the blue beads at her throat, in a way to indicate that she was in hearty sympathy with any question that touched upon gallantry.

"Law! La Chatte, you ain' gwine hinder a gemman f'om payin' intentions to a young lady w'en he a mine to."

"Dat all I got to say," returned La Chatte, seating herself lazily and heavily on the doorstep. "Nobody don' know dem Sanchun boys bettah 'an I does. Did n' I done part raise 'em? W'at you reckon my ha'r all tu'n plumb w'ite dat-a-way ef it warn't dat Placide w'at done it?"

"How come he make yo' ha'r tu'n w'ite, La Chatte?"

"Dev'ment, pu' dev'ment, Rose. Did n' he come in dat same cabin one day, w'en he warn't no bigga 'an dat Pres'dent Hayes[8] w'at you sees gwine 'long de road wid dat cotton sack 'crost 'im? He come an' sets down by de do', on dat same t'ree-laigged stool w'at you's a-settin' on now, wid his gun in his han', an' he say: 'La Chatte, I wants some croquignoles,[9] an' I wants 'em quick, too.' I 'low: 'G' 'way f'om dah, boy. Don' you see I's flutin' yo' ma's petticoat?' He say: 'La Chatte, put 'side dat ar flutin'-i'on an' dat ar petticoat;' an' he cock dat gun an' p'int it to my head. 'Dar de ba'el,' he say; 'git out dat flour, git out dat butta an' dat aigs; step roun' dah, ole 'oman. Dis heah gun don' quit yo' head tell dem croqui-

gnoles is on de table, wid a w'ite tableclof an' a cup o' coffee.' Ef I
goes to de ba'el, de gun's a-p'intin'. Ef I goes to de fiah, de gun's a-
p'intin'. W'en I rolls out de dough, de gun 's a-p'intin'; an' him neva
say nuttin', an' me a-trim'lin' like ole Uncle Noah w'en de mis'ry
strike 'im."

"Lordy! w'at you reckon he do ef he tu'n roun' an' git mad wid
dat young gemman f'om de city?"

"I don' reckon nuttin'; I knows w'at he gwine do,—same w'at
his pa done."

"W'at his pa done, La Chatte?"

"G' 'long 'bout yo' business; you 's axin' too many questions."
And La Chatte arose slowly and went to gather her party-colored
wash that hung drying on the jagged and irregular points of a dilapidated picket-fence.

But the darkies were mistaken in supposing that Offdean was
paying attention to Euphrasie. Those little jaunts in the wood were
purely of a business character. Offdean had made a contract with a
neighboring mill for fencing, in exchange for a certain amount of
uncut timber. He had made it his work—with the assistance of Euphrasie—to decide upon what trees he wanted felled, and to mark
such for the woodman's axe.

If they sometimes forgot what they had gone into the woods for,
it was because there was so much to talk about and to laugh about.
Often, when Offdean had blazed a tree with the sharp hatchet
which he carried at his pommel, and had further discharged his
duty by calling it "a fine piece of timber," they would sit upon some
fallen and decaying trunk, maybe to listen to a chorus of mocking-
birds above their heads, or to exchange confidences, as young people will.

Euphrasie thought she had never heard any one talk quite so
pleasantly as Offdean did. She could not decide whether it was his
manner or the tone of his voice, or the earnest glance of his dark
and deep-set blue eyes, that gave such meaning to everything he
said; for she found herself afterward thinking of his every word.

One afternoon it rained in torrents, and Rose was forced to drag
buckets and tubs into Offdean's room to catch the streams that
threatened to flood it. Euphrasie said she was glad of it; now he
could see for himself.

And when he had seen for himself, he went to join her out on a corner of the gallery, where she stood with a cloak around her, close up against the house. He leaned against the house, too, and they stood thus together, gazing upon as desolate a scene as it is easy to imagine.

The whole landscape was gray, seen through the driving rain. Far away the dreary cabins seemed to sink and sink to earth in abject misery. Above their heads the live-oak branches were beating with sad monotony against the blackened roof. Great pools of water had formed in the yard, which was deserted by every living thing; for the little darkies had scampered away to their cabins, the dogs had run to their kennels, and the hens were puffing big with wretchedness under the scanty shelter of a fallen wagon-body.

Certainly a situation to make a young man groan with ennui, if he is used to his daily stroll on Canal Street, and pleasant afternoons at the club. But Offdean thought it delightful. He only wondered that he had never known, or some one had never told him, how charming a place an old, dismantled plantation can be—when it rains. But as well as he liked it, he could not linger there forever. Business called him back to New Orleans, and after a few days he went away.

The interest which he felt in the improvement of this plantation was of so deep a nature, however, that he found himself thinking of it constantly. He wondered if the timber had all been felled, and how the fencing was coming on. So great was his desire to know such things that much correspondence was required between himself and Euphrasie, and he watched eagerly for those letters that told him of her trials and vexations with carpenters, bricklayers, and shingle-bearers. But in the midst of it, Offdean suddenly lost interest in the progress of work on the plantation. Singularly enough, it happened simultaneously with the arrival of a letter from Euphrasie which announced in a modest postscript that she was going down to the city with the Duplans for Mardi Gras.

VI

When Offdean learned that Euphrasie was coming to New Orleans, he was delighted to think he would have an opportunity to make some return for the hospitality which he had received from her father. He decided at once that she must see everything: day processions and night parades, balls and tableaux, operas and plays. He would arrange for it all, and he went to the length of begging to be relieved of certain duties that had been assigned him at the club, in order that he might feel himself perfectly free to do so.

The evening following Euphrasie's arrival, Offdean hastened to call upon her, away down on Esplanade Street. She and the Duplans were staying there with old Mme. Carantelle, Mrs. Duplan's mother, a delightfully conservative old lady who had not "crossed Canal Street" for many years.

He found a number of people gathered in the long high-ceiled drawing-room,—young people and old people, all talking French, and some talking louder than they would have done if Madame Carantelle had not been so very deaf.

When Offdean entered, the old lady was greeting some one who had come in just before him. It was Placide, and she was calling him Grégoire, and wanting to know how the crops were up on Red River. She met every one from the country with this stereotyped inquiry, which placed her at once on the agreeable and easy footing she liked.

Somehow Offdean had not counted on finding Euphrasie so well provided with entertainment, and he spent much of the evening in trying to persuade himself that the fact was a pleasing one in itself. But he wondered why Placide was with her, and sat so persistently beside her, and danced so repeatedly with her when Mrs. Duplan played upon the piano. Then he could not see by what right these young creoles had already arranged for the Proteus ball, and every other entertainment that he had meant to provide for her.

He went away without having had a word alone with the girl whom he had gone to see. The evening had proved a failure. He did not go to the club as usual, but went to his rooms in a mood which inclined him to read a few pages from a stoic philosopher whom he sometimes affected. But the words of wisdom that had often before helped him over disagreeable places left no impress tonight. They were powerless to banish from his thoughts the look of a pair of brown eyes, or to drown the tones of a girl's voice that kept singing in his soul.

Placide was not very well acquainted with the city; but that made no difference to him so long as he was at Euphrasie's side. His brother Hector, who lived in some obscure corner of the town, would willingly have made his knowledge a more intimate one; but Placide did not choose to learn the lessons that Hector was ready to teach. He asked nothing better than to walk with Euphrasie along the streets, holding her parasol at an agreeable angle over her pretty head, or to sit beside her in the evening at the play, sharing her frank delight.

When the night of the Mardi Gras ball came, he felt like a lost spirit during the hours he was forced to remain away from her. He stood in the dense crowd on the street gazing up at her, where she sat on the club-house balcony amid a bevy of gayly dressed women. It was not easy to distinguish her, but he could think of no more agreeable occupation than to stand down there on the street trying to do so.

She seemed during all this pleasant time to be entirely his own, too. It made him very fierce to think of the possibility of her not being entirely his own. But he had no cause whatever to think this. She had grown conscious and thoughtful of late about him and their relationship. She often communed with herself, and as a result tried to act toward him as an engaged girl would toward her *fiancé*. Yet a wistful look came sometimes into the brown eyes when she walked the streets with Placide, and eagerly scanned the faces of passers-by.

Offdean had written her a note, very studied, very formal, asking to see her a certain day and hour, to consult about matters on the plantation, saying he had found it so difficult to obtain a word with her, that he was forced to adopt this means, which he trusted would not be offensive.

This seemed perfectly right to Euphrasie. She agreed to see him one afternoon—the day before leaving town—in the long, stately drawing-room, quite alone.

It was a sleepy day, too warm for the season. Gusts of moist air were sweeping lazily through the long corridors, rattling the slats of the half-closed green shutters, and bringing a delicious perfume from the courtyard where old Charlot was watering the spreading palms and brilliant parterres. A group of little children had stood awhile quarreling noisily under the windows, but had moved on down the street and left quietness reigning.

Offdean had not long to wait before Euphrasie came to him. She had lost some of that ease which had marked her manner during their first acquaintance. Now, when she seated herself before him, she showed a disposition to plunge at once into the subject that had brought him there. He was willing enough that it should play some rôle, since it had been his pretext for coming; but he soon dismissed it, and with it much restraint that had held him till now. He simply looked into her eyes, with a gaze that made her shiver a little, and began to complain because she was going away next day and he had seen nothing of her; because he had wanted to do so many things when she came—why had she not let him?

"You fo'get I'm no stranger here," she told him. "I know many people. I've been coming so often with Mme. Duplan. I wanted to see mo' of you, Mr. Offdean"—

"Then you ought to have managed it; you could have done so. It 's—it 's aggravating," he said, far more bitterly than the subject warranted, "when a man has so set his heart upon something."

"But it was n' anything ver' important," she interposed; and they both laughed, and got safely over a situation that would soon have been strained, if not critical.

Waves of happiness were sweeping through the soul and body of the girl as she sat there in the drowsy afternoon near the man whom she loved. It mattered not what they talked about, or whether they talked at all. They were both scintillant with feeling. If Offdean had taken Euphrasie's hands in his and leaned forward and kissed her lips, it would have seemed to both only the rational outcome of things that stirred them. But he did not do this. He knew now that overwhelming passion was taking possession of him. He had not to heap more coals upon the fire; on the contrary, it was a moment to put on the brakes, and he was a young gentleman able to do this when circumstances required.

However, he held her hand longer than he needed to when he bade her good-by. For he got entangled in explaining why he should have to go back to the plantation to see how matters stood there, and he dropped her hand only when the rambling speech was ended.

He left her sitting by the window in a big brocaded armchair. She drew the lace curtain aside to watch him pass in the street. He lifted his hat and smiled when he saw her. Any other man she knew would have done the same thing, but this simple act caused the blood to surge to her cheeks. She let the curtain drop, and sat there like one dreaming. Her eyes, intense with the unnatural light that glowed in them, looked steadily into vacancy, and her lips stayed parted in the half-smile that did not want to leave them.

Placide found her thus, a good while afterward, when he came in, full of bustle, with theatre tickets in his pocket for the last night. She started up, and went eagerly to meet him.

"W'ere have you been, Placide?" she asked with unsteady voice, placing her hands on his shoulders with a freedom that was new and strange to him.

He appeared to her suddenly as a refuge from something, she did not know what, and she rested her hot cheek against his breast. This made him mad, and he lifted her face and kissed her passionately upon the lips.

She crept from his arms after that, and went away to her room, and locked herself in. Her poor little inexperienced soul was torn and sore. She knelt down beside her bed, and sobbed a little and prayed a little. She felt that she had sinned, she did not know exactly in what; but a fine nature warned her that it was in Placide's kiss.

VII

The spring came early in Orville, and so subtly that no one could tell exactly when it began. But one morning the roses were so luscious in Placide's sunny parterres, the peas and bean-vines and borders of strawberries so rank in his trim vegetable patches, that he called out lustily, "No mo' winta, Judge!" to the staid Judge Blount, who went ambling by on his gray pony.

"There 's right smart o' folks don't know it, Santien," responded the judge, with occult meaning that might be applied to certain indebted clients back on the bayou who had not broken land yet. Ten minutes later the judge observed sententiously, and apropos of nothing, to a group that stood waiting for the post-office to open:—

"I see Santien 's got that noo fence o' his painted. And a pretty piece o' work it is," he added reflectively.

"Look lack Placide goin' pent mo' 'an de fence," sagaciously snickered 'Tit-Edouard, a strolling *maigre-échine*[10] of indefinite occupation. "I seen 'im, me, pesterin' wid all kine o' pent on a piece o' bo'd yistiday."

"I knows he gwine paint mo' 'an de fence," emphatically announced Uncle Abner, in a tone that carried conviction. "He gwine paint de house; dat what he gwine do. Did n' Marse Luke Williams orda de paints? An' did n' I done kyar' 'em up dah myse'f?"

Seeing the deference with which this positive piece of knowledge was received, the judge coolly changed the subject by announcing that Luke Williams's Durham bull had broken a leg the night before in Luke's new pasture ditch,—a piece of news that fell among his hearers with telling, if paralytic effect.

But most people wanted to see for themselves these astonishing things that Placide was doing. And the young ladies of the village strolled slowly by of afternoons in couples and arm in arm. If Placide happened to see them, he would leave his work to hand them a fine rose or a bunch of geraniums over the dazzling white fence. But if it chanced to be 'Tit-Edouard or Luke Williams, or any of the young men of Orville, he pretended not to see them, or to hear the ingratiating cough that accompanied their lingering footsteps.

In his eagerness to have his home sweet and attractive for Euphrasie's coming, Placide had gone less frequently than ever before up to Natchitoches. He worked and whistled and sang until the yearning for the girl's presence became a driving need; then he would put away his tools and mount his horse as the day was closing, and away he would go across bayous and hills and fields until he was with her again. She had never seemed to Placide so lovable as she was then. She had grown more womanly and thoughtful. Her cheek had lost much of its color, and the light in her eyes flashed less often. But her manner had gained a something of pathetic tenderness toward her lover that moved him with an intoxicating happiness. He could hardly wait with patience for that day in early April which would see the fulfillment of his lifelong hopes.

After Euphrasie's departure from New Orleans, Offdean told himself honestly that he loved the girl. But being yet unsettled in life, he felt it was no time to think of marrying, and, like the worldly-wise young gentleman that he was, resolved to forget the little Natchitoches girl. He knew it would be an affair of some diffi-culty, but not an impossible thing, so he set about forgetting her.

The effort made him singularly irascible. At the office he was gloomy and taciturn; at the club he was a bear. A few young ladies whom he called upon were astonished and distressed at the cynical views of life which he had so suddenly adopted.

When he had endured a week or more of such humor, and in-flicted it upon others, he abruptly changed his tactics. He decided not to fight against his love for Euphrasie. He would not marry her,—certainly not; but he would let himself love her to his heart's bent, until that love should die a natural death, and not a violent one as he had designed. He abandoned himself completely to his passion, and dreamed of the girl by day and thought of her by night. How delicious had been the scent of her hair, the warmth of her breath, the nearness of her body, that rainy day when they stood close together upon the veranda! He recalled the glance of her honest, beautiful eyes, that told him things which made his heart beat fast now when he thought of them. And then her voice! Was there another like it when she laughed or when she talked! Was there another woman in the world possessed of so alluring a charm as this one he loved!

He was not bearish now, with these sweet thoughts crowding his brain and thrilling his blood; but he sighed deeply, and worked lan-guidly, and enjoyed himself listlessly.

One day he sat in his room puffing the air thick with sighs and smoke, when a thought came suddenly to him—an inspiration, a very message from heaven, to judge from the cry of joy with which he greeted it. He sent his cigar whirling through the window, over the stone paving of the street, and he let his head fall down upon his arms, folded upon the table.

It had happened to him, as it does to many, that the solution of a vexed question flashed upon him when he was hoping least for it. He positively laughed aloud, and somewhat hysterically. In the space of a moment he saw the whole delicious future which a kind fate had mapped out for him: those rich acres upon the Red River his own, bought and embellished with his inheritance; and Eu-phrasie, whom he loved, his wife and companion throughout a life such as he knew now he had craved for,—a life that, imposing bodily activity, admits the intellectual repose in which thought unfolds.

Wallace Offdean was like one to whom a divinity had revealed his vocation in life,—no less a divinity because it was love. If doubts assailed him of Euphrasie's consent, they were soon stilled. For had they not spoken over and over to each other the mute and subtile language of reciprocal love—out under the forest trees, and in the quiet night-time on the plantation when the stars shone? And never so plainly as in the stately old drawing-room down on Esplanade Street. Surely no other speech was needed then, save such as their eyes told. Oh, he knew that she loved him; he was sure of it! The knowledge made him all the more eager now to hasten to her, to tell her that he wanted her for his very own.

VIII

If Offdean had stopped in Natchitoches on his way to the plantation, he would have heard something there to astonish him, to say the very least; for the whole town was talking of Euphrasie's wedding, which was to take place in a few days. But he did not linger. After securing a horse at the stable, he pushed on with all the speed of which the animal was capable, and only in such company as his eager thoughts afforded him.

The plantation was very quiet, with that stillness which broods over broad, clean acres that furnish no refuge for so much as a bird that sings. The negroes were scattered about the fields at work, with hoe and plow, under the sun, and old Pierre, on his horse, was far off in the midst of them.

Placide had arrived in the morning, after traveling all night, and had gone to his room for an hour or two of rest. He had drawn the lounge close up to the window to get what air he might through the closed shutters. He was just beginning to doze when he heard Euphrasie's light footsteps approaching. She stopped and seated herself so near that he could have touched her if he had but reached out his hand. Her nearness banished all desire to sleep, and he lay there content to rest his limbs and think of her.

The portion of the gallery on which Euphrasie sat was facing the river, and away from the road by which Offdean had reached the house. After fastening his horse, he mounted the steps, and traversed the broad hall that intersected the house from end to end, and that was open wide. He found Euphrasie engaged upon a piece of sewing. She was hardly aware of his presence before he had seated himself beside her.

She could not speak. She only looked at him with frightened eyes, as if his presence were that of some disembodied spirit.

"Are you not glad that I have come?" he asked her. "Have I made a mistake in coming?" He was gazing into her eyes, seeking to read the meaning of their new and strange expression.

"Am I glad?" she faltered. "I don' know. W'at has that to do? You 've come to see the work, of co'se. It 's—it 's only half done, Mr. Offdean. They would n' listen to me or to papa, an' you did n' seem to care."

"I have n't come to see the work," he said, with a smile of love and confidence. "I am here only to see you,—to say how much I want you, and need you—to tell you how I love you."

She rose, half choking with words she could not utter. But he seized her hands and held her there.

"The plantation is mine, Euphrasie,—or it will be when you say that you will be my wife," he went on excitedly. "I know that you love me"—

"I do not!" she exclaimed wildly. "W'at do you mean? How do you dare," she gasped, "to say such things w'en you know that in two days I shall be married to Placide?" The last was said in a whisper; it was like a wail.

"Married to Placide!" he echoed, as if striving to understand,—to grasp some part of his own stupendous folly and blindness. "I knew nothing of it," he said hoarsely. "Married to Placide! I would never have spoken to you as I did, if I had known. You believe me, I hope? Please say that you forgive me."

He spoke with long silences between his utterances.

"Oh, there is n' anything to fo'give. You 've only made a mistake. Please leave me, Mr. Offdean. Papa is out in the fiel', I think, if you would like to speak with him. Placide is somew'ere on the place."

"I shall mount my horse and go see what work has been done," said Offdean, rising. An unusual pallor had overspread his face, and his mouth was drawn with suppressed pain. "I must turn my fool's errand to some practical good," he added, with a sad attempt at playfulness; and with no further word he walked quickly away.

She listened to his going. Then all the wretchedness of the past months, together with the sharp distress of the moment, voiced itself in a sob: "O God—O my God, he'p me!"

But she could not stay out there in the broad day for any chance comer to look upon her uncovered sorrow.

Placide heard her rise and go to her room. When he had heard the key turn in the lock, he got up, and with quiet deliberation prepared to go out. He drew on his boots, then his coat. He took his pistol from the dressing-bureau, where he had placed it a while before, and after examining its chambers carefully, thrust it into his pocket. He had certain work to do with the weapon before night. But for Euphrasie's presence he might have accomplished it very surely a moment ago, when the hound—as he called him—stood outside his window. He did not wish her to know anything of his movements, and he left his room as quietly as possible, and mounted his horse, as Offdean had done.

"La Chatte," called Placide to the old woman, who stood in her yard at the washtub, "w'ich way did that man go?"

"W'at man dat? I is n' studyin' 'bout no mans; I got 'nough to do wid dis heah washin'. 'Fo' God, I don' know w'at man you 's talkin' 'bout"—

"La Chatte, w'ich way did that man go? Quick, now!" with the deliberate tone and glance that had always quelled her.

"Ef you's talkin' 'bout dat Noo Orleans man, I could 'a' tole you dat. He done tuck de road to de cocoa-patch," plunging her black arms into the tub with unnecessary energy and disturbance.

"That 's enough. I know now he 's gone into the woods. You always was a liar, La Chatte."

"Dat his own lookout, de smoove-tongue' raskil," soliloquized the woman a moment later. "I done said he did n'have no call to come heah, caperin' roun' Miss 'Phrasie."

Placide was possessed by only one thought, which was a want as well,—to put an end to this man who had come between him and his love. It was the same brute passion that drives the beast to slay when he sees the object of his own desire laid hold of by another.

He had heard Euphrasie tell the man she did not love him, but what of that? Had he not heard her sobs, and guessed what her distress was? It needed no very flexible mind to guess as much, when a hundred signs besides, unheeded before, came surging to his memory. Jealousy held him, and rage and despair.

Offdean, as he rode along under the trees in apathetic despondency, heard some one approaching him on horseback, and turned aside to make room in the narrow pathway.

It was not a moment for punctilious scruples, and Placide had not been hindered by such from sending a bullet into the back of his rival. The only thing that stayed him was that Offdean must know why he had to die.

"Mr. Offdean," Placide said, reining his horse with one hand, while he held his pistol openly in the other, "I was in my room 'w'ile ago, and yeared w'at you said to Euphrasie. I would 'a' killed you then if she had n' been 'longside o' you. I could 'a' killed you jus' now w'en I come up behine you."

"Well, why did n't you?" asked Offdean, meanwhile gathering his faculties to think how he had best deal with this madman.

"Because I wanted you to know who done it, an' w'at he done it for."

"Mr. Santien, I suppose to a person in your frame of mind it will make no difference to know that I 'm unarmed. But if you make any attempt upon my life, I shall certainly defend myself as best I can."

"Defen' yo'se'f, then."

"You must be mad," said Offdean, quickly, and looking straight into Placide's eyes, "to want to soil your happiness with murder. I thought a creole knew better than that how to love a woman."

"By———! are you goin' to learn me how to love a woman?"

"No, Placide," said Offdean eagerly, as they rode slowly along; "your own honor is going to tell you that. The way to love a woman is to think first of her happiness. If you love Euphrasie, you must go to her clean. I love her myself enough to want you to do that. I shall leave this place tomorrow; you will never see me again if I can help it. Is n't that enough for you? I 'm going to turn here and leave you. Shoot me in the back if you like; but I know you won't." And Offdean held out his hand.

"I don' want to shake han's with you," said Placide sulkily. "Go 'way f'om me."

He stayed motionless watching Offdean ride away. He looked at the pistol in his hand, and replaced it slowly in his pocket; then he removed the broad felt hat which he wore, and wiped away the moisture that had gathered upon his forehead.

Offdean's words had touched some chord within him and made it vibrant; but they made him hate the man no less.

"The way to love a woman is to think firs' of her happiness," he muttered reflectively. "He thought a creole knew how to love. Does he reckon he 's goin' to learn a creole how to love?"

His face was white and set with despair now. The rage had all left it as he rode deeper on into the wood.

IX

Offdean rose early, wishing to take the morning train to the city. But he was not before Euphrasie, whom he found in the large hall arranging the breakfast-table. Old Pierre was there too, walking slowly about with hands folded behind him, and with bowed head.

A restraint hung upon all of them, and the girl turned to her father and asked him if Placide were up, seemingly for want of something to say. The old man fell heavily into a chair, and gazed upon her in the deepest distress.

"Oh, my po' li'le Euphrasie! my po' li'le chile! Mr. Offde'n, you ain't no stranger."

"*Bon Dieu!* Papa!" cried the girl sharply, seized with a vague terror. She quitted her occupation at the table, and stood in nervous apprehension of what might follow.

"I yaired people say Placide was one no-'count creole. I nevair want to believe dat, me. Now I know dat 's true. Mr. Offde'n, you ain't no stranger, you."

Offdean was gazing upon the old man in amazement.

"In de night," Pierre continued, "I yaired some noise on de winder. I go open, an' dere Placide, standin' wid his big boot' on, an' his w'ip w'at he knocked wid on de winder, an' his hoss all saddle'. Oh, my po' li'le chile! He say, 'Pierre, I yaired say Mr. Luke William' want his house pent down in Orville. I reckon I go git de job befo' somebody else teck it.' I say, 'You come straight back, Placide?' He say, 'Don' look fer me.' An w'en I ax 'im w'at I goin' tell to my li'le chile, he say, 'Tell Euphrasie Placide know better 'an anybody livin' w'at goin' make her happy.' An' he start 'way; den he come back an' say, 'Tell dat man'—I don' know who he was talk' 'bout—'tell 'im he ain't goin' learn nuttin' to a creole.' *Mon Dieu! Mon Dieu!* I don' know w'at all dat mean."

He was holding the half-fainting Euphrasie in his arms, and stroking her hair.

"I always yaired say he was one no-'count creole. I nevair want to believe dat."

"Don't—don't say that again, papa," she whisperingly entreated, speaking in French. "Placide has saved me!"

"He has save' you f'om w'at, Euphrasie?" asked her father, in dazed astonishment.

"From sin," she replied to him under her breath.

"I don' know w'at all dat mean," the old man muttered, bewildered, as he arose and walked out on the gallery.

Offdean had taken coffee in his room, and would not wait for breakfast. When he went to bid Euphrasie good-by, she sat beside the table with her head bowed upon her arm.

He took her hand and said good-by to her, but she did not look up.

"Euphrasie," he asked eagerly, "I may come back? Say that I may—after a while."

She gave him no answer, and he leaned down and pressed his cheek caressingly and entreatingly against her soft thick hair.

"May I, Euphrasie?" he begged. "So long as you do not tell me no, I shall come back, dearest one."

She still made him no reply, but she did not tell him no.

So he kissed her hand and her cheek,—what he could touch of it, that peeped out from her folded arm,—and went away.

An hour later, when Offdean passed through Natchitoches, the old town was already ringing with the startling news that Placide had been dismissed by his *fiancée,* and the wedding was off, information which the young creole was taking the trouble to scatter broadcast as he went.

In and Out of Old Natchitoches

PRECISELY at eight o'clock every morning except Saturdays and Sundays, Mademoiselle Suzanne St. Denys Godolph would cross the railroad trestle that spanned Bayou Boispourri. She might have crossed in the flat which Mr. Alphonse Laballière kept for his own convenience; but the method was slow and unreliable; so, every morning at eight, Mademoiselle St. Denys Godolph crossed the trestle.

She taught public school in a picturesque little white frame structure that stood upon Mr. Laballière's land, and hung upon the very brink of the bayou.

Laballière himself was comparatively a new-comer in the parish. It was barely six months since he decided one day to leave the sugar and rice to his brother Alcée, who had a talent for their cultivation, and to try his hand at cotton-planting. That was why he was up in Natchitoches parish on a piece of rich, high, Cane River land, knocking into shape a tumbled-down plantation that he had bought for next to nothing.

He had often during his perambulations observed the trim, graceful figure stepping cautiously over the ties, and had sometimes shivered for its safety. He always exchanged a greeting with the girl, and once threw a plank over a muddy pool for her to step upon. He caught but glimpses of her features, for she wore an enormous sun-bonnet to shield her complexion, that seemed marvelously fair; while loosely-fitting leather gloves protected her hands. He knew she was the school-teacher, and also that she was the daughter of that very pig-headed old Madame St. Denys Godolph who was hoarding her barren acres across the bayou as a miser hoards gold. Starving over them, some people said. But that was nonsense; nobody starves on a Louisiana plantation, unless it be with suicidal intent.

These things he knew, but he did not know why Mademoiselle St. Denys Godolph always answered his salutation with an air of chilling hauteur that would easily have paralyzed a less sanguine man.

The reason was that Suzanne, like every one else, had heard the stories that were going the rounds about him. People said he was entirely too much at home with the free mulattoes.[1] It seems a dreadful thing to say, and it would be a shocking thing to think of a Laballière; but it was n't true.

When Laballière took possession of his land, he found the plantation-house occupied by one Giestin and his swarming family. It was past reckoning how long the free mulatto and his people had been there. The house was a six-room, long, shambling affair, shrinking together from decrepitude. There was not an entire pane of glass in the structure; and the Turkey-red curtains flapped in and out of the broken apertures. But there is no need to dwell upon details; it was wholly unfit to serve as a civilized human habitation; and Alphonse Laballière would no sooner have disturbed its contented occupants than he would have scattered a family of partridges nesting in a corner of his field. He established himself with a few belongings in the best cabin he could find on the place, and, without further ado, proceeded to supervise the building of house, of gin, of this, that, and the other, and to look into the hundred details that go to set a neglected plantation in good working order. He took his meals at the free mulatto's, quite apart from the family, of course; and they attended, not too skillfully, to his few domestic wants.

Some loafer whom he had snubbed remarked one day in town that Laballière had more use for a free mulatto than he had for a white man. It was a sort of catching thing to say, and suggestive, and was repeated with the inevitable embellishments.

One morning when Laballière sat eating his solitary breakfast, and being waited upon by the queenly Madame Giestin and a brace of her weazened boys, Giestin himself came into the room. He was about half the size of his wife, puny and timid. He stood beside the table, twirling his felt hat aimlessly and balancing himself insecurely on his high-pointed boot-heels.

"Mr. Laballière," he said, "I reckon I tell you; it 's betta you git shed o' me en' my fambly. Jis like you want, yas."

"What in the name of common sense are you talking about?" asked Laballière, looking up abstractedly from his New Orleans paper. Giestin wriggled uncomfortably.

"It 's heap o' story goin' roun' 'bout you, if you want b'lieve me." And he snickered and looked at his wife, who thrust the end of her shawl into her mouth and walked from the room with a tread like the Empress Eugenie's,[2] in that elegant woman's palmiest days.

"Stories!" echoed Laballière, his face the picture of astonishment. "Who—where—what stories?"

"Yon'a in town en' all about. It 's heap o' tale goin' roun', yas. They say how come you mighty fon' o' mulatta. You done shoshiate wid de mulatta down yon'a on de suga plantation, tell you can't res' lessen it 's mulatta roun' you."

Laballière had a distressingly quick temper. His fist, which was a strong one, came down upon the wobbling table with a crash that sent half of Madame Giestin's crockery bouncing and crashing to the floor. He swore an oath that sent Madame Giestin and her father and grandmother, who were all listening in the next room, into suppressed convulsions of mirth.

"Oh, ho! so I 'm not to associate with whom I please in Natchitoches parish. We 'll see about that. Draw up your chair, Giestin. Call your wife and your grandmother and the rest of the tribe, and we 'll breakfast together. By thunder! if I want to hobnob with mulattoes, or negroes or Choctaw Indians or South Sea savages, whose business is it but my own?"

"I don' know, me. It 's jis like I tell you, Mr. Laballière," and Giestin selected a huge key from an assortment that hung against the wall, and left the room.

A half hour later, Laballière had not yet recovered his senses. He appeared suddenly at the door of the schoolhouse, holding by the shoulder one of Giestin's boys. Mademoiselle St. Denys Godolph stood at the opposite extremity of the room. Her sunbonnet hung upon the wall, now, so Laballière could have seen how charming she was, had he not at the moment been blinded by stupidity. Her blue eyes that were fringed with dark lashes reflected astonishment at seeing him there. Her hair was dark like her lashes, and waved softly about her smooth, white forehead.

"Mademoiselle," began Laballière at once, "I have taken the liberty of bringing a new pupil to you."

Mademoiselle St. Denys Godolph paled suddenly and her voice was unsteady when she replied:—

"You are too considerate, Monsieur. Will you be so kine to give me the name of the scholar whom you desire to int'oduce into this school?" She knew it as well as he.

"What 's your name, youngster? Out with it!" cried Laballière, striving to shake the little free mulatto into speech; but he stayed as dumb as a mummy.

"His name is André Giestin. You know him. He is the son"—

"Then, Monsieur," she interrupted, "permit me to remine you that you have made a se'ious mistake. This is not a school conducted fo' the education of the colored population. You will have to go elsew'ere with yo' protégé."

"I shall leave my protégé right here, Mademoiselle, and I trust you 'll give him the same kind attention you seem to accord to the others;" saying which Laballière bowed himself out of her presence. The little Giestin, left to his own devices, took only the time to give a quick, wary glance round the room, and the next instant he bounded through the open door, as the nimblest of four-footed creatures might have done.

Mademoiselle St. Denys Godolph conducted school during the hours that remained, with a deliberate calmness that would have seemed ominous to her pupils, had they been better versed in the ways of young women. When the hour for dismissal came, she rapped upon the table to demand attention.

"Chil'ren," she began, assuming a resigned and dignified mien, "you all have been witness to-day of the insult that has been offered to yo' teacher by the person upon whose lan' this schoolhouse stan's. I have nothing further to say on that subjec'. I only shall add that to-morrow yo' teacher shall sen' the key of this schoolhouse, together with her resignation, to the gentlemen who compose the school-boa'd." There followed visible disturbance among the young people.

"I ketch that li'le m'latta, I make 'im see sight', yas," screamed one.

"Nothing of the kine, Mathurin, you mus' take no such step, if only out of consideration fo' my wishes. The person who has offered the affront I consider beneath my notice. André, on the other han', is a chile of good impulse, an' by no means to blame. As you all perceive, he has shown mo' taste and judgment than those above him, f'om whom we might have espected good breeding, at least."

She kissed them all, the little boys and the little girls, and had a kind word for each. "*Et toi, mon petit Numa, j'espère qu'un autre*"[3]—She could not finish the sentence, for little Numa, her favorite, to whom she had never been able to impart the first word of English, was blubbering at a turn of affairs which he had only miserably guessed at.

She locked the schoolhouse door and walked away towards the bridge. By the time she reached it, the little 'Cadians had already disappeared like rabbits, down the road and through and over the fences.

Mademoiselle St. Denys Godolph did not cross the trestle the following day, nor the next nor the next. Laballière watched for her; for his big heart was already sore and filled with shame. But more, it stung him with remorse to realize that he had been the stupid instrument in taking the bread, as it were, from the mouth of Mademoiselle St. Denys Godolph.

He recalled how unflinchingly and haughtily her blue eyes had challenged his own. Her sweetness and charm came back to him and he dwelt upon them and exaggerated them, till no Venus, so far unearthed, could in any way approach Mademoiselle St. Denys Godolph. He would have liked to exterminate the Giestin family, from the great-grandmother down to the babe unborn.

Perhaps Giestin suspected this unfavorable attitude, for one morning he piled his whole family and all his effects into wagons, and went away; over into that part of the parish known as *l'Isle des Mulâtres*.[4]

Laballière's really chivalrous nature told him, beside, that he owed an apology, at least, to the young lady who had taken his whim so seriously. So he crossed the bayou one day and penetrated into the wilds where Madame St. Denys Godolph ruled.

An alluring little romance formed in his mind as he went; he fancied how easily it might follow the apology. He was almost in love with Mademoiselle St. Denys Godolph when he quitted his plantation. By the time he had reached hers, he was wholly so.

He was met by Madame mère, a sweet-eyed, faded woman, upon whom old age had fallen too hurriedly to completely efface all traces of youth. But the house was old beyond question; decay had eaten slowly to the heart of it during the hours, the days, and years that it had been standing.

"I have come to see your daughter, Madame," began Laballière, all too bluntly; for there is no denying he was blunt.

"Mademoiselle St. Denys Godolph is not presently at home, sir," Madame replied. "She is at the time in New Orleans. She fills there a place of high trus' an' employment, Monsieur Laballière."

When Suzanne had ever thought of New Orleans, it was always in connection with Hector Santien, because he was the only soul she knew who dwelt there. He had had no share in obtaining for her the position she had secured with one of the leading dry-goods firms; yet it was to him she addressed herself when her arrangements to leave home were completed.

He did not wait for her train to reach the city, but crossed the river and met her at Gretna. The first thing he did was to kiss her, as he had done eight years before when he left Natchitoches parish. An hour later he would no more have thought of kissing Suzanne than he would have tendered an embrace to the Empress of China. For by that time he had realized that she was no longer twelve nor he twenty-four.

She could hardly believe the man who met her to be the Hector of old. His black hair was dashed with gray on the temples; he wore a short, parted beard and a small moustache that curled. From the crown of his glossy silk hat down to his trimly-gaitered feet, his attire was faultless. Suzanne knew her Natchitoches, and she had been to Shreveport and even penetrated as far as Marshall, Texas, but in all her travels she had never met a man to equal Hector in the elegance of his mien.

They entered a cab, and seemed to drive for an interminable time through the streets, mostly over cobble-stones that rendered conversation difficult. Nevertheless he talked incessantly, while she peered from the windows to catch what glimpses she could, through the night, of that New Orleans of which she had heard so much. The sounds were bewildering; so were the lights, that were uneven, too, serving to make the patches of alternating gloom more mysterious.

She had not thought of asking him where he was taking her. And it was only after they crossed Canal and had penetrated some distance into Royal Street, that he told her. He was taking her to a friend of his, the dearest little woman in town. That was Maman Chavan, who was going to board and lodge her for a ridiculously small consideration.

Maman Chavan lived within comfortable walking distance of Canal Street, on one of those narrow, intersecting streets between Royal and Chartres. Her house was a tiny, single-story one, with overhanging gable, heavily shuttered door and windows and three wooden steps leading down to the banquette. A small garden flanked it on one side, quite screened from outside view by a high fence, over which appeared the tops of orange trees and other luxuriant shrubbery.

She was waiting for them—a lovable, fresh-looking, white-haired, black-eyed, small, fat little body, dressed all in black. She understood no English; which made no difference. Suzanne and Hector spoke but French to each other.

Hector did not tarry a moment longer than was needed to place his young friend and charge in the older woman's care. He would not even stay to take a bite of supper with them. Maman Chavan watched him as he hurried down the steps and out into the gloom. Then she said to Suzanne: "That man is an angel, Mademoiselle, *un ange du bon Dieu*."[5]

"Women, my dear Maman Chavan, you know how it is with me in regard to women. I have drawn a circle round my heart, so—at pretty long range, mind you—and there is not one who gets through it, or over it or under it."

"*Blagueur, va!*"[6] laughed Maman Chavan, replenishing her glass from the bottle of sauterne.

It was Sunday morning. They were breakfasting together on the pleasant side gallery that led by a single step down to the garden. Hector came every Sunday morning, an hour or so before noon, to breakfast with them. He always brought a bottle of sauterne, a paté,

or a mess of artichokes or some tempting bit of *charcuterie.*[7] Sometimes he had to wait till the two women returned from hearing mass
at the cathedral. He did not go to mass himself. They were both
making a Novena on that account, and had even gone to the expense of burning a round dozen of candles before the good St.
Joseph, for his conversion. When Hector accidentally discovered
the fact, he offered to pay for the candles, and was distressed at not
being permitted to do so.

Suzanne had been in the city more than a month. It was already
the close of February, and the air was flower-scented, moist, and deliciously mild.

"As I said: women, my dear Maman Chavan"—

"Let us hear no more about women!" cried Suzanne, impatiently.
"*Cher Maître!*[8] but Hector can be tiresome when he wants. Talk,
talk; to say what in the end?"

"Quite right, my cousin; when I might have been saying how
charming you are this morning. But don't think that I have n't noticed it," and he looked at her with a deliberation that quite unsettled her. She took a letter from her pocket and handed it to him.

"Here, read all the nice things mamma has to say of you, and the
love messages she sends to you." He accepted the several closely
written sheets from her and began to look over them.

"*Ah, la bonne tante,*"[9] he laughed, when he came to the tender
passages that referred to himself. He had pushed aside the glass of
wine that he had only partly filled at the beginning of breakfast and
that he had scarcely touched. Maman Chavan again replenished her
own. She also lighted a cigarette. So did Suzanne, who was learning
to smoke. Hector did not smoke; he did not use tobacco in any
form, he always said to those who offered him cigars.

Suzanne rested her elbows on the table, adjusted the ruffles
about her wrists, puffed awkwardly at her cigarette that kept going
out, and hummed the Kyrie Eleison that she had heard so beauti-
fully rendered an hour before at the Cathedral, while she gazed off
into the green depths of the garden. Maman Chavan slipped a little
silver medal toward her, accompanying the action with a pantomine
that Suzanne readily understood. She, in turn, secretly and adroitly
transferred the medal to Hector's coat-pocket. He noticed the action plainly enough, but pretended not to.

"Natchitoches has n't changed," he commented. "The everlasting

can-cans![10] when will they have done with them? This is n't little
Athénaïse Miché, getting married! *Sapristi!*[11] but it makes one old!
And old Papa Jean-Pierre only dead now? I thought he was out of
purgatory five years ago. And who is this Laballière? One of the
Laballières of St. James?"

"St. James, *mon cher.*[12] Monsieur Alphonse Laballière; an aristo-
crat from the 'golden coast.' But it is a history, if you will believe
me. *Figurez vous,* Maman Chavan,—*pensez donc, mon ami*"[13]—
And with much dramatic fire, during which the cigarette went ir-
revocably out, she proceeded to narrate her experiences with
Laballière.

"Impossible!" exclaimed Hector when the climax was reached;
but his indignation was not so patent as she would have liked it
to be.

"And to think of an affront like that going unpunished!" was
Maman Chavan's more sympathetic comment.

"Oh, the scholars were only too ready to offer violence to poor
little André, but that, you can understand, I would not permit. And
now, here is mamma gone completely over to him; entrapped, God
only knows how!"

"Yes," agreed Hector, "I see he has been sending her tamales and
boudin blanc."[14]

"*Boudin blanc,* my friend! If it were only that! But I have a stack
of letters, so high,—I could show them to you,—singing of Laballière, Laballière, enough to drive one distracted. He visits her constantly. He is a man of attainment, she says, a man of courage, a man
of heart; and the best of company. He has sent her a bunch of fat
robins as big as a tub"—

"There is something in that—a good deal in that, mignonne,"[15]
piped Maman Chavan, approvingly.

"And now *boudin blanc!* and she tells me it is the duty of a
Christian to forgive. Ah, no; it 's no use; mamma's ways are past
finding out."

Suzanne was never in Hector's company elsewhere than at Maman Chavan's. Beside the Sunday visit, he looked in upon them
sometimes at dusk, to chat for a moment or two. He often treated
them to theatre tickets, and even to the opera, when business was
brisk. Business meant a little notebook that he carried in his pocket,

in which he sometimes dotted down orders from the country people for wine, that he sold on commission. The women always went
together, unaccompanied by any male escort; trotting along, arm in
arm, and brimming with enjoyment.

That same Sunday afternoon Hector walked with them a short
distance when they were on their way to vespers. The three walking
abreast almost occupied the narrow width of the banquette. A gentleman who had just stepped out of the Hotel Royal stood aside to
better enable them to pass. He lifted his hat to Suzanne, and cast a
quick glance, that pictured stupefaction and wrath, upon Hector.

"It 's he!" exclaimed the girl, melodramatically seizing Maman
Chavan's arm.

"Who, he?"

"Laballière!"

"No!"

"Yes!"

"A handsome fellow, all the same," nodded the little lady, approvingly. Hector thought so too. The conversation again turned
upon Laballière, and so continued till they reached the side door of
the cathedral, where the young man left his two companions.

In the evening Laballière called upon Suzanne. Maman Chavan
closed the front door carefully after he entered the small parlor, and
opened the side one that looked into the privacy of the garden.
Then she lighted the lamp and retired, just as Suzanne entered.

The girl bowed a little stiffly, if it may be said that she did anything stiffly. "Monsieur Laballière." That was all she said.

"Mademoiselle St. Denys Godolph," and that was all he said. But
ceremony did not sit easily upon him.

"Mademoiselle," he began, as soon as seated, "I am here as the
bearer of a message from your mother. You must understand that
otherwise I would not be here."

"I do understan', sir, that you an' maman have become very
warm frien's during my absence," she returned, in measured, conventional tones.

"It pleases me immensely to hear that from you," he responded,
warmly; "to believe that Madame St. Denys Godolph is my friend."

Suzanne coughed more affectedly than was quite nice, and patted
her glossy braids. "The message, if you please, Mr. Laballière."

"To be sure," pulling himself together from the momentary abstraction into which he had fallen in contemplating her. "Well, it 's just this; your mother, you must know, has been good enough to sell me a fine bit of land—a deep strip along the bayou"—

"Impossible! *Mais* w'at sorcery did you use to obtain such a thing of my mother, Mr. Laballière? Lan' that has been in the St. Denys Godolph family since time untole!"

"No sorcery whatever, Mademoiselle, only an appeal to your mother's intelligence and common sense; and she is well supplied with both. She wishes me to say, further, that she desires your presence very urgently and your immediate return home."

"My mother is unduly impatient, surely," replied Suzanne, with chilling politeness.

"May I ask, mademoiselle," he broke in, with an abruptness that was startling, "the name of the man with whom you were walking this afternoon?"

She looked at him with unaffected astonishment, and told him: "I hardly understan' yo' question. That gentleman is Mr. Hector Santien, of one of the firs' families of Natchitoches; a warm ole frien' an' far distant relative of mine."

"Oh, that's his name, is it, Hector Santien? Well, please don't walk on the New Orleans streets again with Mr. Hector Santien."

"Yo' remarks would be insulting if they were not so highly amusing, Mr. Laballière."

"I beg your pardon if I am insulting; and I have no desire to be amusing," and then Laballière lost his head. "You are at liberty to walk the streets with whom you please, of course," he blurted, with ill-suppressed passion, "but if I encounter Mr. Hector Santien in your company again, in public, I shall wring his neck, then and there, as I would a chicken; I shall break every bone in his body"— Suzanne had arisen.

"You have said enough, sir. I even desire no explanation of yo' words."

"I did n't intend to explain them," he retorted, stung by the insinuation.

"You will escuse me further," she requested icily, motioning to retire.

"Not till—oh, not till you have forgiven me," he cried impulsively, barring her exit; for repentance had come swiftly this time.

But she did not forgive him. "I can wait," she said. Then he stepped aside and she passed by him without a second glance.

She sent word to Hector the following day to come to her. And when he was there, in the late afternoon, they walked together to the end of the vine-sheltered gallery,—where the air was redolent with the odor of spring blossoms.

"Hector," she began, after a while, "some one has told me I should not be seen upon the streets of New Orleans with you."

He was trimming a long rose-stem with his sharp penknife. He did not stop nor start, nor look embarrassed, nor anything of the sort.

"Indeed!" he said.

"But, you know," she went on, "if the saints came down from heaven to tell me there was a reason for it, I could n't believe them."

"You would n't believe them, *ma petite Suzanne?*"[16] He was getting all the thorns off nicely, and stripping away the heavy lower leaves.

"I want you to look me in the face, Hector, and tell me if there is any reason."

He snapped the knife-blade and replaced the knife in his pocket; then he looked in her eyes, so unflinchingly, that she hoped and believed it presaged a confession of innocence that she would gladly have accepted. But he said indifferently: "Yes, there are reasons."

"Then I say there are not," she exclaimed excitedly; "you are amusing yourself—laughing at me, as you always do. There are no reasons that I will hear or believe. You will walk the streets with me, will you not, Hector?" she entreated, "and go to church with me on Sunday; and, and—oh, it 's nonsense, nonsense for you to say things like that!"

He held the rose by its long, hardy stem, and swept it lightly and caressingly across her forehead, along her cheek, and over her pretty mouth and chin, as a lover might have done with his lips. He noticed how the red rose left a crimson stain behind it.

She had been standing, but now she sank upon the bench that was there, and buried her face in her palms. A slight convulsive movement of the muscles indicated a suppressed sob.

"Ah, Suzanne, Suzanne, you are not going to make yourself un-happy about a *bon à rien*[17] like me. Come, look at me; tell me that you are not." He drew her hands down from her face and held them a while, bidding her good-by. His own face wore the quizzical look it often did, as if he were laughing at her.

"That work at the store is telling on your nerves, *mignonne*. Promise me that you will go back to the country. That will be best."

"Oh, yes; I am going back home, Hector."

"That is right, little cousin," and he patted her hands kindly, and laid them both down gently into her lap.

He did not return; neither during the week nor the following Sunday. Then Suzanne told Maman Chavan she was going home. The girl was not too deeply in love with Hector; but imagination counts for something, and so does youth.

Laballière was on the train with her. She felt, somehow, that he would be. And yet she did not dream that he had watched and waited for her each morning since he parted from her.

He went to her without preliminary of manner or speech, and held out his hand; she extended her own unhesitatingly. She could not understand why, and she was a little too weary to strive to do so. It seemed as though the sheer force of his will would carry him to the goal of his wishes.

He did not weary her with attentions during the time they were together. He sat apart from her, conversing for the most time with friends and acquaintances who belonged in the sugar district through which they traveled in the early part of the day.

She wondered why he had ever left that section to go up into Natchitoches. Then she wondered if he did not mean to speak to her at all. As if he had read the thought, he went and sat down beside her.

He showed her, away off across the country, where his mother lived, and his brother Alcée, and his cousin Clarisse.

On Sunday morning, when Maman Chavan strove to sound the depth of Hector's feeling for Suzanne, he told her again: "Women,

my dear Maman Chavan, you know how it is with me in regard to
women,"—and he refilled her glass from the bottle of sauterne.

"*Farceur va!*"[18] and Maman Chavan laughed, and her fat shoulders quivered under the white *volante*[19] she wore.

A day or two later, Hector was walking down Canal Street at
four in the afternoon. He might have posed, as he was, for a fash-
ion-plate. He looked not to the right nor to the left; not even at the
women who passed by. Some of them turned to look at him.

When he approached the corner of Royal, a young man who
stood there nudged his companion.

"You know who that is?" he said, indicating Hector.

"No; who?"

"Well, you are an innocent. Why, that 's Deroustan, the most
notorious gambler in New Orleans."

In Sabine

THE SIGHT of a human habitation, even if it was a rude log cabin with a mud chimney at one end, was a very gratifying one to Grégoire.

He had come out of Natchitoches parish, and had been riding a great part of the day through the big lonesome parish of Sabine. He was not following the regular Texas road, but, led by his erratic fancy, was pushing toward the Sabine River by circuitous paths through the rolling pine forests.

As he approached the cabin in the clearing, he discerned behind a palisade of pine saplings an old negro man chopping wood.

"Howdy, Uncle," called out the young fellow, reining his horse. The negro looked up in blank amazement at so unexpected an apparition, but he only answered: "How you do, suh," accompanying his speech by a series of polite nods.

"Who lives yere?"

"Hit 's Mas' Bud Aiken w'at live' heah, suh."

"Well, if Mr. Bud Aiken c'n affo'd to hire a man to chop his wood, I reckon he won't grudge me a bite o' suppa an' a couple hours' res' on his gall'ry. W'at you say, ole man?"

"I say dit Mas' Bud Aiken don't hires me to chop 'ood. Ef I don't chop dis heah, his wife got it to do. Dat w'y I chops 'ood, suh. Go right 'long in, suh; you g'ine fine Mas' Bud some'eres roun', ef he ain't drunk an' gone to bed."

Grégoire, glad to stretch his legs, dismounted, and led his horse into the small inclosure which surrounded the cabin. An unkempt, vicious-looking little Texas pony stopped nibbling the stubble there to look maliciously at him and his fine sleek horse, as they passed by. Back of the hut, and running plumb up against the pine wood, was a small, ragged specimen of a cotton-field.

Grégoire was rather undersized, with a square, well-knit figure, upon which his clothes sat well and easily. His corduroy trousers were thrust into the legs of his boots; he wore a blue flannel shirt; his coat was thrown across the saddle. In his keen black eyes had come a puzzled expression, and he tugged thoughtfully at the brown moustache that lightly shaded his upper lip.

He was trying to recall when and under what circumstances he had before heard the name of Bud Aiken. But Bud Aiken himself saved Grégoire the trouble of further speculation on the subject. He appeared suddenly in the small doorway, which his big body quite filled; and then Grégoire remembered. This was the disreputable so-called "Texan" who a year ago had run away with and married Baptiste Choupic's pretty daughter, 'Tite Reine, yonder on Bayou Pierre, in Natchitoches parish. A vivid picture of the girl as he remembered her appeared to him: her trim rounded figure; her piquant face with its saucy black coquettish eyes; her little exacting, imperious ways that had obtained for her the nickname of 'Tite Reine, little queen. Grégoire had known her at the 'Cadian balls that he sometimes had the hardihood to attend.

These pleasing recollections of 'Tite Reine lent a warmth that might otherwise have been lacking to Grégoire's manner, when he greeted her husband.

"I hope I fine you well, Mr. Aiken," he exclaimed cordially, as he approached and extended his hand.

"You find me damn' porely, suh; but you 've got the better o' me, ef I may so say." He was a big good-looking brute, with a straw-colored "horse-shoe" moustache quite concealing his mouth, and a several days' growth of stubble on his rugged face. He was fond of reiterating that women's admiration had wrecked his life, quite forgetting to mention the early and sustained influence of "Pike's Magnolia"[1] and other brands, and wholly ignoring certain inborn propensities capable of wrecking unaided any ordinary existence. He had been lying down, and looked frouzy and half asleep.

"Ef I may so say, you 've got the better o' me, Mr.—er"—

"Santien, Grégoire Santien. I have the pleasure o' knowin' the lady you married, suh; an' I think I met you befo',—somew'ere o' 'nother," Grégoire added vaguely.

"Oh," drawled Aiken, waking up, "one o' them Red River

Sanchuns!" and his face brightened at the prospect before him of enjoying the society of one of the Santien boys. "Mortimer!" he called in ringing chest tones worthy a commander at the head of his troop. The negro had rested his axe and appeared to be listening to their talk, though he was too far to hear what they said.

"Mortimer, come along here an' take my frien' Mr. Sanchun's hoss. Git a move thar, git a move!" Then turning toward the entrance of the cabin he called back through the open door: "Rain!" it was his way of pronouncing 'Tite Reine's name. "Rain!" he cried again peremptorily; and turning to Grégoire: "she 's 'tendin' to some or other housekeepin' truck." 'Tite Reine was back in the yard feeding the solitary pig which they owned, and which Aiken had mysteriously driven up a few days before, saying he had bought it at Many.

Grégoire could hear her calling out as she approached: "I 'm comin', Bud. Yere I come. W'at you want, Bud?" breathlessly, as she appeared in the door frame and looked out upon the narrow sloping gallery where stood the two men. She seemed to Grégoire to have changed a good deal. She was thinner, and her eyes were larger, with an alert, uneasy look in them; he fancied the startled expression came from seeing him there unexpectedly. She wore cleanly homespun garments, the same she had brought with her from Bayou Pierre; but her shoes were in shreds. She uttered only a low, smothered exclamation when she saw Grégoire.

"Well, is that all you got to say to my frien' Mr. Sanchun? That 's the way with them Cajuns," Aiken offered apologetically to his guest; "ain't got sense enough to know a white man when they see one." Grégoire took her hand.

"I 'm mighty glad to see you, 'Tite Reine," he said from his heart. She had for some reason been unable to speak; now she panted somewhat hysterically:—

"You mus' escuse me, Mista Grégoire. It 's the truth I did n' know you firs', stan'in' up there." A deep flush had supplanted the former pallor of her face, and her eyes shone with tears and ill-concealed excitement.

"I thought you all lived yonda in Grant," remarked Grégoire carelessly, making talk for the purpose of diverting Aiken's attention away from his wife's evident embarrassment, which he himself was at a loss to understand.

"Why, we did live a right smart while in Grant; but Grant ain't no parish to make a livin' in. Then I tried Winn and Caddo a spell; they was n't no better. But I tell you, suh, Sabine 's a damn' sight worse than any of 'em. Why, a man can't git a drink o' whiskey here without going out of the parish fer it, or across into Texas. I 'm fixin' to sell out an' try Vernon."

Bud Aiken's household belongings surely would not count for much in the contemplated "selling out." The one room that constituted his home was extremely bare of furnishing,—a cheap bed, a pine table, and a few chairs, that was all. On a rough shelf were some paper parcels representing the larder. The mud daubing had fallen out here and there from between the logs of the cabin; and into the largest of these apertures had been thrust pieces of ragged bagging and wisps of cotton. A tin basin outside on the gallery offered the only bathing facilities to be seen. Notwithstanding these drawbacks, Grégoire announced his intention of passing the night with Aiken.

"I 'm jus' goin' to ask the privilege o' layin' down yere on yo' gall'ry to-night, Mr. Aiken. My hoss ain't in firs'-class trim; an' a night's res' ain't goin' to hurt him o' me either." He had begun by declaring his intention of pushing on across the Sabine, but an imploring look from 'Tite Reine's eyes had stayed the words upon his lips. Never had he seen in a woman's eyes a look of such heartbroken entreaty. He resolved on the instant to know the meaning of it before setting foot on Texas soil. Grégoire had never learned to steel his heart against a woman's eyes, no matter what language they spoke.

An old patchwork quilt folded double and a moss pillow which 'Tite Reine gave him out on the gallery made a bed that was, after all, not too uncomfortable for a young fellow of rugged habits.

Grégoire slept quite soundly after he laid down upon his improvised bed at nine o'clock. He was awakened toward the middle of the night by some one gently shaking him. It was 'Tite Reine stooping over him; he could see her plainly, for the moon was shining. She had not removed the clothing she had worn during the day; but her feet were bare and looked wonderfully small and white. He arose on his elbow, wide awake at once. "W'y, 'Tite Reine! w'at the devil you mean? w'ere 's yo' husban'?"

"The house kin fall on 'im, 't en goin' wake up Bud w'en he 's sleepin'; he drink' too much." Now that she had aroused Grégoire, she stood up, and sinking her face in her bended arm like a child, began to cry softly. In an instant he was on his feet.

"My God, 'Tite Reine! w'at 's the matta? you got to tell me w'at 's the matta." He could no longer recognize the imperious 'Tite Reine, whose will had been the law in her father's household. He led her to the edge of the low gallery and there they sat down.

Grégoire loved women. He liked their nearness, their atmosphere; the tones of their voices and the things they said; their ways of moving and turning about; the brushing of their garments when they passed him by pleased him. He was fleeing now from the pain that a woman had inflicted upon him. When any overpowering sorrow came to Grégoire he felt a singular longing to cross the Sabine River and lose himself in Texas. He had done this once before when his home, the old Santien place, had gone into the hands of creditors. The sight of 'Tite Reine's distress now moved him painfully.

"W'at is it, 'Tite Reine? tell me w'at it is," he kept asking her. She was attempting to dry her eyes on her coarse sleeve. He drew a handkerchief from his back pocket and dried them for her.

"They all well, yonda?" she asked, haltingly, "my popa? my moma? the chil'en?" Grégoire knew no more of the Baptiste Choupic family than the post beside him. Nevertheless he answered: "They all right well, 'Tite Reine, but they mighty lonesome of you."

"My popa, he got a putty good crop this yea'?"

"He made right smart o' cotton fo' Bayou Pierre."

"He done haul it to the relroad?"

"No, he ain't quite finish pickin'."

"I hope they all ent sole 'Putty Girl'?" she inquired solicitously.

"Well, I should say not! Yo' pa says they ain't anotha piece o' hossflesh in the pa'ish he 'd want to swap fo' 'Putty Girl.' " She turned to him with vague but fleeting amazement,—"Putty Girl" was a cow!

The autumn night was heavy about them. The black forest seemed to have drawn nearer; its shadowy depths were filled with the gruesome noises that inhabit a southern forest at night time.

"Ain't you 'fraid sometimes yere, 'Tite Reine?" Grégoire asked, as he felt a light shiver run through him at the weirdness of the scene.

"No," she answered promptly, "I ent 'fred o' nothin' 'cep' Bud."
"Then he treats you mean? I thought so!"

"Mista Grégoire," drawing close to him and whispering in his face, "Bud 's killin' me." He clasped her arm, holding her near him, while an expression of profound pity escaped him. "Nobody don' know, 'cep' Unc' Mort'mer," she went on. "I tell you, he beats me; my back an' arms—you ought to see—it 's all blue. He would 'a' choke' me to death one day w'en he was drunk, if Unc' Mort'mer had n' make 'im lef go—with his axe ov' his head." Grégoire glanced back over his shoulder toward the room where the man lay sleeping. He was wondering if it would really be a criminal act to go then and there and shoot the top of Bud Aiken's head off. He himself would hardly have considered it a crime, but he was not sure of how others might regard the act.

"That 's w'y I wake you up, to tell you," she continued. "Then sometime' he plague me mos' crazy; he tell me 't ent no preacher, it 's a Texas drummer w'at marry him an' me; an' w'en I don' know w'at way to turn no mo', he say no, it 's a Meth'dis' archbishop, an' keep on laughin' 'bout me, an' I don' know w'at the truth!"

Then again, she told how Bud had induced her to mount the vicious little mustang "Buckeye," knowing that the little brute would n't carry a woman; and how it had amused him to witness her distress and terror when she was thrown to the ground.

"If I would know how to read an' write, an' had some pencil an' paper, it 's long 'go I would wrote to my popa. But it 's no pos'of-fice, it 's no relroad,—nothin' in Sabine. An' you know, Mista Gré-goire, Bud say he 's goin' carry me yonda to Vernon, an' fu'ther off yet,—'way yonda, an' he 's goin' turn me loose. Oh, don' leave me yere, Mista Grégoire! don' leave me behine you!" she entreated, breaking once more into sobs.

" 'Tite Reine," he answered, "do you think I 'm such a low-down scound'el as to leave you yere with that"—He finished the sentence mentally, not wishing to offend the ears of 'Tite Reine.

They talked on a good while after that. She would not return to the room where her husband lay; the nearness of a friend had already emboldened her to inward revolt. Grégoire induced her to lie down and rest upon the quilt that she had given to him for a bed. She did so, and broken down by fatigue was soon fast asleep.

He stayed seated on the edge of the gallery and began to smoke

cigarettes which he rolled himself of périque tobacco. He might
have gone in and shared Bud Aiken's bed, but preferred to stay
there near 'Tite Reine. He watched the two horses, tramping slowly
about the lot, cropping the dewy wet tufts of grass.

Grégoire smoked on. He only stopped when the moon sank
down behind the pine-trees, and the long deep shadow reached out
and enveloped him. Then he could no longer see and follow the
filmy smoke from his cigarette, and he threw it away. Sleep was
pressing heavily upon him. He stretched himself full length upon
the rough bare boards of the gallery and slept until day-break.

Bud Aiken's satisfaction was very genuine when he learned that
Grégoire proposed spending the day and another night with him.
He had already recognized in the young creole a spirit not alto-
gether uncongenial to his own.

'Tite Reine cooked breakfast for them. She made coffee; of
course there was no milk to add to it, but there was sugar. From a
meal bag that stood in the corner of the room she took a measure of
meal, and with it made a pone of corn bread. She fried slices of salt
pork. Then Bud sent her into the field to pick cotton with old Uncle Mortimer. The negro's cabin was the counterpart of their own,
but stood quite a distance away hidden in the woods. He and Aiken
worked the crop on shares.

Early in the day Bud produced a grimy pack of cards from behind a parcel of sugar on the shelf. Grégoire threw the cards into
the fire and replaced them with a spic and span new "deck" that he
took from his saddlebags. He also brought forth from the same re-
ceptacle a bottle of whiskey, which he presented to his host, saying
that he himself had no further use for it, as he had "sworn off" since
day before yesterday, when he had made a fool of himself in
Cloutierville.

They sat at the pine table smoking and playing cards all the
morning, only desisting when 'Tite Reine came to serve them with
the gumbo-filé that she had come out of the field to cook at noon.
She could afford to treat a guest to chicken gumbo, for she owned a
half dozen chickens that Uncle Mortimer had presented to her at
various times. There were only two spoons, and 'Tite Reine had to
wait till the men had finished before eating her soup. She waited for
Grégoire's spoon, though her husband was the first to get through.
It was a very childish whim.

In the afternoon she picked cotton again; and the men played cards, smoked, and Bud drank.

It was a very long time since Bud Aiken had enjoyed himself so well, and since he had encountered so sympathetic and appreciative a listener to the story of his evenful career. The story of 'Tite Reine's fall from the horse he told with much spirit, mimicking quite skillfully the way in which she had complained of never being permitted "to teck a li'le pleasure," whereupon he had kindly suggested horseback riding. Grégoire enjoyed the story amazingly, which encouraged Aiken to relate many more of a similar character. As the afternoon wore on, all formality of address between the two had disappeared: they were "Bud" and "Grégoire" to each other, and Grégoire had delighted Aiken's soul by promising to spend a week with him. 'Tite Reine was also touched by the spirit of recklessness in the air; it moved her to fry two chickens for supper. She fried them deliciously in bacon fat. After supper she again arranged Grégoire's bed out on the gallery.

The night fell calm and beautiful, with the delicious odor of the pines floating upon the air. But the three did not sit up to enjoy it. Before the stroke of nine, Aiken had already fallen upon his bed unconscious of everything about him in the heavy drunken sleep that would hold him fast through the night. It even clutched him more relentlessly than usual, thanks to Grégoire's free gift of whiskey.

The sun was high when he awoke. He lifted his voice and called imperiously for 'Tite Reine, wondering that the coffee-pot was not on the hearth, and marveling still more that he did not hear her voice in quick response with its, "I 'm comin', Bud. Yere I come." He called again and again. Then he arose and looked out through the back door to see if she were picking cotton in the field, but she was not there. He dragged himself to the front entrance. Grégoire's bed was still on the gallery, but the young fellow was nowhere to be seen.

Uncle Mortimer had come into the yard, not to cut wood this time, but to pick up the axe which was his own property, and lift it to his shoulder.

"Mortimer," called out Aiken, "whur 's my wife?" at the same time advancing toward the negro. Mortimer stood still, waiting for him. "Whur 's my wife an' that Frenchman? Speak out, I say, before I send you to h—l."

Uncle Mortimer never had feared Bud Aiken; and with the trusty axe upon his shoulder, he felt a double hardihood in the man's presence. The old fellow passed the back of his black, knotty hand unctuously over his lips, as though he relished in advance the words that were about to pass them. He spoke carefully and deliberately:

"Miss Reine," he said, "I reckon she mus' of done struck Natchitoches pa'ish sometime to'ard de middle o' de night, on dat 'ar swif' hoss o' Mr. Sanchun's."

Aiken uttered a terrific oath. "Saddle up Buckeye," he yelled, "before I count twenty, or I 'll rip the black hide off yer. Quick, thar! Thur ain't nothin' fourfooted top o' this earth that Buckeye can't run down." Uncle Mortimer scratched his head dubiously, as he answered:—

"Yas, Mas' Bud, but you see, Mr. Sanchun, he done cross de Sabine befo' sun-up on Buckeye."

A Very Fine Fiddle

WHEN the half dozen little ones were hungry, old Cléophas would take the fiddle from its flannel bag and play a tune upon it. Perhaps it was to drown their cries, or their hunger, or his conscience, or all three. One day Fifine, in a rage, stamped her small foot and clinched her little hands, and declared:

"It 's no two way'! I 'm goin' smash it, dat fiddle, some day in a t'ousan' piece'!"

"You mus' n' do dat, Fifine," expostulated her father. "Dat fiddle been ol'er 'an you an' me t'ree time' put togedder. You done yaird me tell often 'nough 'bout dat *Italien*[1] w'at give it to me w'en he die, 'long yonder befo' de war. An' he say, 'Cléophas, dat fiddle—dat one part my life—w'at goin' live w'en I be dead—*Dieu merci!*[2] You talkin' too fas', Fifine."

"Well, I 'm goin' do some'in' wid dat fiddle, *va!*" returned the daughter, only half mollified. "Mine w'at I say."

So once when there were great carryings-on up at the big plantation—no end of ladies and gentlemen from the city, riding, driving, dancing, and making music upon all manner of instruments—Fifine, with the fiddle in its flannel bag, stole away and up to the big house where these festivities were in progress.

No one noticed at first the little barefoot girl seated upon a step of the veranda and watching, lynx-eyed, for her opportunity.

"It 's one fiddle I got for sell," she announced, resolutely, to the first who questioned her.

It was very funny to have a shabby little girl sitting there wanting to sell a fiddle, and the child was soon surrounded.

The lustreless instrument was brought forth and examined, first with amusement, but soon very seriously, especially by three gentlemen: one with very long hair that hung down, another with equally long hair that stood up, the third with no hair worth mentioning.

These three turned the fiddle upside down and almost inside out. They thumped upon it, and listened. They scraped upon it, and listened. They walked into the house with it, and out of the house with it, and into remote corners with it. All this with much putting of heads together, and talking together in familiar and unfamiliar languages. And, finally, they sent Fifine away with a fiddle twice as beautiful as the one she had brought, and a roll of money besides!

The child was dumb with astonishment, and away she flew. But when she stopped beneath a big chinaberry-tree, to further scan the roll of money, her wonder was redoubled. There was far more than she could count, more than she had ever dreamed of possessing. Certainly enough to top the old cabin with new shingles; to put shoes on all the little bare feet and food into the hungry mouths. Maybe enough—and Fifine's heart fairly jumped into her throat at the vision—maybe enough to buy Blanchette and her tiny calf that Unc' Siméon wanted to sell!

"It's jis like you say, Fifine," murmured old Cléophas, huskily, when he had played upon the new fiddle that night. "It's one fine fiddle; an' like you say, it shine' like satin. But some way or udder, 't ain' de same. Yair, Fifine, take it—put it 'side. I b'lieve, me, I ain' goin' play de fiddle no mo'."

Beyond the Bayou

THE BAYOU curved like a crescent around the point of land on which La Folle's cabin stood. Between the stream and the hut lay a big abandoned field, where cattle were pastured when the bayou sup-plied them with water enough. Through the woods that spread back into unknown regions the woman had drawn an imaginary line, and past this circle she never stepped. This was the form of her only mania.

She was now a large, gaunt black woman, past thirty-five. Her real name was Jacqueline, but every one on the plantation called her La Folle, because in childhood she had been frightened literally "out of her senses," and had never wholly regained them.

It was when there had been skirmishing and sharpshooting all day in the woods. Evening was near when P'tit Maître,[1] black with powder and crimson with blood, had staggered into the cabin of Jacqueline's mother, his pursuers close at his heels. The sight had stunned her childish reason.

She dwelt alone in her solitary cabin, for the rest of the quarters had long since been removed beyond her sight and knowledge. She had more physical strength than most men, and made her patch of cotton and corn and tobacco like the best of them. But of the world beyond the bayou she had long known nothing, save what her mor-bid fancy conceived.

People at Bellissime[2] had grown used to her and her way, and they thought nothing of it. Even when "Old Mis'" died, they did not wonder that La Folle had not crossed the bayou, but had stood upon her side of it, wailing and lamenting.

P'tit Maître was now the owner of Bellissime. He was a middle-aged man, with a family of beautiful daughters about him, and a little son whom La Folle loved as if he had been her own. She called him Chéri,[3] and so did every one else because she did.

None of the girls had ever been to her what Chéri was. They had each and all loved to be with her, and to listen to her wondrous stories of things that always happened "yonda, beyon' de bayou."

But none of them had stroked her black hand quite as Chéri did, nor rested their heads against her knee so confidingly, nor fallen asleep in her arms as he used to do. For Chéri hardly did such things now, since he had become the proud possessor of a gun, and had had his black curls cut off.

That summer—the summer Chéri gave La Folle two black curls tied with a knot of red ribbon—the water ran so low in the bayou that even the little children at Bellissime were able to cross it on foot, and the cattle were sent to pasture down by the river. La Folle was sorry when they were gone, for she loved these dumb companions well, and liked to feel that they were there, and to hear them browsing by night up to her own inclosure.

It was Saturday afternoon, when the fields were deserted. The men had flocked to a neighboring village to do their week's trading, and the women were occupied with household affairs,—La Folle as well as the others. It was then she mended and washed her handful of clothes, scoured her house, and did her baking.

In this last employment she never forgot Chéri. To-day she had fashioned croquignoles[4] of the most fantastic and alluring shapes for him. So when she saw the boy come trudging across the old field with his gleaming little new rifle on his shoulder, she called out gayly to him, "Chéri! Chéri!"

But Chéri did not need the summons, for he was coming straight to her. His pockets all bulged out with almonds and raisins and an orange that he had secured for her from the very fine dinner which had been given that day up at his father's house.

He was a sunny-faced youngster of ten. When he had emptied his pockets, La Folle patted his round red cheek, wiped his soiled hands on her apron, and smoothed his hair. Then she watched him as, with his cakes in his hand, he crosssed her strip of cotton back of the cabin, and disappeared into the wood.

He had boasted of the things he was going to do with his gun out there.

"You think they got plenty deer in the wood, La Folle?" he had inquired, with the calculating air of an experienced hunter.

"*Non, non!*" the woman laughed. "Don't you look fo' no deer, Chéri. Dat 's too big. But you bring La Folle one good fat squirrel fo' her dinner to-morrow, an' she goin' be satisfi'."

"One squirrel ain't a bite. I'll bring you mo' 'an one, La Folle," he had boasted pompously as he went away.

When the woman, an hour later, heard the report of the boy's rifle close to the wood's edge, she would have thought nothing of it if a sharp cry of distress had not followed the sound.

She withdrew her arms from the tub of suds in which they had been plunged, dried them upon her apron, and as quickly as her trembling limbs would bear her, hurried to the spot whence the ominous report had come.

It was as she feared. There she found Chéri stretched upon the ground, with his rifle beside him. He moaned piteously:—

"I'm dead, La Folle! I'm dead! I'm gone!"

"*Non, non!*" she exclaimed resolutely, as she knelt beside him. "Put you' arm 'roun' La Folle's nake, Chéri. Dat 's nuttin'; dat goin' be nuttin'." She lifted him in her powerful arms.

Chéri had carried his gun muzzle-downward. He had stumbled,—he did not know how. He only knew that he had a ball lodged somewhere in his leg, and he thought that his end was at hand. Now, with his head upon the woman's shoulder, he moaned and wept with pain and fright.

"Oh, La Folle! La Folle! it hurt so bad! I can' stan' it, La Folle!"

"Don't cry, *mon bébé, mon bébé, mon Chéri!*"[5] the woman spoke soothingly as she covered the ground with long strides. "La Folle goin' mine you; Doctor Bonfils goin' come make *mon Chéri* well agin."

She had reached the abandoned field. As she crossed it with her precious burden, she looked constantly and restlessly from side to side. A terrible fear was upon her,—the fear of the world beyond the bayou, the morbid and insane dread she had been under since childhood.

When she was at the bayou's edge she stood there, and shouted for help as if a life depended upon it:—

"Oh, P'tit Maître! P'tit Maître! Venez donc! Au secours! Au secours!"[6]

No voice responded. Chéri's hot tears were scalding her neck. She called for each and every one upon the place, and still no answer came.

She shouted, she wailed; but whether her voice remained unheard or unheeded, no reply came to her frenzied cries. And all the while Chéri moaned and wept and entreated to be taken home to his mother.

La Folle gave a last despairing look around her. Extreme terror was upon her. She clasped the child close against her breast, where he could feel her heart beat like a muffled hammer. Then shutting her eyes, she ran suddenly down the shallow bank of the bayou, and never stopped till she had climbed the opposite shore.

She stood there quivering an instant as she opened her eyes. Then she plunged into the footpath through the trees.

She spoke no more to Chéri, but muttered constantly, "Bon Dieu, ayez pitié La Folle! Bon Dieu, ayez pitié moi!"[7]

Instinct seemed to guide her. When the pathway spread clear and smooth enough before her, she again closed her eyes tightly against the sight of that unknown and terrifying world.

A child, playing in some weeds, caught sight of her as she neared the quarters. The little one uttered a cry of dismay.

"La Folle!" she screamed, in her piercing treble. "La Folle done cross de bayer!"

Quickly the cry passed down the line of cabins.

"Yonda, La Folle done cross de bayou!"

Children, old men, old women, young ones with infants in their arms, flocked to doors and windows to see this awe-inspiring spectacle. Most of them shuddered with superstitious dread of what it might portend. "She totin' Chéri!" some of them shouted.

Some of the more daring gathered about her, and followed at her heels, only to fall back with new terror when she turned her distorted face upon them. Her eyes were bloodshot and the saliva had gathered in a white foam on her black lips.

Some one had run ahead of her to where P'tit Maître sat with his family and guests upon the gallery.

"P'tit Maître! La Folle done cross de bayou! Look her! Look her yonda totin' Chéri!" This startling intimation was the first which they had of the woman's approach.

She was now near at hand. She walked with long strides. Her

eyes were fixed desperately before her, and she breathed heavily, as a tired ox.

At the foot of the stairway, which she could not have mounted, she laid the boy in his father's arms. Then the world that had looked red to La Folle suddenly turned black,—like that day she had seen powder and blood.

She reeled for an instant. Before a sustaining arm could reach her, she fell heavily to the ground.

When La Folle regained consciousness, she was at home again, in her own cabin and upon her own bed. The moon rays, streaming in through the open door and windows, gave what light was needed to the old black mammy who stood at the table concocting a tisane[8] of fragrant herbs. It was very late.

Others who had come, and found that the stupor clung to her, had gone again. P'tit Maître had been there, and with him Doctor Bonfils, who said that La Folle might die.

But death had passed her by. The voice was very clear and steady with which she spoke to Tante Lizette, brewing her tisane there in a corner.

"Ef you will give me one good drink tisane, Tante Lizette, I b'lieve I'm goin' sleep, me."

And she did sleep; so soundly, so healthfully, that old Lizette without compunction stole softly away, to creep back through the moonlit fields to her own cabin in the new quarters.

The first touch of the cool gray morning awoke La Folle. She arose, calmly, as if no tempest had shaken and threatened her existence but yesterday.

She donned her new blue cottonade and white apron, for she remembered that this was Sunday. When she had made for herself a cup of strong black coffee, and drunk it with relish, she quitted the cabin and walked across the old familiar field to the bayou's edge again.

She did not stop there as she had always done before, but crossed with a long, steady stride as if she had done this all her life.

When she had made her way through the brush and scrub cottonwood-trees that lined the opposite bank, she found herself upon the border of a field where the white, bursting cotton, with the dew upon it, gleamed for acres and acres like frosted silver in the early dawn.

La Folle drew a long, deep breath as she gazed across the country. She walked slowly and uncertainly, like one who hardly knows how, looking about her as she went.

The cabins, that yesterday had sent a clamor of voices to pursue her, were quiet now. No one was yet astir at Bellissime. Only the birds that darted here and there from hedges were awake, and singing their matins.

When La Folle came to the broad stretch of velvety lawn that surrounded the house, she moved slowly and with delight over the springy turf, that was delicious beneath her tread.

She stopped to find whence came those perfumes that were assailing her senses with memories from a time far gone.

There they were, stealing up to her from the thousand blue violets that peeped out from green, luxuriant beds. There they were, showering down from the big waxen bells of the magnolias far above her head, and from the jessamine clumps around her.

There were roses, too, without number. To right and left palms spread in broad and graceful curves. It all looked like enchantment beneath the sparkling sheen of dew.

When La Folle had slowly and cautiously mounted the many steps that led up to the veranda, she turned to look back at the perilous ascent she had made. Then she caught sight of the river, bending like a silver bow at the foot of Bellissime. Exultation possessed her soul.

La Folle rapped softly upon a door near at hand. Chéri's mother soon cautiously opened it. Quickly and cleverly she dissembled the astonishment she felt at seeing La Folle.

"Ah, La Folle! Is it you, so early?"

"*Oui*, madame. I come ax how my po' li'le Chéri to, 's mo'nin'."

"He is feeling easier, thank you, La Folle. Dr. Bonfils says it will be nothing serious. He's sleeping now. Will you come back when he awakes?"

"*Non*, madame. I'm goin' wait yair tell Chéri wake up." La Folle seated herself upon the topmost step of the veranda.

A look of wonder and deep content crept into her face as she watched for the first time the sun rise upon the new, the beautiful world beyond the bayou.

Old Aunt Peggy

WHEN the war was over, old Aunt Peggy went to Monsieur, and said:—

"Massa, I ain't never gwine to quit yer. I'm gittin' ole an' feeble, an' my days is few in dis heah lan' o' sorrow an' sin. All I axes is a li'le co'ner whar I kin set down an' wait peaceful fu de en'."

Monsieur and Madame were very much touched at this mark of affection and fidelity from Aunt Peggy. So, in the general reconstruction of the plantation which immediately followed the surrender, a nice cabin, pleasantly appointed, was set apart for the old woman. Madame did not even forget the very comfortable rocking-chair in which Aunt Peggy might "set down," as she herself feelingly expressed it, "an' wait fu de en'."

She has been rocking ever since.

At intervals of about two years Aunt Peggy hobbles up to the house, and delivers the stereotyped address which has become more than familiar:—

"Mist'ess, I 's come to take a las' look at you all. Le' me look at you good. Le' me look at de chillun,—de big chillun an' de li'le chillun. Le' me look at de picters an' de photygraphts an' de pianny, an' eve'ything 'fo' it 's too late. One eye is done gone, an' de udder 's a-gwine fas'. Any mo'nin' yo' po' ole Aunt Peggy gwine wake up an' fin' herse'f stone-bline."

After such a visit Aunt Peggy invariably returns to her cabin with a generously filled apron.

The scruple which Monsieur one time felt in supporting a woman for so many years in idleness has entirely disappeared. Of late his attitude towards Aunt Peggy is simply one of profound astonishment,—wonder at the surprising age which an old black woman may attain when she sets her mind to it, for Aunt Peggy is a hundred and twenty-five, so she says.

It may not be true, however. Possibly she is older.

The Return of Alcibiade

MR. FRED BARTNER was sorely perplexed and annoyed to find that a wheel and tire of his buggy threatened to part company.

"Ef you want," said the negro boy who drove him, "we kin stop yonda at ole M'sié Jean Ba's an' fix it; he got de bes' blacksmif shop in de pa'ish on his place."

"Who in the world is old Monsieur Jean Ba," the young man inquired.

"How come, suh, you don' know old M'sié Jean Baptiste Plochel? He ole, ole. He sorter quare in he head ev' sence his son M'sié Alcibiade got kill' in de wah. Yonda he live'; whar you sees dat che'okee hedge takin' up half de road."

Little more than twelve years ago, before the "Texas and Pacific" had joined the cities of New Orleans and Shreveport with its steel bands, it was a common thing to travel through miles of central Louisiana in a buggy. Fred Bartner, a young commission merchant of New Orleans, on business bent, had made the trip in this way by easy stages from his home to a point on Cane River, within a half day's journey of Natchitoches. From the mouth of Cane River he had passed one plantation after another,—large ones and small ones. There was nowhere sight of anything like a town, except the little hamlet of Cloutierville, through which they had sped in the gray dawn. "Dat town, hit's ole, ole; mos' a hund'ed year' ole, dey say. Uh, uh, look to me like it heap ol'r an' dat," the darkey had commented. Now they were within sight of Monsieur Jean Ba's towering Cherokee hedge.

It was Christmas morning, but the sun was warm and the air so soft and mild that Bartner found the most comfortable way to wear his light overcoat was across his knees. At the entrance to the plantation he dismounted and the negro drove away toward the smithy which stood on the edge of the field.

From the end of the long avenue of magnolias that led to it, the house which confronted Bartner looked grotesquely long in comparison with its height. It was one story, of pale, yellow stucco; its massive wooden shutters were a faded green. A wide gallery, topped by the overhanging roof, encircled it.

At the head of the stairs a very old man stood. His figure was small and shrunken, his hair long and snow-white. He wore a broad, soft felt hat, and a brown plaid shawl across his bent shoulders. A tall, graceful girl stood beside him; she was clad in a warm-colored blue stuff gown. She seemed to be expostulating with the old gentleman, who evidently wanted to descend the stairs to meet the approaching visitor. Before Bartner had had time to do more than lift his hat, Monsieur Jean Ba had thrown his trembling arms about the young man and was exclaiming in his quavering old tones: "À la fin! mon fils! à la fin!"[1] Tears started to the girl's eyes and she was rosy with confusion. "Oh, escuse him, sir; please escuse him," she whisperingly entreated, gently striving to disengage the old gentleman's arms from around the astonished Bartner. But a new line of thought seemed fortunately to take possession of Monsieur Jean Ba, for he moved away and went quickly, pattering like a baby, down the gallery. His fleecy white hair streamed out on the soft breeze, and his brown shawl flapped as he turned the corner.

Bartner, left alone with the girl, proceeded to introduce himself and to explain his presence there.

"Oh! Mr. Fred Bartna of New Orleans? The commission merchant!" she exclaimed, cordially extending her hand. "So well known in Natchitoches parish. Not *our* merchant, Mr. Bartna," she added, naïvely, "but jus' as welcome, all the same, at my gran'father's."

Bartner felt like kissing her, but he only bowed and seated himself in the big chair which she offered him. He wondered what was the longest time it could take to mend a buggy tire.

She sat before him with her hands pressed down into her lap, and with an eagerness and pretty air of being confidential that were extremely engaging, explained the reasons for her grandfather's singular behavior.

Years ago, her uncle Alcibiade, in going away to the war, with the cheerful assurance of youth, had promised his father that he would return to eat Christmas dinner with him. He never returned. And now, of late years, since Monsieur Jean Ba had begun to fail in body and mind, that old, unspoken hope of long ago had come back to live anew in his heart. Every Christmas Day he watched for the coming of Alcibiade.

"Ah! if you knew, Mr. Bartna, how I have endeavor' to distrac' his mine from that thought! Weeks ago, I tole to all the negroes, big and li'le, 'If one of you dare to say the word, Christmas gif', in the hearing of Monsieur Jean Baptiste, you will have to answer it to me.' "

Bartner could not recall when he had been so deeply interested in a narration.

"So las' night, Mr. Bartna, I said to grandpère, 'Pépère, you know to-morrow will be the great feas' of la Trinité; we will read our litany together in the morning and say a *chapelet*.'[2] He did not answer a word; *il est malin, oui.*[3] But this morning at daylight he was rapping his cane on the back gallery, calling together the negroes. Did they not know it was Christmas Day, an' a great dinner mus' be prepare' for his son Alcibiade, whom he was especting!"

"And so he has mistaken me for his son Alcibiade. It is very unfortunate," said Bartner, sympathetically. He was a good-looking, honest-faced young fellow.

The girl arose, quivering with an inspiration. She approached Bartner, and in her eagerness laid her hand upon his arm.

"Oh, Mr. Bartna, if you will do me a favor! The greates' favor of my life!"

He expressed his absolute readiness.

"Let him believe, jus' for this one Christmas day, that you are his son. Let him have that Christmas dinner with Alcibiade, that he has been longing for so many year'."

Bartner's was not a puritanical conscience, but truthfulness was a habit as well as a principle with him, and he winced. "It seems to me it would be cruel to deceive him; it would not be"—he did not like to say "right," but she guessed that he meant it.

"Oh, for that," she laughed, "you may stay as w'ite as snow, Mr. Bartna. *I* will take all the sin on my conscience. I assume all the responsibility on my shoulder'."

"Esmée!" the old man was calling as he came trotting back, "Es-

mée, my child," in his quavering French, "I have ordered the dinner. Go see to the arrangements of the table, and have everything
faultless."

The dining-room was at the end of the house, with windows opening upon the side and back galleries. There was a high, simply
carved wooden mantelpiece, bearing a wide, slanting, old-fashioned
mirror that reflected the table and its occupants. The table was
laden with an overabundance. Monsieur Jean Ba sat at one end, Esmée at the other, and Bartner at the side.

Two *"grif"*[4] boys, a big black woman and a little mulatto girl
waited upon them; there was a reserve force outside within easy
call, and the little black and yellow faces kept bobbing up constantly above the windowsills. Windows and doors were open, and
a fire of hickory branches blazed on the hearth.

Monsieur Jean Ba ate little, but that little greedily and rapidly;
then he stayed in rapt contemplation of his guest.

"You will notice, Alcibiade, the flavor of the turkey," he said. "It
is dressed with pecans; those big ones from the tree down on the
bayou. I had them gathered expressly." The delicate and rich flavor
of the nut was indeed very perceptible.

Bartner had a stupid impression of acting on the stage, and had
to pull himself together every now and then to throw off the stiff-
ness of the amateur actor. But this discomposure amounted almost
to paralysis when he found Mademoiselle Esmée taking the situation as seriously as her grandfather.

"*Mon Dieu!* uncle Alcibiade, you are not eating! *Mais* w'ere have
you lef' your appetite? Corbeau, fill your young master's glass. Do-
ralise, you are neglecting Monsieur Alcibiade; he is without bread."

Monsieur Jean Ba's feeble intelligence reached out very dimly; it
was like a dream which clothes the grotesque and unnatural with
the semblance of reality. He shook his head up and down with
pleased approbation of Esmée's "Uncle Alcibiade," that tripped so
glibly on her lips. When she arranged his after-dinner *brûlot*,—a
lump of sugar in a flaming teaspoonful of brandy, dropped into a
tiny cup of black coffee,—he reminded her, "Your Uncle Alcibiade
takes two lumps, Esmée. The scamp! he is fond of sweets. Two or
three lumps, Esmée." Bartner would have relished his *brûlot*

greatly, prepared so gracefully as it was by Esmée's deft hands, had it not been for that superfluous lump.

After dinner the girl arranged her grandfather comfortably in his big armchair on the gallery, where he loved to sit when the weather permitted. She fastened his shawl about him and laid a second one across his knees. She shook up the pillow for his head, patted his sunken cheek and kissed his forehead under the soft-brimmed hat. She left him there with the sun warming his feet and old shrunken knees.

Esmée and Bartner walked together under the magnolias. In walking they trod upon the violet borders that grew rank and sprawling, and the subtle perfume of the crushed flowers scented the air deliciously. They stooped and plucked handfuls of them. They gathered roses, too, that were blooming yet against the warm south end of the house; and they chattered and laughed like children. When they sat in the sunlight upon the low steps to arrange the flowers they had broken, Bartner's conscience began to prick him anew.

"You know," he said, "I can't stay here always, as well as I should like to. I shall have to leave presently; then your grandfather will discover that we have been deceiving him,—and you can see how cruel that will be."

"Mr. Bartna," answered Esmée, daintily holding a rosebud up to her pretty nose, "W'en I awoke this morning an' said my prayers, I prayed to the good God that He would give one happy Christmas day to my gran'father. He has answered my prayer; an' He does not sen' his gif's incomplete. He will provide.

"Mr. Bartna, this morning I agreed to take all responsibility on my shoulder', you remember? Now, I place all that responsibility on the shoulder' of the blessed Virgin."

Bartner was distracted with admiration; whether for this beautiful and consoling faith, or its charming votary, was not quite clear to him.

Every now and then Monsieur Jean Ba would call out, "Alcibiade, *mon fils!*" and Bartner would hasten to his side. Sometimes the old man had forgotten what he wanted to say. Once it was to ask if the salad had been to his liking, or if he would, perhaps, not have preferred the turkey *aux truffes*.[5]

"Alcibiade, *mon fils!*" Again Bartner amiably answered the summons. Monsieur Jean Ba took the young man's hand affectionately in his, but limply, as children hold hands. Bartner's closed firmly around it.

"Alcibiade, I am going to take a little nap now. If Robert McFarlane[6] comes while I am sleeping, with more talk of wanting to buy Nég Sévérin, tell him I will sell none of my slaves; not the least little *négrillon*.[7] Drive him from the place with the shot-gun. Don't be afraid to use the shot-gun, Alcibiade,—when I am asleep,—if he comes."

Esmée and Bartner forgot that there was such a thing as time, and that it was passing. There were no more calls of "Alcibiade, *mon fils!*" As the sun dipped lower and lower in the west, its light was creeping, creeping up and illuming the still body of Monsieur Jean Ba. It lighted his waxen hands, folded so placidly in his lap; it touched his shrunken bosom. When it reached his face, another brightness had come there before it,—the glory of a quiet and peaceful death.

Bartner remained over night, of course, to add what assistance he could to that which kindly neighbors offered.

In the early morning, before taking his departure, he was permitted to see Esmée. She was overcome with sorrow, which he could hardly hope to assuage, even with the keen sympathy which he felt.

"And may I be permitted to ask, Mademoiselle, what will be your plans for the future?"

"Oh," she moaned, "I cannot any longer remain upon the ole plantation, which would not be home without grandpère. I suppose I shall go to live in New Orleans with my *tante* Clémentine." The last was spoken in the depths of her handkerchief.

Bartner's heart bounded at this intelligence in a manner which he could not but feel was one of unbecoming levity. He pressed her disengaged hand warmly, and went away.

The sun was again shining brightly, but the morning was crisp and cool; a thin wafer of ice covered what had yesterday been pools of water in the road. Bartner buttoned his coat about him closely. The shrill whistles of steam cotton-gins sounded here and there. One or two shivering negroes were in the field gathering what shreds of cotton were left on the dry, naked stalks. The horses snorted with satisfaction, and their strong hoof-beats rang out against the hard ground.

"Urge the horses," Bartner said; "they 've had a good rest and we want to push on to Natchitoches."

"You right, suh. We done los' a whole blesse' day,—a plumb day."

"Why, so we have," said Bartner, "I had n't thought of it."

A Rude Awakening

"TAKE de do' an' go! You year me? Take de do'!"

Lolotte's brown eyes flamed. Her small frame quivered. She stood with her back turned to a meagre supper-table, as if to guard it from the man who had just entered the cabin. She pointed toward the door, to order him from the house.

"You mighty cross to-night, Lolotte. You mus' got up wid de wrong foot to 's mo'nin'. *Hein,* Veveste? *hein,* Jacques, w'at you say?"

The two small urchins who sat at table giggled in sympathy with their father's evident good humor.

"I'm wo' out, me!" the girl exclaimed, desperately, as she let her arms fall limp at her side. "Work, work! Fu w'at? Fu w'at? Fu feed de lazies' man in Natchitoches pa'ish."

"Now, Lolotte, you think w'at you sayin'," expostulated her father. "Sylveste Bordon don' ax nobody to feed 'im."

"W'en you brought a poun' of suga in de house?" his daughter retorted hotly, "or a poun' of coffee? W'en did you brought a piece o' meat home, you? An' Nonomme all de time sick. Co'n bread an' po'k, dat's good fu Veveste an' me an' Jacques; but Nonomme? no!"

She turned as if choking, and cut into the round, soggy "pone" of corn bread which was the main feature of the scanty supper.

"Po' li'le Nonomme; we mus' fine some'in' to break dat fevah. You want to kill a chicken once a w'ile fu Nonomme, Lolotte." He calmly seated himself at the table.

"Did n' I done put de las' roostah in de pot?" she cried with exasperation. "Now you come axen me fu kill de hen'! W'ere I goen to fine aigg' to trade wid, w'en de hen' be gone? Is I got one picayune in de house fu trade wid, me?"

"Papa," piped the young Jacques, "w'at dat I yeard you drive in de yard, w'ile go?"

"Dat 's it! W'en Lolotte would n' been talken' so fas', I could tole you 'bout dat job I got fu to-morrow. Dat was Joe Duplan's team of mule' an' wagon, wid t'ree bale' of cotton, w'at you yaird. I got to go soon in de mo'nin' wid dat load to de landin'. An' a man mus' eat w'at got to work; dat's sho."

Lolotte's bare brown feet made no sound upon the rough boards as she entered the room where Nonomme lay sick and sleeping. She lifted the coarse mosquito net from about him, sat down in the clumsy chair by the bedside, and began gently to fan the slumbering child.

Dusk was falling rapidly, as it does in the South. Lolotte's eyes grew round and big, as she watched the moon creep up from branch to branch of the moss-draped live-oak just outside her window. Presently the weary girl slept as profoundly as Nonomme. A little dog sneaked into the room, and socially licked her bare feet. The touch, moist and warm, awakened Lolotte.

The cabin was dark and quiet. Nonomme was crying softly, because the mosquitoes were biting him. In the room beyond, old Sylveste and the others slept. When Lolotte had quieted the child, she went outside to get a pail of cool, fresh water at the cistern. Then she crept into bed beside Nonomme, who slept again.

Lolotte's dreams that night pictured her father returning from work, and bringing luscious oranges home in his pocket for the sick child.

When at the very break of day she heard him astir in his room, a certain comfort stole into her heart. She lay and listened to the faint noises of his preparations to go out. When he had quitted the house, she waited to hear him drive the wagon from the yard.

She waited long, but heard no sound of horse's tread or wagon-wheel. Anxious, she went to the cabin door and looked out. The big mules were still where they had been fastened the night before. The wagon was there, too.

Her heart sank. She looked quickly along the low rafters supporting the roof of the narrow porch to where her father's fishing pole and pail always hung. Both were gone.

" 'T ain' no use," she said, as she turned into the house with a look of something like anguish in her eyes.

When the spare breakfast was eaten and the dishes cleared away, Lolotte turned with resolute mien to the two little brothers.

"Veveste," she said to the older, "go see if dey got co'n in dat wagon fu feed dem mule'."

"Yes, dey got co'n. Papa done feed 'em, fur I see de co'n-cob in de trough, me."

"Den you goen he'p me hitch dem mule, to de wagon. Jacques, go down de lane an' ax Aunt Minty if she come set wid Nonomme w'ile I go drive dem mule' to de landin'."

Lolotte had evidently determined to undertake her father's work. Nothing could dissuade her; neither the children's astonishment nor Aunt Minty's scathing disapproval. The fat black negress came laboring into the yard just as Lolotte mounted upon the wagon.

"Git down f'om dah, chile! Is you plumb crazy?" she exclaimed.

"No, I ain't crazy; I'm hungry, Aunt Minty. We all hungry. Somebody got fur work in dis fam'ly."

"Dat ain't no work fur a gal w'at ain't bar' seventeen year ole; drivin' Marse Duplan's mules! W'at I gwine tell yo' pa?"

"Fu me, you kin tell 'im w'at you want. But you watch Nonomme. I done cook his rice an' set it 'side."

"Don't you bodda," replied Aunt Minty; "I got somepin heah fur my boy. I gwine 'ten' to him."

Lolotte had seen Aunt Minty put something out of sight when she came up, and made her produce it. It was a heavy fowl.

"Sence w'en you start raisin' Brahma chicken', you?" Lolotte asked mistrustfully.

"My, but you is a cu'ious somebody! Ev'ything w'at got fedders on its laigs is Brahma chicken wid you. Dis heah ole hen"—

"All de same, you don't got fur give dat chicken to eat to Nonomme. You don't got fur cook 'im in my house."

Aunt Minty, unheeding, turned to the house with blustering inquiry for her boy, while Lolotte drove away with great clatter.

She knew, notwithstanding her injunction, that the chicken would be cooked and eaten. Maybe she herself would partake of it when she came back, if hunger drove her too sharply.

"Nax' thing I'm goen be one rogue," she muttered; and the tears gathered and fell one by one upon her cheeks.

"It *do* look like one Brahma, Aunt Mint," remarked the small and weazened Jacques, as he watched the woman picking the lusty fowl.

"How ole is you?" was her quiet retort.

"I don' know, me."

"Den if you don't know dat much, you betta keep yo' mouf shet, boy."

Then silence fell, but for a monotonous chant which the woman droned as she worked. Jacques opened his lips once more.

"It *do* look like one o' Ma'me Duplan' Brahma, Aunt Mint."

"Yonda, whar I come f'om, befo' de wah"—

"Ole Kaintuck, Aunt Mint?"

"Ole Kaintuck."

"Dat ain't one country like dis yere, Aunt Mint?"

"You mighty right, chile, dat ain't no sech kentry as dis heah. Yonda, in Kaintuck, w'en boys says de word 'Brahma chicken,' we takes an' gags em, an' ties dar han's behines 'em, an' fo'ces 'em ter stan' up watchin' folks settin' down eatin' chicken soup."

Jacques passed the back of his hand across his mouth; but lest the act should not place sufficient seal upon it, he prudently stole away to go and sit beside Nonomme, and wait there as patiently as he could the coming feast.

And what a treat it was! The luscious soup,—a great pot of it,— golden yellow, thickened with the flaky rice that Lolotte had set carefully on the shelf. Each mouthful of it seemed to carry fresh blood into the veins and a new brightness into the eyes of the hungry children who ate of it.

And that was not all. The day brought abundance with it. Their father came home with glistening perch and trout that Aunt Minty broiled deliciously over glowing embers, and basted with the rich chicken fat.

"You see," explained old Sylveste, "w'en I git up to 's mo'nin' an' see it was cloudy, I say to me, 'Sylveste, w'en you go wid dat cotton, rememba you got no tarpaulin. Maybe it rain, an' de cotton was spoil. Betta you go yonda to Lafirme Lake, w'ere de trout was bitin' fas'er 'an mosquito, an' so you git a good mess fur de chil'en.' Lolotte—w'at she goen do yonda? You ought stop Lolotte, Aunt Minty, w'en you see w'at she was want to do."

"Did n' I try to stop 'er? Did n' I ax 'er, 'W'at I gwine tell yo' pa?' An' she 'low, 'Tell 'im to go hang hisse'f, de triflind ole rapscallion! I 's de one w'at 's runnin' dis heah fambly!' "

"Dat don' soun' like Lolotte, Aunt Minty; you mus' yaird 'er crooked; *hein*, Nonomme?"

The quizzical look in his good-natured features was irresistible. Nonomme fairly shook with merriment.

"My head feel so good," he declared. "I wish Lolotte would come, so I could tole 'er." And he turned in his bed to look down the long, dusty lane, with the hope of seeing her appear as he had watched her go, sitting on one of the cotton bales and guiding the mules.

But no one came all through the hot morning. Only at noon a broad-shouldered young negro appeared in view riding through the dust. When he had dismounted at the cabin door, he stood leaning a shoulder lazily against the jamb.

"Well, heah you is," he grumbled, addressing Sylveste with no mark of respect. "Heah you is, settin' down like comp'ny, an' Marse Joe yonda sont me see if you was dead."

"Joe Duplan boun' to have his joke, him," said Sylveste, smiling uneasily.

"Maybe it look like a joke to you, but 't aint no joke to him, man, to have one o' his wagons smoshed to kindlin', an' his bes' team tearin' t'rough de country. You don't want to let 'im lay han's on you, joke o' no joke."

"*Malédiction!*"[1] howled Sylveste, as he staggered to his feet. He stood for one instant irresolute; then he lurched past the man and ran wildly down the lane. He might have taken the horse that was there, but he went tottering on afoot, a frightened look in his eyes, as if his soul gazed upon an inward picture that was horrible.

The road to the landing was little used. As Sylveste went he could readily trace the marks of Lolotte's wagon-wheels. For some distance they went straight along the road. Then they made a track as if a madman had directed their course, over stump and hillock, tearing the bushes and barking the trees on either side.

At each new turn Sylveste expected to find Lolotte stretched senseless upon the ground, but there was never a sign of her.

At last he reached the landing, which was a dreary spot, slanting down to the river and partly cleared to afford room for what desultory freight might be left there from time to time. There were the wagon-tracks, clean down to the river's edge and partly in the water, where they made a sharp and senseless turn. But Sylveste found no trace of his girl.

"Lolotte!" the old man cried out into the stillness. "Lolotte, *ma fille*,[2] Lolotte!" But no answer came; no sound but the echo of his own voice, and the soft splash of the red water that lapped his feet.

He looked down at it, sick with anguish and apprehension.

Lolotte had disappeared as completely as if the earth had opened and swallowed her. After a few days it became the common belief that the girl had been drowned. It was thought that she must have been hurled from the wagon into the water during the sharp turn that the wheel-tracks indicated, and carried away by the rapid current.

During the days of search, old Sylveste's excitement kept him up. When it was over, an apathetic despair seemed to settle upon him.

Madame Duplan, moved by sympathy, had taken the little four-year-old Nonomme to the plantation Les Chêniers,[3] where the child was awed by the beauty and comfort of things that surrounded him there. He thought always that Lolotte would come back, and watched for her every day; for they did not tell him the sad tidings of her loss.

The other two boys were placed in the temporary care of Aunt Minty; and old Sylveste roamed like a persecuted being through the country. He who had been a type of indolent content and repose had changed to a restless spirit.

When he thought to eat, it was in some humble negro cabin that he stopped to ask for food, which was never denied him. His grief had clothed him with a dignity that imposed respect.

One morning very early he appeared before the planter with a disheveled and hunted look.

"M'sieur Duplan," he said, holding his hat in his hand and looking away into vacancy, "I been try ev'thing. I been try settin' down still on de sto' gall'ry. I been walk, I been run; 't ain' no use. Dey got al'ays some'in' w'at push me. I go fishin', an' it's some'in' w'at push me worser 'an ever. By gracious! M'sieur Duplan, gi' me some work!"

The planter gave him at once a plow in hand, and no plow on the whole plantation dug so deep as that one, nor so fast. Sylveste was the first in the field, as he was the last one there. From dawn to nightfall he worked, and after, till his limbs refused to do his bidding.

People came to wonder, and the negroes began to whisper hints of demoniacal possession.

When Mr. Duplan gave careful thought to the subject of Lolotte's mysterious disappearance, an idea came to him. But so fearful was he to arouse false hopes in the breasts of those who grieved for the girl that to no one did he impart his suspicions save to his wife. It was on the eve of a business trip to New Orleans that he told her what he thought, or what he hoped rather.

Upon his return, which happened not many days later, he went out to where old Sylveste was toiling in the field with frenzied energy.

"Sylveste," said the planter, quietly, when he had stood a moment watching the man at work, "have you given up all hope of hearing from your daughter?"

"I don' know, me; I don' know. Le' me work, M'sieur Duplan."

"For my part, I believe the child is alive."

"You b'lieve dat, you?" His rugged face was pitiful in its imploring lines.

"I know it," Mr. Duplan muttered, as calmly as he could. "Hold up! Steady yourself, man! Come; come with me to the house. There is some one there who knows it, too; some one who has seen her."

The room into which the planter led the old man was big, cool, beautiful, and sweet with the delicate odor of flowers. It was shady, too, for the shutters were half closed; but not so darkened but Sylveste could at once see Lolotte, seated in a big wicker chair.

She was almost as white as the gown she wore. Her neatly shod feet rested upon a cushion, and her black hair, that had been closely cut, was beginning to make little rings about her temples.

"Aie!" he cried sharply, at sight of her, grasping his seamed throat as he did so. Then he laughed like a madman, and then he sobbed.

He only sobbed, kneeling upon the floor beside her, kissing her knees and her hands, that sought his. Little Nonomme was close to her, with a health flush creeping into his cheek. Veveste and Jacques

were there, and rather awed by the mystery and grandeur of everything.

"W'ere'bouts you find her, M'sieur Duplan?" Sylveste asked,
when the first flush of his joy had spent itself, and he was wiping his
eyes with his rough cotton shirt sleeve.

"M'sieur Duplan find me 'way yonda to de city, papa, in de hospital," spoke Lolotte, before the planter could steady his voice
to reply. "I did n' know who ev'ybody was, me. I did n' know
me, myse'f, tell I tu'n roun' one day an' see M'sieur Duplan, w'at
stan'en dere."

"You was boun' to know M'sieur Duplan, Lolotte," laughed
Sylveste, like a child.

"Yes, an' I know right 'way how dem mule was git frighten' w'en
de boat w'istle fu stop, an' pitch me plumb on de groun'. An' I rememba it was one *mulâtresse*[4] w'at call herse'f one chembamed, all
de time aside me."

"You must not talk too much, Lolotte," interposed Madame Duplan, coming to place her hand with gentle solicitude upon the girl's
forehead, and to feel how her pulse beat.

Then to save the child further effort of speech, she herself related
how the boat had stopped at this lonely landing to take on a load of
cotton-seed. Lolotte had been found stretched insensible by the
river, fallen apparently from the clouds, and had been taken on
board.

The boat had changed its course into other waters after that trip,
and had not returned to Duplan's Landing. Those who had tended
Lolotte and left her at the hospital supposed, no doubt, that she
would make known her identity in time, and they had troubled
themselves no further about her.

"An' dah you is!" almost shouted aunt Minty, whose black face
gleamed in the doorway; "dah you is, settin' down, lookin' jis' like
w'ite folks!"

"Ain't I always was w'ite folks, Aunt Mint?" smiled Lolotte,
feebly.

"G'long, chile. You knows me. I don' mean no harm."

"And now, Sylveste," said Mr. Duplan, as he rose and started to
walk the floor, with hands in his pockets, "listen to me. It will be a
long time before Lolotte is strong again. Aunt Minty is going to

look after things for you till the child is fully recovered. But what I want to say is this: I shall trust these children into your hands once more, and I want you never to forget again that you are their father—do you hear?—that you are a man!"

Old Sylveste stood with his hand in Lolotte's, who rubbed it lovingly against her cheek.

"By gracious! M'sieur Duplan," he answered, "w'en God want to he'p me, I'm goen try my bes'!"

The Bênitous' Slave

OLD Uncle Oswald believed he belonged to the Bênitous, and there was no getting the notion out of his head. Monsieur tried every way, for there was no sense in it. Why, it must have been fifty years since the Bênitous owned him. He had belonged to others since, and had later been freed. Beside, there was not a Bênitou left in the parish now, except one rather delicate woman, who lived with her little daughter in a corner of Natchitoches town, and constructed "fashionable millinery." The family had dispersed, and almost vanished, and the plantation as well had lost its identity.

But that made no difference to Uncle Oswald. He was always running away from Monsieur—who kept him out of pure kindness—and trying to get back to those Bênitous.

More than that, he was constantly getting injured in such attempts. Once he fell into the bayou and was nearly drowned. Again he barely escaped being run down by an engine. But another time, when he had been lost two days, and finally discovered in an unconscious and half-dead condition in the woods, Monsieur and Doctor Bonfils reluctantly decided that it was time to "do something" with the old man.

So, one sunny spring morning, Monsieur took Uncle Oswald in the buggy, and drove over to Natchitoches with him, intending to take the evening train for the institution in which the poor creature was to be cared for.

It was quite early in the afternoon when they reached town, and Monsieur found himself with several hours to dispose of before train-time. He tied his horses in front of the hotel—the quaintest old stuccoed house, too absurdly unlike a "hotel" for anything—and entered. But he left Uncle Oswald seated upon a shaded bench just within the yard.

There were people occasionally coming in and going out; but no one took the smallest notice of the old negro drowsing over the cane that he held between his knees. The sight was common in Natchitoches.

One who passed in was a little girl about twelve, with dark, kind eyes, and daintily carrying a parcel. She was dressed in blue calico, and wore a stiff white sun-bonnet, extinguisher fashion,[1] over her brown curls.

Just as she passed Uncle Oswald again, on her way out, the old man, half asleep, let fall his cane. She picked it up and handed it back to him, as any nice child would have done.

"Oh, thankee, thankee, missy," stammered Uncle Oswald, all confused at being waited upon by this little lady. "You is a putty li'le gal. W'at 's yo' name, honey?"

"My name 's Susanne; Susanne Bênitou," replied the girl.

Instantly the old negro stumbled to his feet. Without a moment's hesitancy he followed the little one out through the gate, down the street, and around the corner.

It was an hour later that Monsieur, after a distracted search, found him standing upon the gallery of the tiny house in which Madame Bênitou kept "fashionable millinery."

Mother and daughter were sorely perplexed to comprehend the intentions of the venerable servitor, who stood, hat in hand, persistently awaiting their orders.

Monsieur understood and appreciated the situation at once, and he has prevailed upon Madame Bênitou to accept the gratuitous services of Uncle Oswald for the sake of the old darky's own safety and happiness.

Uncle Oswald never tries to run away now. He chops wood and hauls water. He cheerfully and faithfully bears the parcels that Susanne used to carry; and makes an excellent cup of black coffee.

I met the old man the other day in Natchitoches, contentedly stumbling down St. Denis street with a basket of figs that some one was sending to his mistress. I asked him his name.

"My name 's Oswal', Madam; Oswal'—dat's my name. I b'longs to de Bênitous," and some one told me his story then.

Désirée's Baby

As the day was pleasant, Madame Valmondé drove over to L'Abri[1] to see Désirée and the baby.

It made her laugh to think of Désirée with a baby. Why, it seemed but yesterday that Désirée was little more than a baby herself; when Monsieur in riding through the gateway of Valmondé had found her lying asleep in the shadow of the big stone pillar.

The little one awoke in his arms and began to cry for "Dada." That was as much as she could do or say. Some people thought she might have strayed there of her own accord, for she was of the toddling age. The prevailing belief was that she had been purposely left by a party of Texans, whose canvas-covered wagon, late in the day, had crossed the ferry that Coton Maïs kept, just below the plantation. In time Madame Valmondé abandoned every speculation but the one that Désirée had been sent to her by a beneficent Providence to be the child of her affection, seeing that she was without child of the flesh. For the girl grew to be beautiful and gentle, affectionate and sincere,—the idol of Valmondé.

It was no wonder, when she stood one day against the stone pillar in whose shadow she had lain asleep, eighteen years before, that Armand Aubigny riding by and seeing her there, had fallen in love with her. That was the way all the Aubignys fell in love, as if struck by a pistol shot. The wonder was that he had not loved her before; for he had known her since his father brought him home from Paris, a boy of eight, after his mother died there. The passion that awoke in him that day, when he saw her at the gate, swept along like an avalanche, or like a prairie fire, or like anything that drives headlong over all obstacles.

Monsieur Valmondé grew practical and wanted things well considered: that is, the girl's obscure origin. Armand looked into her eyes and did not care. He was reminded that she was nameless. What did it matter about a name when he could give her one of the oldest and proudest in Louisiana? He ordered the *corbeille*[2] from Paris, and contained himself with what patience he could until it arrived; then they were married.

Madame Valmondé had not seen Désirée and the baby for four weeks. When she reached L'Abri she shuddered at the first sight of it, as she always did. It was a sad looking place, which for many years had not known the gentle presence of a mistress, old Monsieur Aubigny having married and buried his wife in France, and she having loved her own land too well ever to leave it. The roof came down steep and black like a cowl, reaching out beyond the wide galleries that encircled the yellow stuccoed house. Big, solemn oaks grew close to it, and their thick-leaved, far-reaching branches shadowed it like a pall. Young Aubigny's rule was a strict one, too, and under it his negroes had forgotten how to be gay, as they had been during the old master's easy-going and indulgent lifetime.

The young mother was recovering slowly, and lay full length, in her soft white muslins and laces, upon a couch. The baby was beside her, upon her arm, where he had fallen asleep, at her breast. The yellow nurse woman sat beside a window fanning herself.

Madame Valmondé bent her portly figure over Désirée and kissed her, holding her an instant tenderly in her arms. Then she turned to the child.

"This is not the baby!" she exclaimed, in startled tones. French was the language spoken at Valmondé in those days.

"I knew you would be astonished," laughed Désirée, "at the way he has grown. The little *cochon de lait*![3] Look at his legs, mamma, and his hands and fingernails,—real finger-nails. Zandrine had to cut them this morning. Is n't it true, Zandrine?"

The woman bowed her turbaned head majestically, "Mais si, Madame."[4]

"And the way he cries," went on Désirée, "is deafening. Armand heard him the other day as far away as La Blanche's[5] cabin."

Madame Valmondé had never removed her eyes from the child. She lifted it and walked with it over to the window that was lightest. She scanned the baby narrowly, then looked as searchingly at Zandrine, whose face was turned to gaze across the fields.

"Yes, the child has grown, has changed," said Madame Valmondé, slowly, as she replaced it beside its mother. "What does Armand say?"

Désirée's face became suffused with a glow that was happiness itself.

"Oh, Armand is the proudest father in the parish, I believe, chiefly because it is a boy, to bear his name; though he says not,—that he would have loved a girl as well. But I know it is n't true. I know he says that to please me. And mamma," she added, drawing Madame Valmondé's head down to her, and speaking in a whisper, "he has n't punished one of them—not one of them—since baby is born. Even Négrillon,[6] who pretended to have burnt his leg that he might rest from work—he only laughed, and said Négrillon was a great scamp. Oh, mamma, I 'm so happy; it frightens me."

What Désirée said was true. Marriage, and later the birth of his son had softened Armand Aubigny's imperious and exacting nature greatly. This was what made the gentle Désirée so happy, for she loved him desperately. When he frowned she trembled, but loved him. When he smiled, she asked no greater blessing of God. But Armand's dark, handsome face had not often been disfigured by frowns since the day he fell in love with her.

When the baby was about three months old, Désirée awoke one day to the conviction that there was something in the air menacing her peace. It was at first too subtle to grasp. It had only been a disquieting suggestion; an air of mystery among the blacks; unexpected visits from far-off neighbors who could hardly account for their coming. Then a strange, an awful change in her husband's manner, which she dared not ask him to explain. When he spoke to her, it was with averted eyes, from which the old love-light seemed to have gone out. He absented himself from home; and when there, avoided her presence and that of her child, without excuse. And the very spirit of Satan seemed suddenly to take hold of him in his dealings with the slaves. Désirée was miserable enough to die.

She sat in her room, one hot afternoon, in her *peignoir*,[7] listlessly drawing through her fingers the strands of her long, silky brown hair that hung about her shoulders. The baby, half naked, lay asleep upon her own great mahogany bed, that was like a sumptuous throne, with its satin-lined half-canopy. One of La Blanche's little quadroon boys—half naked too—stood fanning the child slowly with a fan of peacock feathers. Désirée's eyes had been fixed absently and sadly upon the baby, while she was striving to penetrate the threatening mist that she felt closing about her. She looked from her child to the boy who stood beside him, and back again; over and over. "Ah!" It was a cry that she could not help; which she was not conscious of having uttered. The blood turned like ice in her veins, and a clammy moisture gathered upon her face.

She tried to speak to the little quadroon boy; but no sound would come, at first. When he heard his name uttered, he looked up, and his mistress was pointing to the door. He laid aside the great, soft fan, and obediently stole away, over the polished floor, on his bare tiptoes.

She stayed motionless, with gaze riveted upon her child, and her face the picture of fright.

Presently her husband entered the room, and without noticing her, went to a table and began to search among some papers which covered it.

"Armand," she called to him, in a voice which must have stabbed him, if he was human. But he did not notice. "Armand," she said again. Then she rose and tottered towards him. "Armand," she panted once more, clutching his arm, "look at our child. What does it mean? tell me."

He coldly but gently loosened her fingers from about his arm and thrust the hand away from him. "Tell me what it means!" she cried despairingly.

"It means," he answered lightly, "that the child is not white; it means that you are not white."

A quick conception of all that this accusation meant for her nerved her with unwonted courage to deny it. "It is a lie; it is not true, I am white! Look at my hair, it is brown; and my eyes are gray, Armand, you know they are gray. And my skin is fair," seizing his wrist. "Look at my hand; whiter than yours, Armand," she laughed hysterically.

"As white as La Blanche's," he returned cruelly; and went away leaving her alone with their child.

When she could hold a pen in her hand, she sent a despairing letter to Madame Valmondé.

"My mother, they tell me I am not white. Armand has told me I am not white. For God's sake tell them it is not true. You must know it is not true. I shall die. I must die. I cannot be so unhappy, and live."

The answer that came was as brief:

"My own Désirée: Come home to Valmondé; back to your mother who loves you. Come with your child."

When the letter reached Désirée she went with it to her husband's study, and laid it open upon the desk before which he sat. She was like a stone image: silent, white, motionless after she placed it there.

In silence he ran his cold eyes over the written words. He said nothing. "Shall I go, Armand?" she asked in tones sharp with agonized suspense.

"Yes, go."

"Do you want me to go?"

"Yes, I want you to go."

He thought Almighty God had dealt cruelly and unjustly with him; and felt, somehow, that he was paying Him back in kind when he stabbed thus into his wife's soul. Moreover he no longer loved her, because of the unconscious injury she had brought upon his home and his name.

She turned away like one stunned by a blow, and walked slowly towards the door, hoping he would call her back.

"Good-by, Armand," she moaned.

He did not answer her. That was his last blow at fate.

Désirée went in search of her child. Zandrine was pacing the sombre gallery with it. She took the little one from the nurse's arms with no word of explanation, and descending the steps, walked away, under the live-oak branches.

It was an October afternoon; the sun was just sinking. Out in the still fields the negroes were picking cotton.

Désirée had not changed the thin white garment nor the slippers which she wore. Her hair was uncovered and the sun's rays brought a golden gleam from its brown meshes. She did not take the broad, beaten road which led to the far-off plantation of Valmondé. She walked across a deserted field, where the stubble bruised her tender feet, so delicately shod, and tore her thin gown to shreds.

She disappeared among the reeds and willows that grew thick along the banks of the deep, sluggish bayou; and she did not come back again.

Some weeks later there was a curious scene enacted at L'Abri. In the centre of the smoothly swept back yard was a great bonfire. Armand Aubigny sat in the wide hallway that commanded a view of the spectacle; and it was he who dealt out to a half dozen negroes the material which kept this fire ablaze.

A graceful cradle of willow, with all its dainty furbishings, was laid upon the pyre, which had already been fed with the richness of a priceless *layette*.[8] Then there were silk gowns, and velvet and satin ones added to these; laces, too, and embroideries; bonnets and gloves; for the *corbeille* had been of rare quality.

The last thing to go was a tiny bundle of letters; innocent little scribblings that Désirée had sent to him during the days of their espousal. There was the remnant of one back in the drawer from which he took them. But it was not Désirée's; it was part of an old letter from his mother to his father. He read it. She was thanking God for the blessing of her husband's love:—

"But, above all," she wrote, "night and day, I thank the good God for having so arranged our lives that our dear Armand will never know that his mother, who adores him, belongs to the race that is cursed with the brand of slavery."

A Turkey Hunt

THREE of Madame's finest bronze turkeys were missing from the brood. It was nearing Christmas, and that was the reason, perhaps, that even Monsieur grew agitated when the discovery was made. The news was brought to the house by Séverin's boy, who had seen the troop at noon a half mile up the bayou three short. Others reported the deficiency as even greater. So, at about two in the afternoon, though a cold drizzle had begun to fall, popular feeling in the matter was so strong that all the household forces turned out to search for the missing gobblers.

Alice, the housemaid, went down the river, and Polisson,[1] the yard-boy, went up the bayou. Others crossed the fields, and Artemise was rather vaguely instructed to "go look too."

Artemise is in some respects an extraordinary person. In age she is anywhere between ten and fifteen, with a head not unlike in shape and appearance to a dark chocolate-colored Easter-egg. She talks almost wholly in monosyllables, and has big round glassy eyes, which she fixes upon one with the placid gaze of an Egyptian sphinx.

The morning after my arrival at the plantation, I was awakened by the rattling of cups at my bedside. It was Artemise with the early coffee.

"Is it cold out?" I asked, by way of conversation, as I sipped the tiny cup of ink-black coffee.

"Ya, 'm."

"Where do you sleep, Artemise?" I further inquired, with the same intention as before.

"In uh hole," was precisely what she said, with a pump-like motion of the arm that she habitually uses to indicate a locality. What she meant was that she slept in the hall.

Again, another time, she came with an armful of wood, and having deposited it upon the hearth, turned to stare fixedly at me, with folded hands.

"Did Madame send you to build a fire, Artemise?" I hastened to ask, feeling uncomfortable under the look.

"Ya, 'm."

"Very well; make it."

"Matches!" was all she said.

There happened to be no matches in my room, and she evidently considered that all personal responsibility ceased in face of this first and not very serious obstacle. Pages might be told of her unfathomable ways; but to the turkey hunt.

All afternoon the searching party kept returning, singly and in couples, and in a more or less bedraggled condition. All brought unfavorable reports. Nothing could be seen of the missing fowls. Artemise had been absent probably an hour when she glided into the hall where the family was assembled, and stood with crossed hands and contemplative air beside the fire. We could see by the benign expression of her countenance that she possibly had information to give, if any inducement were offered her in the shape of a question.

"Have you found the turkeys, Artemise?" Madame hastened to ask.

"Ya, 'm."

"You Artemise!" shouted Aunt Florindy, the cook, who was passing through the hall with a batch of newly baked light bread. "She 's a-lyin', mist'ess, if dey ever was! *You* foun' dem turkeys?" turning upon the child. "Whar was you at, de whole blesse' time? Warn't you stan'in' plank up agin de back o' de hen-'ous'? Never budged a inch? Don't jaw me down, gal; don't jaw me!" Artemise was only gazing at Aunt Florindy with unruffled calm. "I warn't gwine tell on 'er, but arter dat untroof, I boun' to."

"Let her alone, Aunt Florindy," Madame interfered. "Where are the turkeys, Artemise?"

"Yon'a," she simply articulated, bringing the pump-handle motion of her arm into play.

"Where 'yonder'?" Madame demanded, a little impatiently.

"In uh hen-'ous'!"

Sure enough! The three missing turkeys had been accidentally locked up in the morning when the chickens were fed.

Artemise, for some unknown reason, had hidden herself during the search behind the hen-house, and had heard their muffled gobble.

Madame Célestin's Divorce

MADAME CÉLESTIN always wore a neat and snugly fitting calico wrapper when she went out in the morning to sweep her small gallery. Lawyer Paxton thought she looked very pretty in the gray one that was made with a graceful Watteau fold[1] at the back: and with which she invariably wore a bow of pink ribbon at the throat. She was always sweeping her gallery when lawyer Paxton passed by in the morning on his way to his office in St. Denis Street.

Sometimes he stopped and leaned over the fence to say good-morning at his ease; to criticise or admire her rosebushes; or, when he had time enough, to hear what she had to say. Madame Célestin usually had a good deal to say. She would gather up the train of her calico wrapper in one hand, and balancing the broom gracefully in the other, would go tripping down to where the lawyer leaned, as comfortably as he could, over her picket fence.

Of course she had talked to him of her troubles. Every one knew Madame Célestin's troubles.

"Really, madame," he told her once, in his deliberate, calculating, lawyer-tone, "it 's more than human nature—woman's nature—should be called upon to endure. Here you are, working your fingers off"—she glanced down at two rosy finger-tips that showed through the rents in her baggy doeskin gloves—"taking in sewing; giving music lessons; doing God knows what in the way of manual labor to support yourself and those two little ones"—Madame Célestin's pretty face beamed with satisfaction at this enumeration of her trials.

"You right, Judge. Not a picayune, not one, not one, have I lay my eyes on in the pas' fo' months that I can say Célestin give it to me or sen' it to me."

90

"The scoundrel!" muttered lawyer Paxton in his beard.

"An' *pourtant*,"[2] she resumed, "they say he 's making money down roun' Alexandria w'en he wants to work."

"I dare say you have n't seen him for months?" suggested the lawyer.

"It 's good six month' since I see a sight of Célestin," she admitted.

"That 's it, that 's what I say; he has practically deserted you; fails to support you. It wouldn't surprise me a bit to learn that he has ill treated you."

"Well, you know, Judge," with an evasive cough, "a man that drinks—w'at can you expec'? An' if you would know the promises he has made me! Ah, If I had as many dolla' as I had promise from Célestin, I would n' have to work, *je vous garantis*."[3]

"And in my opinion, Madame, you would be a foolish woman to endure it longer, when the divorce court is there to offer you redress."

"You spoke about that befo', Judge; I 'm goin' think about that divo'ce. I believe you right."

Madame Célestin thought about the divorce and talked about it, too; and lawyer Paxton grew deeply interested in the theme.

"You know, about that divo'ce, Judge," Madame Célestin was waiting for him that morning, "I been talking to my family an' my frien's, an' it 's me that tells you, they all plumb agains' that divo'ce."

"Certainly, to be sure; that 's to be expected, Madame, in this community of Creoles. I warned you that you would meet with opposition, and would have to face it and brave it."

"Oh, don't fear, I 'm going to face it! Maman says it 's a disgrace like it 's neva been in the family. But it 's good for Maman to talk, her. W'at trouble she ever had? She says I mus' go by all means consult with Père Duchéron—it 's my confessor, you undastan'—Well, I 'll go, Judge, to please Maman. But all the confessor' in the worl' ent goin' make me put up with that conduc' of Célestin any longa."

A day or two later, she was there waiting for him again. "You know, Judge, about that divo'ce."

"Yes, yes," responded the lawyer, well pleased to trace a new determination in her brown eyes and in the curves of her pretty mouth. "I suppose you saw Père Duchéron and had to brave it out with him, too."

"Oh, fo' that, a perfec' sermon, I assho you. A talk of giving scandal an' bad example that I thought would neva en'! He says, fo' him, he wash' his hands; I mus' go see the bishop."

"You won't let the bishop dissuade you, I trust," stammered the lawyer more anxiously than he could well understand.

"You don't know me yet, Judge," laughed Madame Célestin with a turn of the head and a flirt of the broom which indicated that the interview was at an end.

"Well, Madame Célestin! And the bishop!" Lawyer Paxton was standing there holding to a couple of the shaky pickets. She had not seen him. "Oh, it 's you, Judge?" and she hastened towards him with an *empressement*[4] that could not but have been flattering.

"Yes, I saw Monseigneur," she began. The lawyer had already gathered from her expressive countenance that she had not wavered in her determination. "Ah, he 's a eloquent man. It 's not a mo' eloquent man in Natchitoches parish. I was fo'ced to cry, the way he talked to me about my troubles; how he undastan's them, an' feels for me. It would move even you, Judge, to hear how he talk' about that step I want to take; its danga, its temptation. How it is the duty of a Catholic to stan' everything till the las' extreme. An' that life of retirement an' self-denial I would have to lead,—he tole me all that."

"But he has n't turned you from your resolve, I see," laughed the lawyer complacently.

"For that, no," she returned emphatically. "The bishop don't know w'at it is to be married to a man like Célestin, an' have to endu' that conduc' like I have to endu' it. The Pope himse'f can't make me stan' that any longer, if you say I got the right in the law to sen' Célestin sailing."

A noticeable change had come over lawyer Paxton. He discarded his work-day coat and began to wear his Sunday one to the office. He grew solicitous as to the shine of his boots, his collar, and the set of his tie. He brushed and trimmed his whiskers with a care that had not before been apparent. Then he fell into a stupid habit of dreaming as he walked the streets of the old town. It would be very good to take unto himself a wife, he dreamed. And he could dream of no other than pretty Madame Célestin filling that sweet and sacred office as she filled his thoughts, now. Old Natchitoches would not hold them comfortably, perhaps; but the world was surely wide enough to live in, outside of Natchitoches town.

His heart beat in a strangely irregular manner as he neared Madame Célestin's house one morning, and discovered her behind the rosebushes, as usual plying her broom. She had finished the gallery and steps and was sweeping the little brick walk along the edge of the violet border.

"Good-morning, Madame Célestin."

"Ah, it 's you, Judge? Good-morning." He waited. She seemed to be doing the same. Then she ventured, with some hesitancy, "You know, Judge, about that divo'ce. I been thinking,—I reckon you betta neva mine about that divo'ce." She was making deep rings in the palm of her gloved hand with the end of the broomhandle, and looking at them critically. Her face seemed to the lawyer to be unusually rosy; but maybe it was only the reflection of the pink bow at the throat. "Yes, I reckon you need n' mine. You see, Judge, Célestin came home las' night. An' he 's promise me on his word an' honor he 's going to turn ova a new leaf."

Love on the Bon-Dieu

UPON the pleasant veranda of Père Antoine's cottage, that adjoined the church, a young girl had long been seated, awaiting his return. It was the eve of Easter Sunday, and since early afternoon the priest had been engaged in hearing the confessions of those who wished to make their Easters the following day. The girl did not seem impatient at his delay; on the contrary, it was very restful to her to lie back in the big chair she had found there, and peep through the thick curtain of vines at the people who occasionally passed along the village street.

She was slender, with a frailness that indicated lack of wholesome and plentiful nourishment. A pathetic, uneasy look was in her gray eyes, and even faintly stamped her features, which were fine and delicate. In lieu of a hat, a barège veil covered her light brown and abundant hair. She wore a coarse white cotton "josie,"[1] and a blue calico skirt that only half concealed her tattered shoes.

As she sat there, she held carefully in her lap a parcel of eggs securely fastened in a red bandana handkerchief.

Twice already a handsome, stalwart young man in quest of the priest had entered the yard, and penetrated to where she sat. At first they had exchanged the uncompromising "howdy" of strangers, and nothing more. The second time, finding the priest still absent, he hesitated to go at once. Instead, he stood upon the step, and narrowing his brown eyes, gazed beyond the river, off towards the west, where a murky streak of mist was spreading across the sun.

"It look like mo' rain," he remarked, slowly and carelessly.

"We done had 'bout 'nough," she replied, in much the same tone.

"It's no chance to thin out the cotton," he went on.

94

"An' the Bon-Dieu," she resumed, "it's on'y to-day you can cross him on foot."

"You live yonda on the Bon-Dieu, *donc?*" he asked, looking at her for the first time since he had spoken.

"Yas, by Nid d'Hibout,[2] m'sieur."

Instinctive courtesy held him from questioning her further. But he seated himself on the step, evidently determined to wait there for the priest. He said no more, but sat scanning critically the steps, the porch, and pillar beside him, from which he occasionally tore away little pieces of detached wood, where it was beginning to rot at its base.

A click at the side gate that communicated with the churchyard soon announced Père Antoine's return. He came hurriedly across the garden-path, between the tall, lusty rosebushes that lined either side of it, which were now fragrant with blossoms. His long, flapping cassock added something of height to his undersized, middle-aged figure, as did the skullcap which rested securely back on his head. He saw only the young man at first, who rose at his approach.

"Well, Azenor," he called cheerily in French, extending his hand. "How is this? I expected you all the week."

"Yes, monsieur; but I knew well what you wanted with me, and I was finishing the doors for Gros-Léon's new house;" saying which, he drew back, and indicated by a motion and look that some one was present who had a prior claim upon Père Antoine's attention.

"Ah, Lalie!" the priest exclaimed, when he had mounted to the porch, and saw her there behind the vines. "Have you been waiting here since you confessed? Surely an hour ago!"

"Yes, monsieur."

"You should rather have made some visits in the village, child."

"I am not acquainted with any one in the village," she returned.

The priest, as he spoke, had drawn a chair, and seated himself beside her, with his hands comfortably clasping his knees. He wanted to know how things were out on the bayou.

"And how is the grandmother?" he asked. "As cross and crabbed as ever? And with that"—he added reflectively—"good for ten years yet! I said only yesterday to Butrand—you know Butrand, he works on Le Blôt's Bon-Dieu place—'And that Madame Zidore:

how is it with her, Butrand? I believe God has forgotten her here on earth.' 'It is n't that, your reverence,' said Butrand, 'but it's neither God nor the Devil that wants her!' " And Père Antoine laughed with a jovial frankness that took all sting of ill-nature from his very pointed remarks.

Lalie did not reply when he spoke of her grandmother; she only pressed her lips firmly together, and picked nervously at the red bandana.

"I have come to ask, Monsieur Antoine," she began, lower than she needed to speak—for Azenor had withdrawn at once to the far end of the porch—"to ask if you will give me a little scrap of paper—a piece of writing for Monsieur Chartrand at the store over there. I want new shoes and stockings for Easter, and I have brought eggs to trade for them. He says he is willing, yes, if he was sure I would bring more every week till the shoes are paid for."

With good-natured indifference, Père Antoine wrote the order that the girl desired. He was too familiar with distress to feel keenly for a girl who was able to buy Easter shoes and pay for them with eggs.

She went immediately away then, after shaking hands with the priest, and sending a quick glance of her pathetic eyes towards Azenor, who had turned when he heard her rise, and nodded when he caught the look. Through the vines he watched her cross the village street.

"How is it that you do not know Lalie, Azenor? You surely must have seen her pass your house often. It lies on her way to the Bon-Dieu."

"No, I don't know her; I have never seen her," the young man replied, as he seated himself—after the priest—and kept his eyes absently fixed on the store across the road, where he had seen her enter.

"She is the granddaughter of that Madame Izidore"—

"What! Ma'ame Zidore whom they drove off the island last winter?"

"Yes, yes. Well, you know, they say the old woman stole wood and things,—I don't know how true it is,—and destroyed people's property out of pure malice."

"And she lives now on the Bon-Dieu?"

"Yes, on Le Blôt's place, in a perfect wreck of a cabin. You see, she gets it for nothing; not a negro on the place but has refused to live in it."

"Surely, it can't be that old abandoned hovel near the swamp, that Michon occupied ages ago?"

"That is the one, the very one."

"And the girl lives there with that old wretch?" the young man marveled.

"Old wretch to be sure, Azenor. But what can you expect from a woman who never crosses the threshold of God's house—who even tried to hinder the child doing so as well? But I went to her. I said: 'See here, Madame Zidore,'—you know it 's my way to handle such people without gloves,—'you may damn your soul if you choose,' I told her, 'that is a privilege which we all have; but none of us has a right to imperil the salvation of another. I want to see Lalie at mass hereafter on Sundays, or you will hear from me;' and I shook my stick under her nose. Since then the child has never missed a Sunday. But she is half starved, you can see that. You saw how shabby she is—how broken her shoes are? She is at Chartrand's now, trading for new ones with those eggs she brought, poor thing! There is no doubt of her being ill-treated. Butrand says he thinks Madame Zidore even beats the child. I don't know how true it is, for no power can make her utter a word against her grandmother."

Azenor, whose face was a kind and sensitive one, had paled with distress as the priest spoke; and now at these final words he quivered as though he felt the sting of a cruel blow upon his own flesh.

But no more was said of Lalie, for Père Antoine drew the young man's attention to the carpenter-work which he wished to intrust to him. When they had talked the matter over in all its lengthy details, Azenor mounted his horse and rode away.

A moment's gallop carried him outside the village. Then came a half-mile strip along the river to cover. Then the lane to enter, in which stood his dwelling midway, upon a low, pleasant knoll.

As Azenor turned into the lane, he saw the figure of Lalie far ahead of him. Somehow he had expected to find her there, and he watched her again as he had done through Père Antoine's vines. When she passed his house, he wondered if she would turn to look at it. But she did not. How could she know it was his? Upon reaching it himself, he did not enter the yard, but stood there motionless, his eyes always fastened upon the girl's figure. He could not see, away off there, how coarse her garments were. She seemed, through the distance that divided them, as slim and delicate as a flower-stalk. He stayed till she reached the turn of the lane and disappeared into the woods.

Mass had not yet begun when Azenor tiptoed into church on Easter morning. He did not take his place with the congregation, but stood close to the holy-water font, and watched the people who entered.

Almost every girl who passed him wore a white mull, a dotted swiss, or a fresh-starched muslin at least. They were bright with ribbons that hung from their persons, and flowers that bedecked their hats. Some carried fans and cambric handkerchiefs. Most of them wore gloves, and were odorant of *poudre de riz*[3] and nice toilet-waters; while all carried gay little baskets filled with Easter-eggs.

But there was one who came empty-handed, save for the worn prayer-book which she bore. It was Lalie, the veil upon her head, and wearing the blue print and cotton bodice which she had worn the day before.

He dipped his hand into the holy water when she came, and held it out to her, though he had not thought of doing this for the others. She touched his fingers with the tips of her own, making a slight inclination as she did so; and after a deep genuflection before the Blessed Sacrament, passed on to the side. He was not sure if she had known him. He knew she had not looked into his eyes, for he would have felt it.

He was angered against other young women who passed him, because of their flowers and ribbons, when she wore none. He himself did not care, but he feared she might, and watched her narrowly to see if she did.

But it was plain that Lalie did not care. Her face, as she seated herself, settled into the same restful lines it had worn yesterday, when she sat in Père Antoine's big chair. It seemed good to her to be there. Sometimes she looked up at the little colored panes through which the Easter sun was streaming; then at the flaming candles, like stars; or at the embowered figures of Joseph and Mary, flanking the central tabernacle which shrouded the risen Christ. Yet she liked just as well to watch the young girls in their spring fresh-ness, or to sensuously inhale the mingled odor of flowers and in-cense that filled the temple.

Lalie was among the last to quit the church. When she walked down the clean pathway that led from it to the road, she looked with pleased curiosity towards the groups of men and maidens who were gayly matching their Easter-eggs under the shade of the China-berry trees.

Azenor was among them, and when he saw her coming solitary down the path, he approached her and, with a smile, extended his hat, whose crown was quite lined with the pretty colored eggs.

"You mus' of forgot to bring aiggs," he said. "Take some o' mine."

"Non, merci," she replied, flushing and drawing back.

But he urged them anew upon her. Much pleased, then, she bent her pretty head over the hat, and was evidently puzzled to make a selection among so many that were beautiful.

He picked out one for her,—a pink one, dotted with white clover-leaves.

"Yere," he said, handing it to her, "I think this is the pretties'; an' it look' strong too. I'm sho' it will break all of the res'." And he playfully held out another, half-hidden in his fist, for her to try its strength upon. But she refused to. She would not risk the ruin of her pretty egg. Then she walked away, without once having noticed that the girls, whom Azenor had left, were looking curiously at her.

When he rejoined them, he was hardly prepared for their greet-ing; it startled him.

"How come you talk to that girl? She 's real canaille,[4] her," was what one of them said to him.

"Who say' so? Who say she 's canaille? If it's a man, I 'll smash 'is head!" he exclaimed, livid. They all laughed merrily at this.

"An' if it 's a lady, Azenor? W'at you goin' to do 'bout it?" asked another, quizzingly.

" 'T ain' no lady. No lady would say that 'bout a po' girl, w'at she don't even know."

He turned away, and emptying all his eggs into the hat of a little urchin who stood near, walked out of the churchyard. He did not stop to exchange another word with any one; neither with the men who stood all *endimanchés*[5] before the stores, nor the women who were mounting upon horses and into vehicles, or walking in groups to their homes.

He took a short cut across the cotton-field that extended back of the town, and walking rapidly, soon reached his home. It was a pleasant house of few rooms and many windows, with fresh air blowing through from every side; his workshop was beside it. A broad strip of greensward, studded here and there with trees, sloped down to the road.

Azenor entered the kitchen, where an amiable old black woman was chopping onion and sage at a table.

"Tranquiline,"[6] he said abruptly, "they 's a young girl goin' to pass yere afta a w'ile. She 's got a blue dress an' w'ite josie on, an' a veil on her head. W'en you see her, I want you to go to the road an' make her res' there on the bench, an' ask her if she don't want a cup o' coffee. I saw her go to communion, me; so she did n't eat any breakfas'. Eve'ybody else f'om out o' town, that went to communion, got invited somew'ere another. It 's enough to make a person sick to see such meanness."

"An' you want me ter go down to de gate, jis' so, an' ax 'er pineblank ef she wants some coffee?" asked the bewildered Tranquiline.

"I don't care if you ask her poin' blank o' not; but you do like I say." Tranquiline was leaning over the gate when Lalie came along.

"Howdy," offered the woman.

"Howdy," the girl returned.

"Did you see a yalla calf wid black spots a t'arin' down de lane, missy?"

"Non; not yalla, an' not with black spot'. *Mais* I see one li'le w'ite calf tie by a rope, yonda 'roun' the ben'."

"Dat warn't hit. Dis heah one was yalla. I hope he done flung hisse'f down de bank an' broke his nake. Sarve 'im right! But whar you come f'om, chile? You look plum wo' out. Set down dah on dat bench, an' le' me fotch you a cup o' coffee."

Azenor had already in his eagerness arranged a tray, upon which was a smoking cup of *café au lait*. He had buttered and jellied generous slices of bread, and was searching wildly for something when Tranquiline reentered.

"W'at become o' that half of chicken-pie, Tranquiline, that was yere in the *garde manger*[7] yesterday?"

"W'at chicken-pie? W'at *garde manger?*" blustered the woman.

"Like we got mo' 'en one *garde manger* in the house, Tranquiline!"

"You jis' like ole Ma'ame Azenor use' to be, you is! You 'spec' chicken-pie gwine las' eternal? W'en some'pin done sp'ilt, I flings it 'way. Dat's me—dat 's Tranquiline!"

So Azenor resigned himself,—what else could he do?—and sent the tray, incomplete, as he fancied it, out to Lalie.

He trembled at the thought of what he did; he whose nerves were usually as steady as some piece of steel mechanism.

Would it anger her if she suspected? Would it please her if she knew? Would she say this or that to Tranquiline? And would Tranquiline tell him truly what she said—how she looked?

As it was Sunday, Azenor did not work that afternoon. Instead, he took a book out under the trees, as he often did, and sat reading it, from the first sound of the Vesper bell, that came faintly across the fields, till the Angelus. All that time! He turned many a page, yet in the end did not know what he had read. With his pencil he had traced "Lalie" upon every margin, and was saying it softly to himself.

Another Sunday Azenor saw Lalie at mass—and again. Once he walked with her and showed her the short cut across the cotton-field. She was very glad that day, and told him she was going to work—her grandmother said she might. She was going to hoe, up in the fields with Monsieur Le Blôt's hands. He entreated her not to; and when she asked his reason, he could not tell her, but turned and tore shyly and savagely at the elder-blossoms that grew along the fence.

Then they stopped where she was going to cross the fence from the field into the lane. He wanted to tell her that was his house which they could see not far away; but he did not dare to, since he had fed her there on the morning she was hungry.

"An' you say yo' gran'ma 's goin' to let you work? She keeps you f'om workin', *donc?*" He wanted to question her about her grandmother, and could think of no other way to begin.

"Po' ole grand'mère!" she answered. "I don' b'lieve she know mos' time w'at she 's doin'. Sometime she say' I ain't no betta an' one nigga, an' she fo'ce me to work. Then she say she know I 'm goin' be one canaille like maman, an' she make me set down still, like she would want to kill me if I would move. Her, she on'y want' to be out in the wood', day an' night, day an' night. She ain' got her right head, po' grand'mère. I know she ain't."

Lalie had spoken low and in jerks, as if every word gave her pain. Azenor could feel her distress as plainly as he saw it. He wanted to say something to her—to do something for her. But her mere presence paralyzed him into inactivity—except his pulses, that beat like hammers when he was with her. Such a poor, shabby little thing as she was, too!

"I 'm goin' to wait yere nex' Sunday fo' you, Lalie," he said, when the fence was between them. And he thought he had said something very daring.

But the next Sunday she did not come. She was neither at the appointed place of meeting in the lane, nor was she at mass. Her absence—so unexpected—affected Azenor like a calamity. Late in the afternoon, when he could stand the trouble and bewilderment of it no longer, he went and leaned over Père Antoine's fence. The priest was picking the slugs from his roses on the other side.

"That young girl from the Bon-Dieu," said Azenor—"she was not at mass to-day. I suppose her grandmother has forgotten your warning."

"No," answered the priest. "The child is ill, I hear. Butrand tells me she has been ill for several days from overwork in the fields. I shall go out to-morrow to see about her. I would go to-day, if I could."

"The child is ill," was all Azenor heard or understood of Père Antoine's words. He turned and walked resolutely away, like one who determines suddenly upon action after meaningless hesitation.

He walked towards his home and past it, as if it were a spot that did not concern him. He went on down the lane and into the wood where he had seen Lalie disappear that day.

Here all was shadow, for the sun had dipped too low in the west to send a single ray through the dense foliage of the forest.

Now that he found himself on the way to Lalie's home, he strove to understand why he had not gone there before. He often visited other girls in the village and neighborhood,—why not have gone to her, as well? The answer lay too deep in his heart for him to be more than half-conscious of it. Fear had kept him,—dread to see her desolate life face to face. He did not know how he could bear it.

But now he was going to her at last. She was ill. He would stand upon that dismantled porch that he could just remember. Doubtless Ma'ame Zidore would come out to know his will, and he would tell her that Père Antoine had sent to inquire how Mamzelle Lalie was. No! Why drag in Père Antoine? He would simply stand boldly and say, "Ma'ame Zidore, I learn that Lalie is ill. I have come to know if it is true, and to see her, if I may."

When Azenor reached the cabin where Lalie dwelt, all sign of day had vanished. Dusk had fallen swiftly after the sunset. The moss that hung heavy from great live oak branches was making fantastic silhouettes against the eastern sky that the big, round moon was beginning to light. Off in the swamp beyond the bayou, hundreds of dismal voices were droning a lullaby. Upon the hovel itself, a stillness like death rested.

Oftener than once Azenor tapped upon the door, which was closed as well as it could be, without obtaining a reply. He finally approached one of the small unglazed windows, in which coarse mosquito-netting had been fastened, and looked into the room.

By the moonlight slanting in he could see Lalie stretched upon a bed; but of Ma'ame Zidore there was no sign. "Lalie!" he called softly. "Lalie!"

The girl slightly moved her head upon the pillow. Then he boldly opened the door and entered.

Upon a wretched bed, over which was spread a cover of patched calico, Lalie lay, her frail body only half concealed by the single garment that was upon it. One hand was plunged beneath her pillow; the other, which was free, he touched. It was as hot as flame; so was her head. He knelt sobbing upon the floor beside her, and called her his love and his soul. He begged her to speak a word to him,—to look at him. But she only muttered disjointedly that the cotton was all turning to ashes in the fields, and the blades of the corn were in flames.

If he was choked with love and grief to see her so, he was moved by anger as well; rage against himself, against Père Antoine, against the people upon the plantation and in the village, who had so abandoned a helpless creature to misery and maybe death. Because she had been silent—had not lifted her voice in complaint—they believed she suffered no more than she could bear.

But surely the people could not be utterly without heart. There must be one somewhere with the spirit of Christ. Père Antoine would tell him of such a one, and he would carry Lalie to her,—out of this atmosphere of death. He was in haste to be gone with her. He fancied every moment of delay was a fresh danger threatening her life.

He folded the rude bed-cover over Lalie's naked limbs, and lifted her in his arms. She made no resistance. She seemed only loath to withdraw her hand from beneath the pillow. When she did, he saw that she held lightly but firmly clasped in her encircling fingers the pretty Easter-egg he had given her! He uttered a low cry of exultation as the full significance of this came over him. If she had hung for hours upon his neck telling him that she loved him, he could not have known it more surely than by this sign. Azenor felt as if some mysterious bond had all at once drawn them heart to heart and made them one.

No need now to go from door to door begging admittance for her. She was his. She belonged to him. He knew now where her place was, whose roof must shelter her, and whose arms protect her.

So Azenor, with his loved one in his arms, walked through the forest, surefooted as a panther. Once, as he walked, he could hear in the distance the weird chant which Ma'ame Zidore was crooning—to the moon, maybe—as she gathered her wood.

Once, where the water was trickling cool through rocks, he stopped to lave Lalie's hot cheeks and hands and forehead. He had not once touched his lips to her. But now, when a sudden great fear came upon him because she did not know him, instinctively he pressed his lips upon hers that were parched and burning. He held them there till hers were soft and pliant from the healthy moisture of his own.

Then she knew him. She did not tell him so, but her stiffened fingers relaxed their tense hold upon the Easter bauble. It fell to the ground as she twined her arm around his neck; and he understood.

"Stay close by her, Tranquiline," said Azenor, when he had laid Lalie upon his own couch at home. "I'm goin' for the doctor en' for Père Antoine. Not because she is goin' to die," he added hastily, seeing the awe that crept into the woman's face at mention of the priest. "She is goin' to live! Do you think I would let my wife die, Tranquiline?"

Loka

SHE was a half-breed Indian girl, with hardly a rag to her back. To the ladies of the Band of United Endeavor who questioned her, she said her name was Loka, and she did not know where she belonged, unless it was on Bayou Choctaw.

She had appeared one day at the side door of Frobissaint's "oyster saloon" in Natchitoches, asking for food. Frobissaint, a practical philanthropist, engaged her on the spot as tumbler-washer.

She was not successful at that; she broke too many tumblers. But, as Frobissaint charged her with the broken glasses, he did not mind, until she began to break them over the heads of his customers. Then he seized her by the wrist and dragged her before the Band of United Endeavor, then in session around the corner. This was considerate on Frobissaint's part, for he could have dragged her just as well to the police station.

Loka was not beautiful, as she stood in her red calico rags before the scrutinizing band. Her coarse, black, unkempt hair framed a broad, swarthy face without a redeeming feature, except eyes that were not bad; slow in their movements, but frank eyes enough. She was big-boned and clumsy.

She did not know how old she was. The minister's wife reckoned she might be sixteen. The judge's wife thought that it made no difference. The doctor's wife suggested that the girl have a bath and change before she be handled, even in discussion. The motion was not seconded. Loka's ultimate disposal was an urgent and difficult consideration.

Some one mentioned a reformatory. Every one else objected.

Madame Laballière, the planter's wife, knew a respectable family of 'Cadians living some miles below, who, she thought, would give the girl a home, with benefit to all concerned. The 'Cadian woman was a deserving one, with a large family of small children, who had all her own work to do. The husband cropped in a modest way. Loka would not only be taught to work at the Padues', but would receive a good moral training beside.

That settled it. Every one agreed with the planter's wife that it was a chance in a thousand; and Loka was sent to sit on the steps outside, while the band proceeded to the business next in order.

Loka was afraid of treading upon the little Padues when she first got amongst them,—there were so many of them,—and her feet were like leaden weights, encased in the strong brogans with which the band had equipped her.

Madame Padue, a small, black-eyed, aggressive woman, questioned her in a sharp, direct fashion peculiar to herself.

"How come you don't talk French, you?" Loka shrugged her shoulders.

"I kin talk English good 's anybody; an' lit' bit Choctaw, too," she offered, apologetically.

"*Ma foi,*[1] you kin fo'git yo' Choctaw. Soona the betta for me. Now if you willin', an' ent too lazy an' sassy, we 'll git 'long somehow. *Vrai sauvage ça,*"[2] she muttered under her breath, as she turned to initiate Loka into some of her new duties.

She herself was a worker. A good deal more fussy one than her easy-going husband and children thought necessary or agreeable. Loka's slow ways and heavy motions aggravated her. It was in vain Monsieur Padue expostulated:—

"She 's on'y a chile, rememba, Tontine."

"She 's *vrai sauvage,* that 's w'at. It 's got to be work out of her," was Tontine's only reply to such remonstrance.

The girl was indeed so deliberate about her tasks that she had to be urged constantly to accomplish the amount of labor that Tontine required of her. Moreover, she carried to her work a stolid indifference that was exasperating. Whether at the wash-tub, scrubbing the floors, weeding the garden, or learning her lessons and catechism with the children on Sundays, it was the same.

It was only when intrusted with the care of little Bibine, the baby, that Loka crept somewhat out of her apathy. She grew very fond of him. No wonder; such a baby as he was! So good, so fat, and complaisant! He had such a way of clasping Loka's broad face between his pudgy fists and savagely biting her chin with his hard, toothless gums! Such a way of bouncing in her arms as if he were mounted upon springs! At his antics the girl would laugh a wholesome, ringing laugh that was good to hear.

She was left alone to watch and nurse him one day. An accommodating neighbor who had become the possessor of a fine new spring wagon passed by just after the noon-hour meal, and offered to take the whole family on a jaunt to town. The offer was all the more tempting as Tontine had some long-delayed shopping to do; and the opportunity to equip the children with shoes and summer hats could not be slighted. So away they all went. All but Bibine, who was left swinging in his branle with only Loka for company.

This branle consisted of a strong circular piece of cotton cloth, securely but slackly fastened to a large, stout hoop suspended by three light cords to a hook in a rafter of the gallery. The baby who has not swung in a branle does not know the quintessence of baby luxury. In each of the four rooms of the house was a hook from which to hang this swing.

Often it was taken out under the trees. But to-day it swung in the shade of the open gallery; and Loka sat beside it, giving it now and then a slight impetus that sent it circling in slow, sleep-inspiring undulations.

Bibine kicked and cooed as long as he was able. But Loka was humming a monotonous lullaby; the branle was swaying to and fro, the warm air fanning him deliciously; and Bibine was soon fast asleep.

Seeing this, Loka quietly let down the mosquito net, to protect the child's slumber from the intrusion of the many insects that were swarming in the summer air.

Singularly enough, there was no work for her to do; and Tontine, in her hurried departure, had failed to provide for the emergency. The washing and ironing were over; the floors had been scrubbed, and the rooms righted; the yard swept; the chickens fed; vegetables picked and washed. There was absolutely nothing to do, and Loka gave herself up to the dreams of idleness.

As she sat comfortably back in the roomy rocker, she let her eyes sweep lazily across the country. Away off to the right peeped up, from amid densely clustered trees, the pointed roofs and long pipe of the steam-gin of Laballière's. No other habitation was visible except a few low, flat dwellings far over the river, that could hardly be seen.

The immense plantation took up all the land in sight. The few acres that Baptiste Padue cultivated were his own, that Laballière, out of friendly consideration, had sold to him. Baptiste's fine crop of cotton and corn was "laid by" just now, waiting for rain; and Baptiste had gone with the rest of the family to town. Beyond the river and the field and everywhere about were dense woods.

Loka's gaze, that had been slowly traveling along the edge of the horizon, finally fastened upon the woods, and stayed there. Into her eyes came the absent look of one whose thought is projected into the future or the past, leaving the present blank. She was seeing a vision. It had come with a whiff that the strong south breeze had blown to her from the woods.

She was seeing old Marot, the squaw who drank whiskey and plaited baskets and beat her. There was something, after all, in being beaten, if only to scream out and fight back, as at that time in Natchitoches, when she broke a glass on the head of a man who laughed at her and pulled her hair, and called her "fool names."

Old Marot wanted her to steal and cheat, to beg and lie, when they went out with the baskets to sell. Loka did not want to. She did not like to. That was why she had run away—and because she was beaten. But—but ah! the scent of the sassafras leaves hanging to dry in the shade! The pungent camomile! The sound of the bayou tumbling over that old slimy log! Only to lie there for hours and watch the glistening lizards glide in and out was worth a beating.

She knew the birds must be singing in chorus out there in the woods where the gray moss was hanging, and the trumpetvine trailing from the trees, spangled with blossoms. In spirit she heard the songsters.

She wondered if Choctaw Joe and Sambite played dice every night by the campfire, as they used to do; and if they still fought and slashed each other when wild with drink. How good it felt to walk with moccasined feet over the springy turf, under the trees! What fun to trap the squirrels, to skin the otter; to take those swift flights on the pony that Choctaw Joe had stolen from the Texans!

Loka sat motionless; only her breast heaved tumultuously. Her heart was aching with savage homesickness. She could not feel just then that the sin and pain of that life were anything beside the joy of its freedom.

Loka was sick for the woods. She felt she must die if she could not get back to them, and to her vagabond life. Was there anything to hinder her? She stooped and unlaced the brogans that were chafing her feet, removed them and her stockings, and threw the things away from her. She stood up all a-quiver, panting, ready for flight.

But there was a sound that stopped her. It was little Bibine, cooing, sputtering, battling hands and feet with the mosquito net that he had dragged over his face. The girl uttered a sob as she reached down for the baby she had grown to love so, and clasped him in her arms. She could not go and leave Bibine behind.

Tontine began to grumble at once when she discovered that Loka was not at hand to receive them on their return.

"*Bon!*" she exclaimed. "Now w'ere is that Loka? Ah, that girl, she aggravates me too much. Firs' thing she knows I 'm goin' sen' her straight back to them ban' of lady w'ere she come frum."

"Loka!" she called, in short, sharp tones, as she traversed the house and peered into each room. "Lo—ka!" She cried loudly enough to be heard half a mile away when she got out upon the back gallery. Again and again she called.

Baptiste was exchanging the discomfort of his Sunday coat for the accustomed ease of shirt sleeves.

"*Mais* don't git so excite, Tontine," he implored. "I 'm sho she 's yonda to the crib shellin' co'n, or somew'ere like that."

"Run, François, you, an' see to the crib," the mother commanded. "Bibine mus' be starve! Run to the hen-house an' look, Juliette. Maybe she 's fall asleep in some corna. That 'll learn me 'notha time to go trus' *une pareille sauvage*[3] with my baby, *va!*"

When it was discovered that Loka was nowhere in the immediate vicinity, Tontine was furious.

"*Pas possible*[4] she 's walk to Laballière, with Bibine!" she exclaimed.

"I 'll saddle the hoss an' go see, Tontine," interposed Baptiste, who was beginning to share his wife's uneasiness.

"Go, go, Baptiste," she urged. "An' you, boys, run yonda down the road to ole Aunt Judy's cabin an' see."

It was found that Loka had not been seen at Laballière's, nor at Aunt Judy's cabin; that she had not taken the boat, that was still fastened to its moorings down the bank. Then Tontine's excitement left her. She turned pale and sat quietly down in her room, with an unnatural calm that frightened the children.

Some of them began to cry. Baptiste walked restlessly about, anxiously scanning the country in all directions. A wretched hour dragged by. The sun had set, leaving hardly an afterglow, and in a little while the twilight that falls so swiftly would be there.

Baptiste was preparing to mount his horse, to start out again on the round he had already been over. Tontine sat in the same state of intense abstraction when François, who had perched himself among the lofty branches of a chinaberry-tree, called out: "Ent that Loka 'way yon'a, jis' come out de wood? climbin' de fence down by de melon patch?"

It was difficult to distinguish in the gathering dusk if the figure were that of man or beast. But the family was not left long in suspense. Baptiste sped his horse away in the direction indicated by François, and in a little while he was galloping back with Bibine in his arms; as fretful, sleepy and hungry a baby as ever was.

Loka came trudging on behind Baptiste. He did not wait for explanations; he was too eager to place the child in the arms of its mother. The suspense over, Tontine began to cry; that followed naturally, of course. Through her tears she managed to address Loka, who stood all tattered and disheveled in the doorway; "W'ere you been? Tell me that."

"Bibine an' me," answered Loka, slowly and awkwardly, "we was lonesome—we been take lit' 'broad in de wood."

"You did n' know no betta 'an to take 'way Bibine like that? W'at Ma'ame Laballière mean, anyhow, to sen' me such a objec' like you, I want to know?"

"You go'n' sen' me 'way?" asked Loka, passing her hand in a hopeless fashion over her frowzy hair.

"*Par exemple!* straight you march back to that ban' w'ere you come from. To give me such a fright like that! *pas possible.*"

"Go slow, Tontine; go slow," interposed Baptiste.

"Don' sen' me 'way frum Bibine," entreated the girl, with a note in her voice like a lament.

"To-day," she went on, in her dragging manner, "I want to run 'way bad, an' take to de wood; an' go yonda back to Bayou Choctaw to steal an' lie agin. It 's on'y Bibine w'at hole me back. I could n' lef' 'im. I could n' do dat. An' we jis' go take lit' 'broad in de wood, das all, him an' me. Don' sen' me 'way like dat!"

Baptiste led the girl gently away to the far end of the gallery, and spoke soothingly to her. He told her to be good and brave, and he would right the trouble for her. He left her standing there and went back to his wife.

"Tontine," he began, with unusual energy, "you got to listen to the truth—once fo' all." He had evidently determined to profit by his wife's lachrymose and wilted condition to assert his authority.

"I want to say who 's masta in this house—it 's me," he went on. Tontine did not protest; only clasped the baby a little closer, which encouraged him to proceed.

"You been grind that girl too much. She ent a bad girl—I been watch her close, 'count of the chil'ren; she ent bad. All she want, it 's li'le mo' rope. You can't drive a ox with the same gearin' you drive a mule. You got to learn that, Tontine."

He approached his wife's chair and stood beside her.

"That girl, she done tole us how she was temp' to-day to turn *canaille*—[5] like we all temp' sometime'. W'at was it save her? That li'le chile w'at you hole in yo' arm. An' now you want to take her guarjun angel 'way f'om her? *Non, non, ma femme,*"[6] he said, resting his hand gently upon his wife's head. "We got to rememba she ent like you an' me, po' thing; she 's one Injun, her."

Boulôt and Boulotte

WHEN Boulôt and Boulotte,[1] the little piny-wood twins, had reached the dignified age of twelve, it was decided in family council that the time had come for them to put their little naked feet into shoes. They were two brown-skinned, black-eyed 'Cadian roly-polies, who lived with father and mother and a troop of brothers and sisters halfway up the hill, in a neat log cabin that had a substantial mud chimney at one end. They could well afford shoes now, for they had saved many a picayune through their industry of selling wild grapes, blackberries, and "socoes" to ladies in the village who "put up" such things.

Boulôt and Boulotte were to buy the shoes themselves, and they selected a Saturday afternoon for the important transaction, for that is the great shopping time in Natchitoches Parish. So upon a bright Saturday afternoon Boulôt and Boulotte, hand in hand, with their quarters, their dimes, and their picayunes tied carefully in a Sunday handkerchief, descended the hill, and disappeared from the gaze of the eager group that had assembled to see them go.

Long before it was time for their return, this same small band, with ten year old Seraphine at their head, holding a tiny Seraphin in her arms, had stationed themselves in a row before the cabin at a convenient point from which to make quick and careful observation.

Even before the two could be caught sight of, their chattering voices were heard down by the spring, where they had doubtless stopped to drink. The voices grew more and more audible. Then, through the branches of the young pines, Boulotte's blue sunbonnet appeared, and Boulôt's straw hat. Finally the twins, hand in hand, stepped into the clearing in full view.

Consternation seized the band.

"You bof crazy *donc,* Boulôt an' Boulotte," screamed Seraphine. "You go buy shoes, an' come home barefeet like you was go!"

Boulôt flushed crimson. He silently hung his head, and looked sheepishly down at his bare feet, then at the fine stout brogans that he carried in his hand. He had not thought of it.

Boulotte also carried shoes, but of the glossiest, with the highest of heels and brightest of buttons. But she was not one to be disconcerted or to look sheepish; far from it.

"You 'spec' Boulôt an' me we got money fur was'e—us?" she retorted, with withering condescension. "You think we go buy shoes fur ruin it in de dus'? *Comment!*"

And they all walked into the house crestfallen; all but Boulotte, who was mistress of the situation, and Seraphin, who did not care one way or the other.

For Marse Chouchoute

"An' now, young man, w'at you want to remember is this—an' take it fer yo' motto: 'No monkey-shines with Uncle Sam.' You undastan'? You aware now o' the penalties attached to monkeyshinin' with Uncle Sam. I reckon that 's 'bout all I got to say; so you be on han' promp' to-morrow mornin' at seven o'clock, to take charge o' the United States mail-bag."

This formed the close of a very pompous address delivered by the postmaster of Cloutierville to young Armand Verchette, who had been appointed to carry the mails from the village to the railway station three miles away.

Armand—or Chouchoute,[1] as every one chose to call him, following the habit of the Creoles in giving nicknames—had heard the man a little impatiently.

Not so the negro boy who accompanied him. The child had listened with the deepest respect and awe to every word of the rambling admonition.

"How much you gwine git, Marse Chouchoute?" he asked, as they walked down the village street together, the black boy a little behind. He was very black, and slightly deformed; a small boy, scarcely reaching to the shoulder of his companion, whose castoff garments he wore. But Chouchoute was tall for his sixteen years, and carried himself well.

"W'y, I'm goin' to git thirty dolla' a month, Wash; w'at you say to that? Betta 'an hoein' cotton, ain't it?" He laughed with a triumphant ring in his voice.

But Wash did not laugh; he was too much impressed by the importance of this new function, too much bewildered by the vision of sudden wealth which thirty dollars a month meant to his understanding.

He felt, too, deeply conscious of the great weight of responsibility which this new office brought with it. The imposing salary had confirmed the impression left by the postmaster's words.

"*You* gwine git all dat money? Sakes! W'at you reckon Ma'ame Verchette say? I know she gwine mos' take a fit w'en she heah dat."

But Chouchoute's mother did not "mos' take a fit" when she heard of her son's good fortune. The white and wasted hand which she rested upon the boy's black curls trembled a little, it is true, and tears of emotion came into her tired eyes. This step seemed to her the beginning of better things for her fatherless boy.

They lived quite at the end of this little French village, which was simply two long rows of very old frame houses, facing each other closely across a dusty roadway.

Their home was a cottage, so small and so humble that it just escaped the reproach of being a cabin.

Every one was kind to Madame Verchette. Neighbors ran in of mornings to help her with her work—she could do so little for herself. And often the good priest, Père Antoine, came to sit with her and talk innocent gossip.

To say that Wash was fond of Madame Verchette and her son is to be poor in language to express devotion. He worshiped her as if she were already an angel in Paradise.

Chouchoute was a delightful young fellow; no one could help loving him. His heart was as warm and cheery as his own southern sunbeams. If he was born with an unlucky trick of forgetfulness—or better, thoughtlessness—no one ever felt much like blaming him for it, so much did it seem a part of his happy, careless nature. And why was that faithful watch-dog, Wash, always at Marse Chouchoute's heels, if it were not to be hands and ears and eyes to him, more than half the time?

One beautiful spring night, Chouchoute, on his way to the station, was riding along the road that skirted the river. The clumsy mail-bag that lay before him across the pony was almost empty; for the Cloutierville mail was a meagre and unimportant one at best.

But he did not know this. He was not thinking of the mail, in fact; he was only feeling that life was very agreeable this delicious spring night.

There were cabins at intervals upon the road—most of them darkened, for the hour was late. As he approached one of these, which was more pretentious than the others, he heard the sound of a fiddle, and saw lights through the openings of the house.

It was so far from the road that when he stopped his horse and peered through the darkness he could not recognize the dancers who passed before the open doors and windows. But he knew this was Gros-Léon's ball, which he had heard the boys talking about all the week.

Why should he not go and stand in the doorway an instant and exchange a word with the dancers?

Chouchoute dismounted, fastened his horse to the fence-post, and proceeded towards the house.

The room, crowded with people young and old, was long and low, with rough beams across the ceiling, blackened by smoke and time. Upon the high mantelpiece a single coal-oil lamp burned, and none too brightly.

In a far corner, upon a platform of boards laid across two flour barrels, sat Uncle Ben, playing upon a squeaky fiddle, and shouting the "figures."

"Ah! *v'là*² Chouchoute!" some one called.

"Eh! Chouchoute!"

"Jus' in time, Chouchoute; yere 's Miss Léontine waitin' fer a partna."

"S'lute yo' partnas!" Uncle Ben was thundering forth; and Chouchoute, with one hand gracefully behind him, made a profound bow to Miss Léontine, as he offered her the other.

Now Chouchoute was noted far and wide for his skill as a dancer. The moment he stood upon the floor, a fresh spirit seemed to enter into all present. It was with renewed vigor that Uncle Ben intoned his "Balancy all! Fus' fo' fo'ard an' back!"

The spectators drew close about the couples to watch Chouchoute's wonderful performance; his pointing of toes; his pigeon-wings in which his feet seemed hardly to touch the floor.

"It take Chouchoute to show 'em de step, *va!*" proclaimed Gros-Léon, with a fat satisfaction, to the audience at large.

"Look 'im! look 'im yonda! Ole Ben got to work hard' 'an dat, if he want to keep up wid Chouchoute, I tell you!"

So it was; encouragement and adulation on all sides, till, from the praise that was showered on him, Chouchoute's head was soon as light as his feet.

At the windows appeared the dusky faces of negroes, their bright eyes gleaming as they viewed the scene within and mingled their loud guffaws with the medley of sound that was already deafening.

The time was speeding. The air was heavy in the room, but no one seemed to mind this. Uncle Ben was calling the figures now with a rhythmic sing-song:—

"Right an' lef' all 'roun'! Swing co'nas!"

Chouchoute turned with a smile to Miss Félicie on his left, his hand extended, when what should break upon his ear but the long, harrowing wail of a locomotive!

Before the sound ceased he had vanished from the room. Miss Félicie stood as he left her, with hand uplifted, rooted to the spot with astonishment.

It was the train whistling for his station, and he a mile and more away! He knew he was too late, and that he could not make the distance; but the sound had been a rude reminder that he was not at his post of duty.

However, he would do what he could now. He ran swiftly to the outer road, and to the spot where he had left his pony.

The horse was gone, and with it the United States mail-bag!

For an instant Chouchoute stood half-stunned with terror. Then, in one quick flash, came to his mind a vision of possibilities that sickened him. Disgrace overtaking him in this position of trust; poverty his portion again; and his dear mother forced to share both with him.

He turned desperately to some negroes who had followed him, seeing his wild rush from the house:—

"Who saw my hoss? W'at you all did with my hoss, say?"

"Who you reckon tech yo' hoss, boy?" grumbled Gustave, a sullen-looking mulatto. "You did n' have no call to lef' 'im in de road, fus' place."

" 'Pear to me like I heahed a hoss a-lopin' down de road jis' now; did n' you, Uncle Jake?" ventured a second.

"Neva heahed nuttin'—nuttin' 't all, 'cep' dat big-mouf Ben yonda makin' mo' fuss 'an a t'unda-sto'm."

"Boys!" cried Chouchoute, excitedly, "bring me a hoss, quick, one of you. I 'm boun' to have one! I 'm boun' to! I 'll give two dolla' to the firs' man brings me a hoss."

Near at hand, in the "lot" that adjoined Uncle Jake's cabin, was his little creole pony, nibbling the cool, wet grass that he found, along the edges and in the corners of the fence.

The negro led the pony forth. With no further word, and with one bound, Chouchoute was upon the animal's back. He wanted neither saddle nor bridle, for there were few horses in the neighborhood that had not been trained to be guided by the simple motions of a rider's body.

Once mounted, he threw himself forward with a certain violent impulse, leaning till his cheek touched the animal's mane.

He uttered a sharp "Hei!" and at once, as if possessed by sudden frenzy, the horse dashed forward, leaving the bewildered black men in a cloud of dust.

What a mad ride it was! On one side was the river bank, steep in places and crumbling away; on the other, an unbroken line of fencing; now in straight lines of neat planking, now treacherous barbed wire, sometimes the zigzag rail.

The night was black, with only such faint light as the stars were shedding. No sound was to be heard save the quick thud of the horse's hoofs upon the hard dirt road, the animal's heavy breathing, and the boy's feverish "hei-hei!" when he fancied the speed slackened.

Occasionally a marauding dog started from the obscurity to bark and give useless chase.

"To the road, to the road, Bon-à-rien!"[3] panted Chouchoute, for the horse in his wild race had approached so closely to the river's edge that the bank crumbled beneath his flying feet. It was only by a desperate lunge and bound that he saved himself and rider from plunging into the water below.

Chouchoute hardly knew what he was pursuing so madly. It was rather something that drove him; fear, hope, desperation.

He was rushing to the station, because it seemed to him, naturally, the first thing to do. There was the faint hope that his own horse had broken rein and gone there of his own accord; but such hope was almost lost in a wretched conviction that had seized him the instant he saw "Gustave the thief" among the men gathered at Gros-Léon's.

"Hei! hei, Bon-à-rien!"

The lights of the railway station were gleaming ahead, and Chouchoute's hot ride was almost at an end.

With sudden and strange perversity of purpose, Chouchoute, as he drew closer upon the station, slackened his horse's speed. A low fence was in his way. Not long before, he would have cleared it at a bound, for Bon-à-rien could do such things. Now he cantered easily to the end of it, to go through the gate which was there.

His courage was growing faint, and his heart sinking within him as he drew nearer and nearer.

He dismounted, and holding the pony by the mane, approached with some trepidation the young station-master, who was taking note of some freight that had been deposited near the tracks.

"Mr. Hudson," faltered Chouchoute, "did you see my pony 'roun' yere anywhere? an'—an' the mail-sack?"

"Your pony 's safe in the woods, Chou'te. The mail-bag 's on its way to New Orleans"—

"Thank God!" breathed the boy.

"But that poor little fool darkey of yours has about done it for himself, I guess."

"Wash? Oh, Mr. Hudson! w'at 's—w'at 's happen' to Wash?"

"He 's inside there, on my mattress. He 's hurt, and he 's hurt bad; that 's what 's the matter. You see the ten forty-five had come in, and she did n't make much of a stop; she was just pushing out, when bless me if that little chap of yours did n't come tearing along on Spunky as if Old Harry[4] was behind him.

"You know how No. 22 can pull at the start; and there was that little imp keeping abreast of her 'most under the thing's wheels.

"I shouted at him. I could n't make out what he was up to, when blamed if he did n't pitch the mail-bag clean into the car! Buffalo Bill[5] could n't have done it neater.

"Then Spunky, she shied; and Wash he bounced against the side of that car and back, like a rubber ball, and laid in the ditch till we carried him inside.

"I 've wired down the road for Doctor Campbell to come up on 14 and do what he can for him."

Hudson had related these events to the distracted boy while they made their way toward the house.

Inside, upon a low pallet, lay the little negro, breathing heavily, his black face pinched and ashen with approaching death. He had wanted no one to touch him further than to lay him upon the bed.

The few men and colored women gathered in the room were looking upon him with pity mingled with curiosity.

When he saw Chouchoute he closed his eyes, and a shiver passed through his small frame. Those about him thought he was dead. Chouchoute knelt, choking, at his side and held his hand.

"O Wash, Wash! W'at you did that for? W'at made you, Wash?"

"Marse Chouchoute," the boy whispered, so low that no one could hear him but his friend, "I was gwine 'long de big road, pas' Marse Gros-Léon's, an' I seed Spunky tied dah wid de mail. Dar warn't a minute—I 'clar', Marse Chouchoute, dar warn't a minute—to fotch you. W'at makes my head tu'n 'roun' dat away?"

"Neva mine, Wash; keep still; don't you try to talk," entreated Chouchoute.

"You ain't mad, Marse Chouchoute?"

The lad could only answer with a hand pressure.

"Dar warn't a minute, so I gits top o' Spunky—I neva seed nut-tin' cl'ar de road like dat. I come 'long side—de train—an' fling de sack. I seed 'im kotch it, and I don' know nuttin' mo' 'cep' mis'ry, tell I see you—a-comin' frough de do'. Mebby Ma'ame Verchette know some'pin," he murmured faintly, "w'at gwine make my—head quit tu'nin' 'round dat away. I boun' to git well, 'ca'se who—gwine—watch Marse—Chouchoute?"

A Visit to Avoyelles

EVERY ONE who came up from Avoyelles had the same story to tell of Mentine. *Cher Maître!*[1] but she was changed. And there were babies, more than she could well manage; as good as four already. Jules was not kind except to himself. They seldom went to church, and never anywhere upon a visit. They lived as poorly as pinewoods people. Doudouce had heard the story often, the last time no later than that morning.

"Ho-a!" he shouted to his mule plumb in the middle of the cotton row. He had staggered along behind the plow since early morning, and of a sudden he felt he had had enough of it. He mounted the mule and rode away to the stable, leaving the plow with its polished blade thrust deep in the red Cane River soil. His head felt like a windmill with the recollections and sudden intentions that had crowded it and were whirling through his brain since he had heard the last story about Mentine.

He knew well enough Mentine would have married him seven years ago had not Jules Trodon come up from Avoyelles and captivated her with his handsome eyes and pleasant speech. Doudouce was resigned then, for he held Mentine's happiness above his own. But now she was suffering in a hopeless, common, exasperating way for the small comforts of life. People had told him so. And somehow, to-day, he could not stand the knowledge passively. He felt he must see those things they spoke of with his own eyes. He must strive to help her and her children if it were possible.

Doudouce could not sleep that night. He lay with wakeful eyes watching the moonlight creep across the bare floor of his room; listening to sounds that seemed unfamiliar and weird down among the rushes along the bayou. But towards morning he saw Mentine as he had seen her last in her white wedding gown and veil. She looked at

122

him with appealing eyes and held out her arms for protection,—for rescue, it seemed to him. That dream determined him. The following day Doudouce started for Avoyelles.

Jules Trodon's home lay a mile or two from Marksville. It consisted of three rooms strung in a row and opening upon a narrow gallery. The whole wore an aspect of poverty and dilapidation that summer day, towards noon, when Doudouce approached it. His presence outside the gate aroused the frantic barking of dogs that dashed down the steps as if to attack him. Two little brown barefooted children, a boy and girl, stood upon the gallery staring stupidly at him. "Call off you' dogs," he requested; but they only continued to stare.

"Down, Pluto! down, Achille!" cried the shrill voice of a woman who emerged from the house, holding upon her arm a delicate baby of a year or two. There was only an instant of unrecognition.

"*Mais* Doudouce, that ent you, *comment!* Well, if any one would tole me this mornin'! Git a chair, 'Tit Jules. That 's Mista Doudouce, f'om 'way yonda Natchitoches w'ere yo' maman use' to live. *Mais,* you ent change'; you' lookin' well, Doudouce."

He shook hands in a slow, undemonstrative way, and seated himself clumsily upon the hide-bottomed chair, laying his broad-rimmed felt hat upon the floor beside him. He was very uncomfortable in the cloth Sunday coat which he wore.

"I had business that call' me to Marksville," he began, "an' I say to myse'f, '*Tiens,* you can't pass by without tell' 'em all howdy.' "

"*Par exemple!* w'at Jules would said to that! *Mais,* you' lookin' well; you ent change', Doudouce."

"An' you' lookin' well, Mentine. Jis' the same Mentine." He regretted that he lacked talent to make the lie bolder.

She moved a little uneasily, and felt upon her shoulder for a pin with which to fasten the front of her old gown where it lacked a button. She had kept the baby in her lap. Doudouce was wondering miserably if he would have known her outside her home. He would have known her sweet, cheerful brown eyes, that were not changed; but her figure, that had looked so trim in the wedding gown, was sadly misshapen. She was brown, with skin like parchment, and piteously thin. There were lines, some deep as if old age had cut them, about the eyes and mouth.

"An' how you lef' 'em all, yonda?" she asked, in a high voice that had grown shrill from screaming at children and dogs.

"They all well. It 's mighty li'le sickness in the country this yea'. But they been lookin' fo' you up yonda, straight along, Mentine."

"Don't talk, Doudouce, it 's no chance; with that po' wo' out piece o' lan' w'at Jules got. He say, anotha yea' like that, he 's goin' sell out, him."

The children were clutching her on either side, their persistent gaze always fastened upon Doudouce. He tried without avail to make friends with them. Then Jules came home from the field, riding the mule with which he had worked, and which he fastened outside the gate.

"Yere 's Doudouce f'om Natchitoches, Jules," called out Mentine, "he stop' to tell us howdy, *en passant*."[2] The husband mounted to the gallery and the two men shook hands; Doudouce listlessly, as he had done with Mentine; Jules with some bluster and show of cordiality.

"Well, you' a lucky man, you," he exclaimed with his swagger air, "able to broad like that, *encore!*[3] You could n't do that if you had half a dozen mouth' to feed, *allez!*"[4]

"Non, j'te garantis!"[5] agreed Mentine, with a loud laugh. Doudouce winced, as he had done the instant before at Jules's heartless implication. This husband of Mentine surely had not changed during the seven years, except to grow broader, stronger, handsomer. But Doudouce did not tell him so.

After the mid-day dinner of boiled salt pork, corn bread and molasses, there was nothing for Doudouce but to take his leave when Jules did.

At the gate, the little boy was discovered in dangerous proximity to the mule's heels, and was properly screamed at and rebuked.

"I reckon he likes hosses," Doudouce remarked. "He take' afta you, Mentine. I got a li'le pony yonda home," he said, addressing the child, "w'at ent no use to me. I'm goin' sen' 'im down to you. He 's a good, tough li'le mustang. You jis' can let 'im eat grass an' feed 'im a han'ful o' co'n, once a w'ile. An' he 's gentle, yes. You an' yo' ma can ride 'im to church, Sundays. *Hein!* you want?"

"W'at you say, Jules?" demanded the father. "W'at you say?" echoed Mentine, who was balancing the baby across the gate. " 'Tit sauvage, va!"[6]

Doudouce shook hands all around, even with the baby, and walked off in the opposite direction to Jules, who had mounted the mule. He was bewildered. He stumbled over the rough ground because of tears that were blinding him, and that he had held in check for the past hour.

He had loved Mentine long ago, when she was young and attractive, and he found that he loved her still. He had tried to put all disturbing thought of her away, on that wedding-day, and he supposed he had succeeded. But he loved her now as he never had. Because she was no longer beautiful, he loved her. Because the delicate bloom of her existence had been rudely brushed away; because she was in a manner fallen; because she was Mentine, he loved her; fiercely, as a mother loves an afflicted child. He would have liked to thrust that man aside, and gather up her and her children, and hold them and keep them as long as life lasted.

After a moment or two Doudouce looked back at Mentine, standing at the gate with her baby. But her face was turned away from him. She was gazing after her husband, who went in the direction of the field.

A Wizard from Gettysburg

IT was one afternoon in April, not long ago, only the other day, and the shadows had already begun to lengthen.

Bertrand Delmandé, a fine, bright-looking boy of fourteen years,—fifteen, perhaps,—was mounted, and riding along a pleasant country road, upon a little Creole pony, such as boys in Louisiana usually ride when they have nothing better at hand. He had hunted, and carried his gun before him.

It is unpleasant to state that Bertrand was not so depressed as he should have been, in view of recent events that had come about. Within the past week he had been recalled from the college of Grand Coteau to his home, the Bon-Accueil[1] plantation.

He had found his father and his grand-mother depressed over money matters, awaiting certain legal developments that might result in his permanent withdrawal from school. That very day, directly after the early dinner, the two had driven to town, on this very business, to be absent till the late afternoon. Bertrand, then, had saddled Picayune and gone for a long jaunt, such as his heart delighted in.

He was returning now, and had approached the beginning of the great tangled Cherokee hedge that marked the boundary line of Bon-Accueil, and that twinkled with multiple white roses.

The pony started suddenly and violently at something there in the turn of the road, and just under the hedge. It looked like a bundle of rags at first. But it was a tramp, seated upon a broad, flat stone.

Bertrand had no maudlin consideration for tramps as a species; he had only that morning driven from the place one who was making himself unpleasant at the kitchen window.

But this tramp was old and feeble. His beard was long, and as white as new-ginned cotton, and when Bertrand saw him he was engaged in stanching a wound in his bare heel with a fistful of matted grass.

"What's wrong, old man?" asked the boy, kindly.

The tramp looked up at him with a bewildered glance, but did not answer.

"Well," thought Bertrand, "since it's decided that I'm to be a physician some day, I can't begin to practice too early."

He dismounted, and examined the injured foot. It had an ugly gash. Bertrand acted mostly from impulse. Fortunately his impulses were not bad ones. So, nimbly, and as quickly as he could manage it, he had the old man astride Picayune, whilst he himself was leading the pony down the narrow lane.

The dark green hedge towered like a high and solid wall on one side. On the other was a broad, open field, where here and there appeared the flash and gleam of uplifted, polished hoes, that negroes were plying between the even rows of cotton and tender corn.

"This is the State of Louisiana," uttered the tramp, quaveringly.

"Yes, this is Louisiana," returned Bertrand cheerily.

"Yes, I know it is. I've been in all of them since Gettysburg. Sometimes it was too hot, and sometimes it was too cold; and with that bullet in my head—you don't remember? No, you don't remember Gettysburg."

"Well, no, not vividly," laughed Bertrand.

"Is it a hospital? It is n't a factory, is it?" the man questioned.

"Where we're going? Why, no, it's the Delmandé plantation— Bon-Accueil. Here we are. Wait, I 'll open the gate."

This singular group entered the yard from the rear, and not far from the house. A big black woman, who sat just without a cabin door, picking a pile of rusty-looking moss, called out at sight of them:—

"W'at's dat you's bringin' in dis yard, boy? top dat hoss?"

She received no reply. Bertrand, indeed, took no notice of her inquiry.

"Fu' a boy w'at goes to school like you does—whar's yo' sense?" she went on, with a fine show of indignation; then, muttering to herself, "Ma'ame Bertrand an' Marse St. Ange ain't gwine stan' dat,

I knows dey ain't. Dah! ef he ain't done sot 'im on de gall'ry, plumb down in his pa's rockin'-cheer!"

Which the boy had done; seated the tramp in a pleasant corner of the veranda, while he went in search of bandages for his wound.

The servants showed high disapproval, the housemaid following Bertrand into his grandmother's room, whither he had carried his investigations.

"W'at you tearin' yo' gra'ma's closit to pieces dat away, boy?" she complained in her high soprano.

"I'm looking for bandages."

"Den w'y you don't ax fu' ban'ges, an' lef yo' gra'ma's closit 'lone? You want to listen to me; you gwine git shed o' dat tramp settin' dah naxt to de dinin'-room! W'en de silva be missin', 'tain' you w'at gwine git blame, it's me."

"The silver? Nonsense, 'Cindy; the man's wounded, and can't you see he's out of his head?"

"No mo' outen his head 'an I is. 'T ain' me w'at want to tres' [trust] 'im wid de sto'-room key, ef he is outen his head," she concluded with a disdainful shrug.

But Bertrand's protégé proved so unapproachable in his long-worn rags, that the boy concluded to leave him unmolested till his father's return, and then ask permission to turn the forlorn creature into the bathhouse, and array him afterward in clean, fresh garments.

So there the old tramp sat in the veranda corner, stolidly content, when St. Ange Delmandé and his mother returned from town.

St. Ange was a dark, slender man of middle age, with a sensitive face, and a plentiful sprinkle of gray in his thick black hair; his mother, a portly woman, and an active one for her sixty-five years.

They were evidently in a despondent mood. Perhaps it was for the cheer of her sweet presence that they had brought with them from town a little girl, the child of Madame Delmandé's only daughter, who was married, and lived there.

Madame Delmandé and her son were astonished to find so uninviting an intruder in possession. But a few earnest words from Bertrand reassured them, and partly reconciled them to the man's presence; and it was with wholly indifferent though not unkindly glances that they passed him by when they entered. On any large plantation there are always nooks and corners where, for a night or more, even such a man as this tramp may be tolerated and given shelter.

When Bertrand went to bed that night, he lay long awake thinking of the man, and of what he had heard from his lips in the hushed starlight. The boy had heard of the awfulness of Gettysburg, till it was like something he could feel and quiver at.

On that field of battle this man had received a new and tragic birth. For all his existence that went before was a blank to him. There, in the black desolation of war, he was born again, without friends or kindred; without even a name he could know was his own. Then he had gone forth a wanderer; living more than half the time in hospitals; toiling when he could, starving when he had to.

Strangely enough, he had addressed Bertrand as "St. Ange," not once, but every time he had spoken to him. The boy wondered at this. Was it because he had heard Madame Delmandé address her son by that name, and fancied it?

So this nameless wanderer had drifted far down to the plantation of Bon-Accueil, and at last had found a human hand stretched out to him in kindness.

When the family assembled at breakfast on the following morning, the tramp was already settled in the chair, and in the corner which Bertrand's indulgence had made familiar to him.

If he had turned partly around, he would have faced the flower garden, with its graveled walks and trim parterres, where a tangle of color and perfume were holding high revelry this April morning; but he liked better to gaze into the back yard, where there was always movement: men and women coming and going, bearing implements of work; little negroes in scanty garments, darting here and there, and kicking up the dust in their exuberance.

Madame Delmandé could just catch a glimpse of him through the long window that opened to the floor, and near which he sat.

Mr. Delmandé had spoken to the man pleasantly; but he and his mother were wholly absorbed by their trouble, and talked constantly of that, while Bertrand went back and forth ministering to the old man's wants. The boy knew that the servants would have done the office with ill grace, and he chose to be cup-bearer himself to the unfortunate creature for whose presence he alone was responsible.

Once, when Bertrand went out to him with a second cup of coffee, steaming and fragrant, the old man whispered:—

"What are they saying in there?" pointing over his shoulder to the dining-room.

"Oh, money troubles that will force us to economize for a while," answered the boy. "What father and *mé-mère*[2] feel worst about is that I shall have to leave college now."

"No, no! St. Ange must go to school. The war 's over, the war 's over! St. Ange and Florentine must go to school."

"But if there's no money," the boy insisted, smiling like one who humors the vagaries of a child.

"Money! money!" murmured the tramp. "The war 's over— money! money!"

His sleepy gaze had swept across the yard into the thick of the orchard beyond, and rested there.

Suddenly he pushed aside the light table that had been set before him, and rose, clutching Bertrand's arm.

"St. Ange, you must go to school!" he whispered. "The war 's over," looking furtively around. "Come. Don't let them hear you. Don't let the negroes see us. Get a spade—the little spade that Buck Williams was digging his cistern with."

Still clutching the boy, he dragged him down the steps as he said this, and traversed the yard with long, limping strides, himself leading the way.

From under a shed where such things were to be found, Bertrand selected a spade, since the tramp's whim demanded that he should, and together they entered the orchard.

The grass was thick and tufted here, and wet with the morning dew. In long lines, forming pleasant avenues between, were peach-trees growing, and pear and apple and plum. Close against the fence was the pomegranate hedge, with its waxen blossoms, brick-red. Far down in the centre of the orchard stood a huge pecan-tree, twice the size of any other that was there, seeming to rule like an old-time king.

Here Bertrand and his guide stopped. The tramp had not once hesitated in his movements since grasping the arm of his young companion on the veranda. Now he went and leaned his back against the pecan-tree, where there was a deep knot, and looking steadily before him he took ten paces forward. Turning sharply to the right, he made five additional paces. Then pointing his finger downward, and looking at Bertrand, he commanded:—

"There, dig. I would do it myself, but for my wounded foot. For I've turned many a spade of earth since Gettysburg. Dig, St. Ange, dig! The war's over; you must go to school."

Is there a boy of fifteen under the sun who would not have dug, even knowing he was following the insane dictates of a demented man? Bertrand entered with all the zest of his years and his spirit into the curious adventure; and he dug and dug, throwing great spadefuls of the rich, fragrant earth from side to side.

The tramp, with body bent, and fingers like claws clasping his bony knees, stood watching with eager eyes, that never unfastened their steady gaze from the boy's rhythmic motions.

"That's it!" he muttered at intervals. "Dig, dig! The war's over. You must go to school, St. Ange."

Deep down in the earth, too deep for any ordinary turning of the soil with spade or plow to have reached it, was a box. It was of tin, apparently, something larger than a cigar box, and bound round and round with twine, rotted now and eaten away in places.

The tramp showed no surprise at seeing it there; he simply knelt upon the ground and lifted it from its long resting place.

Bertrand had let the spade fall from his hands, and was quivering with the awe of the thing he saw. Who could this wizard be that had come to him in the guise of a tramp, that walked in cabalistic paces upon his own father's ground, and pointed his finger like a divining-rod to the spot where boxes—may be treasures—lay? It was like a page from a wonder-book.

And walking behind this white-haired old man, who was again leading the way, something of childish superstition crept back into Bertrand's heart. It was the same feeling with which he had often sat, long ago, in the weird firelight of some negro's cabin, listening to tales of witches who came in the night to work uncanny spells at their will.

Madame Delmandé had never abandoned the custom of washing her own silver and dainty china. She sat, when the breakfast was over, with a pail of warm suds before her that 'Cindy had brought to her, with an abundance of soft linen cloths. Her little granddaughter stood beside her playing, as babies will, with the bright spoons and forks, and ranging them in rows on the polished mahogany. St. Ange was at the window making entries in a note-book, and frowning gloomily as he did so.

The group in the dining-room were so employed when the old tramp came staggering in, Bertrand close behind him.

He went and stood at the foot of the table, opposite to where Madame Delmandé sat, and let fall the box upon it.

The thing in falling shattered, and from its bursting sides gold came, clicking, spinning, gliding, some of it like oil; rolling along the table and off it to the floor, but heaped up, the bulk of it, before the tramp.

"Here's money!" he called out, plunging his old hand in the thick of it. "Who says St. Ange shall not go to school? The war's over—here's money! St. Ange, my boy," turning to Bertrand and speaking with quick authority, "tell Buck Williams to hitch Black Bess to the buggy, and go bring Judge Parkerson here."

Judge Parkerson, indeed, who had been dead for twenty years and more!

"Tell him that—that"—and the hand that was not in the gold went up to the withered forehead, "that—Bertrand Delmandé needs him!"

Madame Delmandé, at sight of the man with his box and his gold, had given a sharp cry, such as might follow the plunge of a knife. She lay now in her son's arms, panting hoarsely.

"Your father, St. Ange,—come back from the dead—your father!"

"Be calm, mother!" the man implored. "You had such sure proof of his death in that terrible battle, this *may* not be he."

"I know him! I know your father, my son!" and disengaging herself from the arms that held her, she dragged herself as a wounded serpent might to where the old man stood.

His hand was still in the gold, and on his face was yet the flush which had come there when he shouted out the name Bertrand Delmandé.

"Husband," she gasped, "do you know me—your wife?"

The little girl was playing gleefully with the yellow coin.

Bertrand stood, pulseless almost, like a young Actæon cut in marble.

When the old man had looked long into the woman's imploring face, he made a courtly bow.

"Madame," he said, "an old soldier, wounded on the field of Gettysburg, craves for himself and his two little children your kind hospitality."

Ma'ame Pélagie

I

WHEN the war began, there stood on Côte Joyeuse[1] an imposing mansion of red brick, shaped like the Pantheon. A grove of majestic live-oaks surrounded it.

Thirty years later, only the thick walls were standing, with the dull red brick showing here and there through a matted growth of clinging vines. The huge round pillars were intact; so to some extent was the stone flagging of hall and portico. There had been no home so stately along the whole stretch of Côte Joyeuse. Every one knew that, as they knew it had cost Philippe Valmêt sixty thousand dollars to build, away back in 1840. No one was in danger of forgetting that fact, so long as his daughter Pélagie survived. She was a queenly, white-haired woman of fifty. "Ma'ame Pélagie," they called her, though she was unmarried, as was her sister Pauline, a child in Ma'ame Pélagie's eyes; a child of thirty-five.

The two lived alone in a three-roomed cabin, almost within the shadow of the ruin. They lived for a dream, for Ma'ame Pélagie's dream, which was to rebuild the old home.

It would be pitiful to tell how their days were spent to accomplish this end; how the dollars had been saved for thirty years and the picayunes hoarded; and yet, not half enough gathered! But Ma'ame Pélagie felt sure of twenty years of life before her, and counted upon as many more for her sister. And what could not come to pass in twenty—in forty—years?

Often, of pleasant afternoons, the two would drink their black coffee, seated upon the stone-flagged portico whose canopy was the blue sky of Louisiana. They loved to sit there in the silence, with only each other and the sheeny, prying lizards for company, talking of the old times and planning for the new; while light breezes stirred the tattered vines high up among the columns, where owls nested.

"We can never hope to have all just as it was, Pauline," Ma'ame Pélagie would say; "perhaps the marble pillars of the salon will have to be replaced by wooden ones, and the crystal candelabra left out. Should you be willing, Pauline?"

"Oh, yes Sesoeur,[2] I shall be willing." It was always, "Yes, Sesoeur," or "No, Sesoeur," "Just as you please, Sesoeur," with poor little Mam'selle Pauline. For what did she remember of that old life and that old splendor? Only a faint gleam here and there; the half-consciousness of a young, uneventful existence; and then a great crash. That meant the nearness of war; the revolt of slaves; confusion ending in fire and flame through which she was borne safely in the strong arms of Pélagie, and carried to the log cabin which was still their home. Their brother, Léandre, had known more of it all than Pauline, and not so much as Pélagie. He had left the management of the big plantation with all its memories and traditions to his older sister, and had gone away to dwell in cities. That was many years ago. Now, Léandre's business called him frequently and upon long journeys from home, and his motherless daughter was coming to stay with her aunts at Côte Joyeuse.

They talked about it, sipping their coffee on the ruined portico. Mam'selle Pauline was terribly excited; the flush that throbbed into her pale, nervous face showed it; and she locked her thin fingers in and out incessantly.

"But what shall we do with La Petite,[3] Sesoeur? Where shall we put her? How shall we amuse her? Ah, Seigneur!"[4]

"She will sleep upon a cot in the room next to ours," responded Ma'ame Pélagie, "and live as we do. She knows how we live, and why we live; her father has told her. She knows we have money and could squander it if we chose. Do not fret, Pauline; let us hope La Petite is a true Valmêt."

Then Ma'ame Pélagie rose with stately deliberation and went to saddle her horse, for she had yet to make her last daily round through the fields; and Mam'selle Pauline threaded her way slowly among the tangled grasses toward the cabin.

The coming of La Petite, bringing with her as she did the pungent atmosphere of an outside and dimly known world, was a shock to these two, living their dream-life. The girl was quite as tall as her aunt Pélagie, with dark eyes that reflected joy as a still pool reflects the light of stars; and her rounded cheek was tinged like the pink crèpe myrtle. Mam'selle Pauline kissed her and trembled. Ma'ame Pélagie looked into her eyes with a searching gaze, which seemed to seek a likeness of the past in the living present.

And they made room between them for this young life.

II

La Petite had determined upon trying to fit herself to the strange, narrow existence which she knew awaited her at Côte Joyeuse. It went well enough at first. Sometimes she followed Ma'ame Pélagie into the fields to note how the cotton was opening, ripe and white; or to count the ears of corn upon the hardy stalks. But oftener she was with her aunt Pauline, assisting in household offices, chattering of her brief past, or walking with the older woman arm-in-arm under the trailing moss of the giant oaks.

Mam'selle Pauline's steps grew very buoyant that summer, and her eyes were sometimes as bright as a bird's, unless La Petite were away from her side, when they would lose all other light but one of uneasy expectancy. The girl seemed to love her well in return, and called her endearingly Tan'tante.[5] But as the time went by, La Petite became very quiet,—not listless, but thoughtful, and slow in her movements. Then her cheeks began to pale, till they were tinged like the creamy plumes of the white crèpe myrtle that grew in the ruin.

One day when she sat within its shadow, between her aunts, holding a hand of each, she said: "Tante Pélagie, I must tell you something, you and Tan'tante." She spoke low, but clearly and firmly. "I love you both,—please remember that I love you both. But I must go away from you. I can't live any longer here at Côte Joyeuse."

A spasm passed through Mam'selle Pauline's delicate frame. La Petite could feel the twitch of it in the wiry fingers that were intertwined with her own. Ma'ame Pélagie remained unchanged and

motionless. No human eye could penetrate so deep as to see the satisfaction which her soul felt. She said: "What do you mean, Petite?
Your father has sent you to us, and I am sure it is his wish that you
remain."

"My father loves me, tante Pélagie, and such will not be his wish
when he knows. Oh!" she continued with a restless movement, "it
is as though a weight were pressing me backward here. I must live
another life; the life I lived before. I want to know things that are
happening from day to day over the world, and hear them talked
about. I want my music, my books, my companions. If I had
known no other life but this one of privation, I suppose it would be
different. If I had to live this life, I should make the best of it. But I
do not have to; and you know, tante Pélagie, you do not need to. It
seems to me," she added in a whisper, "that it is a sin against myself.
Ah, Tan'tante!—what is the matter with Tan'tante?"

It was nothing; only a slight feeling of faintness, that would soon
pass. She entreated them to take no notice; but they brought her
some water and fanned her with a palmetto leaf.

But that night, in the stillness of the room, Mam'selle Pauline
sobbed and would not be comforted. Ma'ame Pélagie took her in
her arms.

"Pauline, my little sister Pauline," she entreated, "I never have
seen you like this before. Do you no longer love me? Have we not
been happy together, you and I?"

"Oh, yes, Sesoeur."

"Is it because La Petite is going away?"

"Yes, Sesoeur."

"Then she is dearer to you than I!" spoke Ma'ame Pélagie with
sharp resentment. "Than I, who held you and warmed you in my
arms the day you were born; than I, your mother, father, sister,
everything that could cherish you. Pauline, don't tell me that."

Mam'selle Pauline tried to talk through her sobs.

"I can't explain it to you, Sesoeur. I don't understand it myself. I
love you as I have always loved you; next to God. But if La Petite
goes away I shall die. I can't understand,—help me, Sesoeur. She
seems—she seems like a saviour; like one who had come and taken
me by the hand and was leading me somewhere—somewhere I
want to go."

Ma'ame Pélagie had been sitting beside the bed in her peignoir and slippers. She held the hand of her sister who lay there, and smoothed down the woman's soft brown hair. She said not a word, and the silence was broken only by Mam'selle Pauline's continued sobs. Once Ma'ame Pélagie arose to mix a drink of orange-flower water, which she gave to her sister, as she would have offered it to a nervous, fretful child. Almost an hour passed before Ma'ame Pélagie spoke again. Then she said:—

"Pauline, you must cease that sobbing, now, and sleep. You will make yourself ill. La Petite will not go away. Do you hear me? Do you understand? She will stay, I promise you."

Mam'selle Pauline could not clearly comprehend, but she had great faith in the word of her sister, and soothed by the promise and the touch of Ma'ame Pélagie's strong, gentle hand, she fell asleep.

III

Ma'ame Pélagie, when she saw that her sister slept, arose noiselessly and stepped outside upon the low-roofed narrow gallery. She did not linger there, but with a step that was hurried and agitated, she crossed the distance that divided her cabin from the ruin.

The night was not a dark one, for the sky was clear and the moon resplendent. But light or dark would have made no difference to Ma'ame Pélagie. It was not the first time she had stolen away to the ruin at night-time, when the whole plantation slept; but she never before had been there with a heart so nearly broken. She was going there for the last time to dream her dreams; to see the visions that hitherto had crowded her days and nights, and to bid them farewell.

There was the first of them, awaiting her upon the very portal; a robust old whitehaired man, chiding her for returning home so late. There are guests to be entertained. Does she not know it? Guests from the city and from the near plantations. Yes, she knows it is late. She had been abroad with Félix, and they did not notice how the time was speeding. Félix is there; he will explain it all. He is there beside her, but she does not want to hear what he will tell her father.

Ma'ame Pélagie had sunk upon the bench where she and her sister so often came to sit. Turning, she gazed in through the gaping chasm of the window at her side. The interior of the ruin is ablaze.

Not with the moonlight, for that is faint beside the other one—the sparkle from the crystal candelabra, which negroes, moving noiselessly and respectfully about, are lighting, one after the other. How the gleam of them reflects and glances from the polished marble pillars!

The room holds a number of guests. There is old Monsieur Lucien Santien, leaning against one of the pillars, and laughing at something which Monsieur Lafirme is telling him, till his fat shoulders shake. His son Jules is with him—Jules, who wants to marry her. She laughs. She wonders if Félix has told her father yet. There is young Jérôme Lafirme playing at checkers upon the sofa with Léandre. Little Pauline stands annoying them and disturbing the game. Léandre reproves her. She begins to cry, and old black Clémentine, her nurse, who is not far off, limps across the room to pick her up and carry her away. How sensitive the little one is! But she trots about and takes care of herself better than she did a year or two ago, when she fell upon the stone hall floor and raised a great "bo-bo" on her forehead. Pélagie was hurt and angry enough about it; and she ordered rugs and buffalo robes to be brought and laid thick upon the tiles, till the little one's steps were surer.

"Il ne faut pas faire mal à Pauline."[6] She was saying it aloud—"faire mal à Pauline."

But she gazes beyond the salon, back into the big dining hall, where the white crèpe myrtle grows. Ha! how low that bat has circled. It has struck Ma'ame Pélagie full on the breast. She does not know it. She is beyond there in the dining hall, where her father sits with a group of friends over their wine. As usual they are talking politics. How tiresome! She has heard them say "la guerre"[7] oftener than once. La guerre. Bah! She and Félix have something pleasanter to talk about, out under the oaks, or back in the shadow of the oleanders.

But they were right! The sound of a cannon, shot at Sumter,[8] has rolled across the Southern States, and its echo is heard along the whole stretch of Côte Joyeuse.

Yet Pélagie does not believe it. Not till La Ricaneuse[9] stands before her with bare, black arms akimbo, uttering a volley of vile abuse and of brazen impudence. Pélagie wants to kill her. But yet she will not believe. Not till Félix comes to her in the chamber above the dining hall—there where that trumpet vine hangs—comes to say good-by to her. The hurt which the big brass buttons of his new gray uniform pressed into the tender flesh of her bosom has never left it. She sits upon the sofa, and he beside her, both speechless with pain. That room would not have been altered. Even the sofa would have been there in the same spot, and Ma'ame Pélagie had meant all along, for thirty years, all along, to lie there upon it some day when the time came to die.

But there is no time to weep, with the enemy at the door. The door has been no barrier. They are clattering through the halls now, drinking the wines, shattering the crystal and glass, slashing the portraits.

One of them stands before her and tells her to leave the house. She slaps his face. How the stigma stands out red as blood upon his blanched cheek!

Now there is a roar of fire and the flames are bearing down upon her motionless figure. She wants to show them how a daughter of Louisiana can perish before her conquerors. But little Pauline clings to her knees in an agony of terror. Little Pauline must be saved.

"Il ne faut pas faire mal à Pauline." Again she is saying it aloud— "faire mal à Pauline."

The night was nearly spent; Ma'ame Pélagie had glided from the bench upon which she had rested, and for hours lay prone upon the stone flagging, motionless. When she dragged herself to her feet it was to walk like one in a dream. About the great, solemn pillars, one after the other, she reached her arms, and pressed her cheek and her lips upon the senseless brick.

"Adieu, adieu!"[10] whispered Ma'ame Pélagie.

There was no longer the moon to guide her steps across the familiar pathway to the cabin. The brightest light in the sky was Venus, that swung low in the east. The bats had ceased to beat their wings about the ruin. Even the mocking-bird that had warbled for hours in the old mulberry-tree had sung himself asleep. That darkest hour before the day was mantling the earth. Ma'ame Pélagie hurried through the wet, clinging grass, beating aside the heavy moss that swept across her face, walking on toward the cabin—toward Pauline. Not once did she look back upon the ruin that brooded like a huge monster—a black spot in the darkness that enveloped it.

IV

Little more than a year later the transformation which the old Valmêt place had undergone was the talk and wonder of Côte Joyeuse. One would have looked in vain for the ruin; it was no longer there; neither was the log cabin. But out in the open, where the sun shone upon it, and the breezes blew about it, was a shapely structure fashioned from woods that the forests of the State had furnished. It rested upon a solid foundation of brick.

Upon a corner of the pleasant gallery sat Léandre smoking his afternoon cigar, and chatting with neighbors who had called. This was to be his *pied à terre* now; the home where his sisters and his daughter dwelt. The laughter of young people was heard out under the trees, and within the house where La Petite was playing upon the piano. With the enthusiasm of a young artist she drew from the keys strains that seemed marvelously beautiful to Mam'selle Pauline, who stood enraptured near her. Mam'selle Pauline had been touched by the re-creation of Valmêt. Her cheek was as full and almost as flushed as La Petite's. The years were falling away from her.

Ma'ame Pélagie had been conversing with her brother and his friends. Then she turned and walked away; stopping to listen awhile to the music which La Petite was making. But it was only for a moment. She went on around the curve of the veranda, where she found herself alone. She stayed there, erect, holding to the banister rail and looking out calmly in the distance across the fields.

She was dressed in black, with the white kerchief she always wore folded across her bosom. Her thick, glossy hair rose like a silver diadem from her brow. In her deep, dark eyes smouldered the light of fires that would never flame. She had grown very old. Years instead of months seemed to have passed over her since the night she bade farewell to her visions.

Poor Ma'ame Pélagie! How could it be different! While the outward pressure of a young and joyous existence had forced her footsteps into the light, her soul had stayed in the shadow of the ruin.

At the 'Cadian Ball

BOBINÔT, that big, brown, good-natured Bobinôt, had no intention of going to the ball, even though he knew Calixta would be there. For what came of those balls but heartache, and a sickening disinclination for work the whole week through, till Saturday night came again and his tortures began afresh? Why could he not love Ozéina, who would marry him to-morrow; or Fronie, or any one of a dozen others, rather than that little Spanish vixen? Calixta's slender foot had never touched Cuban soil; but her mother's had, and the Spanish was in her blood all the same. For that reason the prairie people forgave her much that they would not have overlooked in their own daughters or sisters.

Her eyes,—Bobinôt thought of her eyes, and weakened,—the bluest, the drowsiest, most tantalizing that ever looked into a man's; he thought of her flaxen hair that kinked worse than a mulatto's close to her head; that broad, smiling mouth and tiptilted nose, that full figure; that voice like a rich contralto song, with cadences in it that must have been taught by Satan, for there was no one else to teach her tricks on that 'Cadian prairie. Bobinôt thought of them all as he plowed his rows of cane.

There had even been a breath of scandal whispered about her a year ago, when she went to Assumption,—but why talk of it? No one did now. "C'est Espagnol, ça,"[1] most of them said with lenient shoulder-shrugs. "Bon chien tient de race,"[2] the old men mumbled over their pipes, stirred by recollections. Nothing was made of it, except that Fronie threw it up to Calixta when the two quarreled and fought on the church steps after mass one Sunday, about a lover. Calixta swore roundly in fine 'Cadian French and with true Spanish spirit, and slapped Fronie's face. Fronie had slapped her back; "Tiens, cocotte, va!" "Espèce de lionèse; prends ça, et ça!"[3] till the curé himself was obliged to hasten and make peace between them. Bobinôt thought of it all, and would not go to the ball.

But in the afternoon, over at Friedheimer's store, where he was buying a trace-chain, he heard some one say that Alcée Laballière would be there. Then wild horses could not have kept him away. He knew how it would be—or rather he did not know how it would be—if the handsome young planter came over to the ball as he sometimes did. If Alcée happened to be in a serious mood, he might only go to the card-room and play a round or two; or he might stand out on the galleries talking crops and politics with the old people. But there was no telling. A drink or two could put the devil in his head,—that was what Bobinôt said to himself, as he wiped the sweat from his brow with his red bandanna; a gleam from Calixta's eyes, a flash of her ankle, a twirl of her skirts could do the same. Yes, Bobinôt would go to the ball.

That was the year Alcée Laballière put nine hundred acres in rice. It was putting a good deal of money into the ground, but the returns promised to be glorious. Old Madame Laballière, sailing about the spacious galleries in her white *volante*,[4] figured it all out in her head. Clarisse, her goddaughter, helped her a little, and together they built more air-castles than enough. Alcée worked like a mule that time; and if he did not kill himself, it was because his constitution was an iron one. It was an every-day affair for him to come in from the field well-nigh exhausted, and wet to the waist. He did not mind if there were visitors; he left them to his mother and Clarisse. There were often guests: young men and women who came up from the city, which was but a few hours away, to visit his beautiful kinswoman. She was worth going a good deal farther than that to see. Dainty as a lily; hardy as a sunflower; slim, tall, graceful, like one of the reeds that grew in the marsh. Cold and kind and cruel by turn, and everything that was aggravating to Alcée.

He would have liked to sweep the place of those visitors, often. Of the men, above all, with their ways and their manners; their swaying of fans like women, and dandling about hammocks. He could have pitched them over the levee into the river, if it had n't meant murder. That was Alcée. But he must have been crazy the day he came in from the rice-field, and, toil-stained as he was, clasped Clarisse by the arms and panted a volley of hot, blistering love-words into her face. No man had ever spoken love to her like that.

"Monsieur!" she exclaimed, looking him full in the eyes, without a quiver. Alcée's hands dropped and his glance wavered before the chill of her calm, clear eyes.

"*Par exemple!*" she muttered disdainfully, as she turned from him, deftly adjusting the careful toilet that he had so brutally disarranged.

That happened a day or two before the cyclone came that cut into the rice like fine steel. It was an awful thing, coming so swiftly, without a moment's warning in which to light a holy candle or set a piece of blessed palm burning. Old madame wept openly and said her beads, just as her son Didier, the New Orleans one, would have done. If such a thing had happened to Alphonse, the Laballière planting cotton up in Natchitoches, he would have raved and stormed like a second cyclone, and made his surroundings unbearable for a day or two. But Alcée took the misfortune differently. He looked ill and gray after it, and said nothing. His speechlessness was frightful. Clarisse's heart melted with tenderness; but when she offered her soft, purring words of condolence, he accepted them with mute indifference. Then she and her nénaine⁵ wept afresh in each other's arms.

A night or two later, when Clarisse went to her window to kneel there in the moonlight and say her prayers before retiring, she saw that Bruce, Alcée's negro servant, had led his master's saddle-horse noiselessly along the edge of the sward that bordered the gravel-path, and stood holding him near by. Presently, she heard Alcée quit his room, which was beneath her own, and traverse the lower portico. As he emerged from the shadow and crossed the strip of moonlight, she perceived that he carried a pair of well-filled saddle-bags which he at once flung across the animal's back. He then lost no time in mounting, and after a brief exchange of words with Bruce, went cantering away, taking no precaution to avoid the noisy gravel as the negro had done.

Clarisse had never suspected that it might be Alcée's custom to sally forth from the plantation secretly, and at such an hour; for it was nearly midnight. And had it not been for the telltale saddle-bags, she would only have crept to bed, to wonder, to fret and dream unpleasant dreams. But her impatience and anxiety would not be held in check. Hastily unbolting the shutters of her door that opened upon the gallery, she stepped outside and called softly to the old negro.

"Gre't Peter! Miss Clarisse. I was n' sho it was a ghos' o' w'at, stan'in' up dah, plumb in de night, dataway."

He mounted halfway up the long, broad flight of stairs. She was standing at the top.

"Bruce, w'ere has Monsieur Alcée gone?" she asked.

"W'y, he gone 'bout he business, I reckin," replied Bruce, striving to be non-committal at the outset.

"W'ere has Monsieur Alcée gone?" she reiterated, stamping her bare foot. "I won't stan' any nonsense or any lies; mine, Bruce."

"I don' ric'lic ez I eva tole you lie *yit*, Miss Clarisse. Mista Alcée, he all broke up, sho."

"W'ere—has—he gone? Ah, Sainte Vierge! faut de la patience! butor, va!"[6]

"W'en I was in he room, a-breshin' off he clo'es to-day," the darkey began, settling himself against the stair-rail, "he look dat speechless an' down, I say, 'You 'pear to me like some pussun w'at gwine have a spell o' sickness, Mista Alcée.' He say, 'You reckin?' 'I dat he git up, go look hisse'f stiddy in de glass. Den he go to de chimbly an' jerk up de quinine bottle an' po' a gre't hoss-dose on to he han'. An' he swalla dat mess in a wink, an' wash hit down wid a big dram o' w'iskey w'at he keep in he room, aginst he come all soppin' wet outen de fiel'.

"He 'lows, 'No, I ain' gwine be sick, Bruce.' Den he square off. He say, 'I kin mak out to stan' up an' gi' an' take wid any man I knows, lessen hit 's John L. Sulvun.'[7] But w'en God A'mighty an' a 'oman jines fo'ces agin me, dat 's one too many fur me.' I tell 'im, 'Jis so,' whils' I 'se makin' out to bresh a spot off w'at ain' dah, on he coat colla. I tell 'im, 'You wants li'le res', suh.' He say, 'No, I wants li'le fling; dat w'at I wants; an' I gwine git it. Pitch me a fis'-ful o' clo'es in dem 'ar saddle-bags.' Dat w'at he say. Don't you bodda, missy. He jis' gone a-caperin' yonda to de Cajun ball. Uh—uh—de skeeters is fair' a-swarmin' like bees roun' yo' foots!"

The mosquitoes were indeed attacking Clarisse's white feet savagely. She had unconsciously been alternately rubbing one foot over the other during the darkey's recital.

"The 'Cadian ball," she repeated contemptuously. "Humph! *Par exemple!* Nice conduc' for a Laballiére. An' he needs a saddle-bag, fill' with clothes, to go to the 'Cadian ball!"

"Oh, Miss Clarisse; you go on to bed, chile; git yo' soun' sleep. He 'low he come back in couple weeks o' so. I kiarn be repeatin' lot o' truck w'at young mans say, out heah face o' young gal."

Clarisse said no more, but turned and abruptly reëntered the house.

"You done talk too much wid yo' mouf a'ready, you ole fool nigga, you," muttered Bruce to himself as he walked away.

Alcée reached the ball very late, of course—too late for the chicken gumbo which had been served at midnight.

The big, low-ceiled room—they called it a hall—was packed with men and women dancing to the music of three fiddles. There were broad galleries all around it. There was a room at one side where sober-faced men were playing cards. Another, in which babies were sleeping, was called *le parc aux petits.*[8] Any one who is white may go to a 'Cadian ball, but he must pay for his lemonade, his coffee and chicken gumbo. And he must behave himself like a 'Cadian. Grosbœuf was giving this ball. He had been giving them since he was a young man, and he was a middle-aged one, now. In that time he could recall but one disturbance, and that was caused by American railroaders, who were not in touch with their surroundings and had no business there. "Ces maudits gens du raiderode,"[9] Grosbœuf called them.

Alcée Laballière's presence at the ball caused a flutter even among the men, who could not but admire his "nerve" after such misfortune befalling him. To be sure, they knew the Laballières were rich—that there were resources East, and more again in the city. But they felt it took a *brave homme*[10] to stand a blow like that philosophically. One old gentleman, who was in the habit of reading a Paris newspaper and knew things, chuckled gleefully to everybody that Alcée's conduct was altogether *chic, mais chic.*[11] That he had more *panache* than Boulanger.[12] Well, perhaps he had.

But what he did not show outwardly was that he was in a mood

for ugly things to-night. Poor Bobinôt alone felt it vaguely. He discerned a gleam of it in Alcée's handsome eyes, as the young planter
stood in the doorway, looking with rather feverish glance upon the
assembly, while he laughed and talked with a 'Cadian farmer who
was beside him.

Bobinôt himself was dull-looking and clumsy. Most of the men
were. But the young women were very beautiful. The eyes that
glanced into Alcée's as they passed him were big, dark, soft as those
of the young heifers standing out in the cool prairie grass.

But the belle was Calixta. Her white dress was not nearly so
handsome or well made as Fronie's (she and Fronie had quite forgotten the battle on the church steps, and were friends again), nor
were her slippers so stylish as those of Ozéina; and she fanned herself with a handkerchief, since she had broken her red fan at the last
ball, and her aunts and uncles were not willing to give her another.
But all the men agreed she was at her best to-night. Such animation!
and abandon! such flashes of wit!

"Hé, Bobinôt! *Mais* w'at 's the matta? W'at you standin' *planté
là*[13] like ole Ma'ame Tina's cow in the bog, you?"

That was good. That was an excellent thrust at Bobinôt, who had
forgotten the figure of the dance with his mind bent on other
things, and it started a clamor of laughter at his expense. He joined
good-naturedly. It was better to receive even such notice as that
from Calixta than none at all. But Madame Suzonne, sitting in a
corner, whispered to her neighbor that if Ozéina were to conduct
herself in a like manner, she should immediately be taken out to the
mule-cart and driven home. The women did not always approve of
Calixta.

Now and then were short lulls in the dance, when couples
flocked out upon the galleries for a brief respite and fresh air. The
moon had gone down pale in the west, and in the east was yet no
promise of day. After such an interval, when the dancers again assembled to resume the interrupted quadrille, Calixta was not among
them.

She was sitting upon a bench out in the shadow, with Alcée beside her. They were acting like fools. He had attempted to take a little gold ring from her finger; just for the fun of it, for there was
nothing he could have done with the ring but replace it again. But

she clinched her hand tight. He pretended that it was a very difficult matter to open it. Then he kept the hand in his. They seemed to forget about it. He played with her earring, a thin crescent of gold hanging from her small brown ear. He caught a wisp of the kinky hair that had escaped its fastening, and rubbed the ends of it against his shaven cheek.

"You know, last year in Assumption, Calixta?" They belonged to the younger generation, so preferred to speak English.

"Don't come say Assumption to me, M'sieur Alcée. I done yeard Assumption till I 'm plumb sick."

"Yes, I know. The idiots! Because you were in Assumption, and I happened to go to Assumption, they must have it that we went together. But it was nice—*hein*, Calixta?—in Assumption?"

They saw Bobinôt emerge from the hall and stand a moment outside the lighted doorway, peering uneasily and searchingly into the darkness. He did not see them, and went slowly back.

"There is Bobinôt looking for you. You are going to set poor Bobinôt crazy. You 'll marry him some day; *hein*, Calixta?"

"I don't say no, me," she replied, striving to withdraw her hand, which he held more firmly for the attempt.

"But come, Calixta; you know you said you would go back to Assumption, just to spite them."

"No, I neva said that, me. You mus' dreamt that."

"Oh, I thought you did. You know I 'm going down to the city."

"W'en?"

"To-night."

"Betta make has'e, then; it 's mos' day."

"Well, to-morrow 'll do."

"W'at you goin' do, yonda?"

"I don't know. Drown myself in the lake, maybe; unless you go down there to visit your uncle."

Calixta's senses were reeling; and they well-nigh left her when she felt Alcée's lips brush her ear like the touch of a rose.

"Mista Alcée! Is dat Mista Alcée?" the thick voice of a negro was asking; he stood on the ground, holding to the banister-rails near which the couple sat.

"W'at do you want now?" cried Alcée impatiently. "Can't I have a moment of peace?"

"I ben huntin' you high an' low, suh," answered the man. "Dey—dey some one in de road, onda de mulbare-tree, want see you a minute."

"I would n't go out to the road to see the Angel Gabriel. And if you come back here with any more talk, I 'll have to break your neck." The negro turned mumbling away.

Alcée and Calixta laughed softly about it. Her boisterousness was all gone. They talked low, and laughed softly, as lovers do.

"Alcée! Alcée Laballière!"

It was not the negro's voice this time; but one that went through Alcée's body like an electric shock, bringing him to his feet.

Clarisse was standing there in her riding-habit, where the negro had stood. For an instant confusion reigned in Alcée's thoughts, as with one who awakes suddenly from a dream. But he felt that something of serious import had brought his cousin to the ball in the dead of night.

"W'at does this mean, Clarisse?" he asked.

"It means something has happen' at home. You mus' come."

"Happened to maman?" he questioned, in alarm.

"No; nénaine is well, and asleep. It is something else. Not to frighten you. But you mus' come. Come with me, Alcée."

There was no need for the imploring note. He would have followed the voice anywhere.

She had now recognized the girl sitting back on the bench.

"Ah, c'est vous, Calixta? Comment ça va, mon enfant?"[14]

"Tcha va b'en; et vous, mam'zélle?"[15]

Alcée swung himself over the low rail and started to follow Clarisse, without a word, without a glance back at the girl. He had forgotten he was leaving her there. But Clarisse whispered something to him, and he turned back to say "Good-night, Calixta," and offer his hand to press through the railing. She pretended not to see it.

"How come that? You settin' yere by yo'se'f, Calixta?" It was Bobinôt who had found her there alone. The dancers had not yet come out. She looked ghastly in the faint, gray light struggling out of the east.

"Yes, that's me. Go yonda in the *parc aux petits* an' ask Aunt Olisse fu' my hat. She knows w'ere 't is. I want to go home, me."

"How you came?"

"I come afoot, with the Cateaus. But I 'm goin' now. I ent goin' wait fu' 'em. I 'm plumb wo' out, me."

"Kin I go with you, Calixta?"

"I don' care."

They went together across the open prairie and along the edge of the fields, stumbling in the uncertain light. He told her to lift her dress that was getting wet and bedraggled; for she was pulling at the weeds and grasses with her hands.

"I don' care; it 's got to go in the tub, anyway. You been sayin' all along you want to marry me, Bobinôt. Well, if you want, yet, I don' care, me."

The glow of a sudden and overwhelming happiness shone out in the brown, rugged face of the young Acadian. He could not speak, for very joy. It choked him.

"Oh well, if you don' want," snapped Calixta, flippantly, pretending to be piqued at his silence.

"*Bon Dieu!* You know that makes me crazy, w'at you sayin'. You mean that, Calixta? You ent goin' turn roun' agin?"

"I neva tole you that much *yet*, Bobinôt. I mean that. *Tiens,*" and she held out her hand in the business-like manner of a man who clinches a bargain with a hand-clasp. Bobinôt grew bold with happiness and asked Calixta to kiss him. She turned her face, that was almost ugly after the night's dissipation, and looked steadily into his.

"I don' want to kiss you, Bobinôt," she said, turning away again, "not to-day. Some other time. *Bonté divine!*[16] ent you satisfy, *yet!*"

"Oh, I 'm satisfy, Calixta," he said.

Riding through a patch of wood, Clarisse's saddle became ungirted, and she and Alcée dismounted to readjust it.

For the twentieth time he asked her what had happened at home. "But, Clarisse, w'at is it? Is it a misfortune?"

"Ah Dieu sait!"[17] It 's only something that happen' to me."

"To you!"

"I saw you go away las' night, Alcée, with those saddle-bags," she said, haltingly, striving to arrange something about the saddle, "an' I made Bruce tell me. He said you had gone to the ball, an' wouldn' be home for weeks an' weeks. I thought, Alcée—maybe you were going to—to Assumption. I got wild. An' then I knew if you did n't come back, *now*, to-night, I could n't stan' it,—again."

She had her face hidden in her arm that she was resting against the saddle when she said that.

He began to wonder if this meant love. But she had to tell him so, before he believed it. And when she told him, he thought the face of the Universe was changed—just like Bobinôt. Was it last week the cyclone had well-nigh ruined him? The cyclone seemed a huge joke, now. It was he, then, who an hour ago was kissing little Calixta's ear and whispering nonsense into it. Calixta was like a myth, now. The one, only, great reality in the world was Clarisse standing before him, telling him that she loved him.

In the distance they heard the rapid discharge of pistol-shots; but it did not disturb them. They knew it was only the negro musicians who had gone into the yard to fire their pistols into the air, as the custom is, and to announce *"le bal est fini."*[18]

La Belle Zoraïde

THE summer night was hot and still; not a ripple of air swept over the *marais*.[1] Yonder, across Bayou St. John, lights twinkled here and there in the darkness, and in the dark sky above a few stars were blinking. A lugger that had come out of the lake was moving with slow, lazy motion down the bayou. A man in the boat was singing a song.

The notes of the song came faintly to the ears of old Manna-Loulou, herself as black as the night, who had gone out upon the gallery to open the shutters wide.

Something in the refrain reminded the woman of an old, half-forgotten Creole romance, and she began to sing it low to herself while she threw the shutters open:—

> "Lisett' to kité la plaine,
>   Mo perdi bonhair à moué;
>   Ziés à moué semblé fontaine,
>   Dépi mo pa miré toué."[2]

And then this old song, a lover's lament for the loss of his mistress, floating into her memory, brought with it the story she would tell to Madame, who lay in her sumptuous mahogany bed, waiting to be fanned and put to sleep to the sound of one of Manna-Loulou's stories. The old negress had already bathed her mistress's pretty white feet and kissed them lovingly, one, then the other. She had brushed her mistress's beautiful hair, that was as soft and shining as satin, and was the color of Madame's wedding-ring. Now, when she reëntered the room, she moved softly toward the bed, and seating herself there began gently to fan Madame Delisle.

Manna-Loulou was not always ready with her story, for Madame would hear none but those which were true. But to-night the story was all there in Manna-Loulou's head—the story of la belle Zoraïde—and she told it to her mistress in the soft Creole patois, whose music and charm no English words can convey.

"La belle Zoraïde had eyes that were so dusky, so beautiful, that any man who gazed too long into their depths was sure to lose his head, and even his heart sometimes. Her soft, smooth skin was the color of *café-au-lait*. As for her elegant manners, her *svelte* and graceful figure, they were the envy of half the ladies who visited her mistress, Madame Delarivière.

"No wonder Zoraïde was as charming and as dainty as the finest lady of la rue Royale: from a toddling thing she had been brought up at her mistress's side; her fingers had never done rougher work than sewing a fine muslin seam; and she even had her own little black servant to wait upon her. Madame, who was her godmother as well as her mistress, would often say to her:—

" 'Remember, Zoraïde, when you are ready to marry, it must be in a way to do honor to your bringing up. It will be at the Cathedral. Your wedding gown, your *corbeille*,[3] all will be of the best; I shall see to that myself. You know, M'sieur Ambroise is ready whenever you say the word; and his master is willing to do as much for him as I shall do for you. It is a union that will please me in every way.'

"M'sieur Ambroise was then the body servant of Doctor Langlé. La belle Zoraïde detested the little mulatto, with his shining whiskers like a white man's, and his small eyes, that were cruel and false as a snake's. She would cast down her own mischievous eyes, and say:—

" 'Ah, nénaine,[4] I am so happy, so contented here at your side just as I am. I don't want to marry now; next year, perhaps, or the next.' And Madame would smile indulgently and remind Zoraïde that a woman's charms are not everlasting.

"But the truth of the matter was, Zoraïde had seen le beau Mézor[5] dance the Bamboula in Congo Square. That was a sight to hold one rooted to the ground. Mézor was as straight as a cypress-tree and as proud looking as a king. His body, bare to the waist, was like a column of ebony and it glistened like oil.

"Poor Zoraïde's heart grew sick in her bosom with love for le beau Mézor from the moment she saw the fierce gleam of his eye, lighted by the inspiring strains of the Bamboula, and beheld the stately movements of his splendid body swaying and quivering through the figures of the dance.

"But when she knew him later, and he came near her to speak with her, all the fierceness was gone out of his eyes, and she saw only kindness in them and heard only gentleness in his voice; for love had taken possession of him also, and Zoraïde was more distracted than ever. When Mézor was not dancing Bamboula in Congo Square, he was hoeing sugar-cane, barefooted and half naked, in his master's field outside of the city. Doctor Langlé was his master as well as M'sieur Ambroise's.

"One day, when Zoraïde kneeled before her mistress, drawing on Madame's silken stockings, that were of the finest, she said:

" 'Nénaine, you have spoken to me often of marrying. Now, at last, I have chosen a husband, but it is not M'sieur Ambroise; it is le beau Mézor that I want and no other.' And Zoraïde hid her face in her hands when she had said that, for she guessed, rightly enough, that her mistress would be very angry. And, indeed, Madame Delarivière was at first speechless with rage. When she finally spoke it was only to gasp out, exasperated:—

" 'That negro! that negro! Bon Dieu Seigneur,[6] but this is too much!'

" 'Am I white, nénaine?' pleaded Zoraïde.

" 'You white! *Malheureuse!*[7] You deserve to have the lash laid upon you like any other slave; you have proven yourself no better than the worst.'

" 'I am not white,' persisted Zoraïde, respectfully and gently. 'Doctor Langlé gives me his slave to marry, but he would not give me his son. Then, since I am not white, let me have from out of my own race the one whom my heart has chosen.'

"However, you may well believe that Madame would not hear to that. Zoraïde was forbidden to speak to Mézor, and Mézor was cautioned against seeing Zoraïde again. But you know how the negroes are, Ma'zélle Titite," added Manna-Loulou, smiling a little sadly. "There is no mistress, no master, no king nor priest who can hinder them from loving when they will. And these two found ways and means.

"When months had passed by, Zoraïde, who had grown unlike herself,—sober and preoccupied,—said again to her mistress:—

" 'Nénaine, you would not let me have Mézor for my husband; but I have disobeyed you, I have sinned. Kill me if you wish, né-naine: forgive me if you will; but when I heard le beau Mézor say to me, "Zoraïde, mo l'aime toi,"[8] I could have died, but I could not have helped loving him.'

"This time Madame Delarivière was so actually pained, so wounded at hearing Zoraïde's confession, that there was no place left in her heart for anger. She could utter only confused reproaches. But she was a woman of action rather than of words, and she acted promptly. Her first step was to induce Doctor Langlé to sell Mézor. Doctor Langlé, who was a widower, had long wanted to marry Madame Delarivière, and he would willingly have walked on all fours at noon through the Place d'Armes[9] if she wanted him to. Naturally he lost no time in disposing of le beau Mézor, who was sold away into Georgia, or the Carolinas, or one of those distant countries far away, where he would no longer hear his Creole tongue spoken, nor dance Calinda, nor hold la belle Zoraïde in his arms.

"The poor thing was heartbroken when Mézor was sent away from her, but she took comfort and hope in the thought of her baby that she would soon be able to clasp to her breast.

"La belle Zoraïde's sorrows had now begun in earnest. Not only sorrows but sufferings, and with the anguish of maternity came the shadow of death. But there is no agony that a mother will not forget when she holds her first-born to her heart, and presses her lips upon the baby flesh that is her own, yet far more precious than her own.

"So, instinctively, when Zoraïde came out of the awful shadow she gazed questioningly about her and felt with her trembling hands upon either side of her. 'Où li, mo piti a moin? (Where is my little one?)' she asked imploringly. Madame who was there and the nurse who was there both told her in turn, 'To piti à toi, li mouri' ('Your little one is dead'), which was a wicked falsehood that must have caused the angels in heaven to weep. For the baby was living and well and strong. It had at once been removed from its mother's side, to be sent away to Madame's plantation, far up the coast.

Zoraïde could only moan in reply, 'Li mouri, li mouri,' and she turned her face to the wall.

"Madame had hoped, in thus depriving Zoraïde of her child, to have her young waiting-maid again at her side free, happy, and beautiful as of old. But there was a more powerful will than Madame's at work—the will of the good God, who had already designed that Zoraïde should grieve with a sorrow that was never more to be lifted in this world. La belle Zoraïde was no more. In her stead was a sad-eyed woman who mourned night and day for her baby. 'Li mouri, li mouri,' she would sigh over and over again to those about her, and to herself when others grew weary of her complaint.

"Yet, in spite of all, M'sieur Ambroise was still in the notion to marry her. A sad wife or a merry one was all the same to him so long as that wife was Zoraïde. And she seemed to consent, or rather submit, to the approaching marriage as though nothing mattered any longer in this world.

"One day, a black servant entered a little noisily the room in which Zoraïde sat sewing. With a look of strange and vacuous happiness upon her face, Zoraïde arose hastily. 'Hush, hush,' she whispered, lifting a warning finger, 'my little one is asleep; you must not awaken her.'

"Upon the bed was a senseless bundle of rags shaped like an infant in swaddling clothes. Over this dummy the woman had drawn the mosquito bar, and she was sitting contentedly beside it. In short, from that day Zoraïde was demented. Night nor day did she lose sight of the doll that lay in her bed or in her arms.

"And now was Madame stung with sorrow and remorse at seeing this terrible affliction that had befallen her dear Zoraïde. Consulting with Doctor Langlé, they decided to bring back to the mother the real baby of flesh and blood that was now toddling about, and kicking its heels in the dust yonder upon the plantation.

"It was Madame herself who led the pretty, tiny little "griffe"[10] girl to her mother. Zoraïde was sitting upon a stone bench in the courtyard, listening to the soft splashing of the fountain, and watching the fitful shadows of the palm leaves upon the broad, white flagging.

" 'Here,' said Madame, approaching, 'here, my poor dear Zoraïde, is your own little child. Keep her; she is yours. No one will ever take her from you again.'

"Zoraïde looked with sullen suspicion upon her mistress and the child before her. Reaching out a hand she thrust the little one mistrustfully away from her. With the other hand she clasped the rag bundle fiercely to her breast; for she suspected a plot to deprive her of it.

"Nor could she ever be induced to let her own child approach her; and finally the little one was sent back to the plantation, where she was never to know the love of mother or father.

"And now this is the end of Zoraïde's story. She was never known again as la belle Zoraïde, but ever after as Zoraïde la folle,[11] whom no one ever wanted to marry—not even M'sieur Ambroise. She lived to be an old woman, whom some people pitied and others laughed at—always clasping her bundle of rags—her 'piti.'

"Are you asleep, Ma'zélle Titite?"

"No, I am not asleep; I was thinking. Ah, the poor little one, Man Loulou, the poor little one! better had she died!"

But this is the way Madame Delisle and Manna-Loulou really talked to each other:—

"Vou pré droumi, Ma'zélle Titite?"

"Non, pa pré droumi; mo yapré zongler. Ah, la pauv' piti, Man Loulou. La pauv' piti! Mieux li mouri!"

A Gentleman of Bayou Têche

IT was no wonder Mr. Sublet, who was staying at the Hallet plantation, wanted to make a picture of Evariste. The 'Cadian was rather a picturesque subject in his way, and a tempting one to an artist looking for bits of "local color" along the Têche.

Mr. Sublet had seen the man on the back gallery just as he came out of the swamp, trying to sell a wild turkey to the housekeeper. He spoke to him at once, and in the course of conversation engaged him to return to the house the following morning and have his picture drawn. He handed Evariste a couple of silver dollars to show that his intentions were fair, and that he expected the 'Cadian to keep faith with him.

"He tell' me he want' put my picture in one fine '*Mag*'zine,'" said Evariste to his daughter, Martinette, when the two were talking the matter over in the afternoon. "W'at fo' you reckon he want' do dat?" They sat within the low, homely cabin of two rooms, that was not quite so comfortable as Mr. Hallet's negro quarters.

Martinette pursed her red lips that had little sensitive curves to them, and her black eyes took on a reflective expression.

"Mebbe he yeard 'bout that big fish w'at you ketch las' winta in Carancro lake. You know it was all wrote about in the 'Suga Bowl.'" Her father set aside the suggestion with a deprecatory wave of the hand.

"Well, anyway, you got to fix yo'se'f up," declared Martinette, dismissing further speculation; "put on yo' otha pant'loon an' yo' good coat; an' you betta ax Mr. Léonce to cut yo' hair, an' yo' w'sker' a li'le bit."

"It 's w'at I say," chimed in Evariste. "I tell dat gent'man I'm goin' make myse'f fine. He say', 'No, no,' like he ent please'. He want' me like I come out de swamp. So much betta if my pant'loon' an' coat is tore, he say, an' color' like de mud." They could not understand these eccentric wishes on the part of the strange gentleman, and made no effort to do so.

An hour later Martinette, who was quite puffed up over the affair, trotted across to Aunt Dicey's cabin to communicate the news to her. The negress was ironing; her irons stood in a long row before the fire of logs that burned on the hearth. Martinette seated herself in the chimney corner and held her feet up to the blaze; it was damp and a little chilly out of doors. The girl's shoes were considerably worn and her garments were a little too thin and scant for the winter season. Her father had given her the two dollars he had received from the artist, and Martinette was on her way to the store to invest them as judiciously as she knew how.

"You know, Aunt Dicey," she began a little complacently after listening awhile to Aunt Dicey's unqualified abuse of her own son, Wilkins, who was dining-room boy at Mr. Hallet's, "you know that stranger gentleman up to Mr. Hallet's? he want' to make my popa's picture; an' he say' he goin' put it in one fine *Mag*'zine yonda."

Aunt Dicey spat upon her iron to test its heat. Then she began to snicker. She kept on laughing inwardly, making her whole fat body shake, and saying nothing.

"W'at you laughin' 'bout, Aunt Dice?" inquired Martinette mistrustfully.

"I is n' laughin', chile!"

"Yas, you' laughin'."

"Oh, don't pay no 'tention to me. I jis studyin' how simple you an' yo' pa is. You is bof de simplest somebody I eva come 'crost."

"You got to say plumb out w'at you mean, Aunt Dice," insisted the girl doggedly, suspicious and alert now.

"Well, dat w'y I say you is simple," proclaimed the woman, slamming down her iron on an inverted, battered pie pan, "jis like you says, dey gwine put yo' pa's picture yonda in de picture paper. An' you know w'at readin' dey gwine sot down on'neaf dat picture?" Martinette was intensely attentive. "Dey gwine sot down on'neaf: 'Dis heah is one dem low-down 'Cajuns o' Bayeh Têche!'"

The blood flowed from Martinette's face, leaving it deathly pale; in another instant it came beating back in a quick flood, and her eyes smarted with pain as if the tears that filled them had been fiery hot.

"I knows dem kine o' folks," continued Aunt Dicey, resuming her interrupted ironing. "Dat stranger he got a li'le boy w'at ain't none too big to spank. Dat li'le imp he come a hoppin' in heah yistiddy wid a kine o' box on'neaf his arm. He say' 'Good mo'nin', madam. Will you be so kine an' stan' jis like you is dah at yo' i'onin', an' lef me take yo' picture?' I 'lowed I gwine make a picture outen him wid dis heah flati'on, ef he don' cl'ar hisse'f quick. An' he say he baig my pardon fo' his intrudement. All dat kine o' talk to a ole nigga 'oman! Dat plainly sho' he don' know his place."

"W'at you want 'im to say, Aunt Dice?" asked Martinette, with an effort to conceal her distress.

"I wants 'im to come in heah an' say: 'Howdy, Aunt Dicey! will you be so kine and go put on yo' noo calker dress an' yo' bonnit w'at you w'ars to meetin', an' stan' 'side f'om dat i'onin'-boa'd w'ilse I gwine take yo' photygraph.' Dat de way fo' a boy to talk w'at had good raisin'."

Martinette had arisen, and began to take slow leave of the woman. She turned at the cabin door to observe tentatively: "I reckon it 's Wilkins tells you how the folks they talk, yonda up to Mr. Hallet's."

She did not go to the store as she had intended, but walked with a dragging step back to her home. The silver dollars clicked in her pocket as she walked. She felt like flinging them across the field; they seemed to her somehow the price of shame.

The sun had sunk, and twilight was settling like a silver beam upon the bayou and enveloping the fields in a gray mist. Evariste, slim and slouchy, was waiting for his daughter in the cabin door. He had lighted a fire of sticks and branches, and placed the kettle before it to boil. He met the girl with his slow, serious, questioning eyes, astonished to see her empty-handed.

"How come you did n' bring nuttin' f'om de sto', Martinette?"

She entered and flung her gingham sunbonnet upon a chair. "No, I did n' go yonda;" and with sudden exasperation: "You got to go take back that money; you mus' n' git no picture took."

"But, Martinette," her father mildly interposed, "I promise' 'im; an' he 's goin' give me some mo' money w'en he finish."

"If he give you a ba'el o' money, you mus' n' git no picture took. You know w'at he want to put un'neath that picture, fo' ev'body to read?" She could not tell him the whole hideous truth as she had heard it distorted from Aunt Dicey's lips; she would not hurt him that much. "He 's goin' to write: 'This is one *Cajun* o' the Bayou Têche.' " Evariste winced.

"How you know?" he asked.

"I yeard so. I know it 's true."

The water in the kettle was boiling. He went and poured a small quantity upon the coffee which he had set there to drip. Then he said to her: "I reckon you jus' as well go care dat two dolla' back, tomo' mo'nin'; me, I 'll go yonda ketch a mess o' fish in Carancro lake."

Mr. Hallet and a few masculine companions were assembled at a rather late breakfast the following morning. The dining-room was a big, bare one, enlivened by a cheerful fire of logs that blazed in the wide chimney on massive andirons. There were guns, fishing tackle, and other implements of sport lying about. A couple of fine dogs strayed unceremoniously in and out behind Wilkins, the negro boy who waited upon the table. The chair beside Mr. Sublet, usually occupied by his little son, was vacant, as the child had gone for an early morning outing and had not yet returned.

When breakfast was about half over, Mr. Hallet noticed Martinette standing outside upon the gallery. The dining-room door had stood open more than half the time.

"Is n't that Martinette out there, Wilkins?" inquired the jovial-faced young planter.

"Dat 's who, suh," returned Wilkins. "She ben standin' dah sence mos' sun-up; look like she studyin' to take root to de gall'ry."

"What in the name of goodness does she want? Ask her what she wants. Tell her to come in to the fire."

Martinette walked into the room with much hesitancy. Her small, brown face could hardly be seen in the depths of the gingham sun-bonnet. Her blue cottonade skirt scarcely reached the thin ankles that it should have covered.

"Bonjou'," she murmured, with a little comprehensive nod that took in the entire company. Her eyes searched the table for the "stranger gentleman," and she knew him at once, because his hair was parted in the middle and he wore a pointed beard. She went and laid the two silver dollars beside his plate and motioned to retire without a word of explanation.

"Hold on, Martinette!" called out the planter, "what 's all this pantomime business? Speak out, little one."

"My popa don't want any picture took," she offered, a little timorously. On her way to the door she had looked back to say this. In that fleeting glance she detected a smile of intelligence pass from one to the other of the group. She turned quickly, facing them all, and spoke out, excitement making her voice bold and shrill: "My popa ent one low-down 'Cajun. He ent goin' to stan' to have that kine o' writin' put down un'neath his picture!"

She almost ran from the room, half blinded by the emotion that had helped her to make so daring a speech.

Descending the gallery steps she ran full against her father who was ascending, bearing in his arms the little boy, Archie Sublet. The child was most grotesquely attired in garments far too large for his diminutive person—the rough jeans clothing of some negro boy. Evariste himself had evidently been taking a bath without the preliminary ceremony of removing his clothes, that were now half dried upon his person by the wind and sun.

"Yere you' li'le boy," he announced, stumbling into the room. "You ought not lef dat li'le chile go by hisse'f *comme ça*[1] in de pirogue." Mr. Sublet darted from his chair; the others following suit almost as hastily. In an instant, quivering with apprehension, he had his little son in his arms. The child was quite unharmed, only somewhat pale and nervous, as the consequence of a recent very serious ducking.

Evariste related in his uncertain, broken English how he had been fishing for an hour or more in Carancro lake, when he noticed the boy paddling over the deep, black water in a shell-like pirogue. Nearing a clump of cypress-trees that rose from the lake, the pirogue became entangled in the heavy moss that hung from the tree limbs and trailed upon the water. The next thing he knew, the boat had overturned, he heard the child scream, and saw him disappear beneath the still, black surface of the lake.

"W'en I done swim to de sho' wid 'im," continued Evariste, "I hurry yonda to Jake Baptiste's cabin, an' we rub 'im an' warm 'im up, an' dress 'im up dry like you see. He all right now, M'sieur; but you mus'n lef 'im go no mo' by hisse'f in one pirogue."

Martinette had followed into the room behind her father. She was feeling and tapping his wet garments solicitously, and begging him in French to come home. Mr. Hallet at once ordered hot coffee and a warm breakfast for the two; and they sat down at the corner of the table, making no manner of objection in their perfect simplicity. It was with visible reluctance and ill-disguised contempt that Wilkins served them.

When Mr. Sublet had arranged his son comfortably, with tender care, upon the sofa, and had satisfied himself that the child was quite uninjured, he attempted to find words with which to thank Evariste for this service which no treasure of words or gold could pay for. These warm and heart felt expressions seemed to Evariste to exaggerate the importance of his action, and they intimidated him. He attempted shyly to hide his face as well as he could in the depths of his bowl of coffee.

"You will let me make your picture now, I hope, Evariste," begged Mr. Sublet, laying his hand upon the 'Cadian's shoulder. "I want to place it among things I hold most dear, and shall call it 'A hero of Bayou Têche.' " This assurance seemed to distress Evariste greatly.

"No, no," he protested, "it 's nuttin' hero' to take a li'le boy out de water. I jus' as easy do dat like I stoop down an' pick up a li'le chile w'at fall down in de road. I ent goin' to 'low dat, me. I don't git no picture took, *va!*"

Mr. Hallet, who now discerned his friend's eagerness in the matter, came to his aid.

"I tell you, Evariste, let Mr. Sublet draw your picture, and you yourself may call it whatever you want. I 'm sure he 'll let you."

"Most willingly," agreed the artist.

Evariste glanced up at him with shy and child-like pleasure. "It 's a bargain?" he asked.

"A bargain," affirmed Mr. Sublet.

"Popa," whispered Martinette, "you betta come home an' put on yo' otha pant'loon' an' yo' good coat."

"And now, what shall we call the much talked-of picture?" cheerily inquired the planter, standing with his back to the blaze.

Evariste in a business-like manner began carefully to trace on the tablecloth imaginary characters with an imaginary pen; he could not have written the real characters with a real pen—he did not know how.

"You will put on'neat' de picture," he said, deliberately, " 'Dis is one picture of Mista Evariste Anatole Bonamour, a gent'man of de Bayou Têche.' "

A Lady of Bayou St. John

THE days and the nights were very lonely for Madame Delisle. Gustave, her husband, was away yonder in Virginia somewhere, with Beauregard, and she was here in the old house on Bayou St. John, alone with her slaves.

Madame was very beautiful. So beautiful, that she found much diversion in sitting for hours before the mirror, contemplating her own loveliness; admiring the brilliancy of her golden hair, the sweet languor of her blue eyes, the graceful contours of her figure, and the peach-like bloom of her flesh. She was very young. So young that she romped with the dogs, teased the parrot, and could not fall asleep at night unless old black Manna-Loulou sat beside her bed and told her stories.

In short, she was a child, not able to realize the significance of the tragedy whose unfolding kept the civilized world in suspense. It was only the immediate effect of the awful drama that moved her: the gloom that, spreading on all sides, penetrated her own existence and deprived it of joyousness.

Sépincourt found her looking very lonely and disconsolate one day when he stopped to talk with her. She was pale, and her blue eyes were dim with unwept tears. He was a Frenchman who lived near by. He shrugged his shoulders over this strife between brothers, this quarrel which was none of his; and he resented it chiefly upon the ground that it made life uncomfortable; yet he was young enough to have had quicker and hotter blood in his veins.

When he left Madame Delisle that day, her eyes were no longer dim, and a something of the dreariness that weighted her had been lifted away. That mysterious, that treacherous bond called sympathy, had revealed them to each other.

He came to her very often that summer, clad always in cool, white duck, with a flower in his buttonhole. His pleasant brown eyes sought hers with warm, friendly glances that comforted her as a caress might comfort a disconsolate child. She took to watching for his slim figure, a little bent, walking lazily up the avenue between the double line of magnolias.

They would sit sometimes during whole afternoons in the vine-sheltered corner of the gallery, sipping the black coffee that Manna-Loulou brought to them at intervals; and talking, talking incessantly during the first days when they were unconsciously unfolding themselves to each other. Then a time came—it came very quickly—when they seemed to have nothing more to say to one another.

He brought her news of the war; and they talked about it listlessly, between long intervals of silence, of which neither took account. An occasional letter came by round-about ways from Gustave—guarded and saddening in its tone. They would read it and sigh over it together.

Once they stood before his portrait that hung in the drawing-room and that looked out at them with kind, indulgent eyes. Madame wiped the picture with her gossamer handkerchief and impulsively pressed a tender kiss upon the painted canvas. For months past the living image of her husband had been receding further and further into a mist which she could penetrate with no faculty or power that she possessed.

One day at sunset, when she and Sépincourt stood silently side by side, looking across the *marais*,[1] aflame with the western light, he said to her: "*M'amie*,[2] let us go away from this country that is so *triste*.[3] Let us go to Paris, you and me."

She thought that he was jesting, and she laughed nervously. "Yes, Paris would surely be gayer than Bayou St. John," she answered. But he was not jesting. She saw it at once in the glance that penetrated her own; in the quiver of his sensitive lip and the quick beating of a swollen vein in his brown throat.

"Paris, or anywhere—with you—ah, *bon Dieu!*" he whispered, seizing her hands. But she withdrew from him, frightened, and hurried away into the house, leaving him alone.

That night, for the first time, Madame did not want to hear Manna-Loulou's stories, and she blew out the wax candle that till now had burned nightly in her sleeping-room, under its tall, crystal globe. She had suddenly become a woman capable of love or sacrifice. She would not hear Manna-Loulou's stories. She wanted to be alone, to tremble and to weep.

In the morning her eyes were dry, but she would not see Sépincourt when he came. Then he wrote her a letter.

"I have offended you and I would rather die!" it ran. "Do not banish me from your presence that is life to me. Let me lie at your feet, if only for a moment, in which to hear you say that you forgive me."

Men have written just such letters before, but Madame did not know it. To her it was a voice from the unknown, like music, awaking in her a delicious tumult that seized and held possession of her whole being.

When they met, he had but to look into her face to know that he need not lie at her feet craving forgiveness. She was waiting for him beneath the spreading branches of a live-oak that guarded the gate of her home like a sentinel.

For a brief moment he held her hands, which trembled. Then he folded her in his arms and kissed her many times. "You will go with me, *m'amie*? I love you—oh, I love you! Will you not go with me, *m'amie*?"

"Anywhere, anywhere," she told him in a fainting voice that he could scarcely hear.

But she did not go with him. Chance willed it otherwise. That night a courier brought her a message from Beauregard, telling her that Gustave, her husband, was dead.

When the new year was still young, Sépincourt decided that, all things considered, he might, without any appearance of indecent haste, speak again of his love to Madame Delisle. That love was quite as acute as ever; perhaps a little sharper, from the long period of silence and waiting to which he had subjected it. He found her, as he had expected, clad in deepest mourning. She greeted him precisely as she had welcomed the curé, when the kind old priest had brought to her the consolations of religion—clasping his two hands warmly, and calling him *"cher ami."*[4] Her whole attitude and bearing brought to Sépincourt the poignant, the bewildering conviction that he held no place in her thoughts.

They sat in the drawing-room before the portrait of Gustave, which was draped with his scarf. Above the picture hung his sword, and beneath it was an embankment of flowers. Sépincourt felt an almost irresistible impulse to bend his knee before this altar, upon which he saw foreshadowed the immolation of his hopes.

There was a soft air blowing gently over the *marais*. It came to them through the open window, laden with a hundred subtle sounds and scents of the springtime. It seemed to remind Madame of something far, far away, for she gazed dreamily out into the blue firmament. It fretted Sépincourt with impulses to speech and action which he found it impossible to control.

"You must know what has brought me," he began impulsively, drawing his chair nearer to hers. "Through all these months I have never ceased to love you and to long for you. Night and day the sound of your dear voice has been with me; your eyes"—

She held out her hand deprecatingly. He took it and held it. She let it lie unresponsive in his.

"You cannot have forgotten that you loved me not long ago," he went on eagerly, "that you were ready to follow me anywhere,—anywhere; do you remember? I have come now to ask you to fulfill that promise; to ask you to be my wife, my companion, the dear treasure of my life."

She heard his warm and pleading tones as though listening to a strange language, imperfectly understood.

She withdrew her hand from his, and leaned her brow thoughtfully upon it.

"Can you not feel—can you not understand, *mon ami*,"[5] she said calmly, "that now such a thing—such a thought, is impossible to me?"

"Impossible?"

"Yes, impossible. Can you not see that now my heart, my soul, my thought—my very life, must belong to another? It could not be different."

"Would you have me believe that you can wed your young existence to the dead?" he exclaimed with something like horror. Her glance was sunk deep in the embankment of flowers before her.

"My husband has never been so living to me as he is now," she replied with a faint smile of commiseration for Sépincourt's fatuity. "Every object that surrounds me speaks to me of him. I look yonder across the *marais,* and I see him coming toward me, tired and toil-stained from the hunt. I see him again sitting in this chair or in that one. I hear his familiar voice, his footsteps upon the galleries. We walk once more together beneath the magnolias; and at night in dreams I feel that he is there, there, near me. How could it be different! Ah! I have memories, memories to crowd and fill my life, if I live a hundred years!"

Sépincourt was wondering why she did not take the sword from her altar and thrust it through his body here and there. The effect would have been infinitely more agreeable than her words, penetrating his soul like fire. He arose confused, enraged with pain.

"Then, Madame," he stammered, "there is nothing left for me but to take my leave. I bid you adieu."

"Do not be offended, *mon ami,*" she said kindly, holding out her hand. "You are going to Paris, I suppose?"

"What does it matter," he exclaimed desperately, "where I go?"

"Oh, I only wanted to wish you *bon voyage,*"[6] she assured him amiably.

Many days after that Sépincourt spent in the fruitless mental effort of trying to comprehend that psychological enigma, a woman's heart.

Madame still lives on Bayou St. John. She is rather an old lady now, a very pretty old lady, against whose long years of widowhood there has never been a breath of reproach. The memory of Gustave still fills and satisfies her days. She has never failed, once a year, to have a solemn high mass said for the repose of his soul.

A NIGHT IN ACADIE

A NIGHT IN ACADIE

By KATE CHOPIN

AUTHOR OF "BAYOU FOLK"

Published by
Way & Williams
CHICAGO

MDCCCXCVII

A Night in Acadie

THERE was nothing to do on the plantation so Telèsphore, having a few dollars in his pocket, thought he would go down and spend Sunday in the vicinity of Marksville.

There was really nothing more to do in the vicinity of Marksville than in the neighborhood of his own small farm; but Elvina would not be down there, nor Amaranthe, nor any of Ma'me Valtour's daughters to harass him with doubt, to torture him with indecision, to turn his very soul into a weather-cock for love's fair winds to play with.

Telèsphore at twenty-eight had long felt the need of a wife. His home without one was like an empty temple in which there is no altar, no offering. So keenly did he realize the necessity that a dozen times at least during the past year he had been on the point of proposing marriage to almost as many different young women of the neighborhood. Therein lay the difficulty, the trouble which Telèsphore experienced in making up his mind. Elvina's eyes were beautiful and had often tempted him to the verge of a declaration. But her skin was over swarthy for a wife; and her movements were slow and heavy; he doubted she had Indian blood, and we all know what Indian blood is for treachery. Amaranthe presented in her person none of these obstacles to matrimony. If her eyes were not so handsome as Elvina's, her skin was fine, and being slender to a fault, she moved swiftly about her household affairs, or when she walked the country lanes in going to church or to the store. Telèsphore had once reached the point of believing that Amaranthe would make him an excellent wife. He had even started out one day with the intention of declaring himself, when, as the god of chance would have it, Ma'me Valtour espied him passing in the road and enticed him to enter and partake of coffee and "baignés."[1] He would have been a man of stone to have resisted, or to have remained insensible to the charms and accomplishments of the Valtour girls. Finally there was Ganache's widow, seductive rather than handsome, with a good bit of property in her own right. While Telèsphore was considering his chances of happiness or even success with Ganache's widow, she married a younger man.

From these embarrassing conditions, Telèsphore sometimes felt himself forced to escape; to change his environment for a day or two and thereby gain a few new insights by shifting his point of view.

It was Saturday morning that he decided to spend Sunday in the vicinity of Marksville, and the same afternoon found him waiting at the country station for the south-bound train.

He was a robust young fellow with good, strong features and a somewhat determined expression—despite his vacillations in the choice of a wife. He was dressed rather carefully in navy-blue "store clothes" that fitted well because anything would have fitted Telèsphore. He had been freshly shaved and trimmed and carried an umbrella. He wore—a little tilted over one eye—a straw hat in preference to the conventional gray felt; for no other reason than that his uncle Telèsphore would have worn a felt, and a battered one at that. His whole conduct of life had been planned on lines in direct contradistinction to those of his uncle Telèsphore, whom he was thought in early youth to greatly resemble. The elder Telèsphore could not read nor write, therefore the younger had made it the object of his existence to acquire these accomplishments. The uncle pursued the avocations of hunting, fishing and moss-picking; employments which the nephew held in detestation. And as for carrying an umbrella, "Nonc"[2] Telèsphore would have walked the length of the parish in a deluge before he would have so much as thought of one. In short, Telèsphore, by advisedly shaping his course in direct opposition to that of his uncle, managed to lead a rather orderly, industrious, and respectable existence.

It was a little warm for April but the car was not uncomfortably crowded and Telèsphore was fortunate enough to secure the last available window-seat on the shady side. He was not too familiar with railway travel, his expeditions being usually made on horseback or in a buggy, and the short trip promised to interest him.

There was no one present whom he knew well enough to speak to: the district attorney, whom he knew by sight, a French priest from Natchitoches and a few faces that were familiar only because they were native.

But he did not greatly care to speak to anyone. There was a fair stand of cotton and corn in the fields and Telèsphore gathered satisfaction in silent contemplation of the crops, comparing them with his own.

It was toward the close of his journey that a young girl boarded the train. There had been girls getting on and off at intervals and it was perhaps because of the bustle attending her arrival that this one attracted Telèsphore's attention.

She called good-bye to her father from the platform and waved good-bye to him through the dusty, sun-lit window pane after entering, for she was compelled to seat herself on the sunny side. She seemed inwardly excited and preoccupied save for the attention which she lavished upon a large parcel that she carried religiously and laid reverentially down upon the seat before her.

She was neither tall nor short, nor stout nor slender; nor was she beautiful, nor was she plain. She wore a figured lawn, cut a little low in the back, that exposed a round, soft nuque[3] with a few little clinging circlets of soft, brown hair. Her hat was of white straw, cocked up on the side with a bunch of pansies, and she wore gray lisle-thread gloves. The girl seemed very warm and kept mopping her face. She vainly sought her fan, then she fanned herself with her handkerchief, and finally made an attempt to open the window. She might as well have tried to move the banks of Red river.

Telèsphore had been unconsciously watching her the whole time and perceiving her straight he arose and went to her assistance. But the window could not be opened. When he had grown red in the face and wasted an amount of energy that would have driven the plow for a day, he offered her his seat on the shady side. She demurred—there would be no room for the bundle. He suggested that the bundle be left where it was and agreed to assist her in keeping an eye upon it. She accepted Telèsphore's place at the shady window and he seated himself beside her.

He wondered if she would speak to him. He feared she might have mistaken him for a Western drummer, in which event he knew that she would not; for the women of the country caution their daughters against speaking to strangers on the trains. But the girl was not one to mistake an Acadian farmer for a Western traveling man. She was not born in Avoyelles parish for nothing.

"I wouldn' want anything to happen to it," she said.

"It's all right w'ere it is," he assured her, following the direction of her glance, that was fastened upon the bundle.

"The las' time I came over to Foché's ball I got caught in the rain on my way up to my cousin's house, an' my dress! J' vous réponds![4] it was a sight. Li'le mo', I would miss the ball. As it was, the dress looked like I'd wo' it weeks without doin'-up."

"No fear of rain to-day," he reassured her, glancing out at the sky, "but you can have my umbrella if it does rain; you jus' as well take it as not."

"Oh, no! I wrap' the dress roun' in toile-cirée[5] this time. You goin' to Foché's ball? Didn' I meet you once yonda on Bayou Derbanne? Looks like I know yo' face. You mus' come f'om Natchitoches pa'ish."

"My cousins, the Fédeau family, live yonda. Me, I live on my own place in Rapides since '92."

He wondered if she would follow up her inquiry relative to Foché's ball. If she did, he was ready with an answer, for he had decided to go to the ball. But her thoughts evidently wandered from the subject and were occupied with matters that did not concern him, for she turned away and gazed silently out of the window.

It was not a village; it was not even a hamlet at which they descended. The station was set down upon the edge of a cotton field. Near at hand was the post office and store; there was a section house; there were a few cabins at wide intervals, and one in the distance the girl informed him was the home of her cousin, Jules Trodon. There lay a good bit of road before them and she did not hesitate to accept Telèsphore's offer to bear her bundle on the way.

She carried herself boldly and stepped out freely and easily, like a negress. There was an absence of reserve in her manner; yet there was no lack of womanliness. She had the air of a young person accustomed to decide for herself and for those about her.

"You said yo' name was Fédeau?" she asked, looking squarely at Telèsphore. Her eyes were penetrating—not sharply penetrating, but earnest and dark, and a little searching. He noticed that they were handsome eyes; not so large as Elvina's, but finer in their expression. They started to walk down the track before turning into the lane leading to Trodon's house. The sun was sinking and the air was fresh and invigorating by contrast with the stifling atmosphere of the train.

"You said yo' name was Fédeau?" she asked.

"No," he returned. "My name is Telèsphore Baquette."

"An' my name; it's Zaïda Trodon. It looks like you ought to know me; I don' know w'y."

"It looks that way to me, somehow," he replied. They were satisfied to recognize this feeling—almost conviction—of pre-acquaintance, without trying to penetrate its cause.

By the time they reached Trodon's house he knew that she lived over on Bayou de Glaize with her parents and a number of younger brothers and sisters. It was rather dull where they lived and she often came to lend a hand when her cousin's wife got tangled in domestic complications; or, as she was doing now, when Foché's Saturday ball promised to be unusually important and brilliant. There would be people there even from Marksville, she thought; there were often gentlemen from Alexandria. Telèsphore was as unreserved as she, and they appeared like old acquaintances when they reached Trodon's gate.

Trodon's wife was standing on the gallery with a baby in her arms, watching for Zaïda; and four little bare-footed children were sitting in a row on the step, also waiting; but terrified and struck motionless and dumb at sight of a stranger. He opened the gate for the girl but stayed outside himself. Zaïda presented him formally to her cousin's wife, who insisted upon his entering.

"Ah, b'en, pour ça!⁶ you got to come in. It's any sense you goin' to walk yonda to Foché's! Ti Jules, run call yo' pa." As if Ti Jules could have run or walked even, or moved a muscle!

But Telèsphore was firm. He drew forth his silver watch and looked at it in a business-like fashion. He always carried a watch; his uncle Telèsphore always told the time by the sun, or by instinct, like an animal. He was quite determined to walk on to Foché's, a couple of miles away, where he expected to secure supper and a lodging, as well as the pleasing distraction of the ball.

"Well, I reckon I see you all to-night," he uttered in cheerful anticipation as he moved away.

"You'll see Zaïda; yes, an' Jules," called out Trodon's wife good-humoredly. "Me, I got no time to fool with balls, J' vous réponds! with all them chil'ren."

"He's good-lookin'; yes," she exclaimed, when Telèsphore was out of ear-shot. "An' dressed! it's like a prince. I didn' know you knew any Baquettes, you, Zaïda."

"It's strange you don' know 'em yo' se'f, cousine." Well, there had been no question from Ma'me Trodon, so why should there be an answer from Zaïda?

Telèsphore wondered as he walked why he had not accepted the invitation to enter. He was not regretting it; he was simply wondering what could have induced him to decline. For it surely would have been agreeable to sit there on the gallery waiting while Zaïda prepared herself for the dance; to have partaken of supper with the family and afterward accompanied them to Foché's. The whole situation was so novel, and had presented itself so unexpectedly that Telèsphore wished in reality to become acquainted with it, accustomed to it. He wanted to view it from this side and that in comparison with other, familiar situations. The girl had impressed him—affected him in some way; but in some new, unusual way, not as the others always had. He could not recall details of her personality as he could recall such details of Amaranthe or the Valtours, of any of them. When Telèsphore tried to think of her he could not think at all. He seemed to have absorbed her in some way and his brain was not so occupied with her as his senses were. At that moment he was looking forward to the ball; there was no doubt about that. Afterwards, he did not know what he would look forward to; he did not care; afterward made no difference. If he had expected the crash of doom to come after the dance at Foché's, he would only have smiled in his thankfulness that it was not to come before.

There was the same scene every Saturday at Foché's! A scene to have aroused the guardians of the peace in a locality where such commodities abound. And all on account of the mammoth pot of gumbo that bubbled, bubbled, bubbled out in the open air. Foché in shirt-sleeves, fat, red and enraged, swore and reviled, and stormed at old black Douté for her extravagance. He called her every kind of a name of every kind of animal that suggested itself to his lurid imagination. And every fresh invective that he fired at her she hurled it back at him while into the pot went the chickens and the

pans-full of minced ham, and the fists-full of onion and sage and piment rouge and piment vert.[7] If he wanted her to cook for pigs he
had only to say so. She knew how to cook for pigs and she knew
how to cook for people of les Avoyelles.

The gumbo smelled good, and Telèsphore would have liked a
taste of it. Douté was dragging from the fire a stick of wood that
Foché had officiously thrust beneath the simmering pot, and she
muttered as she hurled it smouldering to one side:

"Vaux mieux y s'méle ces affairs, lui; si non!"[8] But she was all
courtesy as she dipped a steaming plate for Telèsphore; though she
assured him it would not be fit for a Christian or a gentleman to
taste till midnight.

Telèsphore having brushed, "spruced" and refreshed himself,
strolled about, taking a view of the surroundings. The house, big,
bulky and weather-beaten, consisted chiefly of galleries in every
stage of decrepitude and dilapidation. There were a few chinaberry
trees and a spreading live oak in the yard. Along the edge of the
fence, a good distance away, was a line of gnarled and distorted
mulberry trees; and it was there, out in the road, that the people
who came to the ball tied their ponies, their wagons and carts.

Dusk was beginning to fall and Telèsphore, looking out across
the prairie, could see them coming from all directions. The little
Creole ponies galloping in a line looked like hobby horses in the
faint distance; the mule-carts were like toy wagons. Zaïda might be
among those people approaching, flying, crawling ahead of the
darkness that was creeping out of the far wood. He hoped so, but
he did not believe so; she would hardly have had time to dress.

Foché was noisily lighting lamps, with the assistance of an inoffensive mulatto boy whom he intended in the morning to butcher,
to cut into sections, to pack and salt down in a barrel, like the Col-
fax woman did to her old husband—a fitting destiny for so stupid a
pig as the mulatto boy. The negro musicians had arrived: two fid-
dlers and an accordion player, and they were drinking whiskey
from a black quart bottle which was passed socially from one to the
other. The musicians were really never at their best till the quart
bottle had been consumed.

The girls who came in wagons and on ponies from a distance
wore, for the most part, calico dresses and sun-bonnets. Their fin-

ery they brought along in pillow-slips or pinned up in sheets and towels. With these they at once retired to an upper room; later to appear be-ribboned and be-furbelowed; their faces masked with starch powder, but never a touch of rouge.

Most of the guests had assembled when Zaïda arrived—"dashed up" would better express her coming—in an open, two-seated buckboard, with her cousin Jules driving. He reined the pony suddenly and viciously before the time-eaten front steps, in order to produce an impression upon those who were gathered around. Most of the men had halted their vehicles outside and permitted their women folk to walk up from the mulberry trees.

But the real, the stunning effect was produced when Zaïda stepped upon the gallery and threw aside her light shawl in the full glare of half a dozen kerosene lamps. She was white from head to foot—literally, for her slippers even were white. No one would have believed, let alone suspected that they were a pair of old black ones which she had covered with pieces of her first communion sash. There is no describing her dress, it was fluffy, like a fresh powder-puff, and stood out. No wonder she had handled it so reverentially! Her white fan was covered with spangles that she herself had sewed all over it; and in her belt and in her brown hair were thrust small sprays of orange blossom.

Two men leaning against the railing uttered long whistles expressive equally of wonder and admiration.

"Tiens! t'es pareille comme ain mariée, Zaïda,"[9] cried out a lady with a baby in her arms. Some young women tittered and Zaïda fanned herself. The women's voices were almost without exception shrill and piercing; the men's, soft and low-pitched.

The girl turned to Telèsphore, as to an old and valued friend: "Tiens! c'est vous?"[10] He had hesitated at first to approach, but at this friendly sign of recognition he drew eagerly forward and held out his hand. The men looked at him suspiciously, inwardly resenting his stylish appearance, which they considered intrusive, offensive and demoralizing.

How Zaïda's eyes sparkled now! What very pretty teeth Zaïda had when she laughed, and what a mouth! Her lips were a revelation, a promise; something to carry away and remember in the night and grow hungry thinking of next day. Strictly speaking, they may not have been quite all that; but in any event, that is the way Telèsphore thought about them. He began to take account of her appearance: her nose, her eyes, her hair. And when she left him to go in and dance her first dance with cousin Jules, he leaned up against a post and thought of them: nose, eyes, hair, ears, lips and round, soft throat.

Later it was like Bedlam.

The musicians had warmed up and were scraping away indoors and calling the figures. Feet were pounding through the dance; dust was flying. The women's voices were piped high and mingled discordantly, like the confused, shrill clatter of waking birds, while the men laughed boisterously. But if some one had only thought of gagging Foché, there would have been less noise. His good humor permeated everywhere, like an atmosphere. He was louder than all the noise; he was more visible than the dust. He called the young mulatto (destined for the knife) "my boy" and sent him flying hither and thither. He beamed upon Douté as he tasted the gumbo and congratulated her: "C'est toi qui s'y connais, ma fille! 'cré tonnerre!"[11]

Telèsphore danced with Zaïda and then he leaned out against the post; then he danced with Zaïda, and then he leaned against the post. The mothers of the other girls decided that he had the manners of a pig.

It was time to dance again with Zaïda and he went in search of her. He was carrying her shawl, which she had given him to hold.

"W'at time is it?" she asked him when he had found and secured her. They were under one of the kerosene lamps on the front gallery and he drew forth his silver watch. She seemed to be still laboring under some suppressed excitement that he had noticed before.

"It's fo'teen minutes pas' twelve," he told her exactly.

"I wish you'd fine out w'ere Jules is. Go look yonda in the cardroom if he's there, an' come tell me." Jules had danced with all the prettiest girls. She knew it was his custom after accomplishing this agreeable feat, to retire to the card-room.

"You'll wait yere till I come back?" he asked.

"I'll wait yere; you go on." She waited but drew back a little into the shadow. Telèsphore lost no time.

"Yes, he's yonda playin' cards with Foché an' some others I don' know," he reported when he had discovered her in the shadow. There had been a spasm of alarm when he did not at once see her where he had left her under the lamp.

"Does he look—look like he's fixed yonda fo' good?"

"He's got his coat off. Looks like he's fixed pretty comf'table fo' the nex' hour or two."

"Gi' me my shawl."

"You cole?" offering to put it around her.

"No, I ain't cole." She drew the shawl about her shoulders and turned as if to leave him. But a sudden generous impulse seemed to move her, and she added:

"Come along yonda with me."

They descended the few rickety steps that led down to the yard. He followed rather than accompanied her across the beaten and trampled sward. Those who saw them thought they had gone out to take the air. The beams of light that slanted out from the house were fitful and uncertain, deepening the shadows. The embers under the empty gumbo-pot glared red in the darkness. There was a sound of quiet voices coming from under the trees.

Zaïda, closely accompanied by Telèsphore, went out where the vehicles and horses were fastened to the fence. She stepped carefully and held up her skirts as if dreading the least speck of dew or of dust.

"Unhitch Jules' ho'se an' buggy there an' turn 'em 'roun' this way, please." He did as instructed, first backing the pony, then leading it out to where she stood in the half-made road.

"You goin' home?" he asked her, "betta let me water the pony."

"Neva mine." She mounted and seating herself grasped the reins. "No, I ain't goin' home," she added. He, too, was holding the reins gathered in one hand across the pony's back.

"W'ere you goin'?" he demanded.

"Neva you mine w'ere I'm goin'."

"You ain't goin' anyw'ere this time o' night by yo'se'f?"

"W'at you reckon I'm 'fraid of?" she laughed. "Turn loose that ho'se," at the same time urging the animal forward. The little brute started away with a bound and Telèsphore, also with a bound, sprang into the buckboard and seated himself beside Zaïda.

"You ain't goin' anyw'ere this time o' night by yo'se'f." It was

not a question now, but an assertion, and there was no denying it.
There was even no disputing it, and Zaïda recognizing the fact
drove on in silence.

There is no animal that moves so swiftly across a 'Cadian prairie
as the little Creole pony. This one did not run nor trot; he seemed
to reach out in galloping bounds. The buckboard creaked, bounced,
jolted and swayed. Zaïda clutched at her shawl while Telèsphore
drew his straw hat further down over his right eye and offered to
drive. But he did not know the road and she would not let him.
They had soon reached the woods.

If there is any animal that can creep more slowly through a
wooded road than the little Creole pony, that animal has not yet
been discovered in Acadie. This particular animal seemed to be ap-
palled by the darkness of the forest and filled with dejection. His
head drooped and he lifted his feet as if each hoof were weighted
with a thousand pounds of lead. Any one unacquainted with the
peculiarities of the breed would sometimes have fancied that he was
standing still. But Zaïda and Telèsphore knew better. Zaïda uttered
a deep sigh as she slackened her hold on the reins and Telèsphore,
lifting his hat, let it swing from the back of his head.

"How you don' ask me w'ere I'm goin'?" she said finally. These
were the first words she had spoken since refusing his offer to drive.

"Oh, it don' make any diff'ence w'ere you goin'."

"Then if it don' make any diff'ence w'ere I'm goin', I jus' as well
tell you." She hesitated, however. He seemed to have no curiosity
and did not urge her.

"I'm goin' to get married," she said.

He uttered some kind of an exclamation; it was nothing articu-
late—more like the tone of an animal that gets a sudden knife
thrust. And now he felt how dark the forest was. An instant before
it had seemed a sweet, black paradise; better than any heaven he had
ever heard of.

"W'y can't you get married at home?" This was not the first
thing that occurred to him to say, but this was the first thing he said.

"Ah, b'en oui!¹² with perfec' mules fo' a father an' mother! it's
good enough to talk."

"W'y couldn' he come an' get you? W'at kine of a scound'el is
that to let you go through the woods at night by yo'se'f?"

"You betta wait till you know who you talkin' about. He didn' come an' get me because he knows I ain't 'fraid; an' because he's got too much pride to ride in Jules Trodon's buckboard afta he done been put out o' Jules Trodon's house."

"W'at's his name an' w'ere you goin' to fine 'im?"

"Yonda on the other side the woods up at ole Wat Gibson's—a kine of justice of the peace or something. Anyhow he's goin' to marry us. An' afta we done married those têtes-de-mulets[13] yonda on bayou de Glaize can say w'at they want."

"W'at's his name?"

"André Pascal."

The name meant nothing to Telèsphore. For all he knew, André Pascal might be one of the shining lights of Avoyelles; but he doubted it.

"You betta turn 'roun'," he said. It was an unselfish impulse that prompted the suggestion. It was the thought of this girl married to a man whom even Jules Trodon would not suffer to enter his house.

"I done give my word," she answered.

"W'at's the matta with 'im? W'y don't yo' father and mother want you to marry 'im?"

"W'y? Because it's always the same tune! W'en a man's down eve'ybody's got stones to throw at 'im. They say he's lazy. A man that will walk from St. Landry plumb to Rapides lookin' fo' work; an' they call that lazy! Then, somebody's been spreadin' yonda on the Bayou that he drinks. I don' b'lieve it. I neva saw 'im drinkin', me. Anyway, he won't drink afta he's married to me; he's too fon' of me fo' that. He say he'll blow out his brains if I don' marry 'im."

"I reckon you betta turn roun'."

"No, I done give my word." And they went creeping on through the woods in silence.

"W'at time is it?" she asked after an interval. He lit a match and looked at his watch.

"It's quarta to one. W'at time did he say?"

"I tole 'im I'd come about one o'clock. I knew that was a good time to get away f'om the ball."

She would have hurried a little but the pony could not be in-duced to do so. He dragged himself, seemingly ready at any mo-ment to give up the breath of life. But once out of the woods he made up for lost time. They were on the open prairie again, and he fairly ripped the air; some flying demon must have changed skins with him.

It was a few minutes of one o'clock when they drew up before Wat Gibson's house. It was not much more than a rude shelter, and in the dim starlight it seemed isolated, as if standing alone in the middle of the black, far-reaching prairie. As they halted at the gate a dog within set up a furious barking; and an old negro who had been smoking his pipe at that ghostly hour, advanced toward them from the shelter of the gallery. Telèsphore descended and helped his companion to alight.

"We want to see Mr. Gibson," spoke up Zaïda. The old fellow had already opened the gate. There was no light in the house.

"Marse Gibson, he yonda to ole Mr. Bodel's playin' kairds. But he neva' stay atter one o'clock. Come in, ma'am; come in, suh; walk right 'long in." He had drawn his own conclusions to explain their appearance. They stood upon the narrow porch waiting while he went inside to light the lamp.

Although the house was small, as it comprised but one room, that room was comparatively a large one. It looked to Telèsphore and Zaïda very large and gloomy when they entered it. The lamp was on a table that stood against the wall, and that held further a rusty looking ink bottle, a pen and an old blank book. A narrow bed was off in the corner. The brick chimney extended into the room and formed a ledge that served as mantel shelf. From the big, low-hanging rafters swung an assortment of fishing tackle, a gun, some discarded articles of clothing and a string of red peppers. The boards of the floor were broad, rough and loosely joined together.

Telèsphore and Zaïda seated themselves on opposite sides of the table and the negro went out to the wood pile to gather chips and pieces of bois-gras[14] with which to kindle a small fire.

It was a little chilly; he supposed the two would want coffee and he knew that Wat Gibson would ask for a cup the first thing on his arrival.

"I wonder w'at's keepin' 'im," muttered Zaïda impatiently. Telèsphore looked at his watch. He had been looking at it at intervals of one minute straight along.

"It's ten minutes pas' one," he said. He offered no further comment.

At twelve minutes past one Zaïda's restlessness again broke into speech.

"I can't imagine, me, w'at's become of André! He said he'd be yere sho' at one." The old negro was kneeling before the fire that he had kindled, contemplating the cheerful blaze. He rolled his eyes toward Zaïda.

"You talkin' 'bout Mr. André Pascal? No need to look fo' him. Mr. André he b'en down to de P'int all day raisin' Cain."

"That's a lie," said Zaïda. Telèsphore said nothing.

"Tain't no lie, ma'am; he b'en sho' raisin' de ole Nick." She looked at him, too contemptuous to reply.

The negro told no lie so far as his bald statement was concerned. He was simply mistaken in his estimate of André Pascal's ability to "raise Cain" during an entire afternoon and evening and still keep a rendezvous with a lady at one o'clock in the morning. For André was even then at hand, as the loud and menacing howl of the dog testified. The negro hastened out to admit him.

André did not enter at once; he stayed a while outside abusing the dog and communicating to the negro his intention of coming out to shoot the animal after he had attended to more pressing business that was awaiting him within.

Zaïda arose, a little flurried and excited when he entered. Telèsphore remained seated.

Pascal was partially sober. There had evidently been an attempt at dressing for the occasion at some early part of the previous day, but such evidences had almost wholly vanished. His linen was soiled and his whole appearance was that of a man who, by an effort, had aroused himself from a debauch. He was a little taller than Telèsphore, and more loosely put together. Most women would have called him a handsomer man. It was easy to imagine that when sober, he might betray by some subtle grace of speech or manner, evidences of gentle blood.

"W'y did you keep me waitin', André? w'en you knew—" she got no further, but backed up against the table and stared at him with earnest, startled eyes.

"Keep you waiting, Zaïda? my dear li'le Zaïdé, how can you say such a thing! I started up yere an hour ago an' that—w'ere's that damned ole Gibson?" He had approached Zaïda with the evident intention of embracing her, but she seized his wrist and held him at arm's length away. In casting his eyes about for old Gibson his glance alighted upon Telèsphore.

The sight of the 'Cadian seemed to fill him with astonishment. He stood back and began to contemplate the young fellow and lose himself in speculation and conjecture before him, as if before some unlabeled wax figure. He turned for information to Zaïda.

"Say, Zaïda, w'at you call this? W'at kine of damn fool you got sitting yere? Who let him in? W'at you reckon he's lookin' fo'? trouble?"

Telèsphore said nothing; he was awaiting his cue from Zaïda.

"André Pascal," she said, "you jus' as well take the do' an' go. You might stan' yere till the day o' judgment on yo' knees befo' me; an' blow out yo' brains if you a mine to. I ain't neva goin' to marry you."

"The hell you ain't!"

He had hardly more than uttered the words when he lay prone on his back. Telèsphore had knocked him down. The blow seemed to complete the process of sobering that had begun in him. He gathered himself together and rose to his feet; in doing so he reached back for his pistol. His hold was not yet steady, however, and the weapon slipped from his grasp and fell to the floor. Zaïda picked it up and laid it on the table behind her. She was going to see fair play.

The brute instinct that drives men at each other's throat was awake and stirring in these two. Each saw in the other a thing to be wiped out of his way—out of existence if need be. Passion and blind rage directed the blows which they dealt, and steeled the tension of muscles and clutch of fingers. They were not skillful blows, however.

The fire blazed cheerily; the kettle which the negro had placed upon the coals was steaming and singing. The man had gone in search of his master. Zaïda had placed the lamp out of harm's way on the high mantel ledge and she leaned back with her hands behind her upon the table.

She did not raise her voice or lift her finger to stay the combat that was acting before her. She was motionless, and white to the lips; only her eyes seemed to be alive and burning and blazing. At one moment she felt that André must have strangled Telèsphore; but she said nothing. The next instant she could hardly doubt that the blow from Telèsphore's doubled fist could be less than a killing one; but she did nothing.

How the loose boards swayed and creaked beneth the weight of the struggling men! the very old rafters seemed to groan; and she felt that the house shook.

The combat, if fierce, was short, and it ended out on the gallery whither they had staggered through the open door—or one had dragged the other—she could not tell. But she knew when it was over, for there was a long moment of utter stillness. Then she heard one of the men descend the steps and go away, for the gate slammed after him. The other went out to the cistern; the sound of the tin bucket splashing in the water reached her where she stood. He must have been endeavoring to remove traces of the encounter.

Presently Telèsphore entered the room. The elegance of his apparel had been somewhat marred; the men over at the 'Cadian ball would hardly have taken exception now to his appearance.

"W'ere is André?" the girl asked.

"He's gone," said Telésphore.

She had never changed her position and now when she drew herself up her wrists ached and she rubbed them a little. She was no longer pale; the blood had come back into her cheeks and lips, staining them crimson. She held out her hand to him. He took it gratefully enough, but he did not know what to do with it; that is, he did not know what he might dare to do with it, so he let it drop gently away and went to the fire.

"I reckon we betta be goin', too," she said. He stooped and poured some of the bubbling water from the kettle upon the coffee which the negro had set upon the hearth.

"I'll make a li'le coffee firs'," he proposed, "an' anyhow we betta wait till ole man w'at's-his-name comes back. It wouldn't look well to leave his house that way without some kine of excuse or explanation."

She made no reply, but seated herself submissively beside the table.

Her will, which had been overmastering and aggressive, seemed to have grown numb under the disturbing spell of the past few hours. An illusion had gone from her, and had carried her love with it. The absence of regret revealed this to her. She realized, but could not comprehend it, not knowing that the love had been part of the illusion. She was tired in body and spirit, and it was with a sense of restfulness that she sat all drooping and relaxed and watched Telèsphore make the coffee.

He made enough for them both and a cup for old Wat Gibson when he should come in, and also one for the negro. He supposed the cups, the sugar and spoons were in the safe over there in the corner, and that is where he found them.

When he finally said to Zaïda, "Come, I'm going to take you home now," and drew her shawl around her, pinning it under the chin, she was like a little child and followed whither he led in all confidence.

It was Telèsphore who drove on the way back, and he let the pony cut no capers, but held him to a steady and tempered gait. The girl was still quiet and silent; she was thinking tenderly—a little tearfully of those two old têtes-de-mulets yonder on Bayou de Glaize.

How they crept through the woods! and how dark it was and how still!

"W'at time it is?" whispered Zaïda. Alas! he could not tell her; his watch was broken. But almost for the first time in his life, Telèsphore did not care what time it was.

Athénaïse

I

ATHÉNAÏSE went away in the morning to make a visit to her parents, ten miles back on rigolet de Bon Dieu.[1] She did not return in the evening, and Cazeau, her husband, fretted not a little. He did not worry much about Athénaïse, who, he suspected, was resting only too content in the bosom of her family; his chief solicitude was manifestly for the pony she had ridden. He felt sure those "lazy pigs," her brothers, were capable of neglecting it seriously. This misgiving Cazeau communicated to his servant, old Félicité, who waited upon him at supper.

His voice was low pitched, and even softer than Félicité's. He was tall, sinewy, swarthy, and altogether severe looking. His thick black hair waved, and it gleamed like the breast of a crow. The sweep of his mustache, which was not so black, outlined the broad contour of the mouth. Beneath the under lip grew a small tuft which he was much given to twisting, and which he permitted to grow, apparently for no other purpose. Cazeau's eyes were dark blue, narrow and overshadowed. His hands were coarse and stiff from close acquaintance with farming tools and implements, and he handled his fork and knife clumsily. But he was distinguished looking, and succeeded in commanding a good deal of respect, and even fear sometimes.

He ate his supper alone, by the light of a single coal-oil lamp that but faintly illuminated the big room, with its bare floor and huge rafters, and its heavy pieces of furniture that loomed dimly in the gloom of the apartment. Félicité, ministering to his wants, hovered about the table like a little, bent, restless shadow.

She served him with a dish of sunfish fried crisp and brown. There was nothing else set before him beside the bread and butter and the bottle of red wine which she locked carefully in the buffet after he had poured his second glass. She was occupied with her mistress's absence, and kept reverting to it after he had expressed his solicitude about the pony.

"Dat beat me! on'y marry two mont', an' got de head turn' a'ready to go 'broad. C'est pas Chrétien, tenez!"[2]

Cazeau shrugged his shoulders for answer, after he had drained his glass and pushed aside his plate. Félicité's opinion of the unchristianlike behavior of his wife in leaving him thus alone after two months of marriage weighed little with him. He was used to solitude, and did not mind a day or a night or two of it. He had lived alone ten years, since his first wife died, and Félicité might have known better than to suppose that he cared. He told her she was a fool. It sounded like a compliment in his modulated, caressing voice. She grumbled to herself as she set about clearing the table, and Cazeau arose and walked outside on the gallery; his spur, which he had not removed upon entering the house, jangled at every step.

The night was beginning to deepen, and to gather black about the clusters of trees and shrubs that were grouped in the yard. In the beam of light from the open kitchen door a black boy stood feeding a brace of snarling, hungry dogs; further away, on the steps of a cabin, some one was playing the accordion; and in still another direction a little negro baby was crying lustily. Cazeau walked around to the front of the house, which was square, squat and one-story.

A belated wagon was driving in at the gate, and the impatient driver was swearing hoarsely at his jaded oxen. Félicité stepped out on the gallery, glass and polishing towel in hand, to investigate, and to wonder, too, who could be singing out on the river. It was a party of young people paddling around, waiting for the moon to rise, and they were singing Juanita,[3] their voices coming tempered and melodious through the distance and the night.

Cazeau's horse was waiting, saddled, ready to be mounted, for Cazeau had many things to attend to before bed-time; so many things that there was not left to him a moment in which to think of Athénaïse. He felt her absence, though, like a dull, insistent pain.

However, before he slept that night he was visited by the thought of her, and by a vision of her fair young face with its drooping lips and sullen and averted eyes. The marriage had been a blunder; he had only to look into her eyes to feel that, to discover her growing aversion. But it was a thing not by any possibility to be undone. He was quite prepared to make the best of it, and expected no less than a like effort on her part. The less she revisited the rigolet, the better. He would find means to keep her at home hereafter.

These unpleasant reflections kept Cazeau awake far into the night, notwithstanding the craving of his whole body for rest and sleep. The moon was shining, and its pale effulgence reached dimly into the room, and with it a touch of the cool breath of the spring night. There was an unusual stillness abroad; no sound to be heard save the distant, tireless, plaintive notes of the accordion.

II

Athénaïse did not return the following day, even though her husband sent her word to do so by her brother, Montéclin, who passed on his way to the village early in the morning.

On the third day Cazeau saddled his horse and went himself in search of her. She had sent no word, no message, explaining her absence, and he felt that he had good cause to be offended. It was rather awkward to have to leave his work, even though late in the afternoon,—Cazeau had always so much to do; but among the many urgent calls upon him, the task of bringing his wife back to a sense of her duty seemed to him for the moment paramount.

The Michés, Athénaïse's parents, lived on the old Gotrain place. It did not belong to them; they were "running" it for a merchant in Alexandria. The house was far too big for their use. One of the lower rooms served for the storing of wood and tools; the person "occupying" the place before Miché having pulled up the flooring in despair of being able to patch it. Upstairs, the rooms were so large, so bare, that they offered a constant temptation to lovers of the dance, whose importunities Madame Miché was accustomed to meet with amiable indulgence. A dance at Miché's and a plate of Madame Miché's gumbo filé at midnight were pleasures not to be neglected or despised, unless by such serious souls as Cazeau.

Long before Cazeau reached the house his approach had been observed, for there was nothing to obstruct the view of the outer road; vegetation was not yet abundantly advanced, and there was but a patchy, straggling stand of cotton and corn in Miché's field.

Madame Miché, who had been seated on the gallery in a rocking-chair, stood up to greet him as he drew near. She was short and fat, and wore a black skirt and loose muslin sack fastened at the throat with a hair brooch. Her own hair, brown and glossy, showed but a few threads of silver. Her round pink face was cheery, and her eyes were bright and good humored. But she was plainly perturbed and ill at ease as Cazeau advanced.

Montéclin, who was there too, was not ill at ease, and made no attempt to disguise the dislike with which his brother-in-law inspired him. He was a slim, wiry fellow of twenty-five, short of stature like his mother, and resembling her in feature. He was in shirt-sleeves, half leaning, half sitting, on the insecure railing of the gallery, and fanning himself with his broad-rimmed felt hat.

"Cochon!" he muttered under his breath as Cazeau mounted the stairs,—"sacré cochon!"[4]

"Cochon" had sufficiently characterized the man who had once on a time declined to lend Montéclin money. But when this same man had had the presumption to propose marriage to his well-beloved sister, Athénaïse, and the honor to be accepted by her, Montéclin felt that a qualifying epithet was needed fully to express his estimate of Cazeau.

Miché and his oldest son were absent. They both esteemed Cazeau highly, and talked much of his qualities of head and heart, and thought much of his excellent standing with city merchants.

Athénaïse had shut herself up in her room. Cazeau had seen her rise and enter the house at perceiving him. He was a good deal mystified, but no one could have guessed it when he shook hands with Madame Miché. He had only nodded to Montéclin, with a muttered "Comment ça va?"[5]

"Tiens! something tole me you were coming to-day!" exclaimed Madame Miché, with a little blustering appearance of being cordial and at ease, as she offered Cazeau a chair.

He ventured a short laugh as he seated himself.

"You know, nothing would do," she went on, with much gesture

of her small, plump hands, "nothing would do but Athénaïse mus'
stay las' night fo' a li'le dance. The boys wouldn' year to their sister
leaving."

Cazeau shrugged his shoulders significantly, telling as plainly as
words that he knew nothing about it.

"Comment! Montéclin didn' tell you we were going to keep
Athénaïse?" Montéclin had evidently told nothing.

"An' how about the night befo'," questioned Cazeau, "an' las'
night? It isn't possible you dance every night out yere on the Bon
Dieu!"

Madame Miché laughed, with amiable appreciation of the sar-
casm; and turning to her son, "Montéclin, my boy, go tell yo' sister
that Monsieur Cazeau is yere."

Montéclin did not stir except to shift his position and settle himself more securely on the railing.

"Did you year me, Montéclin?"

"Oh yes, I yeard you plain enough," responded her son, "but
you know as well as me it's no use to tell 'Thénaïse anything. You
been talkin' to her yo'se'f since Monday; an' pa's preached himse'f
hoa'se on the subject; an' you even had uncle Achille down yere
yesterday to reason with her. W'en 'Thénaïse said she wasn' goin' to
set her foot back in Cazeau's house, she meant it."

This speech, which Montéclin delivered with thorough uncon-
cern, threw his mother into a condition of painful but dumb embarrassment. It brought two fiery red spots to Cazeau's cheeks, and for
the space of a moment he looked wicked.

What Montéclin had spoken was quite true, though his taste in
the manner and choice of time and place in saying it were not of the
best. Athénaïse, upon the first day of her arrival, had announced
that she came to stay, having no intention of returning under
Cazeau's roof. The announcement had scattered consternation, as
she knew it would. She had been implored, scolded, entreated,
stormed at, until she felt herself like a dragging sail that all the
winds of heaven had beaten upon. Why in the name of God had she
married Cazeau? Her father had lashed her with the question a
dozen times. Why indeed? It was difficult now for her to understand why, unless because she supposed it was customary for girls
to marry when the right opportunity came. Cazeau, she knew,

would make life more comfortable for her; and again, she had liked him, and had even been rather flustered when he pressed her hands and kissed them, and kissed her lips and cheeks and eyes, when she accepted him.

Montéclin himself had taken her aside to talk the thing over. The turn of affairs was delighting him.

"Come, now, 'Thénaïse, you mus' explain to me all about it, so we can settle on a good cause, an' secu' a separation fo' you. Has he been mistreating an' abusing you, the sacré cochon?" They were alone together in her room, whither she had taken refuge from the angry domestic elements.

"You please to reserve yo' disgusting expressions, Montéclin. No, he has not abused me in any way that I can think."

"Does he drink? Come 'Thénaïse, think well over it. Does he ever get drunk?"

"Drunk! Oh, mercy, no,—Cazeau never gets drunk."

"I see; it's jus' simply you feel like me; you hate him."

"No, I don't hate him," she returned reflectively; adding with a sudden impulse, "It's jus' being married that I detes' an' despise. I hate being Mrs. Cazeau, an' would want to be Athénaïse Miché again. I can't stan' to live with a man; to have him always there; his coats an' pantaloons hanging in my room; his ugly bare feet—washing them in my tub, befo' my very eyes, ugh!" She shuddered with recollections, and resumed, with a sigh that was almost a sob; "Mon Dieu, mon Dieu! Sister Marie Angélique knew w'at she was saying; she knew me better than myse'f w'en she said God had sent me a vocation an' I was turning deaf ears. W'en I think of a blessed life in the convent, at peace! Oh, w'at was I dreaming of!" and then the tears came.

Montéclin felt disconcerted and greatly disappointed at having obtained evidence that would carry no weight with a court of justice. The day had not come when a young woman might ask the court's permission to return to her mamma on the sweeping ground of a constitutional disinclination for marriage. But if there was no way of untying this Gordian knot of marriage, there was surely a way of cutting it.

"Well, 'Thénaïse, I'm mighty durn sorry you got no better groun's 'an w'at you say. But you can count on me to stan' by you w'atever you do. God knows I don' blame you fo' not wantin' to live with Cazeau."

And now there was Cazeau himself, with the red spots flaming in his swarthy cheeks, looking and feeling as if he wanted to thrash Montéclin into some semblance of decency. He arose abruptly, and approaching the room which he had seen his wife enter, thrust open the door after a hasty preliminary knock. Athénaïse, who was standing erect at a far window, turned at his entrance.

She appeared neither angry nor frightened, but thoroughly unhappy, with an appeal in her soft dark eyes and a tremor on her lips that seemed to him expressions of unjust reproach, that wounded and maddened him at once. But whatever he might feel, Cazeau knew only one way to act toward a woman.

"Athénaïse, you are not ready?" he asked in his quiet tones. "It's getting late; we havn' any time to lose."

She knew that Montéclin had spoken out, and she had hoped for a wordy interview, a stormy scene, in which she might have held her own as she had held it for the past three days against her family, with Montéclin's aid. But she had no weapon with which to combat subtlety. Her husband's looks, his tones, his mere presence, brought to her a sudden sense of hopelessness, an instinctive realization of the futility of rebellion against a social and sacred institution.

Cazeau said nothing further, but stood waiting in the doorway. Madame Miché had walked to the far end of the gallery, and pretended to be occupied with having a chicken driven from her parterre. Montéclin stood by, exasperated, fuming, ready to burst out.

Athénaïse went and reached for her riding skirt that hung against the wall. She was rather tall, with a figure which, though not robust, seemed perfect in its fine proportions. "La fille de son père,"[6] she was often called, which was a great compliment to Miché. Her brown hair was brushed all fluffily back from her temples and low forehead, and about her features and expression lurked a softness, a prettiness, a dewiness, that were perhaps too childlike, that savored of immaturity.

She slipped the riding-skirt, which was of black alpaca, over her head, and with impatient fingers hooked it at the waist over her pink linen-lawn. Then she fastened on her white sunbonnet and reached for her gloves on the mantelpiece.

"If you don' wan' to go, you know w'at you got to do, 'Thé-naïse," fumed Montéclin. "You don' set yo' feet back on Cane River, by God, unless you want to,—not w'ile I'm alive."

Cazeau looked at him as if he were a monkey whose antics fell short of being amusing.

Athénaïse still made no reply, said not a word. She walked rapidly past her husband, past her brother; bidding good-bye to no one, not even to her mother. She descended the stairs, and without assistance from any one mounted the pony, which Cazeau had ordered to be saddled upon his arrival. In this way she obtained a fair start of her husband, whose departure was far more leisurely, and for the greater part of the way she managed to keep an appreciable gap between them. She rode almost madly at first, with the wind inflating her skirt balloon-like about her knees, and her sunbonnet falling back between her shoulders.

At no time did Cazeau make an effort to overtake her until traversing an old fallow meadow that was level and hard as a table. The sight of a great solitary oak-tree, with its seemingly immutable outlines, that had been a landmark for ages—or was it the odor of elderberry stealing up from the gully to the south? or what was it that brought vividly back to Cazeau, by some association of ideas, a scene of many years ago? He had passed that old live-oak hundreds of times, but it was only now that the memory of one day came back to him. He was a very small boy that day, seated before his father on horse-back. They were proceeding slowly, and Black Gabe was moving on before them at a little dog-trot. Black Gabe had run away, and had been discovered back in the Gotrain swamp. They had halted beneath this big oak to enable the negro to take breath; for Cazeau's father was a kind and considerate master, and every one had agreed at the time that Black Gabe was a fool, a great idiot indeed, for wanting to run away from him.

The whole impression was for some reason hideous, and to dispel it Cazeau spurred his horse to a swift gallop. Overtaking his wife, he rode the remainder of the way at her side in silence.

It was late when they reached home. Félicité was standing on the grassy edge of the road, in the moonlight, waiting for them.

Cazeau once more ate his supper alone; for Athénaïse went to her room, and there she was crying again.

III

Athénaïse was not one to accept the inevitable with patient resignation, a talent born in the souls of many women; neither was she the one to accept it with philosophical resignation, like her husband. Her sensibilities were alive and keen and responsive. She met the pleasurable things of life with frank, open appreciation, and against distasteful conditions she rebelled. Dissimulation was as foreign to her nature as guile to the breast of a babe, and her rebellious outbreaks, by no means rare, had hitherto been quite open and aboveboard. People often said that Athénaïse would know her own mind some day, which was equivalent to saying that she was at present unacquainted with it. If she ever came to such knowledge, it would be by no intellectual research, by no subtle analyses or tracing the motives of actions to their source. It would come to her as the song to the bird, the perfume and color to the flower.

Her parents had hoped—not without reason and justice—that marriage would bring the poise, the desirable pose, so glaringly lacking in Athénaïse's character. Marriage they knew to be a wonderful and powerful agent in the development and formation of a woman's character; they had seen its effect too often to doubt it.

"And if this marriage does nothing else," exclaimed Miché in an outburst of sudden exasperaton, "it will rid us of Athénaïse; for I am at the end of my patience with her! You have never had the firmness to manage her,"—he was speaking to his wife,—"I have not had the time, the leisure, to devote to her training; and what good we might have accomplished, that maudit[7] Montéclin—Well, Cazeau is the one! It takes just such a steady hand to guide a disposition like Athénaïse's, a master hand, a strong will that compels obedience."

And now, when they had hoped for so much, here was Athénaïse, with gathered and fierce vehemence, beside which her former outbursts appeared mild, declaring that she would not, and she would not, and she would not continue to enact the role of wife to Cazeau. If she had had a reason! as Madame Miché lamented; but it could not be discovered that she had any sane one. He had never scolded, or called names, or deprived her of comforts, or been guilty of any of the many reprehensible acts commonly attributed to objectionable husbands. He did not slight nor neglect her. Indeed, Cazeau's chief offense seemed to be that he loved her, and Athénaïse was not the woman to be loved against her will. She called marriage a trap set for the feet of unwary and unsuspecting girls, and in round, unmeasured terms reproached her mother with treachery and deceit.

"I told you Cazeau was the man," chuckled Miché, when his wife had related the scene that had accompanied and influenced Athénaïse's departure.

Athénaïse again hoped, in the morning, that Cazeau would scold or make some sort of a scene, but he apparently did not dream of it. It was exasperating that he should take her acquiescence so for granted. It is true he had been up and over the fields and across the river and back long before she was out of bed, and he may have been thinking of something else, which was no excuse, which was even in some sense an aggravation. But he did say to her at breakfast, "That brother of yo's, that Montéclin, is unbearable."

"Montéclin? Par exemple!"

Athénaïse, seated opposite to her husband, was attired in a white morning wrapper. She wore a somewhat abused, long face, it is true,—an expression of countenance familiar to some husbands,—but the expression was not sufficiently pronounced to mar the charm of her youthful freshness. She had little heart to eat, only playing with the food before her, and she felt a pang of resentment at her husband's healthy appetite.

"Yes, Montéclin," he reasserted. "He's developed into a firs'-class nuisance; an' you better tell him, Athénaïse,—unless you want me to tell him,—to confine his energies after this to matters that concern him. I have no use fo' him or fo' his interference in w'at regards you an' me alone."

This was said with unusual asperity. It was the little breach that Athénaïse had been watching for, and she charged rapidly: "It's strange, if you detes' Montéclin so heartily, that you would desire to marry his sister." She knew it was a silly thing to say, and was not surprised when he told her so. It gave her a little foothold for further attack, however. "I don't see, anyhow, w'at reason you had to marry me, w'en there were so many others," she complained, as if accusing him of persecution and injury. "There was Marianne running after you fo' the las' five years till it was disgraceful; an' any one of the Dortrand girls would have been glad to marry you. But no, nothing would do; you mus' come out on the rigolet fo' me." Her complaint was pathetic, and at the same time so amusing that Cazeau was forced to smile.

"I can't see w'at the Dortrand girls or Marianne have to do with it," he rejoined; adding, with no trace of amusement, "I married you because I loved you; because you were the woman I wanted to marry, an' the only one. I reckon I tole you that befo'. I thought— of co'se I was a fool fo' taking things fo' granted—but I did think that I might make you happy in making things easier an' mo' comfortable fo' you. I expected—I was even that big a fool—I believed that yo' coming yere to me would be like the sun shining out of the clouds, an' that our days would be like w'at the story-books promise after the wedding. I was mistaken. But I can't imagine w'at induced you to marry me. W'atever it was, I reckon you foun' out you made a mistake, too. I don' see anything to do but make the best of a bad bargain, an' shake han's over it." He had arisen from the table, and, approaching, held out his hand to her. What he had said was commonplace enough, but it was significant, coming from Cazeau, who was not often so unreserved in expressing himself.

Athénaïse ignored the hand held out to her. She was resting her chin in her palm, and kept her eyes fixed moodily upon the table. He rested his hand, that she would not touch, upon her head for an instant, and walked away out of the room.

She heard him giving orders to workmen who had been waiting for him out on the gallery, and she heard him mount his horse and ride away. A hundred things would distract him and engage his attention during the day. She felt that he had perhaps put her and her grievance from his thoughts when he crossed the threshold; whilst she—

Old Félicité was standing there holding a shining tin pail, asking for flour and lard and eggs from the storeroom, and meal for the chicks.

Athénaïse seized the bunch of keys which hung from her belt and flung them at Félicité's feet.

"Tiens! tu vas les garder comme tu as jadis fait. Je ne veux plus de ce train là, moi!"[8]

The old woman stooped and picked up the keys from the floor. It was really all one to her that her mistress returned them to her keeping, and refused to take further account of the ménage.

IV

It seemed now to Athénaïse that Montéclin was the only friend left to her in the world. Her father and mother had turned from her in what appeared to be her hour of need. Her friends laughed at her, and refused to take seriously the hints which she threw out,—feeling her way to discover if marriage were as distasteful to other women as to herself. Montéclin alone understood her. He alone had always been ready to act for her and with her, to comfort and solace her with his sympathy and his support. Her only hope for rescue from her hateful surroundings lay in Montéclin. Of herself she felt powerless to plan, to act, even to conceive a way out of this pitfall into which the whole world seemed to have conspired to thrust her.

She had a great desire to see her brother, and wrote asking him to come to her. But it better suited Montéclin's spirit of adventure to appoint a meeting-place at the turn of the lane, where Athénaïse might appear to be walking leisurely for health and recreation, and where he might seem to be riding along, bent on some errand of business or pleasure.

There had been a shower, a sudden downpour, short as it was sudden, that had laid the dust in the road. It had freshened the pointed leaves of the live-oaks, and brightened up the big fields of cotton on either side of the lane till they seemed carpeted with green, glittering gems.

Athénaïse walked along the grassy edge of the road, lifting her crisp skirts with one hand, and with the other twirling a gay sunshade over her bare head. The scent of the fields after the rain was delicious. She inhaled long breaths of their freshness and perfume, that soothed and quieted her for the moment. There were birds splashing and spluttering in the pools, pluming themselves on the fence-rails, and sending out little sharp cries, twitters, and shrill rhapsodies of delight.

She saw Montéclin approaching from a great distance,—almost as far away as the turn of the woods. But she could not feel sure it was he; it appeared too tall for Montéclin, but that was because he was riding a large horse. She waved her parasol to him; she was so glad to see him. She had never been so glad to see Montéclin before; not even the day when he had taken her out of the convent, against her parents' wishes, because she had expressed a desire to remain there no longer. He seemed to her, as he drew near, the embodiment of kindness, of bravery, of chivalry, even of wisdom; for she had never known Montéclin at a loss to extricate himself from a disagreeable situation.

He dismounted, and, leading his horse by the bridle, started to walk beside her, after he had kissed her affectionately and asked her what she was crying about. She protested that she was not crying, for she was laughing, though drying her eyes at the same time on her handkerchief, rolled in a soft mop for the purpose.

She took Montéclin's arm, and they strolled slowly down the lane; they could not seat themselves for a comfortable chat, as they would have liked, with the grass all sparkling and bristling wet.

Yes, she was quite as wretched as ever, she told him. The week which had gone by since she saw him had in no wise lightened the burden of her discontent. There had even been some additional provocations laid upon her, and she told Montéclin all about them,—about the keys, for instance, which in a fit of temper she had returned to Félicité's keeping; and she told how Cazeau had brought them back to her as if they were something she had accidentally lost, and he had recovered; and how he had said, in that aggravating tone of his, that it was not the custom on Cane river for the negro servants to carry the keys, when there was a mistress at the head of the household.

But Athénaïse could not tell Montéclin anything to increase the disrespect which he already entertained for his brother-in-law; and it was then he unfolded to her a plan which he had conceived and worked out for her deliverance from this galling matrimonial yoke.

It was not a plan which met with instant favor, which she was at once ready to accept, for it involved secrecy and dissimulation, hateful alternatives, both of them. But she was filled with admiration for Montéclin's resources and wonderful talent for contrivance. She accepted the plan; not with the immediate determination to act upon it, rather with the intention to sleep and to dream upon it.

Three days later she wrote to Montéclin that she had abandoned herself to his counsel. Displeasing as it might be to her sense of honesty, it would yet be less trying than to live on with a soul full of bitterness and revolt, as she had done for the past two months.

V

When Cazeau awoke, one morning at his usual very early hour, it was to find the place at his side vacant. This did not surprise him until he discovered that Athénaïse was not in the adjoining room, where he had often found her sleeping in the morning on the lounge. She had perhaps gone out for an early stroll, he reflected, for her jacket and hat were not on the rack where she had hung them the night before. But there were other things absent,—a gown or two from the armoire; and there was a great gap in the piles of lingerie on the shelf; and her traveling-bag was missing, and so were her bits of jewelry from the toilet tray—and Athénaïse was gone!

But the absurdity of going during the night, as if she had been a prisoner, and he the keeper of a dungeon! So much secrecy and mystery, to go sojourning out on the Bon Dieu! Well, the Michés might keep their daughter after this. For the companionship of no woman on earth would he again undergo the humiliating sensation of baseness that had overtaken him in passing the old oak-tree in the fallow meadow.

But a terrible sense of loss overwhelmed Cazeau. It was not new or sudden; he had felt it for weeks growing upon him, and it seemed to culminate with Athénaïse's flight from home. He knew that he could again compel her return as he had done once before,—compel her to return to the shelter of his roof, compel her cold and unwilling submission to his love and passionate transports; but the loss of self-respect seemed to him too dear a price to pay for a wife.

He could not comprehend why she had seemed to prefer him above others; why she had attracted him with eyes, with voice, with a hundred womanly ways, and finally distracted him with love which she seemed, in her timid, maidenly fashion, to return. The great sense of loss came from the realization of having missed a chance for happiness,—a chance that would come his way again only through a miracle. He could not think of himself loving any other woman, and could not think of Athénaïse ever—even at some remote date—caring for him.

He wrote her a letter, in which he disclaimed any further intention of forcing his commands upon her. He did not desire her presence ever again in his home unless she came of her free will, uninfluenced by family or friends; unless she could be the companion he had hoped for in marrying her, and in some measure return affection and respect for the love which he continued and would always continue to feel for her. This letter he sent out to the rigolet by a messenger early in the day. But she was not out on the rigolet, and had not been there.

The family turned instinctively to Montéclin, and almost literally fell upon him for an explanation; he had been absent from home all night. There was much mystification in his answers, and a plain desire to mislead in his assurances of ignorance and innocence.

But with Cazeau there was no doubt or speculation when he accosted the young fellow. "Montéclin, w'at have you done with Athénaïse?" he questioned bluntly. They had met in the open road on horseback, just as Cazeau ascended the river bank before his house.

"W'at have you done to Athénaïse?" returned Montéclin for answer.

"I don't reckon you've considered yo' conduct by any light of decency an' propriety in encouraging yo' sister to such an action, but let me tell you"—

"Voyons!⁹ you can let me alone with yo' decency an' morality an' fiddlesticks. I know you mus' 'a' done Athénaïse pretty mean that she can't live with you; an' fo' my part, I'm mighty durn glad she had the spirit to quit you."

"I ain't in the humor to take any notice of yo' impertinence, Montéclin; but let me remine you that Athénaïse is nothing but a chile in character; besides that, she's my wife, an' I hole you responsible fo' her safety an' welfare. If any harm of any description happens to her, I'll strangle you, by God, like a rat, and fling you in Cane river, if I have to hang fo' it!" He had not lifted his voice. The only sign of anger was a savage gleam in his eyes.

"I reckon you better keep yo' big talk fo' the women, Cazeau," replied Montéclin, riding away.

But he went doubly armed after that, and intimated that the pre-caution was not needless, in view of the threats and menaces that were abroad touching his personal safety.

VI

Athénaïse reached her destination sound of skin and limb, but a good deal flustered, a little frightened, and altogether excited and interested by her unusual experiences.

Her destination was the house of Sylvie, on Dauphine Street, in New Orleans,—a three-story gray brick, standing directly on the banquette, with three broad stone steps leading to the deep front entrance. From the second-story balcony swung a small sign, con-veying to passers-by the intelligence that within were "*chambres garnies.*"[10]

It was one morning in the last week of April that Athénaïse pre-sented herself at the Dauphine Street house. Sylvie was expecting her, and introduced her at once to her apartment, which was in the second story of the back ell, and accessible by an open, outside gallery. There was a yard below, paved with broad stone flagging; many fragrant flowering shrubs and plants grew in a bed along the side of the opposite wall, and others were distributed about in tubs and green boxes.

It was a plain but large enough room into which Athénaïse was ushered, with matting on the floor, green shades and Nottingham-lace curtains at the windows that looked out on the gallery, and fur-nished with a cheap walnut suit. But everything looked exquisitely clean, and the whole place smelled of cleanliness.

Athénaïse at once fell into the rocking-chair, with the air of ex-haustion and intense relief of one who has come to the end of her troubles. Sylvie, entering behind her, laid the big traveling-bag on the floor and deposited the jacket on the bed.

She was a portly quadroon of fifty or there-about, clad in an am-ple *volante*[11] of the old-fashioned purple calico so much affected by her class. She wore large golden hoop-earrings, and her hair was combed plainly, with every appearance of effort to smooth out the kinks. She had broad, coarse features, with a nose that turned up, exposing the wide nostrils, and that seemed to emphasize the lofti-

ness and command of her bearing,—a dignity that in the presence of
white people assumed a character of respectfulness, but never of ob-
sequiousness. Sylvie believed firmly in maintaining the color line,
and would not suffer a white person, even a child, to call her
"Madame Sylvie,"—a title which she exacted religiously, however,
from those of her own race.

"I hope you be please' wid yo' room, madame," she observed
amiably. "Dat's de same room w'at yo' brother, M'sieur Miché, all
time like w'en he come to New Orlean'. He well, M'sieur Miché? I
receive' his letter las' week, an' dat same day a gent'man want I give
'im dat room. I say, 'No, dat room already ingage'.' Ev-body like
dat room on 'count it so quite (quiet). M'sieur Gouvernail, dere in
nax' room, you can't pay 'im! He been stay t'ree year' in dat room;
but all fix' up fine wid his own furn'ture an' books, 'tel you can't
see! I say to 'im plenty time', 'M'sieur Gouvernail, w'y you don't
take dat t'ree-story front, now, long it's empty?' He tells me, 'Leave
me 'lone, Sylvie; I know a good room w'en I fine it, me.' "

She had been moving slowly and majestically about the apartment, straightening and smoothing down bed and pillows, peering
into ewer and basin, evidently casting an eye around to make sure
that everything was as it should be.

"I sen' you some fresh water, madame," she offered upon retiring from the room. "An' w'en you want an't'ing, you jus' go out on
de gall'ry an' call Pousette: she year you plain,—she right down
dere in de kitchen."

Athénaïse was really not so exhausted as she had every reason to
be after that interminable and circuitous way by which Montéclin
had seen fit to have her conveyed to the city.

Would she ever forget that dark and truly dangerous midnight
ride along the "coast" to the mouth of Cane river! There Montéclin
had parted with her, after seeing her aboard the St. Louis and
Shreveport packet which he knew would pass there before dawn.
She had received instructions to disembark at the mouth of Red
river, and there transfer to the first south-bound steamer for New
Orleans; all of which instructions she had followed implicitly, even
to making her way at once to Sylvie's upon her arrival in the city.
Montéclin had enjoined secrecy and much caution; the clandestine
nature of the affair gave it a savor of adventure which was highly

pleasing to him. Eloping with his sister was only a little less engaging than eloping with some one else's sister.

But Montéclin did not do the *grand seigneur*[12] by halves. He had paid Sylvie a whole month in advance for Athénaïse's board and lodging. Part of the sum he had been forced to borrow, it is true, but he was not niggardly.

Athénaïse was to take her meals in the house, which none of the other lodgers did; the one exception being that Mr. Gouvernail was served with breakfast on Sunday mornings.

Sylvie's clientèle came chiefly from the southern parishes; for the most part, people spending but a few days in the city. She prided herself upon the quality and highly respectable character of her patrons, who came and went unobtrusively.

The large parlor opening upon the front balcony was seldom used. Her guests were permitted to entertain in this sanctuary of elegance,—but they never did. She often rented it for the night to parties of respectable and discreet gentlemen desiring to enjoy a quiet game of cards outside the bosom of their families. The second-story hall also led by a long window out on the balcony. And Sylvie advised Athénaïse, when she grew weary of her back room, to go and sit on the front balcony, which was shady in the afternoon, and where she might find diversion in the sounds and sights of the street below.

Athénaïse refreshed herself with a bath, and was soon unpacking her few belongings, which she ranged neatly away in the bureau drawers and the armoire.

She had revolved certain plans in her mind during the past hour or so. Her present intention was to live on indefinitely in this big, cool, clean back room on Dauphine street. She had thought seriously, for moments, of the convent, with all readiness to embrace the vows of poverty and chastity; but what about obedience? Later, she intended, in some round-about way, to give her parents and her husband the assurance of her safety and welfare; reserving the right to remain unmolested and lost to them. To live on at the expense of Montéclin's generosity was wholly out of the question, and Athénaïse meant to look about for some suitable and agreeable employment.

The imperative thing to be done at present, however, was to go out in search of material for an inexpensive gown or two; for she found herself in the painful predicament of a young woman having almost literally nothing to wear. She decided upon pure white for one, and some sort of a sprigged muslin for the other.

VII

On Sunday morning, two days after Athénaïse's arrival in the city, she went in to breakfast somewhat later than usual, to find two covers laid at table instead of the one to which she was accustomed. She had been to mass, and did not remove her hat, but put her fan, parasol, and prayer-book aside. The dining-room was situated just beneath her own apartment, and, like all rooms of the house, was large and airy; the floor was covered with a glistening oil-cloth.

The small, round table, immaculately set, was drawn near the open window. There were some tall plants in boxes on the gallery outside; and Pousette, a little, old, intensely black woman, was splashing and dashing buckets of water on the flagging, and talking loud in her Creole patois to no one in particular.

A dish piled with delicate river-shrimps and crushed ice was on the table; a caraffe of crystal-clear water, a few *hors d'œuvres*,[13] beside a small golden-brown crusty loaf of French bread at each plate. A half-bottle of wine and the morning paper were set at the place opposite Athénaïse.

She had almost completed her breakfast when Gouvernail came in and seated himself at table. He felt annoyed at finding his cherished privacy invaded. Sylvie was removing the remains of a mutton-chop from before Athénaïse, and serving her with a cup of café au lait.

"M'sieur Gouvernail," offered Sylvie in her most insinuating and impressive manner, "you please leave me make you acquaint' wid Madame Cazeau. Dat's M'sieur Miché's sister; you meet 'im two t'ree time', you rec'lec', an' been one day to de race wid 'im. Madame Cazeau, you please leave me make you acquaint' wid M'sieur Gouvernail."

Gouvernail expressed himself greatly pleased to meet the sister of Monsieur Miché, of whom he had not the slightest recollection. He inquired after Monsieur Miché's health, and politely offered

Athénaïse a part of his newspaper,—the part which contained the Woman's Page and the social gossip.

Athénaïse faintly remembered that Sylvie had spoken of a Monsieur Gouvernail occupying the room adjoining hers, living amid luxurious surroundings and a multitude of books. She had not thought of him further than to picture him a stout, middle-aged gentleman, with a bushy beard turning gray, wearing large gold-rimmed spectacles, and stooping somewhat from much bending over books and writing material. She had confused him in her mind with the likeness of some literary celebrity that she had run across in the advertising pages of a magazine.

Gouvernail's appearance was, in truth, in no sense striking. He looked older than thirty and younger than forty, was of medium height and weight, with a quiet, unobtrusive manner which seemed to ask that he be let alone. His hair was light brown, brushed carefully and parted in the middle. His mustache was brown, and so were his eyes, which had a mild, penetrating quality. He was neatly dressed in the fashion of the day; and his hands seemed to Athénaïse remarkably white and soft for a man's.

He had been buried in the contents of his newspaper, when he suddenly realized that some further little attention might be due to Miché's sister. He started to offer her a glass of wine, when he was surprised and relieved to find that she had quietly slipped away while he was absorbed in his own editorial on Corrupt Legislation.

Gouvernail finished his paper and smoked his cigar out on the gallery. He lounged about, gathered a rose for his buttonhole, and had his regular Sunday-morning confab with Pousette, to whom he paid a weekly stipend for brushing his shoes and clothing. He made a great pretense of haggling over the transaction, only to enjoy her uneasiness and garrulous excitement.

He worked or read in his room for a few hours, and when he quitted the house, at three in the afternoon, it was to return no more till late at night. It was his almost invariable custom to spend Sunday evenings out in the American quarter, among a congenial set of men and women,—*des esprits forts*,[14] all of them, whose lives were irreproachable, yet whose opinions would startle even the traditional "sapeur,"[15] for whom "nothing is sacred." But for all his "advanced" opinions, Gouvernail was a liberal-minded fellow; a man or woman lost nothing of his respect by being married.

When he left the house in the afternoon, Athénaïse had already ensconced herself on the front balcony. He could see her through the jalousies when he passed on his way to the front entrance. She had not yet grown lonesome or homesick; the newness of her surroundings made them sufficiently entertaining. She found it diverting to sit there on the front balcony watching people pass by, even though there was no one to talk to. And then the comforting, comfortable sense of not being married!

She watched Gouvernail walk down the street, and could find no fault with his bearing. He could hear the sound of her rockers for some little distance. He wondered what the "poor little thing" was doing in the city, and meant to ask Sylvie about her when he should happen to think of it.

VIII

The following morning, towards noon, when Gouvernail quitted his room, he was confronted by Athénaïse, exhibiting some confusion and trepidation at being forced to request a favor of him at so early a stage of their acquaintance. She stood in her doorway, and had evidently been sewing, as the thimble on her finger testified, as well as a long-threaded needle thrust in the bosom of her gown. She held a stamped but unaddressed letter in her hand.

And would Mr. Gouvernail be so kind as to address the letter to her brother, Mr. Montéclin Miché? She would hate to detain him with explanations this morning,—another time, perhaps,—but now she begged that he would give himself the trouble.

He assured her that it made no difference, that it was no trouble whatever; and he drew a fountain pen from his pocket and addressed the letter at her dictation, resting it on the inverted rim of his straw hat. She wondered a little at a man of his supposed erudition stumbling over the spelling of "Montéclin" and "Miché."

She demurred at overwhelming him with the additional trouble of posting it, but he succeeded in convincing her that so simple a task as the posting of a letter would not add an iota to the burden of the day. Moreover, he promised to carry it in his hand, and thus avoid any possible risk of forgetting it in his pocket.

After that, and after a second repetition of the favor, when she had told him that she had had a letter from Montéclin, and looked as if she wanted to tell him more, he felt that he knew her better. He felt that he knew her well enough to join her out on the balcony, one night, when he found her sitting there alone. He was not one who deliberately sought the society of women, but he was not wholly a bear. A little commiseration for Athénaïse's aloneness, perhaps some curiosity to know further what manner of woman she was, and the natural influence of her feminine charm were equal unconfessed factors in turning his steps towards the balcony when he discovered the shimmer of her white gown through the open hall window.

It was already quite late, but the day had been intensely hot, and neighboring balconies and doorways were occupied by chattering groups of humanity, loath to abandon the grateful freshness of the outer air. The voices about her served to reveal to Athénaïse the feeling of loneliness that was gradually coming over her. Notwithstanding certain dormant impulses, she craved human sympathy and companionship.

She shook hands impulsively with Gouvernail, and told him how glad she was to see him. He was not prepared for such an admission, but it pleased him immensely, detecting as he did that the expression was as sincere as it was outspoken. He drew a chair up within comfortable conversational distance of Athénaïse, though he had no intention of talking more than was barely necessary to encourage Madame—He had actually forgotten her name!

He leaned an elbow on the balcony rail, and would have offered an opening remark about the oppressive heat of the day, but Athénaïse did not give him the opportunity. How glad she was to talk to some one, and how she talked!

An hour later she had gone to her room, and Gouvernail stayed smoking on the balcony. He knew her quite well after that hour's talk. It was not so much what she had said as what her half saying had revealed to his quick intelligence. He knew that she adored Montéclin, and he suspected that she adored Cazeau without being herself aware of it. He had gathered that she was self-willed, impulsive, innocent, ignorant, unsatisfied, dissatisfied; for had she not complained that things seemed all wrongly arranged in this world, and no one was permitted to be happy in his own way? And he told her he was sorry she had discovered that primordial fact of existence so early in life.

He commiserated her loneliness, and scanned his bookshelves next morning for something to lend her to read, rejecting everything that offered itself to his view. Philosophy was out of the question, and so was poetry; that is, such poetry as he possessed. He had not sounded her literary tastes, and strongly suspected she had none; that she would have rejected The Duchess[16] as readily as Mrs. Humphry Ward.[17] He compromised on a magazine.

It had entertained her passably, she admitted, upon returning it. A New England story had puzzled her, it was true, and a Creole tale had offended her, but the pictures had pleased her greatly, especially one which had reminded her so strongly of Montéclin after a hard day's ride that she was loath to give it up. It was one of Remington's Cowboys,[18] and Gouvernail insisted upon her keeping it,—keeping the magazine.

He spoke to her daily after that, and was always eager to render her some service or to do something towards her entertainment.

One afternoon he took her out to the lake end. She had been there once, some years before, but in winter, so the trip was comparatively new and strange to her. The large expanse of water studded with pleasure-boats, the sight of children playing merrily along the grassy palisades, the music, all enchanted her. Gouvernail thought her the most beautiful woman he had ever seen. Even her gown—the sprigged muslin—appeared to him the most charming one imaginable. Nor could anything be more becoming than the arrangement of her brown hair under the white sailor hat, all rolled back in a soft puff from her radiant face. And she carried her parasol and lifted her skirts and used her fan in ways that seemed quite unique and peculiar to herself, and which he considered almost worthy of study and imitation.

They did not dine out there at the water's edge, as they might have done, but returned early to the city to avoid the crowd. Athénaïse wanted to go home, for she said Sylvie would have dinner prepared and would be expecting her. But it was not difficult to persuade her to dine instead in the quiet little restaurant that he knew and liked, with its sanded floor, its secluded atmosphere, its delicious menu, and its obsequious waiter wanting to know what he might have the honor of serving to "monsieur et madame."[19] No wonder he made the mistake, with Gouvernail assuming such an air of proprietorship! But Athénaïse was very tired after it all; the sparkle went out of her face, and she hung draggingly on his arm in walking home.

He was reluctant to part from her when she bade him good-night at her door and thanked him for the agreeable evening. He had hoped she would sit outside until it was time for him to regain the newspaper office. He knew that she would undress and get into her peignoir and lie upon her bed; and what he wanted to do, what he would have given much to do, was to go and sit beside her, read to her something restful, soothe her, do her bidding, whatever it might be. Of course there was no use in thinking of that. But he was surprised at his growing desire to be serving her. She gave him an opportunity sooner than he looked for.

"Mr. Gouvernail," she called from her room, "will you be so kine as to call Pousette an' tell her she fo'got to bring my ice-water?"

He was indignant at Pousette's negligence, and called severely to her over the banisters. He was sitting before his own door, smoking. He knew that Athénaïse had gone to bed, for her room was dark, and she had opened the slats of the door and windows. Her bed was near a window.

Pousette came flopping up with the ice-water, and with a hundred excuses: "Mo pa oua vou à tab c'te lanuite, mo cri vou pé gagni déja là-bas; parole! Vou pas cri conté ça Madame Sylvie?" She had not seen Athénaïse at table, and thought she was gone. She swore to this, and hoped Madame Sylvie would not be informed of her remissness.

A little later Athénaïse lifted her voice again: "Mr. Gouvernail, did you remark that young man sitting on the opposite side from us, coming in, with a gray coat an' a blue ban' aroun' his hat?"

Of course Gouvernail had not noticed any such individual, but he assured Athénaïse that he had observed the young fellow particularly.

"Don't you think he looked something,—not very much, of co'se,—but don't you think he had a little faux-air[20] of Montéclin?"

"I think he looked strikingly like Montéclin," asserted Gouvernail, with the one idea of prolonging the conversation. "I meant to call your attention to the resemblance, and something drove it out of my head."

"The same with me," returned Athénaïse. "Ah, my dear Montéclin! I wonder w'at he is doing now?"

"Did you receive any news, any letter from him to-day?" asked Gouvernail, determined that if the conversation ceased it should not be through lack of effort on his part to sustain it.

"Not to-day, but yesterday. He tells me that maman was so distracted with uneasiness that finally, to pacify her, he was fo'ced to confess that he knew w'ere I was, but that he was boun' by a vow of secrecy not to reveal it. But Cazeau has not noticed him or spoken to him since he threaten' to throw po' Montéclin in Cane river. You know Cazeau wrote me a letter the morning I lef', thinking I had gone to the rigolet. An' maman opened it, an' said it was full of the mos' noble sentiments, an' she wanted Montéclin to sen' it to me; but Montéclin refuse' poin' blank, so he wrote to me."

Gouvernail preferred to talk of Montéclin. He pictured Cazeau as unbearable, and did not like to think of him.

A little later Athénaïse called out, "Good-night, Mr. Gouvernail."

"Good-night," he returned reluctantly. And when he thought that she was sleeping, he got up and went away to the midnight pandemonium of his newspaper office.

IX

Athénaïse could not have held out through the month had it not been for Gouvernail. With the need of caution and secrecy always uppermost in her mind, she made no new acquaintances, and she did not seek out persons already known to her; however, she knew so few, it required little effort to keep out of their way. As for Sylvie, almost every moment of her time was occupied in looking after her house; and, moreover, her deferential attitude towards her lodgers forbade anything like the gossipy chats in which Athénaïse might have condescended sometimes to indulge with her land-lady. The transient lodgers, who came and went, she never had occasion to meet. Hence she was entirely dependent upon Gouvernail for company.

He appreciated the situation fully; and every moment that he could spare from his work he devoted to her entertainment. She liked to be out of doors, and they strolled together in the summer twilight through the mazes of the old French quarter. They went again to the lake end, and stayed for hours on the water; returning so late that the streets through which they passed were silent and deserted. On Sunday morning he arose at an unconscionable hour to take her to the French market, knowing that the sights and sounds there would interest her. And he did not join the intellectual coterie in the afternoon, as he usually did, but placed himself all day at the disposition and service of Athénaïse.

Notwithstanding all, his manner toward her was tactful, and evinced intelligence and a deep knowledge of her character, surprising upon so brief an acquaintance. For the time he was everything to her that she would have him; he replaced home and friends. Sometimes she wondered if he had ever loved a woman. She could not fancy him loving any one passionately, rudely, offensively, as Cazeau loved her. Once she was so naïve as to ask him outright if he had ever been in love, and he assured her promptly that he had not. She thought it an admirable trait in his character, and esteemed him greatly therefor.

He found her crying one night, not openly or violently. She was leaning over the gallery rail, watching the toads that hopped about in the moonlight, down on the damp flagstones of the courtyard. There was an oppressively sweet odor rising from the cape jessamine. Pousette was down there, mumbling and quarreling with some one, and seeming to be having it all her own way,—as well she might, when her companion was only a black cat that had come in from a neighboring yard to keep her company.

Athénaïse did admit feeling heart-sick, body-sick, when he questioned her; she supposed it was nothing but homesick. A letter from Montéclin had stirred her all up. She longed for her mother, for Montéclin; she was sick for a sight of the cotton-fields, the scent of the ploughed earth, for the dim, mysterious charm of the woods, and the old tumble-down home on the Bon Dieu.

As Gouvernail listened to her, a wave of pity and tenderness swept through him. He took her hands and pressed them against him. He wondered what would happen if he were to put his arms around her.

He was hardly prepared for what happened, but he stood it courageously. She twined her arms around his neck and wept outright on his shoulder; the hot tears scalding his cheek and neck, and her whole body shaken in his arms. The impulse was powerful to strain her to him; the temptation was fierce to seek her lips; but he did neither.

He understood a thousand times better than she herself understood it that he was acting as substitute for Montéclin. Bitter as the conviction was, he accepted it. He was patient; he could wait. He hoped some day to hold her with a lover's arms. That she was married made no particle of difference to Gouvernail. He could not conceive or dream of it making a difference. When the time came that she wanted him,—as he hoped and believed it would come,— he felt he would have a right to her. So long as she did not want him, he had no right to her,—no more than her husband had. It was very hard to feel her warm breath and tears upon his cheek, and her struggling bosom pressed against him and her soft arms clinging to him and his whole body and soul aching for her, and yet to make no sign.

He tried to think what Montéclin would have said and done, and to act accordingly. He stroked her hair, and held her in a gentle embrace, until the tears dried and the sobs ended. Before releasing herself she kissed him against the neck; she had to love somebody in her own way! Even that he endured like a stoic. But it was well he left her, to plunge into the thick of rapid, breathless, exacting work till nearly dawn.

Athénaïse was greatly soothed, and slept well. The touch of friendly hands and caressing arms had been very grateful. Henceforward she would not be lonely and unhappy, with Gouvernail there to comfort her.

X

The fourth week of Athénaïse's stay in the city was drawing to a close. Keeping in view the intention which she had of finding some suitable and agreeable employment, she had made a few tentatives in that direction. But with the exception of two little girls who had promised to take piano lessons at a price that would be embarrassing to mention, these attempts had been fruitless. Morever, the homesickness kept coming back, and Gouvernail was not always there to drive it away.

She spent much of her time weeding and pottering among the flowers down in the courtyard. She tried to take an interest in the black cat, and a mockingbird that hung in a cage outside the kitchen door, and a disreputable parrot that belonged to the cook next door, and swore hoarsely all day long in bad French.

Beside, she was not well; she was not herself, as she told Sylvie. The climate of New Orleans did not agree with her. Sylvie was distressed to learn this, as she felt in some measure responsible for the health and well-being of Monsieur Miché's sister; and she made it her duty to inquire closely into the nature and character of Athénaïse's malaise.

Sylvie was very wise, and Athénaïse was very ignorant. The extent of her ignorance and the depth of her subsequent enlightenment were bewildering. She stayed a long, long time quite still, quite stunned, after her interview with Sylvie, except for the short, uneven breathing that ruffled her bosom. Her whole being was steeped in a wave of ecstasy. When she finally arose from the chair in which she had been seated, and looked at herself in the mirror, a face met hers which she seemed to see for the first time, so transfigured was it with wonder and rapture.

One mood quickly followed another, in this new turmoil of her senses, and the need of action became uppermost. Her mother must know at once, and her mother must tell Montéclin. And Cazeau must know. As she thought of him, the first purely sensuous tremor of her life swept over her. She half whispered his name, and the sound of it brought red blotches into her cheeks. She spoke it over and over, as if it were some new, sweet sound born out of darkness and confusion, and reaching her for the first time. She was impatient to be with him. Her whole passionate nature was aroused as if by a miracle.

She seated herself to write to her husband. The letter he would get in the morning, and she would be with him at night. What would he say? How would he act? She knew that he would forgive her, for had he not written a letter?—and a pang of resentment toward Montéclin shot through her. What did he mean by withholding that letter? How dared he not have sent it?

Athénaïse attired herself for the street, and went out to post the letter which she had penned with a single thought, a spontaneous impulse. It would have seemed incoherent to most people, but Cazeau would understand.

She walked along the street as if she had fallen heir to some magnificent inheritance. On her face was a look of pride and satisfaction that passers-by noticed and admired. She wanted to talk to some one, to tell some person; and she stopped at the corner and told the oyster-woman, who was Irish, and who God-blessed her, and wished prosperity to the race of Cazeaus for generations to come. She held the oyster-woman's fat, dirty little baby in her arms and scanned it curiously and observingly, as if a baby were a phenomenon that she encountered for the first time in life. She even kissed it!

Then what a relief it was to Athénaïse to walk the streets without dread of being seen and recognized by some chance acquaintance from Red river! No one could have said now that she did not know her own mind.

She went directly from the oyster-woman's to the office of Harding & Offdean, her husband's merchants; and it was with such an air of partnership, almost proprietorship, that she demanded a sum of money on her husband's account, they gave it to her as unhesitatingly as they would have handed it over to Cazeau himself. When Mr. Harding, who knew her, asked politely after her health, she turned so rosy and looked so conscious, he thought it a great pity for so pretty a woman to be such a little goose.

Athénaïse entered a dry-goods store and bought all manner of things,—little presents for nearly everybody she knew. She bought whole bolts of sheerest, softest, downiest white stuff; and when the clerk, in trying to meet her wishes, asked if she intended it for infant's use, she could have sunk through the floor, and wondered how he might have suspected it.

As it was Montéclin who had taken her away from her husband, she wanted it to be Montéclin who should take her back to him. So she wrote him a very curt note,—in fact it was a postal card,—asking that he meet her at the train on the evening following. She felt convinced that after what had gone before, Cazeau would await her at their own home; and she preferred it so.

Then there was the agreeable excitement of getting ready to

leave, of packing up her things. Pousette kept coming and going, coming and going; and each time that she quitted the room it was with something that Athénaïse had given her,—a handkerchief, a petticoat, a pair of stockings with two tiny holes at the toes, some broken prayer-beads, and finally a silver dollar.

Next it was Sylvie who came along bearing a gift of what she called "a set of pattern',"—things of complicated design which never could have been obtained in any new-fangled bazaar or pattern-store, that Sylvie had acquired of a foreign lady of distinction whom she had nursed years before at the St. Charles hotel. Athénaïse accepted and handled them with reverence, fully sensible of the great compliment and favor, and laid them religiously away in the trunk which she had lately acquired.

She was greatly fatigued after the day of unusual exertion, and went early to bed and to sleep. All day long she had not once thought of Gouvernail, and only did think of him when aroused for a brief instant by the sound of his foot-falls on the gallery, as he passed in going to his room. He had hoped to find her up, waiting for him.

But the next morning he knew. Some one must have told him. There was no subject known to her which Sylvie hesitated to discuss in detail with any man of suitable years and discretion.

Athénaïse found Gouvernail waiting with a carriage to convey her to the railway station. A momentary pang visited her for having forgotten him so completely, when he said to her, "Sylvie tells me you are going away this morning."

He was kind, attentive, and amiable, as usual, but respected to the utmost the new dignity and reserve that her manner had developed since yesterday. She kept looking from the carriage window, silent, and embarrassed as Eve after losing her ignorance. He talked of the muddy streets and the murky morning, and of Montéclin. He hoped she would find everything comfortable and pleasant in the country, and trusted she would inform him whenever she came to visit the city again. He talked as if afraid or mistrustful of silence and himself.

At the station she handed him her purse, and he bought her ticket, secured for her a comfortable section, checked her trunk, and got all the bundles and things safely aboard the train. She felt very grateful. He pressed her hand warmly, lifted his hat, and left her. He was a man of intelligence, and took defeat gracefully; that was all. But as he made his way back to the carriage, he was thinking, "By heaven, it hurts, it hurts!"

XI

Athénaïse spent a day of supreme happiness and expectancy. The fair sight of the country unfolding itself before her was balm to her vision and to her soul. She was charmed with the rather unfamiliar, broad, clean sweep of the sugar plantations, with their monster sugar-houses, their rows of neat cabins like little villages of a single street, and their impressive homes standing apart amid clusters of trees. There were sudden glimpses of a bayou curling between sunny, grassy banks, or creeping sluggishly out from a tangled growth of wood, and brush, and fern, and poison-vines, and palmettos. And passing through the long stretches of monotonous woodlands, she would close her eyes and taste in anticipation the moment of her meeting with Cazeau. She could think of nothing but him.

It was night when she reached her station. There was Montéclin, as she had expected, waiting for her with a two-seated buggy, to which he had hitched his own swift-footed, spirited pony. It was good, he felt, to have her back on any terms; and he had no fault to find since she came of her own choice. He more than suspected the cause of her coming; her eyes and her voice and her foolish little manner went far in revealing the secret that was brimming over in her heart. But after he had deposited her at her own gate, and as he continued his way toward the rigolet, he could not help feeling that the affair had taken a very disappointing, an ordinary, a most commonplace turn, after all. He left her in Cazeau's keeping.

Her husband lifted her out of the buggy, and neither said a word until they stood together within the shelter of the gallery. Even then they did not speak at first. But Athénaïse turned to him with an appealing gesture. As he clasped her in his arms, he felt the yielding of her whole body against him. He felt her lips for the first time respond to the passion of his own.

The country night was dark and warm and still, save for the distant notes of an accordion which some one was playing in a cabin away off. A little negro baby was crying somewhere. As Athénaïse withdrew from her husband's embrace, the sound arrested her.

"Listen, Cazeau! How Juliette's baby is crying! Pauvre ti chou,[21] I wonder w'at is the matter with it?"

After the Winter

TRÉZINIE, the blacksmith's daughter, stepped out upon the gallery just as M'sieur Michel passed by. He did not notice the girl but walked straight on down the village street.

His seven hounds skulked, as usual, about him. At his side hung his powder-horn, and on his shoulder a gunny-bag slackly filled with game that he carried to the store. A broad felt hat shaded his bearded face and in his hand he carelessly swung his old-fashioned rifle. It was doubtless the same with which he had slain so many people, Trézinie shudderingly reflected. For Cami, the cobbler's son—who must have known—had often related to her how this man had killed two Choctaws, as many Texans, a free mulatto and numberless blacks, in that vague locality known as "the hills."

Older people who knew better took little trouble to correct this ghastly record that a younger generation had scored against him. They themselves had come to half-believe that M'sieur Michel might be capable of anything, living as he had, for so many years, apart from humanity, alone with his hounds in a kennel of a cabin on the hill. The time seemed to most of them fainter than a memory when, a lusty young fellow of twenty-five, he had cultivated his strip of land across the lane from Les Chêniers;[1] when home and toil and wife and child were so many benedictions that he humbly thanked heaven for having given him.

But in the early '60's he went with his friend Duplan and the rest of the "Louisiana Tigers." He came back with some of them. He came to find—well, death may lurk in a peaceful valley lying in wait to ensnare the toddling feet of little ones. Then, there are women—

there are wives with thoughts that roam and grow wanton with roaming; women whose pulses are stirred by strange voices and eyes that woo; women who forget the claims of yesterday, the hopes of to-morrow, in the impetuous clutch of to-day.

But that was no reason, some people thought, why he should have cursed men who found their blessings where they had left them—cursed God, who had abandoned him.

Persons who met him upon the road had long ago stopped greeting him. What was the use? He never answered them; he spoke to no one; he never so much as looked into men's faces. When he bartered his game and fish at the village store for powder and shot and such scant food as he needed, he did so with few words and less courtesy. Yet feeble as it was, this was the only link that held him to his fellow-beings.

Strange to say, the sight of M'sieur Michel, though more forbidding than ever that delightful spring afternoon, was so suggestive to Trézinie as to be almost an inspiration.

It was Easter eve and the early part of April. The whole earth seemed teeming with new, green, vigorous life everywhere—except the arid spot that immediately surrounded Trézinie. It was no use; she had tried. Nothing would grow among those cinders that filled the yard; in that atmosphere of smoke and flame that was constantly belching from the forge where her father worked at his trade. There were wagon wheels, bolts and bars of iron, plowshares and all manner of unpleasant-looking things littering the bleak, black yard; nothing green anywhere except a few weeds that would force themselves into fence corners. And Trézinie knew that flowers belong to Easter time, just as dyed eggs do. She had plenty of eggs; no one had more or prettier ones; she was not going to grumble about that. But she did feel distressed because she had not a flower to help deck the altar on Easter morning. And every one else seemed to have them in such abundance! There was 'Dame Suzanne among her roses across the way. She must have clipped a hundred since noon. An hour ago Trézinie had seen the carriage from Les Chêniers pass by on its way to church with Mamzelle Euphrasie's pretty head looking like a picture enframed with the Easter lilies that filled the vehicle.

For the twentieth time Trézinie walked out upon the gallery. She saw M'sieur Michel and thought of the pine hill. When she thought of the hill she thought of the flowers that grew there—free as sunshine. The girl gave a joyous spring that changed to a farandole as her feet twinkled across the rough, loose boards of the gallery.

"Hé, Cami!" she cried, clapping her hands together.

Cami rose from the bench where he sat pegging away at the clumsy sole of a shoe, and came lazily to the fence that divided his abode from Trézinie's.

"Well, w'at?" he inquired with heavy amiability. She leaned far over the railing to better communicate with him.

"You'll go with me yonda on the hill to pick flowers fo' Easter, Cami? I'm goin' to take La Fringante² along, too, to he'p with the baskets. W'at you say?"

"No!" was the stolid reply. "I'm boun' to finish them shoe', if it is fo' a nigga."

"Not now," she returned impatiently; "to-morrow mo'nin' at sun-up. An' I tell you, Cami, my flowers'll beat all! Look yonda at 'Dame Suzanne pickin' her roses a'ready. An' Mamzelle Euphrasie she's car'ied her lilies an' gone, her. You tell me all that's goin' be fresh to-moro'!"

"Jus' like you say," agreed the boy, turning to resume his work. "But you want to mine out fo' the ole possum up in the wood. Let M'sieu Michel set eyes on you!" and he raised his arms as if aiming with a gun. "Pim, pam, poum! No mo' Trézinie, no mo' Cami, no mo' La Fringante—all stretch'!"

The possible risk which Cami so vividly foreshadowed but added a zest to Trézinie's projected excursion.

II

It was hardly sun-up on the following morning when the three children—Trézinie, Cami and the little negress, La Fringante—were filling big, flat Indian baskets from the abundance of brilliant flowers that studded the hill.

In their eagerness they had ascended the slope and penetrated deep into the forest without thought of M'sieur Michel or of his abode. Suddenly, in the dense wood, they came upon his hut—low, forbidding, seeming to scowl rebuke upon them for their intrusion.

La Fringante dropped her basket, and, with a cry, fled. Cami looked as if he wanted to do the same. But Trézinie, after the first tremor, saw that the ogre himself was away. The wooden shutter of the one window was closed. The door, so low that even a small man must have stooped to enter it, was secured with a chain. Absolute silence reigned, except for the whirr of wings in the air, the fitful notes of a bird in the treetop.

"Can't you see it's nobody there!" cried Trézinie impatiently.

La Fringante, distracted between curiosity and terror, had crept cautiously back again. Then they all peeped through the wide chinks between the logs of which the cabin was built.

M'sieur Michel had evidently begun the construction of his house by felling a huge tree, whose remaining stump stood in the centre of the hut, and served him as a table. This primitive table was worn smooth by twenty-five years of use. Upon it were such humble utensils as the man required. Everything within the hovel, the sleeping bunk, the one seat, were as rude as a savage would have fashioned them.

The stolid Cami could have stayed for hours with his eyes fastened to the aperture, morbidly seeking some dead, mute sign of that awful pastime with which he believed M'sieur Michel was accustomed to beguile his solitude. But Trézinie was wholly possessed by the thought of her Easter offerings. She wanted flowers and flowers, fresh with the earth and crisp with dew.

When the three youngsters scampered down the hill again there was not a purple verbena left about M'sieur Michel's hut; not a May apple blossom, not a stalk of crimson phlox—hardly a violet.

He was something of a savage, feeling that the solitude belonged to him. Of late there had been forming within his soul a sentiment toward man, keener than indifference, bitter as hate. He was coming to dread even that brief intercourse with others into which his traffic forced him.

So when M'sieur Michel returned to his hut, and with his quick, accustomed eye saw that his woods had been despoiled, rage seized him. It was not that he loved the flowers that were gone more than he loved the stars, or the wind that trailed across the hill, but they belonged to and were a part of that life which he had made for himself, and which he wanted to live alone and unmolested.

Did not those flowers help him to keep his record of time that was passing? They had no right to vanish until the hot May days were upon him. How else should he know? Why had these people, with whom he had nothing in common, intruded upon his privacy and violated it? What would they not rob him of next?

He knew well enough it was Easter; he had heard and seen signs yesterday in the store that told him so. And he guessed that his woods had been rifled to add to the mummery of the day.

M'sieur Michel sat himself moodily down beside his table—centuries old—and brooded. He did not even notice his hounds that were pleading to be fed. As he revolved in his mind the event of the morning—innocent as it was in itself—it grew in importance and assumed a significance not at first apparent. He could not remain passive under pressure of its disturbance. He rose to his feet, every impulse aggressive, urging him to activity. He would go down among those people all gathered together, blacks and whites, and face them for once and all. He did not know what he would say to them, but it would be defiance—something to voice the hate that oppressed him.

The way down the hill, then across a piece of flat, swampy woodland and through the lane to the village was so familiar that it required no attention from him to follow it. His thoughts were left free to revel in the humor that had driven him from his kennel.

As he walked down the village street he saw plainly that the place was deserted save for the appearance of an occasional negress, who seemed occupied with preparing the midday meal. But about the church scores of horses were fastened; and M'sieur Michel could see that the edifice was thronged to the very threshold.

He did not once hesitate, but obeying the force that impelled him to face the people wherever they might be, he was soon standing with the crowd within the entrance of the church. His broad, robust shoulders had forced space for himself, and his leonine head stood higher than any there.

"Take off yo' hat!"

It was an indignant mulatto who addressed him. M'sieur Michel instinctively did as he was bidden. He saw confusedly that there was a mass of humanity close to him, whose contact and atmosphere affected him strangely. He saw his wild-flowers, too. He saw them plainly, in bunches and festoons, among the Easter lilies and roses and geraniums. He was going to speak out, now; he had the right to and he would, just as soon as that clamor overhead would cease.

"Bonté divine![3] M'sieur Michel!" whispered 'Dame Suzanne tragically to her neighbor. Trézinie heard. Cami saw. They exchanged an electric glance, and tremblingly bowed their heads low.

M'sieur Michel looked wrathfully down at the puny mulatto who had ordered him to remove his hat. Why had he obeyed? That initial act of compliance had somehow weakened his will, his resolution. But he would regain firmness just as soon as that clamor above gave him chance to speak.

It was the organ filling the small edifice with volumes of sound. It was the voices of men and women mingling in the "Gloria in excelsis Deo!"

The words bore no meaning for him apart from the old familiar strain which he had known as a child and chanted himself in that same organ-loft years ago. How it went on and on! Would it never cease! It was like a menace; like a voice reaching out from the dead past to taunt him.

"Gloria in excelsis Deo!" over and over! How the deep basso rolled it out! How the tenor and alto caught it up and passed it on to be lifted by the high, flute-like ring of the soprano, till all mingled again in the wild pæan, "Gloria in excelsis!"

How insistent was the refrain! and where, what, was that mysterious, hidden quality in it; the power which was overcoming M'sieur Michel, stirring within him a turmoil that bewildered him?

There was no use in trying to speak, or in wanting to. His throat could not have uttered a sound. He wanted to escape, that was all. "Bonæ voluntatis,"—he bent his head as if before a beating storm. "Gloria! Gloria! Gloria!" He must fly; he must save himself, regain his hill where sights and odors and sounds and saints or devils would cease to molest him. "In excelsis Deo!" He retreated, forcing his way backward to the door. He dragged his hat down over his eyes and staggered away down the road. But the refrain pursued him—"Pax! pax! pax!"—fretting him like a lash. He did not slacken his pace till the tones grew fainter than an echo, floating, dying away in an "in excelsis!" When he could hear it no longer he stopped and breathed a sigh of rest and relief.

III

All day long M'sieur Michel stayed about his hut engaged in some familiar employment that he hoped might efface the unaccountable impressions of the morning. But his restlessness was unbounded. A longing had sprung up within him as sharp as pain and not to be appeased. At once, on this bright, warm Easter morning the voices that till now had filled his solitude became meaningless. He stayed mute and uncomprehending before them. Their significance had vanished before the driving want for human sympathy and companionship that had reawakened in his soul.

When night came on he walked through the woods down the slant of the hill again.

"It mus' be all fill' up with weeds," muttered M'sieur Michel to himself as he went. "Ah, Bon Dieu! with trees, Michel, with trees—in twenty-five years, man."

He had not taken the road to the village, but was pursuing a different one in which his feet had not walked for many days. It led him along the river bank for a distance. The narrow stream, stirred by the restless breeze, gleamed in the moonlight that was flooding the land.

As he went on and on, the scent of the newplowed earth that had been from the first keenly perceptible, began to intoxicate him. He wanted to kneel and bury his face in it. He wanted to dig into it; turn it over. He wanted to scatter the seed again as he had done long ago, and watch the new, green life spring up as if at his bidding.

When he turned away from the river, and had walked a piece down the lane that divided Joe Duplan's plantation from that bit of land that had once been his, he wiped his eyes to drive away the mist that was making him see things as they surely could not be.

He had wanted to plant a hedge that time before he went away, but he had not done so. Yet there was the hedge before him, just as he had meant it to be, and filling the night with fragrance. A broad, low gate divided its length, and over this he leaned and looked before him in amazement. There were no weeds as he had fancied; no trees except the scattered live oaks that he remembered.

Could that row of hardy fig trees, old, squat and gnarled, be the twigs that he himself had set one day into the ground? One raw December day when there was a fine, cold mist falling. The chill of it breathed again upon him; the memory was so real. The land did not look as if it ever had been plowed for a field. It was a smooth, green meadow, with cattle huddled upon the cool sward, or moving with slow, stately tread as they nibbled the tender shoots.

There was the house unchanged, gleaming white in the moon, seeming to invite him beneath its calm shelter. He wondered who dwelt within it now. Whoever it was he would not have them find him, like a prowler, there at the gate. But he would come again and again like this at nighttime, to gaze and refresh his spirit.

A hand had been laid upon M'sieur Michel's shoulder and some one called his name. Startled, he turned to see who accosted him.

"Duplan!"

The two men who had not exchanged speech for so many years stood facing each other for a long moment in silence.

"I knew you would come back some day, Michel. It was a long time to wait, but you have come home at last."

M'sieur Michel cowered instinctively and lifted his hands with expressive deprecatory gesture. "No, no; it's no place for me, Joe; no place!"

"Isn't a man's home a place for him, Michel?" It seemed less a question than an assertion, charged with gentle authority.

"Twenty-five years, Duplan; twenty-five years! It's no use; it's too late."

"You see, I have used it," went on the planter, quietly, ignoring M'sieur Michel's protestations. "Those are my cattle grazing off there. The house has served me many a time to lodge guests or workmen, for whom I had no room at Les Chêniers. I have not exhausted the soil with any crops. I had not the right to do that. Yet am I in your debt, Michel, and ready to settle en bon ami."[4]

The planter had opened the gate and entered the inclosure, leading M'sieur Michel with him. Together they walked toward the house.

Language did not come readily to either—one so unaccustomed

to hold intercourse with men; both so stirred with memories that would have rendered any speech painful. When they had stayed long in a silence which was eloquent of tenderness, Joe Duplan spoke:

"You know how I tried to see you, Michel, to speak with you, and you never would."

M'sieur Michel answered with but a gesture that seemed a supplication.

"Let the past all go, Michel. Begin your new life as if the twenty-five years that are gone had been a long night, from which you have only awakened. Come to me in the morning," he added with quick resolution, "for a horse and a plow." He had taken the key of the house from his pocket and placed it in M'sieur Michel's hand.

"A horse?" M'sieur Michel repeated uncertainly; "a plow! Oh, it's too late, Duplan; too late."

"It isn't too late. The land has rested all these years, man; it's fresh, I tell you; and rich as gold. Your crop will be the finest in the land." He held out his hand and M'sieur Michel pressed it without a word in reply, save a muttered "Mon ami."[5]

Then he stood there watching the planter disappear behind the high, clipped hedge.

He held out his arms. He could not have told if it was toward the retreating figure, or in welcome to an infinite peace that seemed to descend upon him and envelop him.

All the land was radiant except the hill far off that was in black shadow against the sky.

Polydore

IT was often said that Polydore was the stupidest boy to be found "from the mouth of Cane river plumb to Natchitoches." Hence it was an easy matter to persuade him, as meddlesome and mischievous people sometimes tried to do, that he was an overworked and much abused individual.

It occurred one morning to Polydore to wonder what would happen if he did not get up. He hardly expected the world to stop turning on its axis; but he did in a way believe that the machinery of the whole plantation would come to a standstill.

He had awakened at the usual hour,—about daybreak,—and instead of getting up at once, as was his custom, he re-settled himself between the sheets. There he lay, peering out through the dormer window into the gray morning that was deliciously cool after the hot summer night, listening to familiar sounds that came from the barn-yard, the fields and woods beyond, heralding the approach of day.

A little later there were other sounds, no less familiar or significant; the roll of the wagon-wheels; the distant call of a negro's voice; Aunt Siney's shuffling step as she crossed the gallery, bearing to Mamzelle Adélaïde and old Monsieur José their early coffee.

Polydore had formed no plan and had thought only vaguely upon results. He lay in a half-slumber awaiting developments, and philosophically resigned to any turn which the affair might take. Still he was not quite ready with an answer when Jude came and thrust his head in at the door.

"Mista Polydore! O Mista Polydore! You 'sleep?"

"W'at you want?"

"Dan 'low he ain' gwine wait yonda wid de wagon all day. Say

233

does you inspect 'im to pack dat freight f'om de landing by hisse'f?"

"I reckon he got it to do, Jude. I ain' going to get up, me."

"You ain' gwine git up?"

"No; I'm sick. I'm going stay in bed. Go 'long and le' me sleep."

The next one to invade Polydore's privacy was Mamzelle Adélaïde herself. It was no small effort for her to mount the steep, narrow stairway to Polydore's room. She seldom penetrated to these regions under the roof. He could hear the stairs creak beneath her weight, and knew that she was panting at every step. Her presence seemed to crowd the small room; for she was stout and rather tall, and her flowing muslin wrapper swept majestically from side to side as she walked.

Mamzelle Adélaïde had reached middle age, but her face was still fresh with its mignon[1] features; and her brown eyes at the moment were round with astonishment and alarm.

"W'at's that I hear, Polydore? They tell me you're sick!" She went and stood beside the bed, lifting the mosquito bar that settled upon her head and fell about her like a veil.

Polydore's eyes blinked, and he made no attempt to answer. She felt his wrist softly with the tips of her fingers, and rested her hand for a moment on his low forehead beneath the shock of black hair.

"But you don't seem to have any fever, Polydore!"

"No," hesitatingly, feeling himself forced to make some reply. "It's a kine of—a kine of pain, like you might say. It kitch me yere in the knee, and it goes 'long like you stickin' a knife clean down in my heel. Aie! Oh, lala!" expressions of pain wrung from him by Mamzelle Adélaïde gently pushing aside the covering to examine the afflicted member.

"My patience! but that leg is swollen, yes, Polydore." The limb, in fact, seemed dropsical, but if Mamzelle Adélaïde had bethought her of comparing it with the other one, she would have found the two corresponding in their proportions to a nicety. Her kind face expressed the utmost concern, and she quitted Polydore feeling pained and ill at ease.

For one of the aims of Mamzelle Adélaïde's existence was to do the right thing by this boy, whose mother, a 'Cadian hill woman, had begged her with dying breath to watch over the temporal and spiritual welfare of her son; above all, to see that he did not follow in the slothful footsteps of an over-indolent father.

Polydore's scheme worked so marvellously to his comfort and pleasure that he wondered at not having thought of it before. He ate with keen relish the breakfast which Jude brought to him on a tray. Even old Monsieur José was concerned, and made his way up to Polydore, bringing a number of picture-papers for his entertainment, a palm-leaf fan and a cow-bell, with which to summon Jude when necessary and which he placed within easy reach.

As Polydore lay on his back fanning luxuriously, it seemed to him that he was enjoying a foretaste of paradise. Only once did he shudder with apprehension. It was when he heard Aunt Siney, with lifted voice, recommending to "wrop the laig up in bacon fat; de oniest way to draw out de misery."

The thought of a healthy leg swathed in bacon fat on a hot day in July was enough to intimidate a braver heart than Polydore's. But the suggestion was evidently not adopted, for he heard no more of the bacon fat. In its stead he became acquainted with the not unpleasant sting of a soothing liniment which Jude rubbed into the leg at intervals during the day.

He kept the limb propped on a pillow, stiff and motionless, even when alone and unobserved. Toward evening he fancied that it really showed signs of inflammation, and he was quite sure it pained him.

It was a satisfaction to all to see Polydore appear down-stairs the following afternoon. He limped painfully, it is true, and clutched wildly at anything in his way that offered a momentary support. His acting was clumsily overdrawn; and by less guileless souls than Mamzelle Adélaïde and her father would have surely been suspected. But these two only thought with deep concern of means to make him comfortable.

They seated him on the shady back gallery in an easy-chair, with his leg propped up before him.

"He inhe'its dat rheumatism," proclaimed Aunt Siney, who affected the manner of an oracle. "I see dat boy's granpap, many times, all twis' up wid rheumatism twell his head sot down on his body, hine side befo'. He got to keep outen de jew in de mo'nin's, and he 'bleege to w'ar red flannen."

Monsieur José, with flowing white locks enframing his aged face, leaned upon his cane and contemplated the boy with unflagging attention. Polydore was beginning to believe himself a worthy object as a center of interest.

Mamzelle Adélaïde had but just returned from a long drive in the open buggy, from a mission which would have fallen to Polydore had he not been disabled by this unlooked-for illness. She had thoughtlessly driven across the country at an hour when the sun was hottest, and now she sat panting and fanning herself; her face, which she mopped incessantly with her handkerchief, was inflamed from the heat.

Mamzelle Adélaïde ate no supper that night, and went to bed early, with a compress of *eau sédative*[2] bound tightly around her head. She thought it was a simple headache, and that she would be rid of it in the morning; but she was not better in the morning.

She kept her bed that day, and late in the afternoon Jude rode over to town for the doctor, and stopped on the way to tell Mamzelle Adélaïde's married sister that she was quite ill, and would like to have her come down to the plantation for a day or two.

Polydore made round, serious eyes and forgot to limp. He wanted to go for the doctor in Jude's stead; but Aunt Siney, assuming a brief authority, forced him to sit still by the kitchen door and talked further of bacon fat.

Old Monsieur José moved about uneasily and restlessly, in and out of his daughter's room. He looked vacantly at Polydore now, as if the stout young boy in blue jeans and a calico shirt were a sort of a transparency.

A dawning anxiety, coupled to the inertia of the past two days, deprived Polydore of his usual healthful night's rest. The slightest noises awoke him. Once it was the married sister breaking ice down on the gallery. One of the hands had been sent with the cart for ice late in the afternoon; and Polydore himself had wrapped the huge chunk in an old blanket and set it outside of Mamzelle Adélaïde's door.

Troubled and wakeful, he arose from bed and went and stood by the open window. There was a round moon in the sky, shedding its pale glamor over all the country; and the live-oak branches, stirred by the restless breeze, flung quivering, grotesque shadows slanting across the old roof. A mocking-bird had been singing for hours near Polydore's window, and farther away there were frogs croaking. He could see as through a silvery gauze the level stretch of the cotton-field, ripe and white; a gleam of water beyond,—that was the bend of the river,—and farther yet, the gentle rise of the pine hill.

There was a cabin up there on the hill that Polydore remembered well. Negroes were living in it now, but it had been his home once. Life had been pinched and wretched enough up there with the little chap. The bright days had been the days when his godmother, Mamzelle Adélaïde, would come driving her old white horse over the pine needles and crackling fallen twigs of the deserted hill-road. Her presence was connected with the earliest recollections of whatever he had known of comfort and well-being.

And one day when death had taken his mother from him, Mamzelle Adélaïde had brought him home to live with her always. Now she was sick down there in her room; very sick, for the doctor had said so, and the married sister had put on her longest face.

Polydore did not think of these things in any connected or very intelligent way. They were only impressions that penetrated him and made his heart swell, and the tears well up to his eyes. He wiped his eyes on the sleeve of his night-gown. The mosquitoes were stinging him and raising great welts on his brown legs. He went and crept back under the mosquito-bar, and soon he was asleep and dreaming that his *nénaine*[3] was dead and he left alone in the cabin upon the pine hill.

In the morning, after the doctor had seen Mamzelle Adélaïde, he went and turned his horse into the lot and prepared to stay with his patient until he could feel it would be prudent to leave her.

Polydore tiptoed into her room and stood at the foot of the bed. Nobody noticed now whether he limped or not. She was talking very loud, and he could not believe at first that she could be as ill as they said, with such strength of voice. But her tones were unnatural, and what she said conveyed no meaning to his ears.

He understood, however, when she thought she was talking to his mother. She was in a manner apologizing for his illness; and seemed to be troubled with the idea that she had in a way been the indirect cause of it by some oversight or neglect.

Polydore felt ashamed, and went outside and stood by himself near the cistern till some one told him to go and attend to the doctor's horse.

Then there was confusion in the household, when mornings and afternoons seemed turned around; and meals, which were scarcely tasted, were served at irregular and unseasonable hours. And there came one awful night, when they did not know if Mamzelle Adélaïde would live or die.

Nobody slept. The doctor snatched moments of rest in the hammock. He and the priest, who had been summoned, talked a little together with professional callousness about the dry weather and the crops.

Old monsieur walked, walked, like a restless, caged animal. The married sister came out on the gallery every now and then and leaned up against the post and sobbed in her handkerchief. There were many negroes around, sitting on the steps and standing in small groups in the yard.

Polydore crouched on the gallery. It had finally come to him to comprehend the cause of his *nénaine's* sickness—that drive in the sweltering afternoon, when he was shamming illness. No one there could have comprehended the horror of himself, the terror that possessed him, squatting there outside her door like a savage. If she died—but he could not think of that. It was the point at which his reason was stunned and seemed to swoon.

A week or two later Mamzelle Adélaïde was sitting outside for the first time since her convalescence began. They had brought her own rocker around to the side where she could get a sight and whiff of the flower-garden and the blossom-laden rose-vine twining in and out of the banisters. Her former plumpness had not yet returned, and she looked much older, for the wrinkles were visible.

She was watching Polydore cross the yard. He had been putting up his pony. He approached with his heavy, clumsy walk; his round, simple face was hot and flushed from the ride. When he had mounted to the gallery he went and leaned against the railing, facing Mamzelle Adélaïde, mopping his face, his hands and neck with his handkerchief. Then he removed his hat and began to fan himself with it.

"You seem to be perfec'ly cu'ed of yo' rheumatism, Polydore. It doesn' hurt you any mo', my boy?" she questioned.

He stamped the foot and extended the leg violently, in proof of its perfect soundness.

"You know w'ere I been, *nénaine?*" he said. "I been to confession."

"That's right. Now you mus' rememba and not take a drink of water to-morrow morning, as you did las' time, and miss yo' communion, my boy. You are a good child, Polydore, to go like that to confession without bein' told."

"No, I ain' good," he returned, doggedly. He began to twirl his hat on one finger. "Père Cassimelle say he always yeard I was stupid, but he never knew befo' how bad I been."

"Indeed!" muttered Mamzelle Adélaïde, not over well pleased with the priest's estimate of her protégé.

"He gave me a long penance," continued Polydore. "The 'Litany of the Saint' and the 'Litany of the Blessed Virgin,' and three 'Our Father' and three 'Hail Mary' to say ev'ry mo'ning fo' a week. But he say' that ain' enough."

"My patience! W'at does he expec' mo' from you, I like to know?" Polydore was now creasing and scanning his hat attentively.

"He say' w'at I need, it's to be wo' out with the raw-hide. He say' he knows M'sieur José is too ole and feeble to give it to me like I deserve; and if you want, he say' he's willing to give me a good tas'e of the raw-hide himse'f."

Mamzelle Adélaïde found it impossible to disguise her indignation:

"Père Cassimelle sho'ly fo'gets himse'f, Polydore. Don't repeat to me any further his inconsid'ate remarks."

"He's right, *nénaine.* Père Cassimelle is right."

Since the night he crouched outside her door, Polydore had lived with the weight of his unconfessed fault oppressing every moment of existence. He had tried to rid himself of it in going to Father Cassimelle; but that had only helped by indicating the way. He was awkward and unaccustomed to express emotions with coherent speech. The words would not come.

Suddenly he flung his hat to the ground, and falling on his knees, began to sob, with his face pressed down in Mamzelle Adélaïde's lap. She had never seen him cry before, and in her weak condition it made her tremble.

Then somehow he got it out; he told the whole story of his deceit. He told it simply, in a way that bared his heart to her for the first time. She said nothing; only held his hand close and stroked his hair. But she felt as if a kind of miracle had happened. Hitherto her first thought in caring for this boy had been a desire to fulfill his dead mother's wishes.

But now he seemed to belong to herself, and to be her very own. She knew that a bond of love had been forged that would hold them together always.

"I know I can't he'p being stupid," sighed Polydore, "but it's no call fo' me to be bad."

"Neva mine, Polydore; neva mine, my boy," and she drew him close to her and kissed him as mothers kiss.

Regret

MAMZELLE AURÉLIE possessed a good strong figure, ruddy cheeks, hair that was changing from brown to gray, and a determined eye. She wore a man's hat about the farm, and an old blue army overcoat when it was cold, and sometimes topboots.

Mamzelle Aurélie had never thought of marrying. She had never been in love. At the age of twenty she had recieved a proposal, which she had promptly declined, and at the age of fifty she had not yet lived to regret it.

So she was quite alone in the world, except for her dog Ponto, and the negroes who lived in her cabins and worked her crops, and the fowls, a few cows, a couple of mules, her gun (with which she shot chicken-hawks), and her religion.

One morning Mamzelle Aurélie stood upon her gallery, contemplating, with arms akimbo, a small band of very small children who, to all intents and purposes, might have fallen from the clouds, so unexpected and bewildering was their coming, and so unwelcome. They were the children of her nearest neighbor, Odile, who was not such a near neighbor, after all.

The young woman had appeared but five minutes before, accompanied by these four children. In her arms she carried little Elodie; she dragged Ti Nomme[1] by an unwilling hand; while Marcéline and Marcélette followed with irresolute steps.

Her face was red and disfigured from tears and excitement. She had been summoned to a neighboring parish by the dangerous illness of her mother; her husband was away in Texas—it seemed to her a million miles away; and Valsin was waiting with the mule-cart to drive her to the station.

"It's no question, Mamzelle Aurélie; you jus' got to keep those youngsters fo' me tell I come back. Dieu sait,[2] I would n' botha you with 'em if it was any otha way to do! Make 'em mine you, Mamzelle Aurélie; don' spare 'em. Me, there, I'm half crazy between the chil'ren, an' Léon not home, an' maybe not even to fine po' maman alive encore!"[3]—a harrowing possibility which drove Odile to take a final hasty and convulsive leave of her disconsolate family.

She left them crowded into the narrow strip of shade on the porch of the long, low house; the white sunlight was beating in on the white old boards; some chickens were scratching in the grass at the foot of the steps, and one had boldly mounted, and was stepping heavily, solemnly, and aimlessly across the gallery. There was a pleasant odor of pinks in the air, and the sound of negroes' laughter was coming across the flowering cotton-field.

Mamzelle Aurélie stood contemplating the children. She looked with a critical eye upon Marcéline, who had been left staggering beneath the weight of the chubby Elodie. She surveyed with the same calculating air Marcélette mingling her silent tears with the audible grief and rebellion of Ti Nomme. During those few contemplative moments she was collecting herself, determining upon a line of action which should be identical with a line of duty. She began by feeding them.

If Mamzelle Aurélie's responsibilities might have begun and ended there, they could easily have been dismissed; for her larder was amply provided against an emergency of this nature. But little children are not little pigs; they require and demand attentions which were wholly unexpected by Mamzelle Aurélie, and which she was ill prepared to give.

She was, indeed, very inapt in her management of Odile's children during the first few days. How could she know that Marcélette always wept when spoken to in a loud and commanding tone of voice? It was a peculiarity of Marcélette's. She became acquainted with Ti Nomme's passion for flowers only when he had plucked all the choicest gardenias and pinks for the apparent purpose of critically studying their botanical construction.

" 'Tain't enough to tell 'im, Mamzelle Aurélie," Marcéline instructed her; "you got to tie 'im in a chair. It's w'at maman all time do w'en he's bad: she tie 'im in a chair." The chair in which

Mamzelle Aurélie tied Ti Nomme was roomy and comfortable, and he seized the opportunity to take a nap in it, the afternoon being warm.

At night, when she ordered them one and all to bed as she would have shooed the chickens into the hen-house, they stayed uncomprehending before her. What about the little white nightgowns that had to be taken from the pillow-slip in which they were brought over, and shaken by some strong hand till they snapped like ox-whips? What about the tub of water which had to be brought and set in the middle of the floor, in which the little tired, dusty, sun-browned feet had every one to be washed sweet and clean? And it made Marcéline and Marcélette laugh merrily—the idea that Mamzelle Aurélie should for a moment have believed that Ti Nomme could fall asleep without being told the story of *Croquemitaine* or *Loup-garou*,[4] or both; or that Elodie could fall asleep at all without being rocked and sung to.

"I tell you, Aunt Ruby," Mamzelle Aurélie informed her cook in confidence; "me, I'd rather manage a dozen plantation' than fo' chil'ren. It's terrassent! Bonté![5] Don't talk to me about chil'ren!"

" 'Tain' ispected sich as you would know airy thing 'bout 'em, Mamzelle Aurélie. I see dat plainly yistiddy w'en I spy dat li'le chile playin' wid yo' baskit o' keys. You don' know dat makes chillun grow up hard-headed, to play wid keys? Des like it make 'em teeth hard to look in a lookin'-glass. Them's the things you got to know in the raisin' an' manigement o' chillun."

Mamzelle Aurélie certainly did not pretend or aspire to such subtle and far-reaching knowledge on the subject as Aunt Ruby possessed, who had "raised five an' bared (buried) six" in her day. She was glad enough to learn a few little mother-tricks to serve the moment's need.

Ti Nomme's sticky fingers compelled her to unearth white aprons that she had not worn for years, and she had to accustom herself to his moist kisses—the expressions of an affectionate and exuberant nature. She got down her sewing-basket, which she seldom used, from the top shelf of the armoire, and placed it within the ready and easy reach which torn slips and buttonless waists demanded. It took her some days to become accustomed to the laughing, the crying, the chattering that echoed through the house and around it all day long. And it was not the first or the second night that she could sleep comfortably with little Elodie's hot, plump body pressed close against her, and the little one's warm breath beating her cheek like the fanning of a bird's wing.

But at the end of two weeks Mamzelle Aurélie had grown quite used to these things, and she no longer complained.

It was also at the end of two weeks that Mamzelle Aurélie, one evening, looking away toward the crib where the cattle were being fed, saw Valsin's blue cart turning the bend of the road. Odile sat beside the mulatto, upright and alert. As they drew near, the young woman's beaming face indicated that her homecoming was a happy one.

But this coming, unannounced and unexpected, threw Mamzelle Aurélie into a flutter that was almost agitation. The children had to be gathered. Where was Ti Nomme? Yonder in the shed, putting an edge on his knife at the grindstone. And Marcéline and Marcélette? Cutting and fashioning doll-rags in the corner of the gallery. As for Elodie, she was safe enough in Mamzelle Aurélie's arms; and she had screamed with delight at sight of the familiar blue cart which was bringing her mother back to her.

The excitement was all over, and they were gone. How still it was when they were gone! Mamzelle Aurélie stood upon the gallery, looking and listening. She could no longer see the cart; the red sunset and the blue-gray twilight had together flung a purple mist across the fields and road that hid it from her view. She could no longer hear the wheezing and creaking of its wheels. But she could still faintly hear the shrill, glad voices of the children.

She turned into the house. There was much work awaiting her, for the children had left a sad disorder behind them; but she did not at once set about the task of righting it. Mamzelle Aurélie seated herself beside the table. She gave one slow glance through the room, into which the evening shadows were creeping and deepening around her solitary figure. She let her head fall down upon her bended arm, and began to cry. Oh, but she cried! Not softly, as women often do. She cried like a man, with sobs that seemed to tear her very soul. She did not notice Ponto licking her hand.

A Matter of Prejudice

MADAME CARAMBEAU wanted it strictly understood that she was not to be disturbed by Gustave's birthday party. They carried her big rocking-chair from the back gallery, that looked out upon the garden where the children were going to play, around to the front gallery, which closely faced the green levee bank and the Mississippi coursing almost flush with the top of it.

The house—an old Spanish one, broad, low and completely encircled by a wide gallery—was far down in the French quarter of New Orleans. It stood upon a square of ground that was covered thick with a semi-tropical growth of plants and flowers. An impenetrable board fence, edged with a formidable row of iron spikes, shielded the garden from the prying glances of the occasional passer-by.

Madame Carambeau's widowed daughter, Madame Cécile Lalonde, lived with her. This annual party, given to her little son, Gustave, was the one defiant act of Madame Lalonde's existence. She persisted in it, to her own astonishment and the wonder of those who knew her and her mother.

For old Madame Carambeau was a woman of many prejudices—so many, in fact, that it would be difficult to name them all. She detested dogs, cats, organ-grinders, white servants and children's noises. She despised Americans, Germans and all people of a different faith from her own. Anything not French had, in her opinion, little right to existence.

She had not spoken to her son Henri for ten years because he had married an American girl from Prytania street. She would not permit green tea to be introduced into her house, and those who could not or would not drink coffee might drink tisane of *fleur de Laurier*[1] for all she cared.

Nevertheless, the children seemed to be having it all their own way that day, and the organ-grinders were let loose. Old madame, in her retired corner, could hear the screams, the laughter and the music far more distinctly than she liked. She rocked herself noisily, and hummed "Partant pour la Syrie."[2]

She was straight and slender. Her hair was white, and she wore it in puffs on the temples. Her skin was fair and her eyes blue and cold.

Suddenly she became aware that footsteps were approaching, and threatening to invade her privacy—not only footsteps, but screams! Then two little children, one in hot pursuit of the other, darted wildy around the corner near which she sat.

The child in advance, a pretty little girl, sprang excitedly into Madame Carambeau's lap, and threw her arms convulsively around the old lady's neck. Her companion lightly struck her a "last tag," and ran laughing gleefully away.

The most natural thing for the child to do then would have been to wriggle down from madame's lap, without a "thank you" or a "by your leave," after the manner of small and thoughtless children. But she did not do this. She stayed there, panting and fluttering, like a frightened bird.

Madame was greatly annoyed. She moved as if to put the child away from her, and scolded her sharply for being boisterous and rude. The little one, who did not understand French, was not disturbed by the reprimand, and stayed on in madame's lap. She rested her plump little cheek, that was hot and flushed, against the soft white linen of the old lady's gown.

Her cheek was very hot and very flushed. It was dry, too, and so were her hands. The child's breathing was quick and irregular. Madame was not long in detecting these signs of disturbance.

Though she was a creature of prejudice, she was nevertheless a skillful and accomplished nurse, and a connoisseur in all matters pertaining to health. She prided herself upon this talent, and never lost an opportunity of exercising it. She would have treated an organ-grinder with tender consideration if one had presented himself in the character of an invalid.

Madame's manner toward the little one changed immediately. Her arms and her lap were at once adjusted so as to become the most comfortable of resting places. She rocked very gently to and

fro. She fanned the child softly with her palm leaf fan, and sang
"Partant pour la Syrie" in a low and agreeable tone.

The child was perfectly content to lie still and prattle a little in
that language which madame thought hideous. But the brown eyes
were soon swimming in drowsiness, and the little body grew heavy
with sleep in madame's clasp.

When the little girl slept Madame Carambeau arose, and treading
carefully and deliberately, entered her room, that opened near at
hand upon the gallery. The room was large, airy and inviting, with
its cool matting upon the floor, and its heavy, old, polished mahogany furniture. Madame, with the child still in her arms, pulled a
bell-cord; then she stood waiting, swaying gently back and forth.
Presently an old black woman answered the summons. She wore
gold hoops in her ears, and a bright bandanna knotted fantastically
on her head.

"Louise, turn down the bed," commanded madame. "Place that
small, soft pillow below the bolster. Here is a poor little unfortunate creature whom Providence must have driven into my arms."
She laid the child carefully down.

"Ah, those Americans! Do they deserve to have children? Understanding as little as they do how to take care of them!" said
madame, while Louise was mumbling an accompanying assent that
would have been unintelligible to any one unacquainted with the
negro patois.

"There, you see, Louise, she is burning up," remarked madame;
"she is consumed. Unfasten the little bodice while I lift her. Ah, talk
to me of such parents! So stupid as not to perceive a fever like that
coming on, but they must dress their child up like a monkey to go
play and dance to the music of organ-grinders.

"Haven't you better sense, Louise, than to take off a child's shoe
as if you were removing the boot from the leg of a cavalry officer?"
Madame would have required fairy fingers to minister to the sick.
"Now go to Mamzelle Cécile, and tell her to send me one of those
old, soft, thin nightgowns that Gustave wore two summers ago."

When the woman retired, madame busied herself with concocting a cooling pitcher of orange-flower water, and mixing a fresh
supply of *eau sédative*[3] with which agreeably to sponge the little invalid.

Madame Lalonde came herself with the old, soft nightgown. She was a pretty, blonde, plump little woman, with the deprecatory air of one whose will has become flaccid from want of use. She was mildly distressed at what her mother had done.

"But, mamma! But, mamma, the child's parents will be sending the carriage for her in a little while. Really, there was no use. Oh dear! oh dear!"

If the bedpost had spoken to Madame Carambeau, she would have paid more attention, for speech from such a source would have been at least surprising if not convincing. Madame Lalonde did not possess the faculty of either surprising or convincing her mother.

"Yes, the little one will be quite comfortable in this," said the old lady, taking the garment from her daughter's irresolute hands.

"But, mamma! What shall I say, what shall I do when they send? Oh, dear; oh, dear!"

"That is your business," replied madame, with lofty indifference. "My concern is solely with a sick child that happens to be under my roof. I think I know my duty at this time of life, Cécile."

As Madame Lalonde predicted, the carriage soon came, with a stiff English coachman driving it, and a red-cheeked Irish nurse-maid seated inside. Madame would not even permit the maid to see her little charge. She had an original theory that the Irish voice is distressing to the sick.

Madame Lalonde sent the girl away with a long letter of explanation that must have satisfied the parents; for the child was left undisturbed in Madame Carambeau's care. She was a sweet child, gentle and affectionate. And, though she cried and fretted a little throughout the night for her mother, she seemed, after all, to take kindly to madame's gentle nursing. It was not much of a fever that afflicted her, and after two days she was well enough to be sent back to her parents.

Madame, in all her varied experience with the sick, had never before nursed so objectionable a character as an American child. But the trouble was that after the little one went away, she could think of nothing really objectionable against her except the accident of her birth, which was, after all, her misfortune; and her ignorance of the French language, which was not her fault.

But the touch of the caressing baby arms; the pressure of the soft little body in the night; the tones of the voice, and the feeling of the hot lips when the child kissed her, believing herself to be with her mother, were impressions that had sunk through the crust of madame's prejudice and reached her heart.

She often walked the length of the gallery, looking out across the wide, majestic river. Sometimes she trod the mazes of her garden where the solitude was almost that of a tropical jungle. It was during such moments that the seed began to work in her soul—the seed planted by the innocent and undesigning hands of a little child.

The first shoot that it sent forth was Doubt. Madame plucked it away once or twice. But it sprouted again, and with it Mistrust and Dissatisfaction. Then from the heart of the seed, and amid the shoots of Doubt and Misgiving, came the flower of Truth. It was a very beautiful flower, and it bloomed on Christmas morning.

As Madame Carambeau and her daughter were about to enter her carriage on that Christmas morning, to be driven to church, the old lady stopped to give an order to her black coachman, François. François had been driving these ladies every Sunday morning to the French Cathedral for so many years—he had forgotten exactly how many, but ever since he had entered their service, when Madame Lalonde was a little girl. His astonishment may therefore be imagined when Madame Carambeau said to him:

"François, to-day you will drive us to one of the American churches."

"Plait-il, madame?"[4] the negro stammered, doubting the evidence of his hearing.

"I say, you will drive us to one of the American churches. Any one of them," she added, with a sweep of her hand. "I suppose they are all alike," and she followed her daughter into the carriage.

Madame Lalonde's surprise and agitation were painful to see, and they deprived her of the ability to question, even if she had possessed the courage to do so.

François, left to his fancy, drove them to St. Patrick's Church on Camp street. Madame Lalonde looked and felt like the proverbial fish out of its element as they entered the edifice. Madame Carambeau, on the contrary, looked as if she had been attending St. Patrick's church all her life. She sat with unruffled calm through the long service and through a lengthy English sermon, of which she did not understand a word.

When the mass was ended and they were about to enter the carriage again, Madame Carambeau turned, as she had done before, to the coachman.

"François," she said, coolly, "you will now drive us to the residence of my son, M. Henri Carambeau. No doubt Mamzelle Cécile can inform you where it is," she added, with a sharply penetrating glance that caused Madame Lalonde to wince.

Yes, her daughter Cécile knew, and so did François, for that matter. They drove out St. Charles avenue—very far out. It was like a strange city to old madame, who had not been in the American quarter since the town had taken on this new and splendid growth.

The morning was a delicious one, soft and mild; and the roses were all in bloom. They were not hidden behind spiked fences. Madame appeared not to notice them, or the beautiful and striking residences that lined the avenue along which they drove. She held a bottle of smelling-salts to her nostrils, as though she were passing through the most unsavory instead of the most beautiful quarter of New Orleans.

Henri's house was a very modern and very handsome one, standing a little distance away from the street. A well-kept lawn, studded with rare and charming plants, surrounded it. The ladies, dismounting, rang the bell, and stood out upon the banquette, waiting for the iron gate to be opened.

A white maid-servant admitted them. Madame did not seem to mind. She handed her a card with all proper ceremony, and followed with her daughter to the house.

Not once did she show a sign of weakness; not even when her son, Henri, came and took her in his arms and sobbed and wept upon her neck as only a warm-hearted Creole could. He was a big, good-looking, honest-faced man, with tender brown eyes like his dead father's and a firm mouth like his mother's.

Young Mrs. Carambeau came, too, her sweet, fresh face transfigured with happiness. She led by the hand her little daughter, the "American child" whom madame had nursed so tenderly a month before, never suspecting the little one to be other than an alien to her.

"What a lucky chance was that fever! What a happy accident!" gurgled Madame Lalonde.

"Cécile, it was no accident, I tell you; it was Providence," spoke madame, reprovingly, and no one contradicted her.

They all drove back together to eat Christmas dinner in the old house by the river. Madame held her little granddaughter upon her lap; her son Henri sat facing her, and beside her was her daughter-in-law.

Henri sat back in the carriage and could not speak. His soul was possessed by a pathetic joy that would not admit of speech. He was going back again to the home where he was born, after a banishment of ten long years.

He would hear again the water beat against the green levee-bank with a sound that was not quite like any other that he could remember. He would sit within the sweet and solemn shadow of the deep and overhanging roof; and roam through the wild, rich solitude of the old garden, where he had played his pranks of boyhood and dreamed his dreams of youth. He would listen to his mother's voice calling him, "mon fils,"[5] as it had always done before that day he had had to choose between mother and wife. No; he could not speak.

But his wife chatted much and pleasantly—in a French, however, that must have been trying to old madame to listen to.

"I am so sorry, ma mère,"[6] she said, "that our little one does not speak French. It is not my fault, I assure you," and she flushed and hesitated a little. "It—it was Henri who would not permit it."

"That is nothing," replied madame, amiably, drawing the child close to her. "Her grandmother will teach her French; and she will teach her grandmother English. You see, I have no prejudices. I am not like my son. Henri was always a stubborn boy. Heaven only knows how he came by such a character!"

Caline

THE SUN was just far enough in the west to send inviting shadows. In the centre of a small field, and in the shade of a haystack which was there, a girl lay sleeping. She had slept long and soundly, when something awoke her as suddenly as if it had been a blow. She opened her eyes and stared a moment up in the cloudless sky. She yawned and stretched her long brown legs and arms, lazily. Then she arose, never minding the bits of straw that clung to her black hair, to her red bodice, and the blue cotonade skirt that did not reach her naked ankles.

The log cabin in which she dwelt with her parents was just outside the enclosure in which she had been sleeping. Beyond was a small clearing that did duty as a cotton field. All else was dense wood, except the long stretch that curved round the brow of the hill, and in which glittered the steel rails of the Texas and Pacific road.

When Caline emerged from the shadow she saw a long train of passenger coaches standing in view, where they must have stopped abruptly. It was that sudden stopping which had awakened her; for such a thing had not happened before within her recollection, and she looked stupid, at first, with astonishment. There seemed to be something wrong with the engine; and some of the passengers who dismounted went forward to investigate the trouble. Others came strolling along in the direction of the cabin, where Caline stood under an old gnarled mulberry tree, staring. Her father had halted his mule at the end of the cotton row, and stood staring also, leaning upon his plow.

There were ladies in the party. They walked awkwardly in their high-heeled boots over the rough, uneven ground, and held up their skirts mincingly. They twirled parasols over their shoulders, and laughed immoderately at the funny things which their masculine companions were saying.

They tried to talk to Caline, but could not understand the French patois with which she answered them.

One of the men—a pleasant-faced youngster—drew a sketch book from his pocket and began to make a picture of the girl. She stayed motionless, her hands behind her, and her wide eyes fixed earnestly upon him.

Before he had finished there was a summons from the train; and all went scampering hurriedly away. The engine screeched, it sent a few lazy puffs into the still air, and in another moment or two had vanished, bearing its human cargo with it.

Caline could not feel the same after that. She looked with new and strange interest upon the trains of cars that passed so swiftly back and forth across her vision, each day; and wondered whence these people came, and whither they were going.

Her mother and father could not tell her, except to say that they came from "loin là bas," and were going "Djieu sait é où."[1]

One day she walked miles down the track to talk with the old flagman, who stayed down there by the big water tank. Yes, he knew. Those people came from the great cities in the north, and were going to the city in the south. He knew all about the city; it was a grand place. He had lived there once. His sister lived there now; and she would be glad enough to have so fine a girl as Caline to help her cook and scrub, and tend the babies. And he thought Caline might earn as much as five dollars a month, in the city.

So she went; in a new cotonade, and her Sunday shoes; with a sacredly guarded scrawl that the flagman sent to his sister.

The woman lived in a tiny, stuccoed house, with green blinds, and three wooden steps leading down to the banquette. There seemed to be hundreds like it along the street. Over the house tops loomed the tall masts of ships, and the hum of the French market could be heard on a still morning.

Caline was at first bewildered. She had to readjust all her preconceptions to fit the reality of it. The flagman's sister was a kind and gentle task-mistress. At the end of a week or two she wanted to know how the girl liked it all. Caline liked it very well, for it was pleasant, on Sunday afternoons, to stroll with the children under the great, solemn sugar sheds; or to sit upon the compressed cotton bales, watching the stately steamers, the graceful boats, and noisy little tugs that plied the waters of the Mississippi. And it filled her with agreeable excitement to go to the French market, where the handsome Gascon butchers were eager to present their compliments and little Sunday bouquets to the pretty Acadian girl; and to throw fistfuls of *lagniappe*[2] into her basket.

When the woman asked her again after another week if she were still pleased, she was not so sure. And again when she questioned Caline the girl turned away, and went to sit behind the big, yellow cistern, to cry unobserved. For she knew now that it was not the great city and its crowds of people she had so eagerly sought; but the pleasant-faced boy, who had made her picture that day under the mulberry tree.

A Dresden Lady in Dixie

MADAME VALTOUR had been in the sitting-room some time before she noticed the absence of the Dresden china figure from the corner of the mantel-piece, where it had stood for years. Aside from the intrinsic value of the piece, there were some very sad and tender memories associated with it. A baby's lips that were now forever still had loved once to kiss the painted "pitty 'ady"; and the baby arms had often held it in a close and smothered embrace.

Madame Valtour gave a rapid, startled glance around the room, to see perchance if it had been misplaced; but she failed to discover it.

Viny, the house-maid, when summoned, remembered having carefully dusted it that morning, and was rather indignantly positive that she had not broken the thing to bits and secreted the pieces.

"Who has been in the room during my absence?" questioned Madame Valtour, with asperity. Viny abandoned herself to a moment's reflection.

"Pa-Jeff comed in yere wid de mail—" If she had said St. Peter came in with the mail, the fact would have had as little bearing on the case from Madame Valtour's point of view.

Pa-Jeff's uprightness and honesty were so long and firmly established as to have become proverbial on the plantation. He had not served the family faithfully since boyhood and been all through the war with "old Marse Valtour" to descend at his time of life to tampering with household bric-a-brac.

"Has any one else been here?" Madame Valtour naturally inquired.

"On'y Agapie w'at brung you some Creole aiggs. I tole 'er to sot 'em down in de hall. I don' know she comed in de settin'-room o' not."

Yes, there they were; eight, fresh "Creole eggs" reposing on the muslin in the sewing basket. Viny herself had been seated on the gallery brushing her mistress' gowns during the hours of that lady's absence, and could think of no one else having penetrated to the sitting-room.

Madame Valtour did not entertain the thought that Agapie had stolen the relic. Her worst fear was, that the girl, finding herself alone in the room, had handled the frail bit of porcelain and inadvertently broken it.

Agapie came often to the house to play with the children and amuse them—she loved nothing better. Indeed, no other spot known to her on earth so closely embodied her confused idea of paradise, as this home with its atmosphere of love, comfort and good cheer. She was, herself, a cheery bit of humanity, overflowing with kind impulses and animal spirits.

Madame Valtour recalled the fact that Agapie had often admired this Dresden figure (but what had she not admired!); and she remembered having heard the girl's assurance that if ever she became possessed of "fo' bits" to spend as she liked, she would have some one buy her just such a china doll in town or in the city.

Before night, the fact that the Dresden lady had strayed from her proud eminence on the sitting-room mantel, became, through Viny's indiscreet babbling, pretty well known on the place.

The following morning Madame Valtour crossed the field and went over to the Bedauts' cabin. The cabins on the plantation were not grouped; but each stood isolated upon the section of land which its occupants cultivated. Pa-Jeff's cabin was the only one near enough to the Bedauts to admit of neighborly intercourse.

Seraphine Bedaut was sitting on her small gallery, stringing red peppers, when Madame Valtour approached.

"I'm so distressed, Madame Bedaut," began the planter's wife, abruptly. But the 'Cadian woman arose politely and interrupted, offering her visitor a chair.

"Come in, set down, Ma'me Valtour."

"No, no; it's only for a moment. You know, Madame Bedaut, yesterday when I returned from making a visit, I found that an ornament was missing from my sitting-room mantel-piece. It's a thing I prize very, very much—" with sudden tears filling her eyes—"and I would not willingly part with it for many times its value." Seraphine Bedaut was listening, with her mouth partly open, looking, in truth, stupidly puzzled.

"No one entered the room during my absence," continued Madame Valtour, "but Agapie." Seraphine's mouth snapped like a steel trap and her black eyes gleamed with a flash of anger.

"You wan' say Agapie stole some'in' in yo' house!" she cried out in a shrill voice, tremulous from passion.

"No; oh no! I'm sure Agapie is an honest girl and we all love her; but you know how children are. It was a small Dresden figure. She may have handled and broken the thing and perhaps is afraid to say so. She may have thoughtlessly misplaced it; oh, I don't know what! I want to ask if she saw it."

"Come in; you got to come in, Ma'me Valtour," stubbornly insisted Seraphine, leading the way into the cabin. "I sen' 'er to de house yistiddy wid some Creole aiggs," she went on in her rasping voice, "like I all time do, because you all say you can't eat dem sto' aiggs no mo'. Yere de basket w'at I sen' 'em in," reaching for an Indian basket which hung against the wall—and which was partly filled with cotton seed.

"Oh, never mind," interrupted Madame Valtour, now thoroughly distressed at witnessing the woman's agitation.

"Ah, bien non.[1] I got to show you, Agapie en't no mo' thief 'an yo' own child'en is." She led the way into the adjoining room of the hut.

"Yere all her things w'at she 'muse herse'f wid," continued Seraphine, pointing to a soapbox which stood on the floor just beneath the open window. The box was filled with an indescribable assortment of odds and ends, mostly doll-rags. A catechism and a blue-backed speller poked dog-eared corners from out of the confusion; for the Valtour children were making heroic and patient efforts toward Agapie's training.

Seraphine cast herself upon her knees before the box and dived her thin brown hands among its contents. "I wan' show you; I goin' show you," she kept repeating excitedly. Madame Valtour was standing beside her.

Suddenly the woman drew forth from among the rags, the Dresden lady, as dapper, sound, and smiling as ever. Seraphine's hand shook so violently that she was in danger of letting the image fall to the floor. Madame Valtour reached out and took it very quietly from her. Then Seraphine rose tremblingly to her feet and broke into a sob that was pitiful to hear.

Agapie was approaching the cabin. She was a chubby girl of twelve. She walked with bare, callous feet over the rough ground and bare-headed under the hot sun. Her thick, short, black hair covered her head like a mane. She had been dancing along the path, but slackened her pace upon catching sight of the two women who had returned to the gallery. But when she perceived that her mother was crying she darted impetuously forward. In an instant she had her arms around her mother's neck, clinging so tenaciously in her youthful strength as to make the frail woman totter.

Agapie had seen the Dresden figure in Madame Valtour's possession and at once guessed the whole accusation.

"It en't so! I tell you, maman, it en't so! I neva touch' it. Stop cryin'; stop cryin'!" and she began to cry most piteously herself.

"But Agapie, we fine it in yo' box," moaned Seraphine through her sobs.

"Then somebody put it there. Can't you see somebody put it there? 'Ten't so, I tell you."

The scene was extremely painful to Madame Valtour. Whatever she might tell these two later, for the time she felt herself powerless to say anything befitting, and she walked away. But she turned to remark, with a hardness of expression and intention which she seldom displayed: "No one will know of this through me. But, Agapie, you must not come into my house again; on account of the children; I could not allow it."

As she walked away she could hear Agapie comforting her mother with renewed protestations of innocence.

Pa-Jeff began to fail visibly that year. No wonder, considering his great age, which he computed to be about one hundred. It was, in fact, some ten years less than that, but a good old age all the same. It was seldom that he got out into the field; and then, never to do any heavy work—only a little light hoeing. There were days when the "misery" doubled him up and nailed him down to his chair so that he could not set foot beyond the door of his cabin. He would sit there courting the sunshine and blinking, as he gazed across the fields with the patience of the savage.

The Bedauts seemed to know almost instinctively when Pa-Jeff was sick. Agapie would shade her eyes and look searchingly towards the old man's cabin.

"I don' see Pa-Jeff this mo'nin'," or "Pa-Jeff en't open his winda," or "I didn' see no smoke yet yonda to Pa-Jeff's." And in a little while the girl would be over there with a pail of soup or coffee, or whatever there was at hand which she thought the old negro might fancy. She had lost all the color out of her cheeks and was pining like a sick bird.

She often sat on the steps of the gallery and talked with the old man while she waited for him to finish his soup from her tin pail.

"I tell you, Pa-Jeff, its neva been no thief in the Bedaut family. My pa say he couldn' hole up his head if he think I been a thief, me. An' maman say it would make her sick in bed, she don' know she could ever git up. Sosthène tell me the chil'en been cryin' fo' me up yonda. Li'le Lulu cry so hard M'sieur Valtour want sen' afta me, an' Ma'me Valtour say no."

And with this, Agapie flung herself at length upon the gallery with her face buried in her arms, and began to cry so hysterically as seriously to alarm Pa-Jeff. It was well he had finished his soup, for he could not have eaten another mouthful.

"Hole up yo' head, chile. God save us! W'at you kiarrin' on dat away?" he exclaimed in great distress. "You gwine to take a fit? Hole up yo' head."

Agapie rose slowly to her feet, and drying her eyes upon the sleeve of her "josie,"[2] reached out for the tin bucket. Pa-Jeff handed it to her, but without relinquishing his hold upon it.

"War hit you w'at tuck it?" he questioned in a whisper. "I isn' gwine tell; you knows I isn' gwine tell." She only shook her head, attempting to draw the pail forcibly away from the old man.

"Le' me go, Pa-Jeff. W'at you doin'! Gi' me my bucket!"

He kept his old blinking eyes fastened for a while questioningly upon her disturbed and tear-stained face. Then he let her go and she turned and ran swiftly away towards her home.

He sat very still watching her disappear; only his furrowed old face twitched convulsively, moved by an unaccustomed train of reasoning that was at work in him.

"She w'ite, I is black," he muttered calculatingly. "She young, I is ole; sho I is ole. She good to Pa-Jeff like I her own kin an' color." This line of thought seemed to possess him to the exclusion of every other. Late in the night he was still muttering.

"Sho I is ole. She good to Pa-Jeff, yas."

A few days later, when Pa-Jeff happened to be feeling comparatively well, he presented himself at the house just as the family had assembled at their early dinner. Looking up suddenly, Monsieur Valtour was astonished to see him standing there in the room near the open door. He leaned upon his cane and his grizzled head was bowed upon his breast. There was general satisfaction expressed at seeing Pa-Jeff on his legs once more.

"Why, old man, I'm glad to see you out again," exclaimed the planter, cordially, pouring a glass of wine, which he instructed Viny to hand to the old fellow. Pa-Jeff accepted the glass and set it solemnly down upon a small table near by.

"Marse Albert," he said, "I is come heah to-day fo' to make a statement of de rights an' de wrongs w'at is done hang heavy on my soul dis heah long time. Arter you heahs me an' de missus heahs me an' de chillun an' ev'body, den ef you says: 'Pa-Jeff you kin tech yo' lips to dat glass o' wine,' all well an' right.' "

His manner was impressive and caused the family to exchange surprised and troubled glances. Foreseeing that his recital might be long, a chair was offered to him, but he declined it.

"One day," he began, "w'en I ben hoein' de madam's flower bed close to de fence, Sosthène he ride up, he say: 'Heah, Pa-Jeff, heah de mail.' I takes de mail f'om 'im an' I calls out to Viny w'at settin' on de gallery: 'Heah Marse Albert's mail, gal; come git it.'

"But Viny she answer, pert-like—des like Viny: 'You is got two laigs, Pa-Jeff, des well as me.' I ain't no han' fo' disputin' wid gals, so I brace up an' I come 'long to de house an' goes on in dat settin'-room dah, naix' to de dinin'-room. I lays dat mail down on Marse Albert's table; den I looks roun'.

"Ev'thing do look putty, sho! De lace cu'tains was a-flappin' an' de flowers was a-smellin' sweet, an' de pictures a-settin' back on de wall. I keep on lookin' roun'. To reckly my eye hit fall on de li'le gal w'at al'ays sets on de een' o' de mantel-shelf. She do look mighty

sassy dat day, wid 'er toe a-stickin' out, des so; an' holdin' her skirt
des dat away; an' lookin' at me wid her head twis'.

"I laff out. Viny mus' heahed me. I say, 'g'long 'way f'om dah,
gal.' She keep on smilin'. I reaches out my han'. Den Satan an' de
good Sperrit, dey begins to wrastle in me. De Sperrit say: 'You ole
fool-nigga, you; mine w'at you about.' Satan keep on shovin' my
han'—des so—keep on shovin'. Satan he mighty powerful dat day,
an' he win de fight. I kiar dat li'le trick home in my pocket."

Pa-Jeff lowered his head for a moment in bitter confusion. His
hearers were moved with distressful astonishment. They would
have had him stop the recital right there, but Pa-Jeff resumed, with
an effort:

"Come dat night I heah tell how dat li'le trick, wo'th heap
money; how madam, she cryin' 'cause her li'le blessed lamb was
use' to play wid dat, an' kiar-on ov' it. Den I git scared. I say, 'w'at
I gwine do?' An' up jump Satan an' de Sperrit a-wrastlin' again.

"De Sperrit say: 'Kiar hit back whar it come f'om, Pa-Jeff.' Satan
'low: 'Fling it in de bayeh, you ole fool.' De Sperrit say: 'You won't
fling dat in de bayeh, whar de madam kain't neva sot eyes on hit no
mo'?' Den Satan he kine give in; he 'low he plumb sick o' disputin'
so long; tell me go hide it some 'eres whar day nachelly gwine fine
it. Satan he win dat fight.

"Des w'en de day g'ine break, I creeps out an' goes 'long de fiel'
road. I pass by Ma'me Bedaut's house. I riclic how dey says li'le Bedaut gal ben in de sittin'-room, too, day befo'. De winda war open.
Ev'body sleepin'. I tres' in my head, des like a dog w'at shame
hisse'f. I sees dat box o' rags befo' my eyes; an' I drops dat li'le im-
p'dence 'mongst dem rags.

"Mebby yo' all t'ink Satan an' de Sperrit lef' me 'lone, arter dat?"
continued Pa-Jeff, straightening himself from the relaxed position
in which his members seemed to have settled.

"No, suh; dey ben desputin' straight 'long. Las' night dey come
nigh onto en'in' me up. De Sperrit say: 'Come 'long, I gittin' tired
dis heah, you g'long up yonda an' tell de truf an' shame de devil.'
Satan 'low: 'Stay whar you is; you heah me!' Dey clutches me. Dey
twis'es an' twines me. Dey dashes me down an' jerks me up. But de
Sperrit he win dat fight in de en', an' heah I is, mist'ess, master,
chillun'; heah I is."

Years later Pa-Jeff was still telling the story of his temptation and fall. The negroes especially seemed never to tire of hearing him relate it. He enlarged greatly upon the theme as he went, adding new and dramatic features which gave fresh interest to its every telling.

Agapie grew up to deserve the confidence and favors of the family. She redoubled her acts of kindness toward Pa-Jeff; but somehow she could not look into his face again.

Yet she need not have feared. Long before the end came, poor old Pa-Jeff, confused, bewildered, believed the story himself as firmly as those who had heard him tell it over and over for so many years.

Nég Créol

AT the remote period of his birth he had been named César François Xavier, but no one ever thought of calling him anything but Chicot,[1] or Nég, or Maringouin.[2] Down at the French market, where he worked among the fishmongers, they called him Chicot, when they were not calling him names that are written less freely than they are spoken. But one felt privileged to call him almost anything, he was so black, lean, lame, and shriveled. He wore a headkerchief, and whatever other rags the fishermen and their wives chose to bestow upon him. Throughout one whole winter he wore a woman's discarded jacket with puffed sleeves.

Among some startling beliefs entertained by Chicot was one that "Michié St. Pierre et Michié St. Paul" had created him. Of "Michié bon Dieu" he held his own private opinion, and not a too flattering one at that. This fantastic notion concerning the origin of his being he owed to the early teaching of his young master, a lax believer, and a great *farceur*[3] in his day. Chicot had once been thrashed by a robust young Irish priest for expressing his religious views, and at another time knifed by a Sicilian. So he had come to hold his peace upon that subject.

Upon another theme he talked freely and harped continuously. For years he had tried to convince his associates that his master had left a progeny, rich, cultured, powerful, and numerous beyond belief. This prosperous race of beings inhabited the most imposing mansions in the city of New Orleans. Men of note and position, whose names were familiar to the public, he swore were grandchildren, great-grandchildren, or, less frequently, distant relatives of his master, long deceased. Ladies who came to the market in carriages, or whose elegance of attire attracted the attention and admiration of the fishwomen, were all *des 'tites cousines*[4] to his former master, Jean Boisduré.[5] He never looked for recognition from any of these superior beings, but delighted to discourse by the hour upon their dignity and pride of birth and wealth.

Chicot always carried an old gunny-sack, and into this went his earnings. He cleaned stalls at the market, scaled fish, and did many odd offices for the itinerant merchants, who usually paid in trade for his service. Occasionally he saw the color of silver and got his clutch upon a coin, but he accepted anything, and seldom made terms. He was glad to get a handkerchief from the Hebrew, and grateful if the Choctaws would trade him a bottle of *filé* for it. The butcher flung him a soup bone, and the fishmonger a few crabs or a paper bag of shrimps. It was the big *mulatresse, vendeuse de café,*[6] who cared for his inner man.

Once Chicot was accused by a shoe-vender of attempting to steal a pair of ladies' shoes. He declared he was only examining them. The clamor raised in the market was terrific. Young Dagoes assembled and squealed like rats; a couple of Gascon butchers bellowed like bulls. Matteo's wife shook her fist in the accuser's face and called him incomprehensible names. The Choctaw women, where they squatted, turned their slow eyes in the direction of the fray, taking no further notice; while a policeman jerked Chicot around by the puffed sleeve and brandished a club. It was a narrow escape.

Nobody knew where Chicot lived. A man—even a nég créol— who lives among the reeds and willows of Bayou St. John, in a deserted chicken-coop constructed chiefly of tarred paper, is not going to boast of his habitation or to invite attention to his domestic appointments. When, after market hours, he vanished in the direction of St. Philip street, limping, seemingly bent under the weight of his gunny-bag, it was like the disappearance from the stage of some petty actor whom the audience does not follow in imagination beyond the wings, or think of till his return in another scene.

There was one to whom Chicot's coming or going meant more than this. In *la maison grise*[7] they called her La Chouette,[8] for no earthly reason unless that she perched high under the roof of the old rookery and scolded in shrill sudden outbursts. Forty or fifty years before, when for a little while she acted minor parts with a company of French players (an escapade that had brought her grandmother to the grave), she was known as Mademoiselle de Montallaine. Seventy-five years before she had been christened Aglaé Boisduré.

No matter at what hour the old negro appeared at her threshold, Mamzelle Aglaé always kept him waiting till she finished her prayers. She opened the door for him and silently motioned him to a seat, returning to prostrate herself upon her knees before a crucifix, and a shell filled with holy water that stood on a small table; it represented in her imagination an altar. Chicot knew that she did it to aggravate him; he was convinced that she timed her devotions to begin when she heard his footsteps on the stairs. He would sit with sullen eyes contemplating her long, spare, poorly clad figure as she knelt and read from her book or finished her prayers. Bitter was the religious warfare that had raged for years between them, and Mamzelle Aglaé had grown, on her side, as intolerant as Chicot. She had come to hold St. Peter and St. Paul in such utter detestation that she had cut their pictures out of her prayer-book.

Then Mamzelle Aglaé pretended not to care what Chicot had in his bag. He drew forth a small hunk of beef and laid it in her basket that stood on the bare floor. She looked from the corner of her eye, and went on dusting the table. He brought out a handful of potatoes, some pieces of sliced fish, a few herbs, a yard of calico, and a small pat of butter wrapped in lettuce leaves. He was proud of the butter, and wanted her to notice it. He held it out and asked her for something to put it on. She handed him a saucer, and looked indifferent and resigned, with lifted eyebrows.

"Pas d' sucre, Nég?"[9]

Chicot shook his head and scratched it, and looked like a black picture of distress and mortification. No sugar! But tomorrow he would get a pinch here and a pinch there, and would bring as much as a cupful.

Mamzelle Aglaé then sat down, and talked to Chicot uninterruptedly and confidentially. She complained bitterly, and it was all about a pain that lodged in her leg; that crept and acted like a live, stinging serpent, twining about her waist and up her spine, and coiling round the shoulder-blade. And then *les rheumatismes* in her fingers! He could see for himself how they were knotted. She could not bend them; she could hold nothing in her hands, and had let a saucer fall that morning and broken it in pieces. And if she were to tell him that she had slept a wink through the night, she would be a liar, deserving of perdition. She had sat at the window *la nuit blanche*,[10] hearing the hours strike and the market-wagons rumble. Chicot nodded, and kept up a running fire of sympathetic comment and suggestive remedies for rheumatism and insomnia: herbs, or *tisanes*,[11] or *grigris*,[12] or all three. As if he knew! There was Purgatory Mary, a perambulating soul whose office in life was to pray for the shades in purgatory,—she had brought Mamzelle Aglaé a bottle of *eau de Lourdes*,[13] but so little of it! She might have kept her water of Lourdes, for all the good it did,—a drop! Not so much as would cure a fly or a mosquito! Mamzelle Aglaé was going to show Purgatory Mary the door when she came again, not only because of her avarice with the Lourdes water, but, beside that, she brought in on her feet dirt that could only be removed with a shovel after she left.

And Mamzelle Aglaé wanted to inform Chicot that there would be slaughter and bloodshed in *la maison grise* if the people below stairs did not mend their ways. She was convinced that they lived for no other purpose than to torture and molest her. The woman kept a bucket of dirty water constantly on the landing with the hope of Mamzelle Aglaé falling over it or into it. And she knew that the children were instructed to gather in the hall and on the stairway, and scream and make a noise and jump up and down like galloping horses, with the intention of driving her to suicide. Chicot should notify the policeman on the beat, and have them arrested, if possible, and thrust into the parish prison, where they belonged.

Chicot would have been extremely alarmed if he had ever chanced to find Mamzelle Aglaé in an uncomplaining mood. It never occurred to him that she might be otherwise. He felt that she had a right to quarrel with fate, if ever mortal had. Her poverty was a disgrace, and he hung his head before it and felt ashamed.

One day he found Mamzelle Aglaé stretched on the bed, with her head tied up in a handkerchief. Her sole complaint that day was, "Aïe—aïe—aïe! Aïe—aïe—aïe!" uttered with every breath. He had seen her so before, especially when the weather was damp.

"Vous pas bézouin tisane, Mamzelle Aglaé? Vous pas veux mo cri gagni docteur?"[14]

She desired nothing. "Aïe—aïe—aïe!"

He emptied his bag very quietly, so as not to disturb her; and he wanted to stay there with her and lie down on the floor in case she needed him, but the woman from below had come up. She was an Irishwoman with rolled sleeves.

"It's a shtout shtick I'm afther giving her, Nég, and she do but knock on the flure it's me or Janie or wan of us that'll be hearing her."

"You too good, Brigitte. Aïe—aïe—aïe! Une goutte d'eau sucré, Nég![15] That Purg'tory Marie,—you see hair, ma bonne Brigitte,[16] you tell hair go say li'le prayer là-bas au Cathédral.[17] Aïe—aïe—aïe!"

Nég could hear her lamentation as he descended the stairs. It followed him as he limped his way through the city streets, and seemed part of the city's noise; he could hear it in the rumble of wheels and jangle of car-bells, and in the voices of those passing by.

He stopped at Mimotte the Voudou's shanty and bought a *grigri*—a cheap one for fifteen cents. Mimotte held her charms at all prices. This he intended to introduce next day into Mamzelle Aglaé's room,—somewhere about the altar,—to the confusion and discomfort of "Michié bon Dieu," who persistently declined to concern himself with the welfare of a Boisduré.

At night, among the reeds on the bayou, Chicot could still hear the woman's wail, mingled now with the croaking of the frogs. If he could have been convinced that giving up his life down there in the water would in any way have bettered her condition, he would not have hesitated to sacrifice the remnant of his existence that was wholly devoted to her. He lived but to serve her. He did not know it himself; but Chicot knew so little, and that little in such a distorted way! He could scarcely have been expected, even in his most lucid moments, to give himself over to self-analysis.

Chicot gathered an uncommon amount of dainties at market the following day. He had to work hard, and scheme and whine a little; but he got hold of an orange and a lump of ice and a *chou-fleur*.[18] He did not drink his cup of *café au lait*, but asked Mimi Lambeau to put it in the little new tin pail that the Hebrew notion-vender had just given him in exchange for a mess of shrimps. This time, however, Chicot had his trouble for nothing. When he reached the upper room of *la maison grise,* it was to find that Mamzelle Aglaé had died during the night. He set his bag down in the middle of the floor, and stood shaking, and whined low like a dog in pain.

Everything had been done. The Irishwoman had gone for the doctor, and Purgatory Mary had summoned a priest. Furthermore, the woman had arranged Mamzelle Aglaé decently. She had covered the table with a white cloth, and had placed it at the head of the bed, with the crucifix and two lighted candles in silver candlesticks upon it; the little bit of ornamentation brightened and embellished the poor room. Purgatory Mary, dressed in shabby black, fat and breathing hard, sat reading half audibly from a prayerbook. She was watching the dead and the silver candlesticks, which she had borrowed from a benevolent society, and for which she held herself responsible. A young man was just leaving,—a reporter snuffing the air for items, who had scented one up there in the top room of *la maison grise.*

All the morning Janie had been escorting a procession of street Arabs up and down the stairs to view the remains. One of them—a little girl, who had had her face washed and had made a species of toilet for the occasion—refused to be dragged away. She stayed seated as if at an entertainment, fascinated alternately by the long, still figure of Mamzelle Aglaé, the mumbling lips of Purgatory Mary, and the silver candlesticks.

"Will ye get down on yer knees, man, and say a prayer for the dead!" commanded the woman.

But Chicot only shook his head, and refused to obey. He approached the bed, and laid a little black paw for a moment on the stiffened body of Mamzelle Aglaé. There was nothing for him to do here. He picked up his old ragged hat and his bag and went away.

"The black h'athen!" the woman muttered. "Shut the dure, child."

The little girl slid down from her chair, and went on tiptoe to shut the door which Chicot had left open. Having resumed her seat, she fastened her eyes upon Purgatory Mary's heaving chest.

"You, Chicot!" cried Matteo's wife the next morning. "My man, he read in paper 'bout woman name' Boisduré, use' b'long to big-a famny. She die roun' on St. Philip—po', same-a like church rat. It's any them Boisdurés you alla talk 'bout?"

Chicot shook his head in slow but emphatic denial. No, indeed, the woman was not of kin to his Boisdurés. He surely had told Matteo's wife often enough—how many times did he have to repeat it!—of their wealth, their social standing. It was doubtless some Boisduré of *les Attakapas;*[19] it was none of his.

The next day there was a small funeral procession passing a little distance away,—a hearse and a carriage or two. There was the priest who had attended Mamzelle Aglaé, and a benevolent Creole gentleman whose father had known the Boisdurés in his youth. There was a couple of player-folk, who, having got wind of the story, had thrust their hands into their pockets.

"Look, Chicot!" cried Matteo's wife. "Yonda go the fune'al. Mus-a be that-a Boisduré woman we talken 'bout yesaday."

But Chicot paid no heed. What was to him the funeral of a woman who had died in St. Philip street? He did not even turn his head in the direction of the moving procession. He went on scaling his red-snapper.

The Lilies

THAT little vagabond Mamouche amused himself one afternoon by letting down the fence rails that protected Mr. Billy's young crop of cotton and corn. He had first looked carefully about him to make sure there was no witness to this piece of rascality. Then he crossed the lane and did the same with the Widow Angèle's fence, thereby liberating Toto, the white calf who stood disconsolately penned up on the other side.

It was not ten seconds before Toto was frolicking madly in Mr. Billy's crop, and Mamouche—the young scamp—was running swiftly down the lane, laughing fiendishly to himself as he went.

He could not at first decide whether there could be more fun in letting Toto demolish things at his pleasure, or in warning Mr. Billy of the calf's presence in the field. But the latter course commended itself as possessing a certain refinement of perfidy.

"Ho, the'a, you!" called out Mamouche to one of Mr. Billy's hands, when he got around to where the men were at work; "you betta go yon'a an' see 'bout that calf o' Ma'me Angèle; he done broke in the fiel' an' 'bout to finish the crop, him." Then Mamouche went and sat behind a big tree, where, unobserved, he could laugh to his heart's content.

Mr. Billy's fury was unbounded when he learned that Madame Angèle's calf was eating up and trampling down his corn. At once he sent a detachment of men and boys to expel the animal from the field. Others were required to repair the damaged fence; while he himself, boiling with wrath, rode up the lane on his wicked black charger.

But merely to look upon the devastation was not enough for Mr. Billy. He dismounted from his horse, and strode belligerently up to

Madame Angèle's door, upon which he gave, with his riding-whip, a couple of sharp raps that plainly indicated the condition of his mind.

Mr. Billy looked taller and broader than ever as he squared himself on the gallery of Madame Angèle's small and modest house. She herself half-opened the door, a pale, sweet-looking woman, somewhat bewildered, and holding a piece of sewing in her hands. Little Marie Louise was beside her, with big, inquiring, frightened eyes.

"Well, Madam!" blustered Mr. Billy, "this is a pretty piece of work! That young beast of yours is a fence-breaker, Madam, and ought to be shot."

"Oh, non, non, M'sieur. Toto's too li'le; I'm sho he can't break any fence, him."

"Don't contradict me, Madam. I say he's a fence-breaker. There's the proof before your eyes. He ought to be shot, I say, and—don't let it occur again, Madam." And Mr. Billy turned and stamped down the steps with a great clatter of spurs as he went.

Madame Angèle was at the time in desperate haste to finish a young lady's Easter dress, and she could not afford to let Toto's escapade occupy her to any extent, much as she regretted it. But little Marie Louise was greatly impressed by the affair. She went out in the yard to Toto, who was under the fig-tree, looking not half so shamefaced as he ought. The child, with arms clasped around the little fellow's white shaggy neck, scolded him roundly.

"Ain't you shame', Toto, to go eat up Mr. Billy's cotton an' co'n? W'at Mr. Billy ev'a done to you, to go do him that way? If you been hungry, Toto, w'y you did'n' come like always an' put yo' head in the winda? I'm goin' tell yo' maman w'en she come back f'om the woods to 's'evenin', M'sieur."

Marie Louise only ceased her mild rebuke when she fancied she saw a penitential look in Toto's big soft eyes.

She had a keen instinct of right and justice for so young a little maid. And all the afternoon, and long into the night, she was disturbed by the thought of the unfortunate accident. Of course, there could be no question of repaying Mr. Billy with money; she and her mother had none. Neither had they cotton and corn with which to make good the loss he had sustained through them.

But had they not something far more beautiful and precious than cotton and corn? Marie Louise thought with delight of that row of

Easter lilies on their tall green stems, ranged thick along the sunny side of the house.

The assurance that she would, after all, be able to satisfy Mr. Billy's just anger, was a very sweet one. And soothed by it, Marie Louise soon fell asleep and dreamt a grotesque dream: that the lilies were having a stately dance on the green in the moonlight, and were inviting Mr. Billy to join them.

The following day, when it was nearing noon, Marie Louise said to her mamma: "Maman, can I have some of the Easter lily, to do with like I want?"

Madame Angèle was just then testing the heat of an iron with which to press out the seams in the young lady's Easter dress, and she answered a shade impatiently:

"Yes, yes; va t'en, chérie,"[1] thinking that her little girl wanted to pluck a lily or two.

So the child took a pair of old shears from her mother's basket, and out she went to where the tall, perfumed lilies were nodding, and shaking off from their glistening petals the rain-drops with which a passing cloud had just laughingly pelted them.

Snip, snap, went the shears here and there, and never did Marie Louise stop plying them till scores of those long-stemmed lilies lay upon the ground. There were far more than she could hold in her small hands, so she literally clasped the great bunch in her arms, and staggered to her feet with it.

Marie Louise was intent upon her purpose, and lost no time in its accomplishment. She was soon trudging earnestly down the lane with her sweet burden, never stopping, and only once glancing aside to cast a reproachful look at Toto, whom she had not wholly forgiven.

She did not in the least mind that the dogs barked, or that the darkies laughed at her. She went straight on to Mr. Billy's big house, and right into the dining-room, where Mr. Billy sat eating his dinner all alone.

It was a finely-furnished room, but disorderly—very disorderly, as an old bachelor's personal surroundings sometimes are. A black boy stood waiting upon the table. When little Marie Louise suddenly appeared, with that armful of lilies, Mr. Billy seemed for a moment transfixed at the sight.

"Well—bless—my soul! what's all this? What's all this?" he questioned, with staring eyes.

Marie Louise had already made a little courtesy. Her sunbonnet had fallen back, leaving exposed her pretty round head; and her sweet brown eyes were full of confidence as they looked into Mr. Billy's.

"I'm bring some lilies to pay back fo' yo' cotton an' co'n w'at Toto eat all up, M'sieur."

Mr. Billy turned savagely upon Pompey. "What are you laughing at, you black rascal? Leave the room!"

Pompey, who out of mistaken zeal had doubled himself with merriment, was too accustomed to the admonition to heed it literally, and he only made a pretense of withdrawing from Mr. Billy's elbow.

"Lilies! well, upon my—isn't it the little one from across the lane?"

"Dat's who," affirmed Pompey, cautiously insinuating himself again into favor.

"Lilies! who ever heard the like? Why, the baby's buried under 'em. Set 'em down somewhere, little one; anywhere." And Marie Louise, glad to be relieved from the weight of the great cluster, dumped them all on the table close to Mr. Billy.

The perfume that came from the damp, massed flowers was heavy and almost sickening in its pungency. Mr. Billy quivered a little, and drew involuntarily back, as if from an unexpected assailant, when the odor reached him. He had been making cotton and corn for so many years, he had forgotten there were such things as lilies in the world.

"Kiar 'em out? fling 'em 'way?" questioned Pompey, who had observed his master cunningly.

"Let 'em alone! Keep your hands off them! Leave the room, you outlandish black scamp! Whar are you standing there for? Can't you set the Mamzelle a place at table, and draw up a chair?"

So Marie Louise—perched upon a fine old-fashioned chair, supplemented by a Webster's Unabridged—sat down to dine with Mr. Billy.

She had never eaten in company with so peculiar a gentlemen before; so irascible toward the inoffensive Pompey, and so courteous to herself. But she was not ill at ease, and conducted herself properly as her mamma had taught her how.

Mr. Billy was anxious that she should enjoy her dinner, and began by helping her generously to Jambalaya. When she had tasted it she made no remark, only laid down her fork, and looked composedly before her.

"Why, bless me! what ails the little one? You don't eat your rice."

"It ain't cook', M'sieur," replied Marie Louise politely.

Pompey nearly strangled in his attempt to smother an explosion.

"Of course it isn't cooked," echoed Mr. Billy, excitedly, pushing away his plate. "What do you mean, setting a mess of that sort before human beings? Do you take us for a couple of—of rice-birds? What are you standing there for; can't you look up some jam or something to keep the young one from starving? Where's all that jam I saw stewing a while back, here?"

Pompey withdrew, and soon returned with a platter of black-looking jam. Mr. Billy ordered cream for it. Pompey reported there was none.

"No cream, with twenty-five cows on the plantation if there's one!" cried Mr. Billy, almost springing from his chair with indignation.

"Aunt Printy 'low she sot de pan o' cream on de winda-sell, suh, an' Unc' Jonah come 'long an' tu'n it cl'ar ova; neva lef' a drap in de pan."

But evidently the jam, with or without cream, was as distasteful to Marie Louise as the rice was; for after tasting it gingerly she laid away her spoon as she had done before.

"O, no! little one; you don't tell me it isn't cooked this time," laughed Mr. Billy. "I saw the thing boiling a day and a half. Wasn't it a day and a half, Pompey? if you know how to tell the truth."

"Aunt Printy alluz do cooks her p'esarves tell dey plumb done, sho," agreed Pompey.

"It's burn', M'sieur," said Marie Louise, politely, but decidedly, to the utter confusion of Mr. Billy, who was as mortified as could be at the failure of his dinner to please his fastidious little visitor.

Well, Mr. Billy thought of Marie Louise a good deal after that; as long as the lilies lasted. And they lasted long, for he had the whole household employed in taking care of them. Often he would chuckle to himself: "The little rogue, with her black eyes and her lilies! And the rice wasn't cooked, if you please; and the jam was burnt. And the best of it is, she was right."

But when the lilies withered finally, and had to be thrown away, Mr. Billy donned his best suit, a starched shirt and fine silk necktie. Thus attired, he crossed the lane to carry his somewhat tardy apologies to Madame Angèle and Mamzelle Marie Louise, and to pay them a first visit.

Azélie

AZÉLIE crossed the yard with slow, hesitating steps. She wore a pink sunbonnet and a faded calico dress that had been made the summer before, and was now too small for her in every way. She carried a large tin pail on her arm. When within a few yards of the house she stopped under a chinaberry-tree, quite still, except for the occasional slow turning of her head from side to side.

Mr. Mathurin, from his elevation upon the upper gallery, laughed when he saw her; for he knew she would stay there, motionless, till some one noticed and questioned her.

The planter was just home from the city, and was therefore in an excellent humor, as he always was, on getting back to what he called *le grand air*,[1] the space and stillness of the country, and the scent of the fields. He was in shirtsleeves, walking around the gallery that encircled the big square white house. Beneath was a brick-paved portico upon which the lower rooms opened. At wide intervals were large whitewashed pillars that supported the upper gallery.

In one corner of the lower house was the store, which was in no sense a store for the general public, but maintained only to supply the needs of Mr. Mathurin's "hands."

"Eh bien! what do you want, Azélie?" the planter finally called out to the girl in French. She advanced a few paces, and, pushing back her sunbonnet, looked up at him with a gentle, inoffensive face—"to which you would give the good God without confession," he once described it.

"Bon jou', M'si' Mathurin,"[2] she replied; and continued in English: "I come git a li'le piece o' meat. We plumb out o' meat home."

"Well, well, the meat is n' going to walk to you, my chile: it has

276

n' got feet. Go fine Mr. 'Polyte. He's yonda mending his buggy unda the shed." She turned away with an alert little step, and went in search of Mr. 'Polyte.

"That's you again!" the young man exclaimed, with a pretended air of annoyance, when he saw her. He straightened himself, and looked down at her and her pail with a comprehending glance. The sweat was standing in shining beads on his brown, good-looking face. He was in his shirt-sleeves, and the legs of his trousers were thrust into the tops of his fine, high-heeled boots. He wore his straw hat very much on one side, and had an air that was altogether *fanfaron.*[3] He reached to a back pocket for the store key, which was as large as the pistol that he sometimes carried in the same place. She followed him across the thick, tufted grass of the yard with quick, short steps that strove to keep pace with his longer, swinging ones.

When he had unlocked and opened the heavy door of the store, there escaped from the close room the strong, pungent odor of the varied wares and provisions massed within. Azélie seemed to like the odor, and, lifting her head, snuffed the air as people sometimes do upon entering a conservatory filled with fragrant flowers.

A broad ray of light streamed in through the open door, illumining the dingy interior. The double wooden shutters of the windows were all closed, and secured on the inside by iron hooks.

"Well, w'at you want, Azélie?" asked 'Polyte, going behind the counter with an air of hurry and importance. "I ain't got time to fool. Make has'e; say w'at you want."

Her reply was precisely the same that she had made to Mr. Mathurin.

"I come git a li'le piece o' meat. We plumb out o' meat home."

He seemed exasperated.

"Bonté! w'at you all do with meat yonda? You don't reflec' you about to eat up yo' crop befo' it's good out o' the groun', you all. I like to know w'y yo' pa don't go he'p with the killin' once aw'ile, an' git some fresh meat fo' a change."

She answered in an unshaded, unmodulated voice that was penetrating, like a child's: "Popa he do go he'p wid the killin'; but he say he can't work 'less he got salt meat. He got plenty to feed—him. He's got to hire he'p wid his crop, an' he's boun' to feed 'em; they won't year no diffe'nt. An' he's got gra'ma to feed, an' Sauterelle, an' me—"

"An' all the lazy-bone 'Cadians in the country that know w'ere they goin' to fine the coffee-pot always in the corna of the fire," grumbled 'Polyte.

With an iron hook he lifted a small piece of salt meat from the pork barrel, weighed it, and placed it in her pail. Then she wanted a little coffee. He gave it to her reluctantly. He was still more loath to let her have sugar; and when she asked for lard, he refused flatly.

She had taken off her sunbonnet, and was fanning herself with it, as she leaned with her elbows upon the counter, and let her eyes travel lingeringly along the well-lined shelves. 'Polyte stood staring into her face with a sense of aggravation that her presence, her manner, always stirred up in him.

The face was colorless but for the red, curved line of the lips. Her eyes were dark, wide, innocent, questioning eyes, and her black hair was plastered smooth back from the forehead and temples. There was no trace of any intention of coquetry in her manner. He resented this as a token of indifference toward his sex, and thought it inexcusable.

"Well, Azélie, if it's anything you don't see, ask fo' it," he suggested, with what he flattered himself was humor. But there was no responsive humor in Azélie's composition. She seriously drew a small flask from her pocket.

"Popa say, if you want to let him have a li'le dram, 'count o' his pains that's 'bout to cripple him."

"Yo' pa knows as well as I do we don't sell w'isky. Mr. Mathurin don't carry no license."

"I know. He say if you want to give 'im a li'le dram, he's willin' to do some work fo' you."

"No! Once fo' all, no!" And 'Polyte reached for the day-book, in which to enter the articles he had given to her.

But Azélie's needs were not yet satisfied. She wanted tobacco; he would not give it to her. A spool of thread; he rolled one up, together with two sticks of peppermint candy, and placed it in her pail. When she asked for a bottle of coal-oil, he grudgingly consented, but assured her it would be useless to cudgel her brain further, for he would positively let her have nothing more. He disappeared toward the coal-oil tank, which was hidden from view behind the piled-up boxes on the counter. When she heard him searching for an empty quart bottle, and making a clatter with the tin funnels, she herself withdrew from the counter against which she had been leaning.

After they quitted the store, 'Polyte, with a perplexed expression upon his face, leaned for a moment against one of the whitewashed pillars, watching the girl cross the yard. She had folded her sunbonnet into a pad, which she placed beneath the heavy pail that she balanced upon her head. She walked upright, with a slow, careful tread. Two of the yard dogs that had stood a moment before upon the threshold of the store door, quivering and wagging their tails, were following her now, with a little businesslike trot. 'Polyte called them back.

The cabin which the girl occupied with her father, her grandmother, and her little brother Sauterelle, was removed some distance from the plantation house, and only its pointed roof could be discerned like a speck far away across the field of cotton, which was all in bloom. Her figure soon disappeared from view, and 'Polyte emerged from the shelter of the gallery, and started again toward his interrupted task. He turned to say to the planter, who was keeping up his measured tramp above:

"Mr. Mathurin, ain't it 'mos' time to stop givin' credit to Arsène Pauché. Look like that crop o' his ain't goin' to start to pay his account. I don't see, me, anyway, how you come to take that triflin' Li'le river gang on the place."

"I know it was a mistake, 'Polyte, but que voulez-vous?"[4] the planter returned, with a good-natured shrug. "Now they are yere, we can't let them starve, my frien'. Push them to work all you can. Hole back all supplies that are not necessary, an' nex' year we will let some one else enjoy the privilège of feeding them," he ended, with a laugh.

"I wish they was all back on Li'le river," 'Polyte muttered under his breath as he turned and walked slowly away.

Directly back of the store was the young man's sleeping-room. He had made himself quite comfortable there in his corner. He had screened his windows and doors; planted Madeira vines, which now formed a thick green curtain between the two pillars that faced his room; and had swung a hammock out there, in which he liked well to repose himself after the fatigues of the day.

He lay long in the hammock that evening, thinking over the day's happenings and the morrow's work, half dozing, half dreaming, and wholly possessed by the charm of the night, the warm, sweeping air that blew through the long corridor, and the almost unbroken stillness that enveloped him.

At times his random thoughts formed themselves into an almost inaudible speech: "I wish she would go 'way f'om yere."

One of the dogs came and thrust his cool, moist muzzle against 'Polyte's cheek. He caressed the fellow's shaggy head. "I don't know w'at's the matta with her," he sighed; "I don' b'lieve she's got good sense."

It was a long time afterward that he murmured again: "I wish to God she'd go 'way f'om yere!"

The edge of the moon crept up—a keen, curved blade of light above the dark line of the cotton-field. 'Polyte roused himself when he saw it. "I didn't know it was so late," he said to himself—or to his dog. He entered his room at once, and was soon in bed, sleeping soundly.

It was some hours later that 'Polyte was roused from his sleep by—he did not know what; his senses were too scattered and confused to determine at once. There was at first no sound; then so faint a one that he wondered how he could have heard it. A door of his room communicated with the store, but this door was never used, and was almost completely blocked by wares piled up on the other side. The faint noise that 'Polyte heard, and which came from within the store, was followed by a flare of light that he could discern through the chinks, and that lasted as long as a match might burn.

He was now fully aware that some one was in the store. How the intruder had entered he could not guess, for the key was under his pillow with his watch and his pistol.

As cautiously as he could he donned an extra garment, thrust his bare feet into slippers, and crept out into the portico, pistol in hand.

The shutters of one of the store windows were open. He stood close to it, and waited, which he considered surer and safer than to enter the dark and crowded confines of the store to engage in what might prove a bootless struggle with the intruder.

He had not long to wait. In a few moments some one darted through the open window as nimbly as a cat. 'Polyte staggered back as if a heavy blow had stunned him. His first thought and his first exclamation were: "My God! how close I come to killin' you!"

It was Azélie. She uttered no cry, but made one quick effort to run when she saw him. He seized her arm and held her with a brutal grip. He put the pistol back into his pocket. He was shaking like a man with the palsy. One by one he took from her the parcels she was carrying, and flung them back into the store. There were not many: some packages of tobacco, a cheap pipe, some fishing-tackle, and the flask which she had brought with her in the afternoon. This he threw into the yard. It was still empty, for she had not been able to find the "key" to the whisky-barrel.

"So—so, you a thief!" he muttered savagely under his breath.

"You hurtin' me, Mr. 'Polyte," she complained, squirming. He somewhat relaxed, but did not relinquish, his hold upon her.

"I ain't no thief," she blurted.

"You was stealin'," he contradicted her sharply.

"I wasn' stealin'. I was jus' takin' a few li'le things you all too mean to gi' me. You all treat my popa like he was a dog. It's on'y las' week Mr. Mathurin sen' 'way to the city to fetch a fine buck-boa'd fo' Son Ambroise, an' he's on'y a nigga, après tout.[5] An' my popa he want a picayune tobacco? It's 'No'—" She spoke loud in her monotonous, shrill voice. 'Polyte kept saying: "Hush, I tell you! Hush! Somebody'll year you. Hush! It's enough you broke in the sto'—how you got in the sto'?" he added, looking from her to the open window.

"It was w'en you was behine the boxes to the coal-oil tank—I unhook' it," she explained sullenly.

"An' you don' know I could sen' you to Baton Rouge fo' that?" He shook her as though trying to rouse her to a comprehension of her grievous fault.

"Jus' fo' a li'le picayune o' tobacca!" she whimpered.

He suddenly abandoned his hold upon her, and left her free. She mechanically rubbed the arm that he had grasped so violently.

Between the long row of pillars the moon was sending pale beams of light. In one of these they were standing.

"Azélie," he said, "go 'way f'om yere quick; some one might fine you yere. W'en you want something in the sto', fo' yo'se'f or fo' yo'

pa—I don' care—ask me fo' it. But you—but you can't neva set yo'
foot inside that sto' again. Go 'way f'om yere quick as you can, I
tell you!"

She tried in no way to conciliate him. She turned and walked
away over the same ground she had crossed before. One of the big
dogs started to follow her. 'Polyte did not call him back this time.
He knew no harm could come to her, going through those lonely
fields, while the animal was at her side.

He went at once to his room for the store key that was beneath
his pillow. He entered the store, and refastened the window. When
he had made everything once more secure, he sat dejectedly down
upon a bench that was in the portico. He sat for a long time motionless. Then, overcome by some powerful feeling that was at
work within him, he buried his face in his hands and wept, his
whole body shaken by the violence of his sobs.

After that night 'Polyte loved Azélie desperately. The very action
which should have revolted him had seemed, on the contrary, to inflame him with love. He felt that love to be a degradation—something that he was almost ashamed to acknowledge to himself; and
he knew that he was hopelessly unable to stifle it.

He watched now in a tremor for her coming. She came very often, for she remembered every word he had said; and she did not
hesitate to ask him for those luxuries which she considered necessi-
ties to her "popa's" existence. She never attempted to enter the
store, but always waited outside, of her own accord, laughing, and
playing with the dogs. She seemed to have no shame or regret for
what she had done, and plainly did not realize that it was a disgraceful act. 'Polyte often shuddered with disgust to discern in her a
being so wholly devoid of moral sense.

He had always been an industrious, bustling fellow, never idle.
Now there were hours and hours in which he did nothing but long
for the sight of Azélie. Even when at work there was that gnawing
want at his heart to see her, often so urgent that he would leave
everything to wander down by her cabin with the hope of seeing
her. It was even something if he could catch a glimpse of Sauterelle
playing in the weeds, or of Arsène lazily dragging himself about,
and smoking the pipe which rarely left his lips now that he was kept
so well supplied with tobacco.

Once, down the bank of the bayou, when 'Polyte came upon Azélie unexpectedly, and was therefore unprepared to resist the shock of her sudden appearance, he seized her in his arms, and covered her face with kisses. She was not indignant; she was not flustered or agitated, as might have been a susceptible, coquettish girl; she was only astonished, and annoyed.

"W'at you doin', Mr. 'Polyte?" she cried, struggling. "Leave me 'lone, I say! Leave me go!"

"I love you, I love you, I love you!" he stammered helplessly over and over in her face.

"You mus' los' yo' head," she told him, red from the effort of the struggle, when he released her.

"You right, Azélie; I b'lieve I los' my head," and he climbed up the bank of the bayou as fast as he could.

After that his behavior was shameful, and he knew it, and he did not care. He invented pretexts that would enable him to touch her hand with his. He wanted to kiss her again, and told her she might come into the store as she used to do. There was no need for her to unhook a window now; he gave her whatever she asked for, charging it always to his own account on the books. She permitted his caresses without returning them, and yet that was all he seemed to live for now. He gave her a little gold ring.

He was looking eagerly forward to the close of the season, when Arsène would go back to Little River. He had arranged to ask Azélie to marry him. He would keep her with him when the others went away. He longed to rescue her from what he felt to be the demoralizing influences of her family and her surroundings. 'Polyte believed he would be able to awaken Azélie to finer, better impulses when he should have her apart to himself.

But when the time came to propose it, Azélie looked at him in amazement. "Ah, b'en, no. I ain't goin' to stay yere wid you, Mr. 'Polyte; I'm goin' yonda on Li'le river wid my popa."

This resolve frightened him, but he pretended not to believe it.

"You jokin', Azélie; you mus' care a li'le about me. It looked to me all along like you cared some about me."

"An' my popa, donc? Ah, b'en, no."[6]

"You don' remamba how lonesome it is on Li'le river, Azélie," he pleaded. "W'enever I think 'bout Li'le river it always make me

sad—like I think about a graveyard. To me it's like a person mus'
die, one way or otha, w'en they go on Li'le river. Oh, I hate it! Stay
with me, Azélie; don' go 'way f'om me."

She said little, one way or the other, after that, when she had
fully understood his wishes, and her reserve led him to believe,
since he hoped it, that he had prevailed with her and that she had
determined to stay with him and be his wife.

It was a cool, crisp morning in December that they went away.
In a ramshackle wagon, drawn by an ill-mated team, Arsène Pauché
and his family left Mr. Mathurin's plantation for their old familiar
haunts on Little river. The grandmother, looking like a witch, with
a black shawl tied over her head, sat upon a roll of bedding in the
bottom of the wagon. Sauterelle's bead-like eyes glittered with mischief as he peeped over the side. Azélie, with the pink sunbonnet
completely hiding her round young face, sat beside her father, who
drove.

'Polyte caught one glimpse of the group as they passed in the
road. Turning, he hurried into his room, and locked himself in.

It soon became evident that 'Polyte's services were going to
count for little. He himself was the first to realize this. One day he
approached the planter, and said: "Mr. Mathurin, befo' we start anotha year togetha, I betta tell you I'm goin' to quit." 'Polyte stood
upon the steps, and leaned back against the railing. The planter was
a little above on the gallery.

"W'at in the name o' sense are you talking about, 'Polyte!" he
exclaimed in astonishment.

"It's jus' that; I'm boun' to quit."

"You had a better offer?"

"No; I ain't had no offa."

"Then explain yo'se'f, my frien'—explain yo'se'f," requested Mr.
Mathurin, with something of offended dignity. "If you leave me,
w'ere are you going?"

'Polyte was beating his leg with his limp felt hat. "I reckon I jus'
as well go yonda on Li'le river—w'ere Azélie," he said.

Mamouche

MAMOUCHE stood within the open doorway, which he had just entered. It was night; the rain was falling in torrents, and the water trickled from him as it would have done from an umbrella, if he had carried one.

Old Doctor John-Luis, who was toasting his feet before a blazing hickory-wood fire, turned to gaze at the youngster through his spectacles. Marshall, the old negro who had opened the door at the boy's knock, also looked down at him, and indignantly said:

"G'long back on de gall'ry an' drip yo'se'f! W'at Cynthy gwine say tomorrow w'en she see dat flo' mess' up dat away?"

"Come to the fire and sit down," said Doctor John-Luis.

Doctor John-Luis was a bachelor. He was small and thin; he wore snuff-colored clothes that were a little too large for him, and spectacles. Time had not deprived him of an abundant crop of hair that had once been red, and was not now more than half-bleached.

The boy looked irresolutely from master to man; then went and sat down beside the fire on a splint-bottom chair. He sat so close to the blaze that had he been an apple he would have roasted. As he was but a small boy, clothed in wet rags, he only steamed.

Marshall grumbled audibly, and Doctor John-Luis continued to inspect the boy through his glasses.

"Marsh, bring him something to eat," he commanded, tentatively.

Marshall hesitated, and challenged the child with a speculating look.

"Is you wi'te o' is you black?" he asked. "Dat w'at I wants ter know 'fo' I kiar' victuals to yo in de settin'-room."

"I'm w'ite, me," the boy responded, promptly.

"I ain't disputin'; go ahead. All right fer dem w'at wants ter take yo' wud fer it." Doctor John-Luis coughed behind his hand and said nothing.

Marshall brought a platter of cold food to the boy, who rested the dish upon his knees and ate from it with keen appetite.

"Where do you come from?" asked Doctor John-Luis, when his caller stopped for breath. Mamouche turned a pair of big, soft, dark eyes upon his questioner.

"I come frum Cloutierville this mo'nin'. I been try to git to the twenty-fo'-mile ferry w'en de rain ketch me."

"What were you going to do at the twenty-four-mile ferry?"

The boy gazed absently into the fire. "I don' know w'at I was goin' to do yonda to the twenty-fo'-mile ferry," he said.

"Then you must be a tramp, to be wandering aimlessly about the country in that way!" exclaimed the doctor.

"No; I don' b'lieve I'm a tramp, me." Mamouche was wriggling his toes with enjoyment of the warmth and palatable food.

"Well, what's your name?" continued Doctor John-Luis.

"My name it's Mamouche."

" 'Mamouche.' Fiddlesticks! That's no name."

The boy looked as if he regretted the fact, while not being able to help it.

"But my pa, his name it was Mathurin Peloté," he offered in some palliation.

"Peloté! Peloté!" mused Doctor John-Luis. "Any kin to Théodule Peloté who lived formerly in Avoyelles parish?"

"W'y, yas!" laughed Mamouche. "Théodule Peloté, it was my gran'pa."

"Your grandfather? Well, upon my word!" He looked again, critically, at the youngster's rags. "Then Stéphanie Galopin must have been your grandmother!"

"Yas," responded Mamouche, complacently; "that who was my gran'ma. She die two year ago down by Alexandria."

"Marsh," called Doctor John-Luis, turning in his chair, "bring him a mug of milk and another piece of pie!"

When Mamouche had eaten all the good things that were set before him, he found that one side of him was quite dry, and he transferred himself over to the other corner of the fire so as to turn to the blaze the side which was still wet.

The action seemed to amuse Doctor John-Luis, whose old head began to fill with recollections.

"That reminds me of Théodule," he laughed. "Ah, he was a great fellow, your father, Théodule!"

"My gran'pa," corrected Mamouche.

"Yes, yes, your grandfather. He was handsome; I tell you, he was good-looking. And the way he could dance and play the fiddle and sing! Let me see, how did that song go that he used to sing when we went out serenading: 'A ta—á ta—'

> 'A ta fenêtre
> Daignes paraître—tra la la la!' "[1]

Doctor John-Luis' voice, even in his youth, could not have been agreeable; and now it bore no resemblance to any sound that Mamouche had ever heard issue from a human throat. The boy kicked his heels and rolled sideward on his chair with enjoyment. Doctor John-Luis laughed even more heartily, finished the stanza, and sang another one through.

"That's what turned the girls' heads, I tell you, my boy," said he, when he had recovered his breath; "that fiddling and dancing and tra la la."

During the next hour the old man lived again through his youth; through any number of alluring experiences with his friend Théodule, that merry fellow who had never done a steady week's work in his life; and Stéphanie, the pretty Acadian girl, whom he had never wholly understood, even to this day.

It was quite late when Doctor John-Luis climbed the stairs that led from the sitting-room up to his bedchamber. As he went, followed by the ever attentive Marshall, he was singing:

> "A ta fenêtre
> Daignes paraître,"

but very low, so as not to awaken Mamouche, whom he left sleeping upon a bed that Marshall at his order had prepared for the boy beside the sitting-room fire.

At a very early hour next morning Marshall appeared at his master's bedside with the accustomed morning coffee.

"What is he doing?" asked Doctor John-Luis, as he sugared and stirred the tiny cup of black coffee.

"Who dat, sah?"

"Why, the boy, Mamouche. What is he doing?"

"He gone, sah. He done gone."

"Gone!"

"Yas, sah. He roll his bed up in de corner; he onlock de do'; he gone. But de silver an' ev'thing dah; he ain't kiar' nuttin' off."

"Marshall," snapped Doctor John-Luis, ill-humoredly, "there are times when you don't seem to have sense and penetration enough to talk about! I think I'll take another nap," he grumbled, as he turned his back upon Marshall. "Wake me at seven."

It was no ordinary thing for Doctor John-Luis to be in a bad humor, and perhaps it is not strictly true to say that he was now. He was only in a little less amiable mood than usual when he pulled on his high rubber boots and went splashing out in the wet to see what his people were doing.

He might have owned a large plantation had he wished to own one, for a long life of persistent, intelligent work had left him with a comfortable fortune in his old age; but he preferred the farm on which he lived contentedly and raised an abundance to meet his modest wants.

He went down to the orchard, where a couple of men were busying themselves in setting out a line of young fruit-trees.

"Tut, tut, tut!" They were doing it all wrong; the line was not straight; the holes were not deep. It was strange that he had to come down there and discover such things with his old eyes!

He poked his head into the kitchen to complain to Prudence about the ducks that she had not seasoned properly the day before, and to hope that the accident would never occur again.

He tramped over to where a carpenter was working on a gate; securing it—as he meant to secure all the gates upon his place—with great patent clamps and ingenious hinges, intended to baffle utterly the designs of the evil-disposed persons who had lately been tampering with them. For there had been a malicious spirit abroad, who played tricks, it seemed, for pure wantonness upon the farmers and planters, and caused them infinite annoyance.

As Dr. John-Luis contemplated the carpenter at work, and remembered how his gates had recently all been lifted from their hinges one night and left lying upon the ground, the provoking nature of the offense dawned upon him as it had not done before. He turned swiftly, prompted by a sudden determination, and re-entered the house.

Then he proceeded to write out in immense black characters a half-dozen placards. It was an offer of twenty-five dollars' reward for the capture of the person guilty of the malicious offence already described. These placards were sent abroad with the same eager haste that had conceived and executed them.

After a day or two, Doctor John-Luis' ill humor had resolved it-self into a pensive melancholy.

"Marsh," he said, "you know, after all, it's rather dreary to be liv-ing alone as I do, without any companion—of my own color, you understand."

"I knows dat, sah. It sho' am lonesome," replied the sympathetic Marshall.

"You see, Marsh, I've been thinking lately," and Doctor John-Luis coughed, for he disliked the inaccuracy of that "lately." "I've been thinking that this property and wealth that I've worked so hard to accumulate, are after all doing no permanent, practical good to any one. Now, if I could find some well-disposed boy whom I might train to work, to study, to lead a decent, honest life—a boy of good heart who would care for me in my old age; for I am still com-paratively—hem—not old? hey, Marsh?"

"Dey ain't one in de pa'ish hole yo' own like you does, sah."

"That's it. Now, can you think of such a boy? Try to think."

Marshall slowly scratched his head and looked reflective.

"If you can think of such a boy," said Doctor John-Luis, "you might bring him here to spend an evening with me, you know, without hinting at my intentions, of course. In that way I could sound him; study him up, as it were. For a step of such importance is not to be taken without due consideration, Marsh."

Well, the first whom Marshall brought was one of Baptiste Choupie's boys. He was a very timid child, and sat on the edge of his chair, fearfully. He replied in jerky monosyllables when Doctor John-Luis spoke to him, "Yas, sah—no, sah," as the case might be; with a little nervous bob of the head.

His presence made the doctor quite uncomfortable. He was glad to be rid of the boy at nine o'clock, when he sent him home with some oranges and a few sweetmeats.

Then Marshall had Theodore over; an unfortunate selection that evinced little judgment on Marshall's part. Not to mince matters, the boy was painfully forward. He monopolized the conversation; asked impertinent questions and handled and inspected everything in the room. Dr. John-Luis sent him home with an orange and not a single sweet.

Then there was Hyppolite, who was too ugly to be thought of; and Cami, who was heavy and stupid, and fell asleep in his chair with his mouth wide open. And so it went. If Doctor John-Luis had hoped in the company of any of these boys to repeat the agreeable evening he had passed with Mamouche, he was sadly deceived.

At last he instructed Marshall to discontinue the search of that ideal companion he had dreamed of. He was resigned to spend the remainder of his days without one.

Then, one day when it was raining again, and very muddy and chill, a red-faced man came driving up to Doctor John-Luis' door in a dilapidated buggy. He lifted a boy from the vehicle, whom he held with a vise-like clutch, and whom he straightway dragged into the astonished presence of Doctor John-Luis.

"Here he is, sir," shouted the red-faced man. "We've got him at last! Here he is."

It was Mamouche, covered with mud, the picture of misery. Doctor John-Luis stood with his back to the fire. He was startled, and visibly and painfully moved at the sight of the boy.

"Is it possible!" he exclaimed. "Then it was you, Mamouche, who did this mischievous thing to me? Lifting my gates from their hinges; letting the chickens in among my flowers to ruin them; and the hogs and cattle to trample and uproot my vegetables!"

"Ha! ha!" laughed the red-faced man, "that game's played out, now;" and Doctor John-Luis looked as if he wanted to strike him.

Mamouche seemed unable to reply. His lower lip was quivering.

"Yas, it's me!" he burst out. "It's me w'at take yo' gates off the hinge. It's me w'at turn loose Mr. Morgin's hoss, w'en Mr. Morgin was passing *veillée*[2] wid his sweetheart. It's me w'at take down Ma'ame Angèle's fence, an' lef her calf loose to tramp in Mr. Billy's cotton. It's me w'at play like a ghos' by the graveyard las' Toussaint to scare the darkies passin' in the road. It's me w'at—"

The confession had burst out from the depth of Mamouche's heart like a torrent, and there is no telling when it would have stopped if Doctor John-Luis had not enjoined silence.

"And pray tell me," he asked, as severely as he could, "why you left my house like a criminal, in the morning, secretly?"

The tears had begun to course down Mamouche's brown cheeks.

"I was 'shame' of myse'f, that's w'y. If you wouldn' gave me no suppa, an' no bed, an' no fire, I don' say. I wouldn' been 'shame' then."

"Well, sir," interrupted the red-faced man, "you've got a pretty square case against him, I see. Not only for malicious trespass, but of theft. See this bolt?" producing a piece of iron from his coat pocket. "That's what gave him away."

"I en't no thief!" blurted Mamouche, indignantly. "It's one piece o' iron w'at I pick up in the road."

"Sir," said Doctor John-Luis with dignity, "I can understand how the grandson of Théodule Peloté might be guilty of such mischievous pranks as this boy has confessed to. But I know that the grandson of Stéphanie Galopin could not be a thief."

And he at once wrote out the check for twenty-five dollars, and handed it to the red-faced man with the tips of his fingers.

It seemed very good to Doctor John-Luis to have the boy sitting again at his fireside; and so natural, too. He seemed to be the incarnation of unspoken hopes; the realization of vague and fitful memories of the past.

When Mamouche kept on crying, Doctor John-Luis wiped away the tears with his own brown silk handkerchief.

"Mamouche," he said, "I want you to stay here; to live here with me always. To learn how to work; to learn how to study; to grow up to be an honorable man. An honorable man, Mamouche, for I want you for my own child."

His voice was pretty low and husky when he said that.

"I shall not take the key from the door tonight," he continued. "If you do not choose to stay and be all this that I say, you may open the door and walk out. I shall use no force to keep you."

"What is he doing, Marsh?" asked Doctor John-Luis the following morning, when he took the coffee that Marshall had brought to him in bed.

"Who dat, sah?"

"Why, the boy Mamouche, of course. What is he doing?"

Marshall laughed.

"He kneelin' down dah on de flo'. He keep on sayin', 'Hail, Mary, full o' grace, de Lord is wid dee. Hail, Mary, full o' grace'— t'ree, fo' times, sah. I tell 'im, 'W'at you sayin' yo' prayer dat away, boy?' He 'low dat w'at his gran'ma larn 'im, ter keep outen mischief. W'en de devil say, 'Take dat gate offen de hinge; do dis; do dat,' he gwine say t'ree Hail Mary, an' de devil gwine tu'n tail an' run."

"Yes, yes," laughed Doctor John-Luis. "That's Stéphanie all over."

"An' I tell 'im: See heah, boy, you drap a couple o' dem Hail Mary, an' quit studyin' 'bout de devil, an' sot yo'se'f down ter wuk. Dat the oniest way to keep outen mischief."

"What business is it of yours to interfere?" broke in Doctor John-Luis, irritably. "Let the boy do as his grandmother instructed him."

"I ain't desputin', sah," apologized Marshall.

"But you know, Marsh," continued the doctor, recovering his usual amiability. "I think we'll be able to do something with the boy. I'm pretty sure of it. For, you see, he has his grandmother's eyes; and his grandmother was a very intelligent woman; a clever woman, Marsh. Her one great mistake was when she married Théodule Peloté."

A Sentimental Soul

I

LACODIE stayed longer than was his custom in Mamzelle Fleurette's little store that evening. He had been tempted by the vapid utterances of a conservative bellhanger to loudly voice his radical opinions upon the rights and wrongs of humanity at large and his fellow-workingmen in particular. He was quite in a tremble when he finally laid his picayune down upon Mamzelle Fleurette's counter and helped himself to *l' Abeille*[1] from the top of the diminished pile of newspapers which stood there.

He was small, frail and hollow-chested, but his head was magnificent with its generous adornment of waving black hair; its sunken eyes that glowed darkly and steadily and sometimes flamed, and its moustaches which were formidable.

"Eh bien, Mamzelle Fleurette, à demain, à demain!"[2] and he waved a nervous good-bye as he let himself quickly and noiselessly out.

However violent Lacodie might be in his manner toward conservatives, he was always gentle, courteous and low-voiced with Mamzelle Fleurette, who was much older than he, much taller; who held no opinions, and whom he pitied, and even in a manner revered: Mamzelle Fleurette at once dismissed the bellhanger, with whom, on general principles, she had no sympathy.

She wanted to close the store, for she was going over to the cathedral to confession. She stayed a moment in the doorway watching Lacodie walk down the opposite side of the street. His step was something between a spring and a jerk, which to her partial eyes seemed the perfection of motion. She watched him until he entered his own small low doorway, over which hung a huge wooden key painted red, the emblem of his trade.

For many months now, Lacodie had been coming daily to Mamzelle Fleurette's little notion store to buy the morning paper, which he only bought and read, however, in the afternoon. Once he had crossed over with his box of keys and tools to open a cupboard, which would unlock for no inducements of its owner. He would not suffer her to pay him for the few moments' work; it was nothing, he assured her; it was a pleasure; he would not dream of accepting payment for so trifling a service from a camarade and fellow-worker. But she need not fear that he would lose by it, he told her with a laugh; he would only charge an extra quarter to the rich lawyer around the corner, or to the top-lofty druggist down the street when these might happen to need his services, as they sometimes did. This was an alternative which seemed far from right and honest to Mamzelle Fleurette. But she held a vague understanding that men were wickeder in many ways than women; that ungodliness was constitutional with them, like their sex, and inseparable from it.

Having watched Lacodie until he disappeared within his shop, she retired to her room, back of the store, and began her preparations to go out. She brushed carefully the black alpaca skirt, which hung in long nun-like folds around her spare figure. She smoothed down the brown, ill-fitting basque, and readjusted the old-fashioned, rusty black lace collar which she always wore. Her sleek hair was painfully and suspiciously black. She powdered her face abundantly with poudre de riz before starting out, and pinned a dotted black lace veil over her straw bonnet. There was little force or character or anything in her withered face, except a pathetic desire and appeal to be permitted to exist.

Mamzelle Fleurette did not walk down Chartres street with her usual composed tread; she seemed preoccupied and agitated. When she passed the locksmith's shop over the way and heard his voice within, she grew tremulously self-conscious, fingering her veil, swishing the black alpaca and waving her prayer book about with meaningless intention.

Mamzelle Fleurette was in great trouble; trouble which was so bitter, so sweet, so bewildering, so terrifying! It had come so stealthily upon her she had never suspected what it might be. She thought the world was growing brighter and more beautiful; she thought the flowers had redoubled their sweetness and the birds their song, and that the voices of her fellow-creatures had grown kinder and their faces truer.

The day before Lacodie had not come to her for his paper. At six o'clock he was not there, at seven he was not there, nor at eight, and then she knew he would not come. At first, when it was only a little past the time of his coming, she had sat strangely disturbed and distressed in the rear of the store, with her back to the door. When the door opened she turned with fluttering expectancy. It was only an unhappy-looking child, who wanted to buy some foolscap, a pencil and an eraser. The next to come in was an old mulatresse, who was bringing her prayer beads for Mamzelle Fleurette to mend. The next was a gentleman, to buy the *Courier des États Unis*,[3] and then a young girl, who wanted a holy picture for her favorite nun at the Ursulines; it was everybody but Lacodie.

A temptation assailed Mamzelle Fleurette, almost fierce in its intensity, to carry the paper over to his shop herself, when he was not there at seven. She conquered it from sheer moral inability to do anything so daring, so unprecedented. But to-day, when he had come back and had stayed so long discoursing with the bellhanger, a contentment, a rapture, had settled upon her being which she could no longer ignore or mistake. She loved Lacodie. That fact was plain to her now, as plain as the conviction that every reason existed why she should not love him. He was the husband of another woman. To love the husband of another woman was one of the deepest sins which Mamzelle Fleurette knew; murder was perhaps blacker, but she was not sure. She was going to confession now. She was going to tell her sin to Almighty God and Father Fochelle, and ask their forgiveness. She was going to pray and beg the saints and the Holy Virgin to remove the sweet and subtle poison from her soul. It was surely a poison, and a deadly one, which could make her feel that her youth had come back and taken her by the hand.

II

Mamzelle Fleurette had been confessing for many years to old Father Fochelle. In his secret heart he often thought it a waste of his time and her own that she should come with her little babblings,

her little nothings to him, calling them sins. He felt that a wave of
the hand might brush them away, and that it in a manner compromised the dignity of holy absolution to pronounce the act over so
innocent a soul.

To-day she had whispered all her shortcomings into his ear
through the grating of the confessional; he knew them so well!
There were many other penitents waiting to be heard, and he was
about to dismiss her with a hasty blessing when she arrested him,
and in hesitating, faltering accents told him of her love for the locksmith, the husband of another woman. A slap in the face would not
have startled Father Fochelle more forcibly or more painfully. What
soul was there on earth, he wondered, so hedged about with innocence as to be secure from the machinations of Satan! Oh, the thunder of indignation that descended upon Mamzelle Fleurette's head!
She bowed down, beaten to earth beneath it. Then came questions,
one, two, three, in quick succession, that made Mamzelle Fleurette
gasp and clutch blindly before her. Why was she not a shadow, a va-
por, that she might dissolve from before those angry, penetrating
eyes; or a small insect, to creep into some crevice and there hide
herself forevermore?

"Oh, father! no, no, no!" she faltered, "he knows nothing, nothing. I would die a hundred deaths before he should know, before
anyone should know, besides yourself and the good God of whom
I implore pardon."

Father Fochelle breathed more freely, and mopped his face with
a flaming bandana, which he took from the ample pocket of his
soutane. But he scolded Mamzelle Fleurette roundly, unpityingly;
for being a fool, for being a sentimentalist. She had not committed
mortal sin, but the occasion was ripe for it; and look to it she must
that she keep Satan at bay with watchfulness and prayer. "Go, my
child, and sin no more."

Mamzelle Fleurette made a detour in regaining her home by
which she would not have to pass the locksmith's shop. She did not
even look in that direction when she let herself in at the glass door
of her store.

Some time before, when she was yet ignorant of the motive
which prompted the act, she had cut from a newspaper a likeness of
Lacodie, who had served as foreman of the jury during a prominent

murder trial. The likeness happened to be good, and quite did justice to the locksmith's fine physiognomy with its leonine hirsute adornment. This picture Mamzelle Fleurette had kept hitherto between the pages of her prayer book. Here, twice a day, it looked out at her; as she turned the leaves of the holy mass in the morning, and when she read her evening devotions before her own little home altar, over which hung a crucifix and a picture of the Empress Eugénie.[4]

Her first action upon entering her room, even before she unpinned the dotted veil, was to take Lacodie's picture from her prayer book and place it at random between the leaves of a "Dictionnaire de la Langue Française,"[5] which was the undermost of a pile of old books that stood on the corner of the mantelpiece. Between night and morning, when she would approach the holy sacrament, Mamzelle Fleurette felt it to be her duty to thrust Lacodie from her throughts by every means and device known to her.

The following day was Sunday, when there was no occasion or opportunity for her to see the locksmith. Moreover, after partaking of holy communion, Mamzelle Fleurette felt invigorated; she was conscious of a new, if fictitious, strength to combat Satan and his wiles.

On Monday, as the hour approached for Lacodie to appear, Mamzelle Fleurette became harassed by indecision. Should she call in the young girl, the neighbor who relieved her on occasion, and deliver the store into the girl's hands for an hour or so? This might be well enough for once in a while, but she could not conveniently resort to this subterfuge daily. After all, she had her living to make, which consideration was paramount. She finally decided that she would retire to her little back room and when she heard the store door open she would call out:

"Is it you, Monsieur Lacodie? I am very busy; please take your paper and leave your cinq sous on the counter." If it happened not to be Lacodie she would come forward and serve the customer in person. She did not, of course, expect to carry out this performance each day; a fresh device would no doubt suggest itself for tomorrow. Mamzelle Fleurette proceeded to carry out her programme to the letter.

"Is it you, Monsieur Lacodie?" she called out from the little back room, when the front door opened. "I am very busy; please take your paper—"

"Ce n'est pas Lacodie, Mamzelle Fleurette. C'est moi, Augustine."[6]

It was Lacodie's wife, a fat, comely young woman, wearing a blue veil thrown carelessly over her kinky black hair, and carrying some grocery parcels clasped close in her arms. Mamzelle Fleurette emerged from the back room, a prey to the most contradictory emotions; relief and disappointment struggling for the mastery with her.

"No Lacodie to-day, Mamzelle Fleurette," Augustine announced with a certain robust ill-humor; "he is there at home shaking with a chill till the very window panes rattle. He had one last Friday" (the day he had not come for his paper) "and now another and a worse one to-day. God knows, if it keeps on—well, let me have the paper; he will want to read it to-night when his chill is past."

Mamzelle Fleurette handed the paper to Augustine, feeling like an old woman in a dream handing a newspaper to a young woman in a dream. She had never thought of Lacodie having chills or being ill. It seemed very strange. And Augustine was no sooner gone than all the ague remedies she had ever heard of came crowding to Mamzelle Fleurette's mind; an egg in black coffee—or was it a lemon in black coffee? or an egg in vinegar? She rushed to the door to call Augustine back, but the young woman was already far down the street.

III

Augustine did not come the next day, nor the next, for the paper. The unhappy looking child who had returned for more foolscap, informed Mamzelle Fleurette that he had heard his mother say that Monsieur Lacodie was very sick, and the bellhanger had sat up all night with him. The following day Mamzelle Fleurette saw Choppin's coupé pass clattering over the cobblestones and stop before the locksmith's door. She knew that with her class it was only in a case of extremity that the famous and expensive physician was summoned. For the first time she thought of death. She prayed all day, silently, to herself, even while waiting upon customers.

In the evening she took an *Abeille* from the top of the pile on the counter, and throwing a light shawl over her head, started with the paper over to the locksmith's shop. She did not know if she were committing a sin in so doing. She would ask Father Fochelle on Saturday, when she went to confession. She did not think it could be a sin; she would have called long before on any other sick neighbor, and she intuitively felt that in this distinction might lie the possibility of sin.

The shop was deserted except for the presence of Lacodie's little boy of five, who sat upon the floor playing with the tools and contrivances which all his days he had coveted, and which all his days had been denied to him. Mamzelle Fleurette mounted the narrow stairway in the rear of the shop which led to an upper landing and then into the room of the married couple. She stood a while hesitating upon this landing before venturing to knock softly upon the partly open door through which she could hear their voices.

"I thought," she remarked apologetically to Augustine, "that perhaps Monsieur Lacodie might like to look at the paper and you had no time to come for it, so I brought it myself."

"Come in, come in, Mamzelle Fleurette. It's Mamzelle Fleurette who comes to inquire about you, Lacodie," Augustine called out loudly to her husband, whose half consciousness she somehow confounded with deafness.

Mamzelle Fleurette drew mincingly forward, clasping her thin hands together at the waist line, and she peeped timorously at Lacodie lying lost amid the bedclothes. His black mane was tossed wildly over the pillow and lent a fictitious pallor to the yellow waxiness of his drawn features. An approaching chill was sending incipient shudders through his frame, and making his teeth claque. But he still turned his head courteously in Mamzelle Fleurette's direction.

"Bien bon de votre part, Mamzelle Fleurette—mais c'est fini. J'suis flambé, flambé, flambé!"[7]

Oh, the pain of it! to hear him in such extremity thanking her for her visit, assuring her in the same breath that all was over with him. She wondered how Augustine could hear it so composedly. She whisperingly inquired if a priest had been summoned.

"Inutile; il n'en veut pas,"[8] was Augustine's reply. So he would have no priest at his bedside, and here was a new weight of bitterness for Mamzelle Fleurette to carry all her days.

She flitted back to her store through the darkness, herself like a slim shadow. The November evening was chill and misty. A dull aureole shot out from the feeble gas jet at the corner, only faintly and for an instant illumining her figure as it glided rapidly and noiselessly along the banquette. Mamzelle Fleurette slept little and prayed much that night. Saturday morning Lacodie died. On Sunday he was buried and Mamzelle Fleurette did not go to the funeral, because Father Fochelle told her plainly she had no business there.

It seemed inexpressibly hard to Mamzelle Fleurette that she was not permitted to hold Lacodie in tender remembrance now that he was dead. But Father Fochelle, with his practical insight, made no compromise with sentimentality; and she did not question his authority, or his ability to master the subtleties of a situation utterly beyond reach of her own powers.

It was no longer a pleasure for Mamzelle Fleurette to go to confession as it had formerly been. Her heart went on loving Lacodie and her soul went on struggling; for she made this delicate and puzzling distinction between heart and soul, and pictured the two as set in a very death struggle against each other.

"I cannot help it, father. I try, but I cannot help it. To love him is like breathing; I do not know how to help it. I pray, and pray, and it does no good, for half of my prayers are for the repose of his soul. It surely cannot be a sin, to pray for the repose of his soul?"

Father Fochelle was heartily sick and tired of Mamzelle Fleurette and her stupidities. Oftentimes he was tempted to drive her from the confessional, and forbid her return until she should have regained a rational state of mind. But he could not withhold absolution from a penitent who, week after week, acknowledged her shortcoming and strove with all her faculties to overcome it and atone for it.

IV

Augustine had sold out the locksmith's shop and the business, and had removed further down the street over a bakery. Out of her window she had hung a sign, "Blanchisseuse de Fin."⁹ Often, in passing by, Mamzelle Fleurette would catch a glimpse of Augustine up at the window, plying the irons; her sleeves rolled to the elbows, baring her round, white arms, and the little black curls all moist and tangled about her face. It was early spring then, and there was a languor in the air; an odor of jasmine in every passing breeze; the sky was blue, unfathomable, and fleecy white; and people along the narrow street laughed, and sang, and called to one another from windows and doorways. Augustine had set a pot of rose-geranium on her window sill and hung out a bird cage.

Once, Mamzelle Fleurette in passing on her way to confession heard her singing roulades, vying with the bird in the cage. Another time she saw the young woman leaning with half her body from the window, exchanging pleasantries with the baker standing beneath on the banquette.

Still, a little later, Mamzelle Fleurette began to notice a handsome young fellow often passing the store. He was jaunty and debonnaire and wore a rich watchchain, and looked prosperous. She knew him quite well as a fine young Gascon, who kept a stall in the French Market, and from whom she had often bought charcuterie. The neighbors told her the young Gascon was paying his addresses to Mme. Lacodie. Mamzelle Fleurette shuddered. She wondered if Lacodie knew! The whole situation seemed suddenly to shift its base, causing Mamzelle Fleurette to stagger. What ground would her poor heart and soul have to do battle upon now?

She had not yet had time to adjust her conscience to the altered conditions when one Saturday afternoon, as she was about to start out to confession, she noticed an unusual movement down the street. The bellhanger, who happened to be presenting himself in the character of a customer, informed her that it was nothing more nor less than Mme. Lacodie returning from her wedding with the Gascon. He was black and bitter with indignation, and thought she might at least have waited for the year to be out. But the charivari¹⁰ was already on foot; and Mamzelle need not feel alarmed if, in the night, she heard sounds and clamor to rouse the dead as far away as Metairie ridge.

Mamzelle Fleurette sank down in a chair, trembling in all her members. She faintly begged the bellhanger to pour her a glass of water from the stone pitcher behind the counter. She fanned herself and loosened her bonnet strings. She sent the bellhanger away.

She nervously pulled off her rusty black kid gloves, and ten times more nervously drew them on again. To a little customer, who came in for chewing gum, she handed a paper of pins.

There was a great, a terrible upheaval taking place in Mamzelle Fleurette's soul. She was preparing for the first time in her life to take her conscience into her own keeping.

When she felt herself sufficiently composed to appear decently upon the street, she started out to confession. She did not go to Father Fochelle. She did not even go to the Cathedral; but to a church which was much farther away, and to reach which she had to spend a picayune for car fare.

Mamzelle Fleurette confessed herself to a priest who was utterly new and strange to her. She told him all her little venial sins, which she had much difficulty in bringing to a number of any dignity and importance whatever. Not once did she mention her love for Lacodie, the dead husband of another woman.

Mamzelle Fleurette did not ride back to her home; she walked. The sensation of walking on air was altogether delicious; she had never experienced it before. A long time she stood contemplative before a shop window in which were displayed wreaths, mottoes, emblems, designed for the embellishment of tombstones. What a sweet comfort it would be, she reflected, on the 1st of November to carry some such delicate offering to Lacodie's last resting place. Might not the sole care of his tomb devolve upon her, after all! The possibility thrilled her and moved her to the heart. What thought would the merry Augustine and her lover-husband have for the dead lying in cemeteries!

When Mamzelle Fleurette reached home she went through the store directly into her little back room. The first thing which she did, even before unpinning the dotted lace veil, was to take the "Dictionnaire de la Langue Française" from beneath the pile of old books on the mantelpiece. It was not easy to find Lacodie's picture hidden somewhere in its depths. But the search afforded her almost a sensuous pleasure; turning the leaves slowly back and forth.

When she had secured the likeness she went into the store and from her showcase selected a picture frame—the very handsomest there; one of those which sold for thirty-five cents.

Into the frame Mamzelle Fleurette neatly and deftly pasted Lacodie's picture. Then she re-entered her room and deliberately hung it upon the wall—between the crucifix and the portrait of Empress Eugènie—and she did not care if the Gascon's wife ever saw it or not.

Dead Men's Shoes

IT never occurred to any person to wonder what would befall
Gilma now that "le vieux Gamiche"[1] was dead. After the burial
people went their several ways, some to talk over the old man and
his eccentricities, others to forget him before nightfall, and others
to wonder what would become of his very nice property, the hundred-
acre farm on which he had lived for thirty years, and on which he
had just died at the age of seventy.

If Gilma had been a child, more than one motherly heart would
have gone out to him. This one and that one would have bethought
them of carrying him home with them; to concern themselves with
his present comfort, if not his future welfare. But Gilma was not a
child. He was a strapping fellow of nineteen, measuring six feet in
his stockings, and as strong as any healthy youth need be. For ten
years he had lived there on the plantation with Monsieur Gamiche;
and he seemed now to have been the only one with tears to shed at
the old man's funeral.

Gamiche's relatives had come down from Caddo in a wagon the
day after his death, and had settled themselves in his house. There
was Septime, his nephew, a cripple, so horribly afflicted that it was
distressing to look at him. And there was Septime's widowed sister,
Ma'me Brozé, with her two little girls. They had remained at the
house during the burial, and Gilma found them still there upon his
return.

The young man went at once to his room to seek a moment's repose. He had lost much sleep during Monsieur Gamiche's illness;
yet, he was in fact more worn by the mental than the bodily strain
of the past week.

But when he entered his room, there was something so changed in its aspect that it seemed no longer to belong to him. In place of his own apparel which he had left hanging on the row of pegs, there were a few shabby little garments and two battered straw hats, the property of the Brozé children. The bureau drawers were empty, there was not a vestige of anything belonging to him remaining in the room. His first impression was that Ma'me Brozé had been changing things around and had assigned him to some other room.

But Gilma understood the situation better when he discovered every scrap of his personal effects piled up on a bench outside the door, on the back or "false" gallery. His boots and shoes were under the bench,. while coats, trousers and underwear were heaped in an indiscriminate mass together.

The blood mounted to his swarthy face and made him look for the moment like an Indian. He had never thought of this. He did not know what he had been thinking of; but he felt that he ought to have been prepared for anything; and it was his own fault if he was not. But it hurt. This spot was "home" to him against the rest of the world. Every tree, every shrub was a friend; he knew every patch in the fences; and the little old house, gray and weather-beaten, that had been the shelter of his youth, he loved as only few can love inanimate things. A great enmity arose in him against Ma'me Brozé. She was walking about the yard, with her nose in the air, and a shabby black dress trailing behind her. She held the little girls by the hand.

Gilma could think of nothing better to do than to mount his horse and ride away—anywhere. The horse was a spirited animal of great value. Monsieur Gamiche had named him "Jupiter" on account of his proud bearing, and Gilma had nicknamed him "Jupe," which seemed to him more endearing and expressive of his great attachment to the fine creature. With the bitter resentment of youth, he felt that "Jupe" was the only friend remaining to him on earth.

He had thrust a few pieces of clothing in his saddlebags and had requested Ma'me Brozé, with assumed indifference, to put his remaining effects in a place of safety until he should be able to send for them.

As he rode around by the front of the house, Septime, who sat on the gallery all doubled up in his uncle Gamiche's big chair, called out:

"Hé, Gilma! w'ere you boun' fo'?"

"I'm goin' away," replied Gilma, curtly, reining his horse.

"That's all right; but I reckon you might jus' as well leave that hoss behine you."

"The hoss is mine," returned Gilma, as quickly as he would have returned a blow.

"We'll see 'bout that li'le later, my frien'. I reckon you jus' well turn 'im loose."

Gilma had no more intention of giving up his horse than he had of parting with his own right hand. But Monsieur Gamiche had taught him prudence and respect for the law. He did not wish to invite disagreeable complications. So, controlling his temper by a supreme effort, Gilma dismounted, unsaddled the horse then and there, and led it back to the stable. But as he started to leave the place on foot, he stopped to say to Septime:

"You know, Mr. Septime, that hoss is mine; I can collec' a hundred aff'davits to prove it. I'll bring them yere in a few days with a statement f'om a lawyer; an' I'll expec' the hoss an' saddle to be turned over to me in good condition."

"That's all right. We'll see 'bout that. Won't you stay fo' dinna?"

"No, I thank you, suh; Ma'me Brozé already ask' me." And Gilma strode away, down the beaten footpath that led across the sloping grassplot toward the outer road.

A definite destination and a settled purpose ahead of him seemed to have revived his flagging energies of an hour before. It was with no trace of fatigue that he stepped out bravely along the wagon-road that skirted the bayou.

It was early spring, and the cotton had already a good stand. In some places the negroes were hoeing. Gilma stopped alongside the rail fence and called to an old negress who was plying her hoe at no great distance.

"Hello, Aunt Hal'fax! see yere."

She turned, and immediately quitted her work to go and join him, bringing her hoe with her across her shoulder. She was large-boned and very black. She was dressed in the deshabille of the field.

"I wish you'd come up to yo' cabin with me a minute, Aunt Hally," he said; "I want to get an aff'davit f'om you."

She understood, after a fashion, what an affidavit was; but she couldn't see the good of it.

"I ain't got no aff'davis, boy; you g'long an' don' pesta me."

" 'Twon't take you any time, Aunt Hal'fax. I jus' want you to put yo' mark to a statement I'm goin' to write to the effec' that my hoss, Jupe, is my own prop'ty; that you know it, an' willin' to swear to it."

"Who say Jupe don't b'long to you?" she questioned cautiously, leaning on her hoe.

He motioned toward the house.

"Who? Mista Septime and them?"

"Yes."

"Well, I reckon!" she exclaimed, sympathetically.

"That's it," Gilma went on; "an' nex' thing they'll be sayin' yo' ole mule, Policy, don't b'long to you."

She started violently.

"Who say so?"

"Nobody. But I say, nex' thing, that' w'at they'll be sayin'."

She began to move along the inside of the fence, and he turned to keep pace with her, walking on the grassy edge of the road.

"I'll jus' write the aff'davit, Aunt Hally, an' all you got to do"—

"You know des well as me dat mule mine. I done paid ole Mista Gamiche fo' 'im in good cotton; dat year you falled outen de puckhorn tree; an' he write it down hisse'f in his 'count book."

Gilma did not linger a moment after obtaining the desired statement from Aunt Halifax. With the first of those "hundred affidavits" that he hoped to secure, safe in his pocket, he struck out across the country, seeking the shortest way to town.

Aunt Halifax stayed in the cabin door.

" 'Relius," she shouted to a little black boy out in the road, "does you see Pol'cy anywhar? G'long, see ef he 'roun' de ben'. Wouldn' s'prise me ef he broke de fence an' got in yo' pa's corn ag'in." And, shading her eyes to scan the surrounding country, she muttered, uneasily: "Whar dat mule?"

The following morning Gilma entered town and proceeded at once to Lawyer Paxton's office. He had no difficulty in obtaining the testimony of blacks and whites regarding his ownership of the horse; but he wanted to make his claim as secure as possible by consulting the lawyer and returning to the plantation armed with unassailable evidence.

The lawyer's office was a plain little room opening upon the street. Nobody was there, but the door was open; and Gilma entered and took a seat at the bare round table and waited. It was not long before the lawyer came in; he had been in conversation with some one across the street.

"Good-morning, Mr. Pax'on," said Gilma, rising.

The lawyer knew his face well enough, but could not place him, and only returned: "Good-morning, sir—good-morning."

"I come to see you," began Gilma plunging at once into business, and drawing his handful of nondescript affidavits from his pocket, "about a matter of prope'ty, about regaining possession of my hoss that Mr. Septime, ole Mr. Gamiche's nephew, is holdin' f'om me yonder."

The lawyer took the papers and, adjusting his eye-glasses, began to look them through.

"Yes, yes," he said; "I see."

"Since Mr. Gamiche died on Tuesday"—began Gilma.

"Gamiche died!" repeated Lawyer Paxton, with astonishment. "Why, you don't mean to tell me that vieux Gamiche is dead? Well, well. I hadn't heard of it; I just returned from Shreveport this morning. So le vieux Gamiche is dead, is he? And you say you want to get possession of a horse. What did you say your name was?" drawing a pencil from his pocket.

"Gilma Germain is my name, suh."

"Gilma Germain," repeated the lawyer, a little meditatively, scanning his visitor closely. "Yes, I recall your face now. You are the young fellow whom le vieux Gamiche took to live with him some ten or twelve years ago."

"Ten years ago las' November, suh."

Lawyer Paxton arose and went to his safe, from which, after unlocking it, he took a legal-looking document that he proceeded to read carefully through to himself.

"Well, Mr. Germain, I reckon there won't be any trouble about regaining possession of the horse," laughed Lawyer Paxton. "I'm pleased to inform you, my dear sir, that our old friend, Gamiche, has made you sole heir to his property; that is, his plantation, including live stock, farming implements, machinery, household effects, etc. Quite a pretty piece of property," he proclaimed leisurely, seating himself comfortably for a long talk. "And I may add, a pretty piece of luck, Mr. Germain, for a young fellow just starting out in life; nothing but to step into a dead man's shoes! A great chance—great chance. Do you know, sir, the moment you mentioned your name, it came back to me like a flash, how le vieux Gamiche came in here one day, about three years ago, and wanted to make his will"—And the loquacious lawyer went on with his reminiscences and interesting bits of information, of which Gilma heard scarcely a word.

He was stunned, drunk, with the sudden joy of possession; the thought of what seemed to him great wealth, all his own—his own! It seemed as if a hundred different sensations were holding him at once, and as if a thousand intentions crowded upon him. He felt like another being who would have to readjust himself to the new conditions, presenting themselves so unexpectedly. The narrow confines of the office were stifling, and it seemed as if the lawyer's flow of talk would never stop. Gilma arose abruptly, and with a half-uttered apology, plunged from the room into the outer air.

Two days later Gilma stopped again before Aunt Halifax's cabin, on his way back to the plantation. He was walking as before, having declined to avail himself of any one of the several offers of a mount that had been tendered him in town and on the way. A rumor of Gilma's great good fortune had preceded him, and Aunt Halifax greeted him with an almost triumphal shout as he approached.

"God knows you desarve it, Mista Gilma! De Lord knows you does, suh! Come in an' res' yo'se'f, suh. You, 'Relius! git out dis heah cabin; crowdin' up dat away!" She wiped off the best chair available and offered it to Gilma.

He was glad to rest himself and glad to accept Aunt Halifax's proffer of a cup of coffee, which she was in the act of dripping before a small fire. He sat as far as he could from the fire, for the day was warm; he mopped his face, and fanned himself with his broad-rimmed hat.

"I des' can't he'p laughin' w'en I thinks 'bout it," said the old woman, fairly shaking, as she leaned over the hearth. "I wakes up in de night, even, an' has to laugh."

"How's that, Aunt Hal'fax," asked Gilma, almost tempted to laugh himself at he knew not what.

"G'long, Mista Gilma! like you don' know! It's w'en I thinks

'bout Septime an' them like I gwine see 'em in dat wagon to-mor'
mo'nin', on' dey way back to Caddo. Oh, lawsy!"

"That isn' so ver' funny, Aunt Hal'fax," returned Gilma, feeling
himself ill at ease as he accepted the cup of coffee which she presented to him with much ceremony on a platter. "I feel pretty sorry
for Septime, myse'f."

"I reckon he know now who Jupe b'long to," she went on, ignoring his expression of sympathy; "no need to tell him who Pol'cy
b'long to, nuther. An' I tell you, Mista Gilma," she went on, leaning
upon the table without seating herself, "dey gwine back to hard
times in Caddo. I heah tell dey nuva gits 'nough to eat, yonda. Septime, he can't do nuttin' 'cep' set still all twis' up like a sarpint. An'
Ma'me Brozé, she do some kine sewin'; but don't look like she got
sense 'nough to do dat halfway. An' dem li'le gals, dey 'bleege to
run bar'foot mos' all las' winta', twell dat li'les' gal, she got her heel
plum fros' bit, so dey tells me. Oh, lawsy! How dey gwine look to-
mor', all trapsin' back to Caddo!"

Gilma had never found Aunt Halifax's company so intensely disagreeable as at that moment. He thanked her for the coffee, and
went away so suddenly as to startle her. But her good humor never
flagged. She called out to him from the doorway:

"Oh, Mista Gilma! You reckon dey knows who Pol'cy b'longs
to now?"

He somehow did not feel quite prepared to face Septime; and he
lingered along the road. He even stopped a while to rest, apparently,
under the shade of a huge cottonwood tree that overhung the
bayou. From the very first, a subtle uneasiness, a self-dissatisfaction
had mingled with his elation, and he was trying to discover what it
meant.

To begin with, the straightforwardness of his own nature had inwardly resented the sudden change in the bearing of most people
toward himself. He was trying to recall, too, something which the
lawyer had said; a little phrase, out of that multitude of words, that
had fallen in his consciousness. It had stayed there, generating a little festering sore place that was beginning to make itself irritatingly
felt. What was it, that little phrase? Something about—in his excitement he had only half heard it—something about dead men's shoes.

The exuberant health and strength of his big body; the courage, virility, endurance of his whole nature revolted against the expression in itself, and the meaning which it conveyed to him. Dead men's shoes! Were they not for such afflicted beings as Septime? as that helpless, dependent woman up there? as those two little ones, with their poorly fed, poorly clad bodies and sweet, appealing eyes? Yet he could not determine how he would act and what he would say to them.

But there was no room left in his heart for hesitancy when he came to face the group. Septime was still crouched in his uncle's chair; he seemed never to have left it since the day of the funeral. Ma'me Brozé had been crying, and so had the children—out of sympathy, perhaps.

"Mr. Septime," said Gilma, approaching, "I brought those aff'-davits about the hoss. I hope you about made up yo' mind to turn it over without further trouble."

Septime was trembling, bewildered, almost speechless.

"W'at you mean?" he faltered, looking up with a shifting, sideward glance. "The whole place b'longs to you. You tryin' to make a fool out o' me?"

"Fo' me," returned Gilma, "the place can stay with Mr. Gamiche's own flesh an' blood. I'll see Mr. Pax'on again an' make that according to the law. But I want my hoss."

Gilma took something besides his horse—a picture of le vieux Gamiche, which had stood on his mantelpiece. He thrust it into his pocket. He also took his old benefactor's walking-stick and a gun.

As he rode out of the gate, mounted upon his well-beloved "Jupe," the faithful dog following, Gilma felt as if he had awakened from an intoxicating but depressing dream.

At Chênière Caminada

I

THERE was no clumsier looking fellow in church that Sunday morning than Antoine Bocaze—the one they called Tonie. But Tonie did not really care if he were clumsy or not. He felt that he could speak intelligibly to no woman save his mother; but since he had no desire to inflame the hearts of any of the island maidens, what difference did it make?

He knew there was no better fisherman on the Chênière Caminada[1] than himself, if his face was too long and bronzed, his limbs too unmanageable and his eyes too earnest—almost too honest.

It was a midsummer day, with a lazy, scorching breeze blowing from the Gulf straight into the church windows. The ribbons on the young girls' hats fluttered like the wings of birds, and the old women clutched the flapping ends of the veils that covered their heads.

A few mosquitoes, floating through the blistering air, with their nipping and humming fretted the people to a certain degree of attention and consequent devotion. The measured tones of the priest at the altar rose and fell like a song: "Credo in unum Deum patrem omnipotentem"[2] he chanted. And then the people all looked at one another, suddenly electrified.

Some one was playing upon the organ whose notes no one on the whole island was able to awaken; whose tones had not been heard during the many months since a passing stranger had one day listlessly dragged his fingers across its idle keys. A long, sweet strain of music floated down from the loft and filled the church.

It seemed to most of them—it seemed to Tonie standing there

beside his old mother—that some heavenly being must have descended upon the Church of Our Lady of Lourdes[3] and chosen this celestial way of communicating with its people.

But it was no creature from a different sphere; it was only a young lady from Grand Isle. A rather pretty young person with blue eyes and nut-brown hair, who wore a dotted lawn of fine texture and fashionable make, and a white Leghorn sailor-hat.

Tonie saw her standing outside of the church after mass, receiving the priest's voluble praises and thanks for her graceful service.

She had come over to mass from Grand Isle in Baptiste Beaudelet's lugger, with a couple of young men, and two ladies who kept a pension over there. Tonic knew these two ladies—the widow Lebrun and her old mother—but he did not attempt to speak with them; he would not have known what to say. He stood aside gazing at the group, as others were doing, his serious eyes fixed earnestly upon the fair organist.

Tonie was late at dinner that day. His mother must have waited an hour for him, sitting patiently with her coarse hands folded in her lap, in that little still room with its "brick-painted" floor, its gaping chimney and homely furnishings.

He told her that he had been walking—walking he hardly knew where, and he did not know why. He must have tramped from one end of the island to the other; but he brought her no bit of news or gossip. He did not know if the Cotures had stopped for dinner with the Avendettes; whether old Pierre François was worse, or better, or dead, or if lame Philibert was drinking again this morning. He knew nothing; yet he had crossed the village, and passed every one of its small houses that stood close together in a long jagged line facing the sea; they were gray and battered by time and the rude buffets of the salt sea winds.

He knew nothing though the Cotures had all bade him "good day" as they filed into Avendette's, where a steaming plate of crab gumbo was waiting for each. He had heard some woman screaming, and others saying it was because old Pierre François had just passed away. But he did not remember this, nor did he recall the fact that lame Philibert had staggered against him when he stood absently watching a "fiddler" sidling across the sun-baked sand. He could tell his mother nothing of all this; but he said he had noticed that the wind was fair and must have driven Baptiste's boat, like a flying bird, across the water.

Well, that was something to talk about, and old Ma'me Antoine, who was fat, leaned comfortably upon the table after she had helped Tonie to his courtbouillon, and remarked that she found Madame was getting old. Tonie thought that perhaps she was aging and her hair was getting whiter. He seemed glad to talk about her, and reminded his mother of old Madame's kindness and sympathy at the time his father and brothers had perished. It was when he was a little fellow, ten years before, during a squall in Barataria Bay.

Ma'me Antoine declared that she could never forget that sympathy, if she lived till Judgment Day; but all the same she was sorry to see that Madame Lebrun was also not so young or fresh as she used to be. Her chances of getting a husband were surely lessening every year; especially with the young girls around her, budding each spring like flowers to be plucked. The one who had played upon the organ was Mademoiselle Duvigné, Claire Duvigné, a great belle, the daughter of the famous lawyer who lived in New Orleans, on Rampart street. Ma'me Antoine had found that out during the ten minutes she and others had stopped after mass to gossip with the priest.

"Claire Duvigné," muttered Tonie, not even making a pretense to taste his courtbouillon, but picking little bits from the half loaf of crusty brown bread that lay beside his plate. "Claire Duvigné; that is a pretty name. Don't you think so, mother? I can't think of any-one on the Chênière who has so pretty a one, nor at Grand Isle, either, for that matter. And you say she lives on Rampart street?"

It appeared to him a matter of great importance that he should have his mother repeat all that the priest had told her.

II

Early the following morning Tonie went out in search of lame Philibert, than whom there was no cleverer workman on the island when he could be caught sober.

Tonie had tried to work on his big lugger that lay bottom up-ward under the shed, but it had seemed impossible. His mind, his hands, his tools refused to do their office, and in sudden despera-tion he desisted. He found Philibert and set him to work in his own place under the shed. Then he got into his small boat with the red lateen-sail and went over to Grand Isle.

There was no one at hand to warn Tonie that he was acting the part of a fool. He had, singularly, never felt those premonitory symptoms of love which afflict the greater portion of mankind before they reach the age which he had attained. He did not at first recognize this powerful impulse that had, without warning, possessed itself of his entire being. He obeyed it without a struggle, as naturally as he would have obeyed the dictates of hunger and thirst.

Tonie left his boat at the wharf and proceeded at once to Mme. Lebrun's pension, which consisted of a group of plain, stoutly built cottages that stood in mid island, about half a mile from the sea.

The day was bright and beautiful with soft, velvety gusts of wind blowing from the water. From a cluster of orange trees a flock of doves ascended, and Tonie stopped to listen to the beating of their wings and follow their flight toward the water oaks whither he himself was moving.

He walked with a dragging, uncertain step through the yellow, fragrant camomile, his thoughts traveling before him. In his mind was always the vivid picture of the girl as it had stamped itself there yesterday, connected in some mystical way with that celestial music which had thrilled him and was vibrating yet in his soul.

But she did not look the same to-day. She was returning from the beach when Tonie first saw her, leaning upon the arm of one of the men who had accompanied her yesterday. She was dressed differently—in a dainty blue cotton gown. Her companion held a big white sunshade over them both. They had exchanged hats and were laughing with great abandonment.

Two young men walked behind them and were trying to engage her attention. She glanced at Tonie, who was leaning against a tree when the group passed by; but of course she did not know him. She was speaking English, a language which he hardly understood.

There were other young people gathered under the water oaks— girls who were, many of them, more beautiful than Mlle. Duvigné; but for Tonie they simply did not exist. His whole universe had suddenly become converted into a glamorous background for the person of Mlle. Duvigné, and the shadowy figures of men who were about her.

Tonie went to Mme. Lebrun and told her he would bring her oranges next day from the Chênière. She was well pleased, and commissioned him to bring her other things from the stores there, which she could not procure at Grand Isle. She did not question his presence, knowing that these summer days were idle ones for the Chênière fishermen. Nor did she seem surprised when he told her that his boat was at the wharf, and would be there every day at her service. She knew his frugal habits, and supposed he wished to hire it, as others did. He intuitively felt that this could be the only way.

And that is how it happened that Tonie spent so little of his time at the Chênière Caminada that summer. Old Ma'me Antoine grumbled enough about it. She herself had been twice in her life to Grand Isle and once to Grand Terre, and each time had been more than glad to get back to the Chênière. And why Tonie should want to spend his days, and even his nights, away from home, was a thing she could not comprehend, especially as he would have to be away the whole winter; and meantime there was much work to be done at his own hearthside and in the company of his own mother. She did not know that Tonie had much, much more to do at Grand Isle than at the Chênière Caminada.

He had to see how Claire Duvigné sat upon the gallery in the big rocking chair that she kept in motion by the impetus of her slender, slippered foot; turning her head this way and that way to speak to the men who were always near her. He had to follow her lithe motions at tennis or croquet, that she often played with the children under the trees. Some days he wanted to see how she spread her bare, white arms, and walked out to meet the foam-crested waves. Even here there were men with her. And then at night, standing alone like a still shadow under the stars, did he not have to listen to her voice when she talked and laughed and sang? Did he not have to follow her slim figure whirling through the dance, in the arms of men who must have loved her and wanted her as he did. He did not dream that they could help it more than he could help it. But the days when she stepped into his boat, the one with the red lateen sail, and sat for hours within a few feet of him, were days that he would have given up for nothing else that he could think of.

III

There were always others in her company at such times, young people with jests and laughter on their lips. Only once she was alone.

She had foolishly brought a book with her, thinking she would want to read. But with the breath of the sea stinging her she could not read a line. She looked precisely as she had looked the day he first saw her, standing outside of the church at Chênière Caminada.

She laid the book down in her lap, and let her soft eyes sweep dreamily along the line of the horizon where the sky and water met. Then she looked straight at Tonie, and for the first time spoke directly to him.

She called him Tonie, as she had heard others do, and questioned him about his boat and his work. He trembled, and answered her vaguely and stupidly. She did not mind, but spoke to him anyhow, satisfied to talk herself when she found that he could not or would not. She spoke French, and talked about the Chênière Caminada, its people and its church. She talked of the day she had played upon the organ there, and complained of the instrument being woefully out of tune.

Tonie was perfectly at home in the familiar task of guiding his boat before the wind that bellied its taut, red sail. He did not seem clumsy and awkward as when he sat in church. The girl noticed that he appeared as strong as an ox.

As she looked at him and surprised one of his shifting glances, a glimmer of the truth began to dawn faintly upon her. She remembered how she had encountered him daily in her path, with his earnest, devouring eyes always seeking her out. She recalled—but there was no need to recall anything. There are women whose perception of passion is very keen; they are the women who most inspire it.

A feeling of complacency took possession of her with this conviction. There was some softness and sympathy mingled with it. She would have liked to lean over and pat his big, brown hand, and tell him she felt sorry and would have helped it if she could. With this belief he ceased to be an object of complete indifference in her eyes. She had thought, awhile before, of having him turn about and take her back home. But now it was really piquant to pose for an hour longer before a man—even a rough fisherman—to whom she felt herself to be an object of silent and consuming devotion. She could think of nothing more interesting to do on shore.

She was incapable of conceiving the full force and extent of his infatuation. She did not dream that under the rude, calm exterior before her a man's heart was beating clamorously, and his reason yielding to the savage instinct of his blood.

"I hear the Angelus ringing at Chênière, Tonie," she said. "I didn't know it was so late; let us go back to the island." There had been a long silence which her musical voice interrupted.

Tonie could now faintly hear the Angelus bell himself. A vision of the church came with it, the odor of incense and the sound of the organ. The girl before him was again that celestial being whom our Lady of Lourdes had once offered to his immortal vision.

It was growing dusk when they landed at the pier, and frogs had begun to croak among the reeds in the pools. There were two of Mlle. Duvigné's usual attendants anxiously awaiting her return. But she chose to let Tonie assist her out of the boat. The touch of her hand fired his blood again.

She said to him very low and half-laughing, "I have no money tonight, Tonie; take this instead," pressing into his palm a delicate silver chain, which she had worn twined about her bare wrist. It was purely a spirit of coquetry that prompted the action, and a touch of the sentimentality which most women possess. She had read in some romance of a young girl doing something like that.

As she walked away between her two attendants she fancied Tonie pressing the chain to his lips. But he was standing quite still, and held it buried in his tightly-closed hand; wanting to hold as long as he might the warmth of the body that still penetrated the bauble when she thrust it into his hand.

He watched her retreating figure like a blotch against the fading sky. He was stirred by a terrible, an overmastering regret, that he had not clasped her in his arms when they were out there alone, and sprung with her into the sea. It was what he had vaguely meant to do when the sound of the Angelus had weakened and palsied his resolution. Now she was going from him, fading away into the mist with those figures on either side of her, leaving him alone. He resolved within himself that if ever again she were out there on the sea at his mercy, she would have to perish in his arms. He would go far, far out where the sound of no bell could reach him. There was some comfort for him in the thought.

But as it happened, Mlle. Duvigné never went out alone in the boat with Tonie again.

IV

It was one morning in January. Tonie had been collecting a bill from one of the fishmongers at the French Market, in New Orleans, and had turned his steps toward St. Philip street. The day was chilly; a keen wind was blowing. Tonie mechanically buttoned his rough, warm coat and crossed over into the sun.

There was perhaps not a more wretched-hearted being in the whole district, that morning, than he. For months the woman he so hopelessly loved had been lost to his sight. But all the more she dwelt in his thoughts, preying upon his mental and bodily forces until his unhappy condition became apparent to all who knew him. Before leaving his home for the winter fishing grounds he had opened his whole heart to his mother, and told her of the trouble that was killing him. She hardly expected that he would ever come back to her when he went away. She feared that he would not, for he had spoken wildly of the rest and peace that could only come to him with death.

That morning when Tonie had crossed St. Philip street he found himself accosted by Madame Lebrun and her mother. He had not noticed them approaching, and, moreover, their figures in winter garb appeared unfamiliar to him. He had never seen them elsewhere than at Grand Isle and the Chênière during the summer. They were glad to meet him, and shook his hand cordially. He stood as usual a little helplessly before them. A pulse in his throat was beating and almost choking him, so poignant were the recollections which their presence stirred up.

They were staying in the city this winter, they told him. They wanted to hear the opera as often as possible, and the island was really too dreary with everyone gone. Madame Lebrun had left her son there to keep order and superintend repairs, and so on.

"You are both well?" stammered Tonie.

"In perfect health, my dear Tonie," Madame Lebrun replied. She was wondering at his haggard eyes and thin, gaunt cheeks; but possessed too much tact to mention them.

"And—the young lady who used to go sailing—is she well?" he inquired lamely.

"You mean Mlle. Favette? She was married just after leaving Grand Isle."

"No; I mean the one you called Claire—Mamzelle Duvigné—is she well?"

Mother and daughter exclaimed together: "Impossible! You haven't heard? Why, Tonie," madame continued, "Mlle. Duvigné died three weeks ago! But that was something sad, I tell you . . . Her family heartbroken . . . Simply from a cold caught by standing in thin slippers, waiting for her carriage after the opera . . . . What a warning!"

The two were talking at once. Tonie kept looking from one to the other. He did not know what they were saying, after madame had told him, "Elle est morte."[4]

As in a dream he finally heard that they said good-by to him, and sent their love to his mother.

He stood still in the middle of the banquette when they had left him, watching them go toward the market. He could not stir. Something had happened to him—he did not know what. He wondered if the news was killing him.

Some women passed by, laughing coarsely. He noticed how they laughed and tossed their heads. A mockingbird was singing in a cage which hung from a window above his head. He had not heard it before.

Just beneath the window was the entrance to a barroom. Tonie turned and plunged through its swinging doors. He asked the bartender for whisky. The man thought he was already drunk, but pushed the bottle toward him nevertheless. Tonie poured a great quantity of the fiery liquor into a glass and swallowed it at a draught. The rest of the day he spent among the fishermen and Barataria oystermen; and that night he slept soundly and peacefully until morning.

He did not know why it was so; he could not understand. But

from that day he felt that he began to live again, to be once more a part of the moving world about him. He would ask himself over and over again why it was so, and stay bewildered before this truth that he could not answer or explain, and which he began to accept as a holy mystery.

One day in early spring Tonie sat with his mother upon a piece of drift-wood close to the sea.

He had returned that day to the Chênière Caminada. At first she thought he was like his former self again, for all his old strength and courage had returned. But she found that there was a new brightness in his face which had not been there before. It made her think of the Holy Ghost descending and bringing some kind of light to a man.

She knew that Mademoiselle Duvigné was dead, and all along had feared that this knowledge would be the death of Tonie. When she saw him come back to her like a new being, at once she dreaded that he did not know. All day the doubt had been fretting her, and she could bear the uncertainty no longer.

"You know, Tonie—that young lady whom you cared for—well, some one read it to me in the papers—she died last winter." She had tried to speak as cautiously as she could.

"Yes, I know she is dead. I am glad."

It was the first time he had said this in words, and it made his heart beat quicker.

Ma'me Antoine shuddered and drew aside from him. To her it was somehow like murder to say such a thing.

"What do you mean? Why are you glad?" she demanded, indignantly.

Tonie was sitting with his elbows on his knees. He wanted to answer his mother, but it would take time; he would have to think. He looked out across the water that glistened gem-like with the sun upon it, but there was nothing there to open his thought. He looked down into his open palm and began to pick at the callous flesh that was hard as a horse's hoof. Whilst he did this his ideas began to gather and take form.

"You see, while she lived I could never hope for anything," he began, slowly feeling his way. "Despair was the only thing for me. There were always men about her. She walked and sang and danced with them. I knew it all the time, even when I didn't see her. But I saw her often enough. I knew that some day one of them would please her and she would give herself to him—she would marry him. That thought haunted me like an evil spirit."

Tonie passed his hand across his forehead as if to sweep away anything of the horror that might have remained there.

"It kept me awake at night," he went on. "But that was not so bad; the worst torture was to sleep, for then I would dream that it was all true.

"Oh, I could see her married to one of them—his wife—coming year after year to Grand Isle and bringing her little children with her! I can't tell you all that I saw—all that was driving me mad! But now"—and Tonie clasped his hands together and smiled as he looked again across the water—"she is where she belongs; there is no difference up there; the curé has often told us there is no difference between men. It is with the soul that we approach each other there. Then she will know who has loved her best. That is why I am so contented. Who knows what may happen up there?"

Ma'me Antoine could not answer. She only took her son's big, rough hand and pressed it against her.

"And now, ma mère," he exclaimed, cheerfully, rising, "I shall go light the fire for your bread; it is a long time since I have done anything for you," and he stooped and pressed a warm kiss on her withered old cheek.

With misty eyes she watched him walk away in the direction of the big brick oven that stood open-mouthed under the lemon trees.

Odalie Misses Mass

ODALIE sprang down from the mulecart, shook out her white skirts, and firmly grasping her parasol, which was blue to correspond with her sash, entered Aunt Pinky's gate and proceeded towards the old woman's cabin. She was a thick-waisted young thing who walked with a firm tread and carried her head with a determined poise. Her straight brown hair had been rolled up over night in papillotes, and the artificial curls stood out in clusters, stiff and uncompromising beneath the rim of her white chip hat. Her mother, sister and brother remained seated in the cart before the gate.

It was the fifteenth of August, the great feast of the Assumption, so generally observed in the Catholic parishes of Louisiana. The Chotard family were on their way to mass, and Odalie had insisted upon stopping to "show herself" to her old friend and protegée, Aunt Pinky.

The helpless, shrivelled old negress sat in the depths of a large, rudely-fashioned chair. A loosely hanging unbleached cotton gown enveloped her mite of a figure. What was visible of her hair beneath the bandana turban, looked like white sheep's wool. She wore round, silver-rimmed spectacles, which gave her an air of wisdom and respectability, and she held in her hand the branch of a hickory sapling, with which she kept mosquitoes and flies at bay, and even chickens and pigs that sometimes penetrated the heart of her domain.

Odalie walked straight up to the old woman and kissed her on the cheek.

"Well, Aunt Pinky, yere I am," she announced with evident self-complacency, turning herself slowly and stiffly around like a mechanical dummy. In one hand she held her prayer-book, fan and handkerchief, in the other the blue parasol, still open; and on her plump hands were blue cotton mitts. Aunt Pinky beamed and chuckled; Odalie hardly expected her to be able to do more.

"Now you saw me," the child continued. "I reckon you satisfied. I mus' go; I ain't got a minute to was'e." But at the threshold she turned to inquire, bluntly:

"W'ere's Pug?"

"Pug," replied Aunt Pinky, in her tremulous old-woman's voice. "She's gone to chu'ch; done gone; she done gone," nodding her head in seeming approval of Pug's action.

"To church!" echoed Odalie with a look of consternation settling in her round eyes.

"She gone to chu'ch," reiterated Aunt Pinky. "Say she kain't miss chu'ch on de fifteent'; de debble gwine pester her twell jedgment, she miss chu'ch on de fifteent'."

Odalie's plump cheeks fairly quivered with indignation and she stamped her foot. She looked up and down the long, dusty road that skirted the river. Nothing was to be seen save the blue cart with its dejected looking mule and patient occupants. She walked to the end of the gallery and called out to a negro boy whose black bullet-head showed up in bold relief against the white of the cotton patch:

"He, Baptiste! w'ere's yo' ma? Ask yo' ma if she can't come set with Aunt Pinky."

"Mammy, she gone to chu'ch," screamed Baptiste in answer.

"Bonté! w'at's taken you all darkies with yo' 'church' to-day? You come along yere Baptiste an' set with Aunt Pinky. That Pug! I'm goin' to make yo' ma wear her out fo' that trick of hers—leavin' Aunt Pinky like that."

But at the first intimation of what was wanted of him, Baptiste dipped below the cotton like a fish beneath water, leaving no sight nor sound of himself to answer Odalie's repeated calls. Her mother and sister were beginning to show signs of impatience.

"But, I can't go," she cried out to them. "It's nobody to stay with Aunt Pinky. I can't leave Aunt Pinky like that, to fall out of her chair, maybe, like she already fell out once."

"You goin' to miss mass on the fifteenth, you, Odalie! W'at you thinkin' about?" came in shrill rebuke from her sister. But her mother offering no objection, the boy lost not a moment in starting the mule forward at a brisk trot. She watched them disappear in a cloud of dust; and turning with a dejected, almost tearful countenance, re-entered the room.

Aunt Pinky seemed to accept her reappearance as a matter of course; and even evinced no surprise at seeing her remove her hat and mitts, which she laid carefully, almost religiously, on the bed, together with her book, fan and handkerchief.

Then Odalie went and seated herself some distance from the old woman in her own small, low rocking-chair. She rocked herself furiously, making a great clatter with the rockers over the wide, uneven boards of the cabin floor; and she looked out through the open door.

"Puggy, she done gone to chu'ch; done gone. Say de debble gwine pester her twell jedgment—"

"You done tole me that, Aunt Pinky; neva mine; don't le's talk about it."

Aunt Pinky thus rebuked, settled back into silence and Odalie continued to rock and stare out of the door.

Once she arose, and taking the hickory branch from Aunt Pinky's nerveless hand, made a bold and sudden charge upon a little pig that seemed bent upon keeping her company. She pursued him with flying heels and loud cries as far as the road. She came back flushed and breathless and her curls hanging rather limp around her face; she began again to rock herself and gaze silently out of the door.

"You gwine make yo' fus' c'mmunion?"

This seemingly sober inquiry on the part of Aunt Pinky at once shattered Odalie's ill-humor and dispelled every shadow of it. She leaned back and laughed with wild abandonment.

"Mais w'at you thinkin' about, Aunt Pinky? How you don't remember I made my firs' communion las' year, with this same dress w'at maman let out the tuck," holding up the altered skirt for Aunt Pinky's inspection. "An' with this same petticoat w'at maman added this ruffle an' crochet' edge; excep' I had a w'ite sash."

These evidences proved beyond question convincing and seemed to satisfy Aunt Pinky. Odalie rocked as furiously as ever, but she sang now, and the swaying chair had worked its way nearer to the old woman.

"You gwine git mar'ied?"

"I declare, Aunt Pinky," said Odalie, when she had ceased laughing and was wiping her eyes, "I declare, sometime' I think you gittin' plumb foolish. How you expec' me to git married w'en I'm on'y thirteen?"

Evidently Aunt Pinky did not know why or how she expected anything so preposterous; Odalie's holiday attire that filled her with contemplative rapture, had doubtless incited her to these vagaries.

The child now drew her chair quite close to the old woman's knee after she had gone out to the rear of the cabin to get herself some water and had brought a drink to Aunt Pinky in the gourd dipper.

There was a strong, hot breeze blowing from the river, and it swept fitfully and in gusts through the cabin, bringing with it the weedy smell of cacti that grew thick on the bank, and occasionally a shower of reddish dust from the road. Odalie for a while was greatly occupied in keeping in place her filmy skirt, which every gust of wind swelled balloon-like about her knees. Aunt Pinky's little black, scrawny hand had found its way among the droopy curls, and strayed often caressingly to the child's plump neck and shoulders.

"You riclics, honey, dat day yo' granpappy say it wur pinchin' times an' he reckin he bleege to sell Yallah Tom an' Susan an' Pinky? Don' know how come he think 'bout Pinky, 'less caze he sees me playin' an' trapsin' roun' wid you alls, day in an' out. I riclics yit how you tu'n w'ite like milk an' fling yo' arms roun' li'le black Pinky; an' you cries out you don' wan' no saddle-mar'; you don' wan' no silk dresses and fing' rings an' sich; an' don' wan' no idication; des wants Pinky. An' you cries an' screams an' kicks, an' 'low you gwine kill fus' pusson w'at dar come an' buy Pinky an' kiars her off. You riclics dat, honey?"

Odalie had grown accustomed to these flights of fancy on the part of her old friend; she liked to humor her as she chose to sometimes humor very small children; so she was quite used to impersonating one dearly beloved but impetuous, "Paulette," who seemed to have held her place in old Pinky's heart and imagination through all the years of her suffering life.

"I rec'lec' like it was yesterday, Aunt Pinky. How I scream an' kick an' maman gave me some med'cine; an' how you scream an' kick an' Susan took you down to the quarters an' give you 'twenty'."

"Das so, honey; des like you says," chuckled Aunt Pinky. "But you don' riclic dat time you cotch Pinky cryin' down in de holler behine de gin; an' you say you gwine give me 'twenty' ef I don' tell you w'at I cryin' 'bout?"

"I rec'lec' like it happen'd to-day, Aunt Pinky. You been cryin' because you want to marry Hiram, ole Mr. Benitou's servant."

"Das true like you says, Miss Paulette; an' you goes home an' cries and kiars on an' won' eat, an' breaks dishes, an' pesters yo' gran'pap 'tell he bleedge to buy Hi'um f'om de Benitous."

"Don't talk, Aunt Pink! I can see all that jus' as plain!" responded Odalie sympathetically, yet in truth she took but a languid interest in these reminiscences which she had listened to so often before.

She leaned her flushed cheek against Aunt Pinky's knee.

The air was rippling now, and hot and caressing. There was the hum of bumble bees outside; and busy mud-daubers kept flying in and out through the door. Some chickens had penetrated to the very threshold in their aimless roamings, and the little pig was approaching more cautiously. Sleep was fast overtaking the child, but she could still hear through her drowsiness the familiar tones of Aunt Pinky's voice.

"But Hi'um, he done gone; he nuva come back; an' Yallah Tom nuva come back; an' ole Marster an' de chillun—all gone—nuva come back. Nobody nuva come back to Pinky 'cep you, my honey. You ain' gwine 'way f'om Pinky no mo', is you, Miss Paulette?"

"Don' fret, Aunt Pinky—I'm goin'—to stay with—you."

"No pussun nuva come back 'cep' you."

Odalie was fast asleep. Aunt Pinky was asleep with her head leaning back on her chair and her fingers thrust into the mass of tangled brown hair that swept across her lap. The chickens and little pig walked fearlessly in and out. The sunlight crept close up to the cabin door and stole away again.

Odalie awoke with a start. Her mother was standing over her arousing her from sleep. She sprang up and rubbed her eyes. "Oh, I been asleep!" she exclaimed. The cart was standing in the road waiting. "An' Aunt Pinky, she's asleep, too."

"Yes, chérie, Aunt Pinky is asleep," replied her mother, leading Odalie away. But she spoke low and trod softly as gentle-souled women do, in the presence of the dead.

Cavanelle

I WAS always sure of hearing something pleasant from Cavanelle across the counter. If he was not mistaking me for the freshest and prettiest girl in New Orleans, he was reserving for me some bit of silk, or lace, or ribbon of a nuance marvelously suited to my complexion, my eyes or my hair! What an innocent, delightful humbug Cavanelle was! How well I knew it and how little I cared! For when he had sold me the confection or bit of dry-goods in question, he always began to talk to me of his sister Mathilde, and then I knew that Cavanelle was an angel.

I had known him long enough to know why he worked so faithfully, so energetically and without rest—it was because Mathilde had a voice. It was because of her voice that his coats were worn till they were out of fashion and almost out at elbows. But for a sister whose voice needed only a little training to rival that of the nightingale, one might do such things without incurring reproach.

"You will believe, madame, that I did not know you las' night at the opera? I remark' to Mathilde, 'tiens! Mademoiselle Montreville,' an' I only rec'nize my mistake when I finally adjust my opera glass . . . . . . I guarantee you will be satisfied, madame. In a year from now you will come an' thank me for having secu' you that bargain in a poult-de-soie[1] . . . . . Yes, yes; as you say, Tolville was in voice. But," with a shrug of the narrow shoulders and a smile of commiseration that wrinkled the lean olive cheeks beneath the thin beard, "but to hear that cavatina render' as I have heard it render' by Mathilde, is another affair! A quality, madame, that moves, that penetrates. Perhaps not yet enough volume, but that will accomplish itself with time, when she will become more robus' in health. It is my intention to sen' her for the summer to Gran' Isle; that

329

good air an' surf bathing will work miracles. An artiste, voyez vous,[2] it is not to be treated like a human being of every day; it needs des petits soins;[3] perfec' res' of body an' mind; good red wine an' plenty . . . . . oh yes, madame, the stage; that is our intention; but never with my consent in light opera. Patience is what I counsel to Mathilde. A little more stren'th; a little dev'lopment of the chest to give that soupçon[4] of compass which is lacking, an' gran' opera is what I aspire for my sister."

I was curious to know Mathilde and to hear her sing; and thought it a great pity that a voice so marvelous as she doubtless possessed should not gain the notice that might prove the step toward the attainment of her ambition. It was such curiosity and a half-formed design or desire to interest myself in her career that prompted me to inform Cavanelle that I should greatly like to meet his sister; and I asked permission to call upon her the following Sunday afternoon.

Cavanelle was charmed. He otherwise would not have been Cavanelle. Over and over I was given the most minute directions for finding the house. The green car—or was it the yellow or blue one? I can no longer remember. But it was near Goodchildren street, and would I kindly walk this way and turn that way? At the corner was an ice dealer's. In the middle of the block, their house—one-story; painted yellow; a knocker; a banana tree nodding over the side fence. But indeed, I need not look for the banana tree, the knocker, the number or anything, for if I but turn the corner in the neighborhood of five o'clock I would find him planted at the door awaiting me.

And there he was! Cavanelle himself; but seeming to me not himself; apart from the entourage with which I was accustomed to associate him. Every line of his mobile face, every gesture emphasized the welcome which his kind eyes expressed as he ushered me into the small parlor that opened upon the street.

"Oh, not that chair, madame! I entreat you. This one, by all means. Thousan' times more comfortable."

"Mathilde! Strange; my sister was here but an instant ago. Mathilde! Où es tu donc?"[5] Stupid Cavanelle! He did not know when I had already guessed it—that Mathilde had retired to the adjoining room at my approach, and would appear after a sufficient delay to give an appropriate air of ceremony to our meeting.

And what a frail little piece of mortality she was when she did appear! At beholding her I could easily fancy that when she stepped outside of the yellow house, the zephyrs would lift her from her feet and, given a proper adjustment of the balloon sleeves, gently waft her in the direction of Goodchildren street, or wherever else she might want to go.

Hers was no physique for grand opera—certainly no stage presence; apparently so slender a hold upon life that the least tension might snap it. The voice which could hope to overcome these glaring disadvantages would have to be phenomenal.

Mathilde spoke English imperfectly, and with embarrassment, and was glad to lapse into French. Her speech was languid, unaffectedly so; and her manner was one of indolent repose; in this respect offering a striking contrast to that of her brother. Cavanelle seemed unable to rest. Hardly was I seated to his satisfaction than he darted from the room and soon returned followed by a limping old black woman bringing in a sirop d'orgeat[6] and layer cake on a tray.

Mathilde's face showed feeble annoyance at her brother's want of savoir vivre[7] in thus introducing the refreshments at so early a stage of my visit.

The servant was one of those cheap black women who abound in the French quarter, who speak Creole patois in preference to English, and who would rather work in a petit ménage[8] in Goodchildren street for five dollars a month than for fifteen in the fourth district. Her presence, in some unaccountable manner, seemed to reveal to me much of the inner working of this small household. I pictured her early morning visit to the French market, where picayunes were doled out sparingly, and lagniappes[9] gathered in with avidity.

I could see the neatly appointed dinner table; Cavanelle extolling his soup and bouillie[10] in extravagant terms; Mathilde toying with her papabotte or chicken-wing, and pouring herself a demi-verre[11] from her very own half-bottle of St. Julien; Pouponne, as they called her, mumbling and grumbling through habit, and serving them as faithfully as a dog through instinct. I wondered if they knew that Pouponne "played the lottery" with every spare "quarter" gathered from a judicious management of lagniappe. Perhaps they would not have cared, or have minded, either, that she as often consulted the Voudoo priestess around the corner as her father confessor.

My thoughts had followed Pouponne's limping figure from the room, and it was with an effort I returned to Cavanelle twirling the piano stool this way and that way. Mathilde was languidly turning over musical scores, and the two warmly discussing the merits of a selection which she had evidently decided upon.

The girl seated herself at the piano. Her hands were thin and anæmic, and she touched the keys without firmness or delicacy. When she had played a few introductory bars, she began to sing. Heaven only knows what she sang; it made no difference then, nor can it make any now.

The day was a warm one, but that did not prevent a creepy chilliness seizing hold of me. The feeling was generated by disappointment, anger, dismay and various other disagreeable sensations which I cannot find names for. Had I been intentionally deceived and misled? Was this some impertinent pleasantry on the part of Cavanelle? Or rather had not the girl's voice undergone some hideous transformation since her brother had listened to it? I dreaded to look at him, fearing to see horror and astonishment depicted on his face. When I did look, his expression was earnestly attentive and beamed approval of the strains to which he measured time by a slow, satisfied motion of the hand.

The voice was thin to attenuation, I fear it was not even true. Perhaps my disappointment exaggerated its simple deficiencies into monstrous defects. But it was an unsympathetic voice that never could have been a blessing to possess or to listen to.

I cannot recall what I said at parting—doubtless conventional things which were not true. Cavanelle politely escorted me to the car, and there I left him with a hand-clasp which from my side was tender with sympathy and pity.

"Poor Cavanelle! poor Cavanelle!" The words kept beating time in my brain to the jingle of the car bells and the regular ring of the mules' hoofs upon the cobble stones. One moment I resolved to have a talk with him in which I would endeavor to open his eyes to the folly of thus casting his hopes and the substance of his labor to the winds. The next instant I had decided that chance would possibly attend to Cavanelle's affair less clumsily than I could. "But all the same," I wondered, "is Cavanelle a fool? is he a lunatic? is he under a hypnotic spell?" And then—strange that I did not think of it before—I realized that Cavanelle loved Mathilde intensely, and we all know that love is blind, but a god just the same.

Two years passed before I saw Cavanelle again. I had been absent that length of time from the city. In the meanwhile Mathilde had died. She and her little voice—the apotheosis of insignificance—were no more. It was perhaps a year after my visit to her that I read an account of her death in a New Orleans paper. Then came a momentary pang of commiseration for my good Cavanelle. Chance had surely acted here the part of a skillful though merciless surgeon; no temporizing, no half measures. A deep, sharp thrust of the scalpel; a moment of agonizing pain; then rest, rest; convalescence; health; happiness! Yes, Mathilde had been dead a year and I was prepared for great changes in Cavanelle.

He had lived like a hampered child who does not recognize the restrictions hedging it about, and lives a life of pathetic contentment in the midst of them. But now all that was altered. He was, doubtless, regaling himself with the half-bottles of St. Julien, which were never before for him; with, perhaps, an occasional petit souper[12] at Moreau's, and there was no telling what little pleasures beside.

Cavanelle would certainly have bought himself a suit of clothes or two of modern fit and finish. I would find him with a brightened eye, a fuller cheek, as became a man of his years; perchance, even, a waxed moustache! So did my imagination run rampant with me.

And after all, the hand which I clasped across the counter was that of the self-same Cavanelle I had left. It was no fuller, no firmer. There were even some additional lines visible through the thin, brown beard.

"Ah, my poor Cavanelle! you have suffered a grievous loss since we parted." I saw in his face that he remembered the circumstance of our last meeting, so there was no use in avoiding the subject. I had rightly conjectured that the wound had been a cruel one, but in a year such wounds heal with a healthy soul.

He could have talked for hours of Mathilde's unhappy taking-off, and if the subject had possessed for me the same touching fascination which it held for him, doubtless, we would have done so, but—

"And how is it now, mon ami?[13] Are you living in the same place? running your little ménage as before, my poor Cavanelle?"

"Oh, yes, madame, except that my Aunt Félicie is making her home with me now. You have heard me speak of my aunt—No? You never have heard me speak of my Aunt Félicie Cavanelle of Terrebonne! That, madame, is a noble woman who has suffer' the mos' cruel affliction, an' deprivation, since the war.—No, madame, not in good health, unfortunately, by any means. It is why I esteem that a blessed privilege to give her declining years those little comforts, ces petits soins, that is a woman's right to expec' from men."

I knew what "des petits soins" meant with Cavanelle; doctors' visits, little jaunts across the lake, friandises[14] of every description showered upon "Aunt Félicie," and he himself relegated to the soup and bouillie which typified his prosaic existence.

I was unreasonably exasperated with the man for awhile, and would not even permit myself to notice the beauty in texture and design of the mousseline de laine[15] which he had spread across the counter in tempting folds. I was forced to restrain a brutal desire to say something stinging and cruel to him for his fatuity.

However, before I had regained the street, the conviction that Cavanelle was a hopeless fool seemed to reconcile me to the situation and also afforded me some diversion.

But even this estimate of my poor Cavanelle was destined not to last. By the time I had seated myself in the Prytania street car and passed up my nickel, I was convinced that Cavanelle was an angel.

Tante Cat'rinette

IT happened just as every one had predicted. Tante Cat'rinette was beside herself with rage and indignation when she learned that the town authorities had for some reason condemned her house and intended to demolish it.

"Dat house w'at Vieumaite[1] gi' me his own se'f, out his own mout', w'en he gi' me my freedom! All wrote down en règle[2] befo' de cote! Bon dieu Seigneur,[3] w'at dey talkin' 'bout!"

Tante Cat'rinette stood in the doorway of her home, resting a gaunt black hand against the jamb. In the other hand she held her corncob pipe. She was a tall, large-boned woman of a pronounced Congo type. The house in question had been substantial enough in its time. It contained four rooms: the lower two of brick, the upper ones of adobe. A dilapidated gallery projected from the upper story and slanted over the narrow banquette, to the peril of passers-by.

"I don't think I ever heard why the property was given to you in the first place, Tante Cat'rinette," observed Lawyer Paxton, who had stopped in passing, as so many others did, to talk the matter over with the old negress. The affair was attracting some attention in town, and its development was being watched with a good deal of interest. Tante Cat'rinette asked nothing better than to satisfy the lawyer's curiosity.

"Vieumaite all time say Cat'rinette wort' gole to 'im; de way I make dem nigga' walk chalk. But," she continued, with recovered seriousness, "w'en I nuss 'is li'le gal w'at all de doctor' 'low it 's goin' die, an' I make it well, me, den Vieumaite, he can't do 'nough, him. He name' dat li'le gal Cat'rine fo' me. Das Miss Kitty w'at marry Miché Raymond yon' by Gran' Eco'. Den he gi' me my freedom; he got plenty slave', him; one don' count in his pocket. An' he gi' me dat house w'at I'm stan'in' in de do'; he got plenty house' an' lan', him. Now dey want pay me t'ousan' dolla', w'at I don' axen' fo', an' tu'n me out dat house! I waitin' fo' 'em, Miché Paxtone," and a wicked gleam shot into the woman's small, dusky eyes. "I got my axe grine fine. Fus' man w'at touch Cat'rinette fo' tu'n her out dat house, he git 'is head bus' like I bus' a gode."

"Dat's nice day, ainty, Miché Paxtone? Fine wedda fo' dry my close." Upon the gallery above hung an array of shirts, which gleamed white in the sunshine, and flapped in the rippling breeze.

The spectacle of Tante Cat'rinette defying the authorities was one which offered much diversion to the children of the neighborhood. They played numberless pranks at her expense; daily serving upon her fictitious notices purporting to be to the last degree official. One youngster, in a moment of inspiration, composed a couplet, which they recited, sang, shouted at all hours, beneath her windows.

> "Tante Cat'rinette, she go in town;
> W'en she come back, her house pull' down."

So ran the production. She heard it many times during the day, but, far from offending her, she accepted it as a warning,—a prediction, as it were,—and she took heed not to offer to fate the conditions for its fulfillment. She no longer quitted her house even for a moment, so great was her fear and so firm her belief that the town authorities were lying in wait to possess themselves of it. She would not cross the street to visit a neighbor. She waylaid passers-by and pressed them into service to do her errands and small shopping. She grew distrustful and suspicious, ever on the alert to scent a plot in the most innocent endeavor to induce her to leave the house.

One morning, as Tante Cat'rinette was hanging out her latest batch of washing, Eusèbe, a "free mulatto"[4] from Red River, stopped his pony beneath her gallery.

"Hé, Tante Cat'rinette!" he called up to her.

She turned to the railing just as she was, in her bare arms and neck that gleamed ebony-like against the unbleached cotton of her chemise. A coarse skirt was fastened about her waist, and a string of many-colored beads knotted around her throat. She held her smoking pipe between her yellow teeth.

"How you all come on, Miché Eusèbe?" she questioned, pleasantly.

"We all middlin', Tante Cat'rinette. But Miss Kitty, she putty bad
off out yon'a. I see Mista Raymond dis mo'nin' w'en I pass by his
house; he say look like de feva don' wan' to quit 'er. She been axen'
fo' you all t'rough de night. He 'low he reckon I betta tell you. Nice
wedda we got fo' plantin', Tante Cat'rinette."

"Nice wedda fo' lies, Miché Eusèbe," and she spat contemptuously down upon the banquette. She turned away without noticing
the man further, and proceeded to hang one of Lawyer Paxton's fine
linen shirts upon the line.

"She been axen' fo' you all t'rough de night."

Somehow Tante Cat'rinette could not get that refrain out of her
head. She would not willingly believe that Eusèbe had spoken the
truth, but—"She been axen' fo' you all t'rough de night—all t'rough
de night." The words kept ringing in her ears, as she came and went
about her daily tasks. But by degrees she dismissed Eusèbe and his
message from her mind. It was Miss Kitty's voice that she could
hear in fancy following her, calling out through the night, "W'ere
Tante Cat'rinette? W'y Tante Cat'rinette don' come? W'y she don'
come—w'y she don' come?"

All day the woman muttered and mumbled to herself in her Creole patois; invoking council of "Vieumaite," as she always did in her
troubles. Tante Cat'rinette's religion was peculiarly her own; she
turned to heaven with her grievances, it is true, but she felt that
there was no one in Paradise with whom she was quite so well acquainted as with "Vieumaite."

Late in the afternoon she went and stood on her doorstep, and
looked uneasily and anxiously out upon the almost deserted street.
When a little girl came walking by,—a sweet child with a frank and
innocent face, upon whose word she knew she could rely,—Tante
Cat'rinette invited her to enter.

"Come yere see Tante Cat'rinette, Lolo. It's long time you en't
come see Tante Cat'rine; you gittin' proud." She made the little one
sit down, and offered her a couple of cookies, which the child accepted with pretty avidity.

"You putty good li'le gal, you, Lolo. You keep on go confession
all de time?"

"Oh, yes. I'm goin' make my firs' communion firs' of May, Tante Cat'rinette." A dog-eared catechism was sticking out of Lolo's apron pocket.

"Das right; be good li'le gal. Mine yo' maman ev't'ing she say; an' neva tell no story. It's nuttin' bad in dis worl' like tellin' lies. You know Eusèbe?"

"Eusèbe?"

"Yas; dat li'le ole Red River free m'latto. Uh, uh! dat one man w'at kin tell lies, yas! He come tell me Miss Kitty down sick yon'a. You ev' yeard such big story like dat, Lolo?"

The child looked a little bewildered, but she answered promptly, " 'Tain't no story, Tante Cat'rinette. I yeard papa sayin', dinner time, Mr. Raymond sen' fo' Dr. Chalon. An' Dr. Chalon says he ain't got time to go yonda. An' papa says it's because Dr. Chalon on'y want to go w'ere it's rich people; an' he's 'fraid Mista Raymond ain' goin' pay 'im."

Tante Cat'rinette admired the little girl's pretty gingham dress, and asked her who had ironed it. She stroked her brown curls, and talked of all manner of things quite foreign to the subject of Eusèbe and his wicked propensity for telling lies.

She was not restless as she had been during the early part of the day, and she no longer mumbled and muttered as she had been doing over her work.

At night she lighted her coal-oil lamp, and placed it near a window where its light could be seen from the street through the half-closed shutters. Then she sat herself down, erect and motionless, in a chair.

When it was near upon midnight, Tante Cat'rinette arose, and looked cautiously, very cautiously, out of the door. Her house lay in the line of deep shadow that extended along the street. The other side was bathed in the pale light of the declining moon. The night was agreeably mild, profoundly still, but pregnant with the subtle quivering life of early spring. The earth seemed asleep and breathing,—a scent-laden breath that blew in soft puffs against Tante Cat'rinette's face as she emerged from the house. She closed and locked her door noiselessly; then she crept slowly away, treading softly, stealthily as a cat, in the deep shadow.

There were but few people abroad at that hour. Once she ran

upon a gay party of ladies and gentlemen who had been spending the evening over cards and anisette. They did not notice Tante Cat'rinette almost effacing herself against the black wall of the cathedral. She breathed freely and ventured from her retreat only when they had disappeared from view. Once a man saw her quite plainly, as she darted across a narrow strip of moonlight. But Tante Cat'rinette need not have gasped with fright as she did. He was too drunk to know if she were a thing of flesh, or only one of the fantastic, maddening shadows that the moon was casting across his path to bewilder him. When she reached the outskirts of the town, and had to cross the broad piece of open country which stretched out toward the pine wood, an almost paralyzing terror came over her. But she crouched low, and hurried through the marsh and weeds, avoiding the open road. She could have been mistaken for one of the beasts browsing there where she passed.

But once in the Grand Ecore road that lay through the pine wood, she felt secure and free to move as she pleased. Tante Cat'rinette straightened herself, stiffened herself in fact, and unconsciously assuming the attitude of the professional sprinter, she sped rapidly beneath the Gothic interlacing branches of the pines. She talked constantly to herself as she went, and to the animate and inanimate objects around her. But her speech, far from intelligent, was hardly intelligible.

She addressed herself to the moon, which she apostrophized as an impertinent busybody spying upon her actions. She pictured all manner of troublesome animals, snakes, rabbits, frogs, pursuing her, but she defied them to catch Cat'rinette, who was hurrying toward Miss Kitty. "Pa capab trapé Cat'rinette, vouzot; mo pé couri vite coté Miss Kitty." She called up to a mocking-bird warbling upon a lofty limb of a pine tree, asking why it cried out so, and threatening to secure it and put it into a cage. "Ca to pé crié comme ça, ti céléra? Arete, mo trapé zozos la, mo mété li dan ain bon lacage." Indeed, Tante Cat'rinette seemed on very familiar terms with the night, with the forest, and with all the flying, creeping, crawling things that inhabit it. At the speed with which she traveled she soon had covered the few miles of wooded road, and before long had reached her destination.

The sleeping-room of Miss Kitty opened upon the long outside gallery, as did all the rooms of the unpretentious frame house which was her home. The place could hardly be called a plantation; it was too small for that. Nevertheless Raymond was trying to plant; trying to teach school between times, in the end room; and sometimes, when he found himself in a tight place, trying to clerk for Mr. Jacobs over in Campte, across Red River.

Tante Cat'rinette mounted the creaking steps, crossed the gallery, and entered Miss Kitty's room as though she were returning to it after a few moments' absence. There was a lamp burning dimly upon the high mantelpiece. Raymond had evidently not been to bed; he was in shirt sleeves, rocking the baby's cradle. It was the same mahogany cradle which had held Miss Kitty thirty-five years before, when Tante Cat'rinette had rocked it. The cradle had been bought then to match the bed,—that big, beautiful bed on which Miss Kitty lay now in a restless half slumber. There was a fine French clock on the mantel, still telling the hours as it had told them years ago. But there were no carpets or rugs on the floors. There was no servant in the house.

Raymond uttered an exclamation of amazement when he saw Tante Cat'rinette enter.

"How you do, Miché Raymond?" she said, quietly. "I yeard Miss Kitty been sick; Eusèbe tell me dat dis mo'nin'."

She moved toward the bed as lightly as though shod with velvet, and seated herself there. Miss Kitty's hand lay outside the coverlid; a shapely hand, which her few days of illness and rest had not yet softened. The negress laid her own black hand upon it. At the touch Miss Kitty instinctively turned her palm upward.

"It's Tante Cat'rinette!" she exclaimed, with a note of satisfaction in her feeble voice. "W'en did you come, Tante Cat'rinette? They all said you wouldn' come."

"I'm goin' come ev'y night, cher coeur,[5] ev'y night tell you be well. Tante Cat'rinette can't come daytime no mo'."

"Raymond tole me about it. They doin' you mighty mean in town, Tante Cat'rinette."

"Nev' mine, ti chou.[6] I know how take care dat w'at Vieumaite gi' me. You go sleep now. Cat'rinette goin' set yere an' mine you. She goin' make you well like she all time do. We don' wan' no céléra[7] doctor. We drive 'em out wid a stick, dey come roun' yere."

Miss Kitty was soon sleeping more restfully than she had done since her illness began. Raymond had finally succeeded in quieting the baby, and he tiptoed into the adjoining room, where the other children lay, to snatch a few hours of much-needed rest for himself. Cat'rinette sat faithfully beside her charge, administering at intervals to the sick woman's wants.

But the thought of regaining her home before daybreak, and of the urgent necessity for doing so, did not leave Tante Cat'rinette's mind for an instant.

In the profound darkness, the deep stillness of the night that comes before dawn, she was walking again through the woods, on her way back to town.

The mocking-birds were asleep, and so were the frogs and the snakes; and the moon was gone, and so was the breeze. She walked now in utter silence but for the heavy guttural breathing that accompanied her rapid footsteps. She walked with a desperate determination along the road, every foot of which was familiar to her.

When she at last emerged from the woods, the earth about her was faintly, very faintly, beginning to reveal itself in the tremulous, gray, uncertain light of approaching day. She staggered and plunged onward with beating pulses quickened by fear.

A sudden turn, and Tante Cat'rinette stood facing the river. She stopped abruptly, as if at command of some unseen power that forced her. For an instant she pressed a black hand against her tired, burning eyes, and stared fixedly ahead of her.

Tante Cat'rinette had always believed that Paradise was up there overhead where the sun and stars and moon are, and that "Vieumaite" inhabited that region of splendor. She never for a moment doubted this. It would be difficult, perhaps unsatisfying, to explain why Tante Cat'rinette, on that particular morning, when a vision of the rising day broke suddenly upon her, should have believed that she stood in face of a heavenly revelation. But why not, after all? Since she talked so familiarly herself to the unseen, why should it not respond to her when the time came?

Across the narrow, quivering line of water, the delicate budding branches of young trees were limned black against the gold, orange,—what word is there to tell the color of that morning sky! And steeped in the splendor of it hung one pale star; there was not another in the whole heaven.

Tante Cat'rinette stood with her eyes fixed intently upon that star, which held her like a hypnotic spell. She stammered breathlessly:

"Mo pé couté, Vieumaite. Cat'rinette pé couté." (I am listening, Vieumaite. Cat'rinette hears you.)

She stayed there motionless upon the brink of the river till the star melted into the brightness of the day and became part of it.

When Tante Cat'rinette entered Miss Kitty's room for the second time, the aspect of things had changed somewhat. Miss Kitty was with much difficulty holding the baby while Raymond mixed a saucer of food for the little one. Their oldest daughter, a child of twelve, had come into the room with an apronful of chips from the woodpile, and was striving to start a fire on the hearth, to make the morning coffee. The room seemed bare and almost squalid in the daylight.

"Well, yere Tante Cat'rinette come back," she said, quietly announcing herself.

They could not well understand why she was back; but it was good to have her there, and they did not question.

She took the baby from its mother, and, seating herself, began to feed it from the saucer which Raymond placed beside her on a chair.

"Yas," she said, "Cat'rinette goin' stay; dis time she en't nev' goin' 'way no mo'."

Husband and wife looked at each other with surprised, questioning eyes.

"Miché Raymond," remarked the woman, turning her head up to him with a certain comical shrewdness in her glance, "if somebody want len' you t'ousan' dolla', w'at you goin' say? Even if it's ole nigga 'oman?"

The man's face flushed with sudden emotion. "I would say that person was our bes' frien', Tante Cat'rinette. An'," he added, with a smile, "I would give her a mortgage on the place, of co'se, to secu' her f'om loss."

"Das right," agreed the woman practically. "Den Cat'rinette goin' len' you t'ousan' dolla'. Dat w'at Vieumaite give her, dat b'long to her; don' b'long to nobody else. An' we go yon'a to town, Miché Raymond, you an' me. You care me befo' Miché Paxtone. I want 'im fo' put down in writin' befo' de cote dat w'at Cat'rinette got, it fo' Miss Kitty w'en I be dead."

Miss Kitty was crying softly in the depths of her pillow.

"I en't got no head fo' all dat, me," laughed Tante Cat'rinette, good humoredly, as she held a spoonful of pap up to the baby's eager lips. "It's Vieumaite tell me all dat clair an' plain dis mo'nin', w'en I comin' 'long de Gran' Eco' road."

A Respectable Woman

Mrs. Baroda was a little provoked to learn that her husband expected his friend, Gouvernail, up to spend a week or two on the plantation.

They had entertained a good deal during the winter; much of the time had also been passed in New Orleans in various forms of mild dissipation. She was looking forward to a period of unbroken rest, now, and undisturbed tête-à-tête with her husband, when he informed her that Gouvernail was coming up to stay a week or two.

This was a man she had heard much of but never seen. He had been her husband's college friend; was now a journalist, and in no sense a society man or "a man about town," which were, perhaps, some of the reasons she had never met him. But she had unconsciously formed an image of him in her mind. She pictured him tall, slim, cynical; with eye-glasses, and his hands in his pockets; and she did not like him. Gouvernail was slim enough, but he wasn't very tall nor very cynical; neither did he wear eye-glasses nor carry his hands in his pockets. And she rather liked him when he first presented himself.

But why she liked him she could not explain satisfactorily to herself when she partly attempted to do so. She could discover in him none of those brilliant and promising traits which Gaston, her husband, had often assured her that he possessed. On the contrary, he sat rather mute and receptive before her chatty eagerness to make him feel at home and in face of Gaston's frank and wordy hospitality. His manner was as courteous toward her as the most exacting woman could require; but he made no direct appeal to her approval or even esteem.

Once settled at the plantation he seemed to like to sit upon the wide portico in the shade of one of the big Corinthian pillars, smoking his cigar lazily and listening attentively to Gaston's experience as a sugar planter.

"This is what I call living," he would utter with deep satisfaction, as the air that swept across the sugar field caressed him with its warm and scented velvety touch. It pleased him also to get on familiar terms with the big dogs that came about him, rubbing themselves sociably against his legs. He did not care to fish, and displayed no eagerness to go out and kill grosbecs when Gaston proposed doing so.

Gouvernail's personality puzzled Mrs. Baroda, but she liked him. Indeed, he was a lovable, inoffensive fellow. After a few days, when she could understand him no better than at first, she gave over being puzzled and remained piqued. In this mood she left her husband and her guest, for the most part, alone together. Then finding that Gouvernail took no manner of exception to her action, she imposed her society upon him, accompanying him in his idle strolls to the mill and walks along the batture. She persistently sought to penetrate the reserve in which he had unconsciously enveloped himself.

"When is he going—your friend?" she one day asked her husband. "For my part, he tires me frightfully."

"Not for a week yet, dear. I can't understand; he gives you no trouble."

"No. I should like him better if he did; if he were more like others, and I had to plan somewhat for his comfort and enjoyment."

Gaston took his wife's pretty face between his hands and looked tenderly and laughingly into her troubled eyes. They were making a bit of toilet sociably together in Mrs. Baroda's dressing-room.

"You are full of surprises, ma belle,"[1] he said to her. "Even I can never count upon how you are going to act under given conditions." He kissed her and turned to fasten his cravat before the mirror.

"Here you are," he went on, "taking poor Gouvernail seriously and making a commotion over him, the last thing he would desire or expect."

"Commotion!" she hotly resented. "Nonsense! How can you

say such a thing? Commotion, indeed! But, you know, you said he
was clever."

"So he is. But the poor fellow is run down by overwork now.
That's why I asked him here to take a rest."

"You used to say he was a man of ideas," she retorted, unconcil-
iated. "I expected him to be interesting, at least. I'm going to the
city in the morning to have my spring gowns fitted. Let me know
when Mr. Gouvernail is gone; I shall be at my Aunt Octavie's."

That night she went and sat alone upon a bench that stood beneath a live oak tree at the edge of the gravel walk.

She had never known her thoughts or her intentions to be so
confused. She could gather nothing from them but the feeling of a
distinct necessity to quit her home in the morning.

Mrs. Baroda heard footsteps crunching the gravel; but could discern in the darkness only the approaching red point of a lighted
cigar. She knew it was Gouvernail, for her husband did not smoke.
She hoped to remain unnoticed, but her white gown revealed her to
him. He threw away his cigar and seated himself upon the bench
beside her; without a suspicion that she might object to his presence.

"Your husband told me to bring this to you, Mrs. Baroda," he
said, handing her a filmy, white scarf with which she sometimes enveloped her head and shoulders. She accepted the scarf from him
with a murmur of thanks, and let it lie in her lap.

He made some commonplace observation upon the baneful effect of the night air at that season. Then as his gaze reached out into
the darkness, he murmured, half to himself:

" 'Night of south winds—night of the large few stars!
       Still nodding night—' "

She made no reply to this apostrophe to the night, which indeed,
was not addressed to her.

Gouvernail was in no sense a diffident man, for he was not a self-
conscious one. His periods of reserve were not constitutional, but
the result of moods. Sitting there beside Mrs. Baroda, his silence
melted for the time.

He talked freely and intimately in a low, hesitating drawl that
was not unpleasant to hear. He talked of the old college days when
he and Gaston had been a good deal to each other; of the days of

keen and blind ambitions and large intentions. Now there was left with him, at least, a philosophic acquiescence to the existing order—only a desire to be permitted to exist, with now and then a little whiff of genuine life, such as he was breathing now.

Her mind only vaguely grasped what he was saying. Her physical being was for the moment predominant. She was not thinking of his words, only drinking in the tones of his voice. She wanted to reach out her hand in the darkness and touch him with the sensitive tips of her fingers upon the face or the lips. She wanted to draw close to him and whisper against his cheek—she did not care what—as she might have done if she had not been a respectable woman.

The stronger the impulse grew to bring herself near him, the further, in fact, did she draw away from him. As soon as she could do so without an appearance of too great rudeness, she rose and left him there alone.

Before she reached the house, Gouvernail had lighted a fresh cigar and ended his apostrophe to the night.[2]

Mrs. Baroda was greatly tempted that night to tell her husband—who was also her friend—of this folly that had seized her. But she did not yield to the temptation. Beside being a respectable woman she was a very sensible one; and she knew there are some battles in life which a human being must fight alone.

When Gaston arose in the morning, his wife had already departed. She had taken an early morning train to the city. She did not return till Gouvernail was gone from under her roof.

There was some talk of having him back during the summer that followed. That is, Gaston greatly desired it; but this desire yielded to his wife's strenuous opposition.

However, before the year ended, she proposed, wholly from herself, to have Gouvernail visit them again. Her husband was surprised and delighted with the suggestion coming from her.

"I am glad, chère amie,[3] to know that you have finally overcome your dislike for him; truly he did not deserve it."

"Oh," she told him, laughingly, after pressing a long, tender kiss upon his lips, "I have overcome everything! you will see. This time I shall be very nice to him."

Ripe Figs

MAMAN-NAINAINE[1] said that when the figs were ripe Babette might go to visit her cousins down on the Bayou-Lafourche where the sugar cane grows. Not that the ripening of figs had the least thing to do with it, but that is the way Maman-Nainaine was.

It seemed to Babette a very long time to wait; for the leaves upon the trees were tender yet, and the figs were like little hard, green marbles.

But warm rains came along and plenty of strong sunshine, and though Maman-Nainaine was as patient as the statue of la Madone,[2] and Babette as restless as a humming-bird, the first thing they both knew it was hot summer-time. Every day Babette danced out to where the fig-trees were in a long line against the fence. She walked slowly beneath them, carefully peering between the gnarled, spreading branches. But each time she came disconsolate away again. What she saw there finally was something that made her sing and dance the whole long day.

When Maman-Nainaine sat down in her stately way to break-fast, the following morning, her muslin cap standing like an aureole about her white, placid face, Babette approached. She bore a dainty porcelain platter, which she set down before her godmother. It contained a dozen purple figs, fringed around with their rich, green leaves.

"Ah," said Maman-Nainaine, arching her eyebrows, "how early the figs have ripened this year!"

"Oh," said Babette, "I think they have ripened very late."

"Babette," continued Maman-Nainaine, as she peeled the very plumpest figs with her pointed silver fruit-knife, "you will carry my love to them all down on Bayou-Lafourche. And tell your Tante Frosine I shall look for her at Toussaint[3]—when the chrysanthe-mums are in bloom."

Ozème's Holiday

Ozème often wondered why there was not a special dispensation of providence to do away with the necessity for work. There seemed to him so much created for man's enjoyment in this world, and so little time and opportunity to profit by it. To sit and do nothing but breathe was a pleasure to Ozème; but to sit in the company of a few choice companions, including a sprinkling of ladies, was even a greater delight; and the joy which a day's hunting or fishing or picnicking afforded him is hardly to be described. Yet he was by no means indolent. He worked faithfully on the plantation the whole year long, in a sort of methodical way; but when the time came around for his annual week's holiday, there was no holding him back. It was often decidedly inconvenient for the planter that Ozème usually chose to take his holiday during some very busy season of the year.

He started out one morning in the beginning of October. He had borrowed Mr. Laballière's buckboard and Padue's old gray mare, and a harness from the negro Sévérin. He wore a light blue suit which had been sent all the way from St. Louis, and which had cost him ten dollars; he had paid almost as much again for his boots; and his hat was a broad-rimmed gray felt which he had no cause to be ashamed of. When Ozème went "broading," he dressed—well, regardless of cost. His eyes were blue and mild; his hair was light, and he wore it rather long; he was clean shaven, and really did not look his thirty-five years.

Ozème had laid his plans weeks beforehand. He was going visiting along Cane River; the mere contemplation filled him with pleasure. He counted upon reaching Fédeaus' about noon, and he would stop and dine there. Perhaps they would ask him to stay all night. He really did not hold to staying all night, and was not decided to accept if they did ask him. There were only the two old people, and he rather fancied the notion of pushing on to Beltrans', where he would stay a night, or even two, if urged. He was quite sure that there would be something agreeable going on at Beltrans', with all those young people—perhaps a fish-fry, or possibly a ball!

Of course he would have to give a day to Tante Sophie and another to Cousine Victoire; but none to the St. Annes unless entreated—after St. Anne reproaching him last year with being a fainéant[1] for broading at such a season! At Cloutierville, where he would linger as long as possible, he meant to turn and retrace his course, zigzagging back and forth across Cane River so as to take in the Duplans, the Velcours, and others that he could not at the moment recall. A week seemed to Ozème a very, very little while in which to crowd so much pleasure.

There were steam-gins at work; he could hear them whistling far and near. On both sides of the river the fields were white with cotton, and everybody in the world seemed busy but Ozème. This reflection did not distress or disturb him in the least; he pursued his way at peace with himself and his surroundings.

At Lamérie's cross-roads store, where he stopped to buy a cigar, he learned that there was no use heading for Fédeaus', as the two old people had gone to town for a lengthy visit, and the house was locked up. It was at Fédeaus' that Ozème had intended to dine.

He sat in the buckboard, given up to a moment or two of reflection. The result was that he turned away from the river, and entered the road that led between two fields back to the woods and into the heart of the country. He had determined upon taking a short cut to the Beltrans' plantation, and on the way he meant to keep an eye open for old Aunt Tildy's cabin, which he knew lay in some remote part of this cut-off. He remembered that Aunt Tildy could cook an excellent meal if she had the material at hand. He would induce her to fry him a chicken, drip a cup of coffee, and turn him out a pone of corn-bread, which he thought would be sumptuous enough fare for the occasion.

Aunt Tildy dwelt in the not unusual log cabin, of one room, with its chimney of mud and stone, and its shallow gallery formed by the jutting of the roof. In close proximity to the cabin was a small cotton-field, which from a long distance looked like a field of snow.

The cotton was bursting and overflowing foam-like from bolls on the drying stalk. On the lower branches it was hanging ragged and tattered, and much of it had already fallen to the ground. There were a few chinaberry-trees in the yard before the hut, and under one of them an ancient and rusty-looking mule was eating corn from a wood trough. Some common little Creole chickens were scratching about the mule's feet and snatching at the grains of corn that occasionally fell from the trough.

Aunt Tildy was hobbling across the yard when Ozème drew up before the gate. One hand was confined in a sling; in the other she carried a tin pan, which she let fall noisily to the ground when she recognized him. She was broad, black, and misshapen, with her body bent forward almost at an acute angle. She wore a blue cottonade of large plaids, and a bandana awkwardly twisted around her head.

"Good God A'mighty, man! Whar you come from?" was her startled exclamation at beholding him.

"F'om home, Aunt Tildy; w'ere else do you expec'?" replied Ozème, dismounting composedly.

He had not seen the old woman for several years—since she was cooking in town for the family with which he boarded at the time. She had washed and ironed for him, atrociously, it is true, but her intentions were beyond reproach if her washing was not. She had also been clumsily attentive to him during a spell of illness. He had paid her with an occasional bandana, a calico dress, or a checked apron, and they had always considered the account between themselves square, with no sentimental feeling of gratitude remaining on either side.

"I like to know," remarked Ozème, as he took the gray mare from the shafts, and led her up to the trough where the mule was— "I like to know w'at you mean by makin' a crop like that an' then lettin' it go to was'e? Who you reckon's goin' to pick that cotton? You think maybe the angels goin' to come down an' pick it fo' you, an' gin it an' press it, an' then give you ten cents a poun' fo' it, hein?"

"Ef de Lord don' pick it, I don' know who gwine pick it, Mista Ozème. I tell you, me an' Sandy we wuk dat crap day in an' day out; it's him done de mos' of it."

"Sandy? That little—"

"He ain' dat li'le Sandy no mo' w'at you rec'lec's; he 'mos' a man, an' he wuk like a man now. He wuk mo' 'an fittin' fo' his strenk, an' now he layin' in dah sick—God A'mighty knows how sick. An' me wid a risin' twell I bleeged to walk de flo' o' nights, an' don' know ef I ain' gwine to lose de han' atter all."

"W'y, in the name o' conscience, you don' hire somebody to pick?"

"Whar I got money to hire? An' you knows well as me ev'y chick an' chile is pickin' roun' on de plantations an' gittin' good pay."

The whole outlook appeared to Ozème very depressing, and even menacing, to his personal comfort and peace of mind. He foresaw no prospect of dinner unless he should cook it himself. And there was that Sandy—he remembered well the little scamp of eight, always at his grandmother's heels when she was cooking or washing. Of course he would have to go in and look at the boy, and no doubt dive into his traveling-bag for quinine, without which he never traveled.

Sandy was indeed very ill, consumed with fever. He lay on a cot covered up with a faded patchwork quilt. His eyes were half closed, and he was muttering and rambling on about hoeing and bedding and cleaning and thinning out the cotton; he was hauling it to the gin, wrangling about weight and bagging and ties and the price offered per pound. That bale or two of cotton had not only sent Sandy to bed, but had pursued him there, holding him through his fevered dreams, and threatening to end him. Ozème would never have known the black boy, he was so tall, so thin, and seemingly so wasted, lying there in bed.

"See yere, Aunt Tildy," said Ozème, after he had, as was usual with him when in doubt, abandoned himself to a little reflection; "between us—you an' me—we got to manage to kill an' cook one o' those chickens I see scratchin' out yonda, fo' I'm jus' about starved. I reckon you ain't got any quinine in the house? No; I didn't suppose an instant you had. Well, I'm goin' to give Sandy a good dose o' quinine to-night, an' I'm goin' stay an' see how that'll work on 'im. But sun-up, min' you, I mus' get out o' yere."

Ozème had spent more comfortable nights than the one passed in Aunt Tildy's bed, which she considerately abandoned to him.

In the morning Sandy's fever was somewhat abated, but had not

taken a decided enough turn to justify Ozème in quitting him before noon, unless he was willing "to feel like a dog," as he told himself. He appeared before Aunt Tildy stripped to the undershirt, and
wearing his second-best pair of trousers.

"That's a nice pickle o' fish you got me in, ol' woman. I guarantee, nex' time I go abroad, 'tain't me that'll take any cut-off. W'ere's
that cotton-basket an' cotton-sack o' yo's?"

"I knowed it!" chanted Aunt Tildy—"I knowed de Lord war
gwine sen' somebody to holp me out. He war n' gwine let de crap
was'e atter he give Sandy an' me de strenk to make hit. De Lord
gwine shove you 'long de row, Mista Ozème. De Lord gwine give
you plenty mo' fingers an' han's to pick dat cotton nimble an'
clean."

"Neva you min' w'at the Lord's goin' to do; go get me that
cotton-sack. An' you put that poultice like I tol' you on yo' han',
an' set down there an' watch Sandy. It looks like you are 'bout as
helpless as a' ol' cow tangled up in a potato-vine."

Ozème had not picked cotton for many years, and he took to it a
little awkwardly at first; but by the time he had reached the end of
the first row the old dexterity of youth had come back to his hands,
which flew rapidly back and forth with the motion of a weaver's
shuttle; and his ten fingers became really nimble in clutching the
cotton from its dry shell. By noon he had gathered about fifty
pounds. Sandy was not then quite so well as he had promised to be,
and Ozème concluded to stay that day and one more night. If the
boy were no better in the morning, he would go off in search of a
doctor for him, and he himself would continue on down to Tante
Sophie's; the Beltrans' was out of the question now.

Sandy hardly needed a doctor in the morning. Ozème's doctor-
ing was beginning to tell favorably; but he would have considered it
criminal indifference and negligence to go away and leave the boy
to Aunt Tildy's awkward ministrations just at the critical moment
when there was a turn for the better; so he stayed that day out, and
picked his hundred and fifty pounds.

On the third day it looked like rain, and a heavy rain just then
would mean a heavy loss to Aunt Tildy and Sandy, and Ozème
again went to the field, this time urging Aunt Tildy with him to do
what she might with her one good hand.

"Aunt Tildy," called out Ozème to the bent old woman moving

ahead of him between the white rows of cotton, "if the Lord gets
me safe out o' this ditch, 't ain't to-morro' I'll fall in anotha with
my eyes open, I bet you."

"Keep along, Mista Ozème; don' grumble, don' stumble; de
Lord's a-watchin' you. Look at yo' Aunt Tildy; she doin' mo' wid
her one han' 'an you doin' wid yo' two, man. Keep right along,
honey. Watch dat cotton how it fallin' in yo' Aunt Tildy's bag."

"I am watchin' you, ol' woman; you don' fool me. You got to
work that han' o' yo's spryer than you doin', or I'll take the
rawhide. You done fo'got w'at the rawhide tas'e like, I reckon"—a
reminder which amused Aunt Tildy so powerfully that her big ne-
gro-laugh resounded over the whole cotton-patch, and even caused
Sandy, who heard it, to turn in his bed.

The weather was still threatening on the succeeding day, and a
sort of dogged determination or characteristic desire to see his un-
dertakings carried to a satisfactory completion urged Ozème to
continue his efforts to drag Aunt Tildy out of the mire into which
circumstances seemed to have thrust her.

One night the rain did come, and began to beat softly on the roof
of the old cabin. Sandy opened his eyes, which were no longer brilliant with the fever flame. "Granny," he whispered, "de rain! Des
listen, granny; de rain a-comin', an' I ain' pick dat cotton yit. W'at
time it is? Gi' me my pants—I got to go—"

"You lay whar you is, chile alive. Dat cotton put aside clean and
dry. Me an' de Lord an' Mista Ozème done pick dat cotton."

Ozème drove away in the morning looking quite as spick and
span as the day he left home in his blue suit and his light felt drawn
a little over his eyes.

"You want to take care o' that boy," he instructed Aunt Tildy at
parting, "an' get 'im on his feet. An', let me tell you, the nex' time I
start out to broad, if you see me passin' in this yere cut-off, put on
yo' specs an' look at me good, because it won't be me; it'll be my
ghos', ol' woman."

Indeed, Ozème, for some reason or other, felt quite shamefaced
as he drove back to the plantation. When he emerged from the lane
which he had entered the week before, and turned into the river
road, Lamérie, standing in the store door, shouted out:

"Hé, Ozème! you had good times yonda? I bet you danced holes
in the sole of them new boots."

"Don't talk, Lamérie!" was Ozème's rather ambiguous reply, as he flourished the remainder of a whip over the old gray mare's sway-back, urging her to a gentle trot.

When he reached home, Bodé, one of Padue's boys, who was assisting him to unhitch, remarked:

"How come you didn' go yonda down de coas' like you said, Mista Ozème? Nobody didn' see you in Cloutierville, an' Mailitte say you neva cross' de twenty-fo'-mile ferry, an' nobody didn' see you no place."

Ozème returned, after his customary moment of reflection:

"You see, it's 'mos' always the same thing on Cane riva, my boy; a man gets tired o' that à la fin.[2] This time I went back in the woods, 'way yonda in the Fédeau cut-off; kin' o' campin' an' roughin' like, you might say. I tell you, it was sport, Bodé."

EXPLANATORY NOTES

Reading parts of some stories in *Bayou Folk* and *A Night in Acadie* may be a little confusing at first. The dialects of the Creoles, Acadians, African Americans, Native Americans, and others in the stories reflect their background and social class. Like other writers of her generation, Kate Chopin sought to be faithful to the speech patterns of the people in the region she was writing about. Reading aloud a confusing sentence will often clear up its meaning.

Most of the following notes explain some of the French and Creole expressions Chopin uses in the stories. A few expressions recur frequently:

Bon!: Good! Right!
Bonté!: Good heavens!
Bon Dieu!: Good God!
Comment!: How is this! What's this! (Expresses disapproval.)
Donc: Therefore, so, or then.
Eh, bien!: Well! So!
Hein!: Eh! You hear me!
Mais: But.
Merci: Thank you.
Marse: Master.
Miché, Michié, M'sié: Variants of Monsieur, Mister.
Mon Dieu!: My God!
Non: No.
Oui: Yes.
Par exemple!: Really! Honestly! (Expresses disapproval.)
Tante: Aunt; sometimes applied to an older woman who is not a relative.

Tiens!: Here! Take this!
Va!: Go on! So there!

Expressions Chopin explains in the text itself are not included here.

BAYOU FOLK

A No-Account Creole

1. *Natchitoches*: Pronounced Nack-e-tosh [Kate Chopin's note].
2. *extinguisher*: A protection for what is underneath. Chopin calls a sunbonnet an extinguisher in "The Bênitous' Slave."
3. *tonnerre!*: Thunder and lightning!
4. *en grand seigneur*: Like a lord, in a grand manner.
5. *Les Chêniers*: The oak grove.
6. *La Chatte*: The (female) cat.
7. *tignon*: Headcloth.
8. *Pres'dent Hayes*: The child is named after Rutherford Hayes, President of the United States from 1877–81.
9. *croquignoles*: Crunchy cookies.
10. *maigre-échine*: Thin, skinny person.

In and Out of Old Natchitoches

1. *free mulattoes*: A term still applied in Louisiana to mulattoes who were never in slavery, and whose families in most instances were themselves slave owners [Kate Chopin's note].
2. *the Empress Eugenie*: Eugénie de Montijo, wife of Napoleon III, French emperor from 1852 to 1870.
3. *Et toi, mon petit Numa, j'espère qu'un autre*: And you, little Numa, I hope another. . . .
4. *l'Isle des Mulâtres*: Island of the Mulattoes: a Mulatto colony in Natchitoches Parish.
5. *un ange du bon Dieu*: God's angel.
6. *Blagueur, va!*: You joker!
7. *charcuterie*: Delicatessen food made from pork.
8. *Cher Maître!*: Dear Lord.
9. *Ah, la bonne tante*: Ah, my dear aunt.
10. *can-cans*: Gossip.
11. *Sapristi*: Good heavens.
12. *mon cher*: My dear.

13. *Figurez vous, Maman Chavan,—pensez donc, mon ami*: You see, Maman Chavan,—think about it, my friend.
14. *boudin blanc*: White blood sausage.
15. *mignonne*: My sweet one.
16. *ma petite Suzanne*: My little Suzanne.
17. *bon à rien*: Good for nothing.
18. *Farceur va!*: You're not serious.
19. *volante*: Loose-fitting women's garment.

In Sabine

1. *Pike's Magnolia*: Some sort of liquor.

A Very Fine Fiddle

1. *Italien*: Italian.
2. *Dieu merci!*: God have mercy.

Beyond the Bayou

1. *P'tit Maître*: Little Master.
2. *Bellissime*: The most beautiful.
3. *Chéri*: Dear one.
4. *croquignoles*: Crunchy cookies.
5. *Mon bébé, mon bébé, mon Chéri!*: My baby, my baby, my dear one.
6. *Oh, P'tit Maître! P'tit Maître! Venez donc! Au secours! Au secours!*: Oh, Little Master, Little Master, Come quick! Help! Help!
7. *Bon Dieu, ayez pitié La Folle! Bon Dieu, ayez pitié moi!*: Good God, have mercy on La Folle! Good God, have mercy on me!
8. *tisane*: Herb tea.

The Return of Alcibiade

1. *À la fin! mon fils! à la fin!*: At last, my son, at last!
2. *chapelet*: Rosary.
3. *il est malin, oui*: He's shrewd, he is.
4. *grif*: The child of a mulatto and a black person.
5. *aux truffes*: Stuffed with truffles.
6. *Robert McFarlane*: Chopin's character—here and in her early novel *At Fault*—resembles Robert McAlpin, who once owned a plantation in northern Louisiana and who, according to tradition, was the inspiration for the character Simon Legree in Harriet Beecher Stowe's *Uncle Tom's Cabin*.
7. *négrillon*: Black boy.

A Rude Awakening

1. *Malédiction!*: Damn!
2. *ma fille*: My daughter.
3. *Les Chêniers*: The oak grove.
4. *mulâtresse*: Mulatto woman.

The Bênitous' Slave

1. *extinguisher fashion*: As a protection.

Désirée's Baby

1. *L'Abri*: The Shelter.
2. *corbeille*: Wedding presents (from the groom to the bride).
3. *cochon de lait*: Piglet.
4. *Mais si, Madame*: Yes, indeed, Madam.
5. *La Blanche*: The white woman (the name apparently was given to the slave because of her light complexion).
6. *Négrillon*: Black boy.
7. *peignoir*: Robe or dressing gown.
8. *layette*: Baby's clothing.

A Turkey Hunt

1. *Polisson*: The naughty one.

Madame Célestin's Divorce

1. *Watteau fold*: A fold of the type worn by women in paintings by the eighteenth-century French painter Antoine Watteau.
2. *pourtant*: Furthermore.
3. *je vous garantis*: I give you my word, I assure you.
4. *empressement*: Eagerness.

Love on the Bon-Dieu

1. *josie*: Girl's jacket.
2. *Nid d'Hibout*: Owl's nest.
3. *poudre de riz*: Powder.
4. *canaille*: Low, dishonest.
5. *endimanchés*: Dressed up (for Sunday mass).
6. *Tranquiline*: The quiet one.
7. *garde manger*: Pantry.

Loka

1. *Ma foi*: Well.
2. *Vrai sauvage ça*: A true savage, this one.
3. *une pareille sauvage*: Such a savage.
4. *Pas possible*: It's not possible.
5. *canaille*: Low, dishonest.
6. *Non, non, ma femme*: No, no, my wife.

Boulôt and Boulotte

1. *Boulôt and Boulotte*: The plump ones (boy and girl).

For Marse Chouchoute

1. *Chouchoute*: Dear one, sweet one.
2. *v'là*: Here is.
3. *Bon-à-rien*: Good for nothing.
4. *Old Harry*: The devil.
5. *Buffalo Bill*: William Frederick Cody, a scout and showman who in 1883 organized Buffalo Bill's Wild West Show.

A Visit to Avoyelles

1. *Cher Maître!*: Dear Lord.
2. *en passant*: On his way.
3. *encore!*: Still.
4. *allez!*: You know.
5. *Non, j'te garantis!*: No, I can assure you.
6. *'Tit sauvage, va!*: You little savage.

A Wizard from Gettysburg

1. *Bon-Accueil*: Welcome.
2. *mé-mère*: Grandmother.

Ma'ame Pélagie

1. *Côte Joyeuse*: Happy Coast.
2. *Sesoeur*: Sister.
3. *La Petite*: The little one.
4. *Seigneur*: Lord.
5. *Tan'tante*: Aunt.
6. *Il ne faut pas faire mal à Pauline*: We can't let Pauline get hurt.

7. *la guerre*: War.
8. *Sumter*: Fort Sumter, at the entrance to the harbor at Charleston, South Carolina; site of the first military engagement of the Civil War.
9. *La Ricaneuse*: The sniggering one.
10. *Adieu, adieu!*: Farewell.

At the 'Cadian Ball

1. *C'est Espagnol, ça*: She's Spanish.
2. *Bon chien tient de race*: French proverb: "Children take after their parents." The sense is derogative here, as it usually is when applied to women.
3. *Tiens, cocotte, va! Espèce de lionèse, prends ça, et ça!*: Take this, you bitch! You lioness, take this, and that!
4. *volante*: Loose-fitting women's garment.
5. *nénaine*: Godmother.
6. *Ah, Sainte Vierge! faut de la patience! butor, va!*: Holy Mary! One needs to be patient! You're a disgrace!
7. *John L. Sulvun*: John L. Sullivan, American boxing champion.
8. *le parc aux petits*: The little ones' room.
9. *Ces maudits gens du raiderode*: These people from the railroad.
10. *brave homme*: A good man.
11. *chic, mais chic*: Classy, really classy.
12. *Boulanger*: French general and minister of war who between 1887 and 1889 presented a threat for the recently established French Republican regime.
13. *planté là*: Planted there.
14. *Ah, c'est vous, Calixta? Comment ça va, mon enfant?*: It's you, Calixta? How are you, my child?
15. *Tcha va b'en; et vous, mam'zélle?*: I'm fine. And you, miss?
16. *Bonté divine!*: Good God!
17. *Ah Dieu sait!*: God knows!
18. *le bal est fini*: The ball has ended.

La Belle Zoraïde

1. *marais*: Swamp.
2. *Lisett' to kité la plaine,*
   Mo perdi bonhair à moué;
   Ziés à moué semblé fontaine,
   Dépi mo pa miré toué.

Lisette has left,
I've lost my happiness;
My eyes are like fountains,
Since I can't look at you.

3. *corbeille*: Wedding presents for the bride.
4. *nénaine*: Godmother.
5. *le beau Mézor*: Handsome Mézor.
6. *Bon Dieu Seigneur*: Good Lord God.
7. *Malheureuse*: Poor wretch.
8. *Zoraïde, mo l'aime toi*: Zoraïde, I love you.
9. *Place d'Armes*: A main square.
10. *griffe*: The child of a mulatto and a black person.
11. *Zoraïde la folle*: Zoraïde the mad woman.

A Gentleman of Bayou Têche
1. *comme ça*: Like this.

A Lady of Bayou St. John

1. *marais*: Swamp.
2. *M'amie*: My friend.
3. *triste*: Sad.
4. *cher ami*: Dear friend.
5. *mon ami*: My friend.
6. *bon voyage*: A good journey.

A NIGHT IN ACADIE

A Night in Acadie
1. *baignés*: Doughnuts.
2. *Nonc*: Uncle.
3. *nuque*: Nape.
4. *J' vous réponds!*: I tell you.
5. *toile-cirée*: Oilcloth.
6. *Ah, b'en, pour ça!*: Really!
7. *piment rouge and piment vert*: Red and green peppers.
8. *Vaux mieux y s'méle ces affairs, lui; si non!*: He would do better minding his own business, or else!
9. *Tiens! t'es pareille comme ain mariée, Zaïda*: You look just like a bride, Zaïda.

10. *Tiens! c'est vous?*: Is it you?
11. *C'est toi qui s'y connais, ma fille! 'cré tonnerre!*: You really are the best, my girl! By God!
12. *Ah, b'en oui!*: Oh, yes!
13. *têtes-de-mulets*: Stubborn mules.
14. *bois-gras*: Wood.

Athénaïse

1. *rigolet de Bon Dieu*: The Bon Dieu river.
2. *C'est pas Chrétien, ténez!*: This is not Christian, you know!
3. *Juanita*: A song by Caroline Norton, set to an old Spanish air:

> Soft o'er the fountain, ling'ring falls the southern moon,
> Far o'er the mountain, breaks the day too soon!
> In thy dark eyes' splendor, where the warm light loves to dwell.
> Weary looks, yet tender, speak their fond farewell.
>   Nita! Juanita! Ask thy soul if we should part!
>   Nita! Juanita! Lean thou on my heart.
> When in thy dreaming, moons like these shall shine again,
> And daylight beaming, prove thy dreams are vain;
> Wilt thou not relenting, for thine absent lover sigh?
> In thy heart consenting to a prayer gone by?
>   Nita! Juanita! Let me linger by thy side!
>   Nita! Juanita! Be my own Fair Bride.

4. *Cochon! sacré cochon!*: Swine, dirty swine!
5. *Comment ça va?*: How are you?
6. *La fille de son père*: Her father's daughter.
7. *maudit*: Blasted.
8. *Tiens! tu vas les garder comme tu as jadis fait. Je ne veux plus de ce train là, moi!*: Here! you keep them as you used to do. I don't want to do this anymore!
9. *Voyons!*: Listen!
10. *chambres garnies*: Furnished rooms.
11. *volante*: Loose-fitting women's garment.
12. *do the grand seigneur*: Behave in a grand manner.
13. *hors d'œuvres*: Appetizers.
14. *des esprits forts*: Free spirits, free thinkers.
15. *sapeur*: Sapper, a soldier who is fearless.
16. *The Duchess*: Probably *La Duchesse de Langeais* (published in serial

form in 1833 and 1834 and in book form under the present title in 1839), a novel by Honoré de Balzac about an unhappily married young woman.

17. *Mrs. Humphrey Ward*: English novelist and social worker.
18. *one of Remington's Cowboys*: An illustration by Frederic Remington, American painter, sculptor, and writer.
19. *monsieur et madame*: Husband and wife (in this context).
20. *faux-air*: A (false) resemblance.
21. *Pauvre ti chou*: Poor little thing.

After the Winter

1. *Les Chêniers*: The oak grove.
2. *La Fringante*: The frisky one.
3. *Bonté divine!*: Good Lord!
4. *en bon ami*: Like a good friend.
5. *Mon ami*: My friend.

Polydore

1. *mignon*: Sweet.
2. *eau sédative*: Calming water.
3. *nénaine*: Godmother.

Regret

1. *Ti Nomme*: Little man.
2. *Dieu sait*: God knows.
3. *alive encore*: Still alive.
4. *Croque-mitaine, Loup-garou*: The ogre, the werewolf.
5. *It's terrassent! Bonté!*: It's exhausting! Good heavens!

A Matter of Prejudice

1. *fleur de Laurier*: Laurel's flower.
2. *"Partant pour la Syrie"*: "Leaving for Syria," a nineteenth-century French song of empire, celebrating Napoleon's advance into northern Africa.
3. *eau sédative*: Calming water.
4. *Plait-il, madame?*: Excuse me, ma'am?
5. *mon fils*: My son.
6. *ma mère*: My mother.

Caline

1. *loin là bas. . . . Djieu sait é où*: Far away, over there. . . . God knows where.
2. *lagniappe*: A little something.

A Dresden Lady in Dixie

1. *Ah, bien non*: Oh, no, no way.
2. *josie*: Girl's jacket.

Nég Créol

1. *Chicot*: Stump.
2. *Maringouin*: Insect, mosquito.
3. *farceur*: Trickster.
4. *des 'tites cousines*: Little cousins (girls).
5. *Boisduré*: Durable wood.
6. *mulatresse, vendeuse de café*: A mulatto woman selling coffee.
7. *la maison grise*: The grey house.
8. *La Chouette*: The Owl.
9. *Pas d' sucre, Nég?*: No sugar, Nég?
10. *la nuit blanche*: A sleepless night.
11. *tisanes*: Herb teas.
12. *grigris*: Charms.
13. *eau de Lourdes*: Holy water from the French city of Lourdes, believed to be able to cure sickness.
14. *Vous pas bézouin tisane, Mamzelle Aglaé? Vous pas veux mo cri gagni docteur?*: You don't want your tea, Miss Aglaé? You don't want me to fetch a doctor?
15. *Une goutte d'eau sucré, Nég!*: A drop of sweetened water, Nég!
16. *ma bonne Brigitte*: My good Brigitte.
17. *là-bas au Cathédral*: Over there at the Cathedral.
18. *chou-fleur*: Cauliflower.
19. *les Attakapas*: An area in central Louisiana.

The Lilies

1. *va t'en, chérie*: Go on, my dear!

Azélie

1. *le grand air*: Fresh air.
2. *Bon jou', M'si' Mathurin*: Hello, Mr. Mathurin.

3. *He . . . had an air . . . fanfaron*: He was quite full of himself, very pleased with himself.
4. *que voulez-vous?*: What can you do?
5. *après tout*: After all.
6. *Ah, b'en, no*: Oh, no; no way.

Mamouche

1. *A ta fenêtre, Daignes paraître—tra la la la!*: Please be good enough to come to your window—tra la la la!
2. *veillée*: The evening.

A Sentimental Soul

1. *l'Abeille*: *The Bee*, a French paper published in the States.
2. *Eh bien, Mamzelle Fleurette, à demain, à demain!*: So Miss Fleurette, see you tomorrow, tomorrow!
3. *Courier des États Unis*: Another French paper published in the States.
4. *Empress Eugénie*: Eugénie de Montijo, wife of Napoleon III, French emperor from 1852 to 1870.
5. *Dictionnaire de la Langue Française*: Dictionary of the French Language.
6. *Ce n'est pas Lacodie, Mamzelle Fleurette. C'est moi, Augustine*: It is not Lacodie, Miss Fleurette. It is Augustine.
7. *Bien bon de votre part, Mamzelle Fleurette—mais c'est fini. J'suis flambé, flambé, flambé!*: This is nice of you, Miss Fleurette, but it's over. I'm done for, really done for!
8. *Inutile; il n'en veut pas*: That's pointless; he doesn't want one.
9. *Blanchisseuse de Fin*: Laundress of fine fabrics.
10. *charivari*: Noisy wedding serenade.

Dead Men's Shoes

1. *le vieux Gamiche*: Old Gamiche.

At Chênière Caminada

1. *Chênière Caminada*: A coastal area south of New Orleans, near Grand Isle, where parts of *The Awakening* take place.
2. *Credo in unun Deum patrem omnipotentem*: "I believe in one God, the father almighty." The beginning of the Nicene creed, recited at mass after the gospel.
3. *Church of Our Lady of Lourdes*: Named after the city in southern

France where the Virgin Mary is believed to have appeared to a young woman in 1858.
4. *Elle est morte*: She died.

Cavanelle

1. *poult-de-soie*: Silky material.
2. *voyez vous*: You see.
3. *des petits soins*: Good care, small attentions.
4. *soupçon*: Little bit.
5. *Où es tu donc?*: Where are you?
6. *sirop d'orgeat*: A sweet drink.
7. *savoir vivre*: Social graces.
8. *petit ménage*: Small household.
9. *lagniappes*: Little things.
10. *bouillie*: Gruel.
11. *demi-verre*: Half-glass.
12. *petit souper*: Light supper.
13. *mon ami*: My friend.
14. *friandises*: Sweets.
15. *mousseline de laine*: Wool chiffon.

Tante Cat'rinette

1. *Vieumaite*: Old Master.
2. *en règle*: According to the law.
3. *Bon dieu Seigneur*: Good Lord in heaven.
4. *free mulatto*: According to Kate Chopin, "A term still applied in Louisiana to mulattoes who were never in slavery, and whose families in most instances were themselves slave owners."
5. *cher coeur*: Sweetheart.
6. *ti chou*: Little thing.
7. *céléra*: Wicked.

A Respectable Woman

1. *ma belle*: My beauty.
2. *apostrophe to the night*: Gouvernail has been quoting lines from section 21 of the 1892 edition of Walt Whitman's *Leaves of Grass*. The remaining lines which Gouvernail recites read:

   Press close bare-bosomed night—press close magnetic nourishing night!